INTERNATIONAL GUY
Volume 2

ALSO BY AUDREY CARLAN

International Guy Series

Paris: International Guy Book 1

New York: International Guy Book 2

Copenhagen: International Guy Book 3

Milan: International Guy Book 4

San Francisco: International Guy Book 5

Calendar Girl Series

January

February

March

April

May

June

July

August

September

October

November

December

MILAN • SAN FRANCISCO • MONTREAL

INTERNATIONAL GUY

GUY

Volume 2

#1 *NEW YORK TIMES* BESTSELLING AUTHOR

AUDREY CARLAN

Montlake
Romance

Text copyright © 2018 by Audrey Carlan

Published by Montlake Romance, Seattle

www.apub.com

Amazon, the Amazon logo, and Montlake Romance are trademarks of Amazon.com, Inc., or its affiliates.

ISBN-13: 9781503904644

ISBN-10: 1503904644

Cover design by Letitia Hasser

Cover photography by Wander Aguiar Photography

Printed in the United States of America

MILAN:

INTERNATIONAL GUY

BOOK 4

To my publishing team at Libri Mondadori.
For believing in my stories,
committing to me as an author, and
sharing my work in your beautiful language . . .
I thank you.

I am proud of my Italian heritage
and can't wait to walk the streets of Milan one day.

1

"Bro, answer your phone. It's Wendy, and she called me in hysterics. She's in a panic about something but said she has to talk to you first. Whatever that means," Bo urges me as he lifts his suitcase off the airport conveyer belt. Of course his would come off first. We've landed back in Boston from Copenhagen. After a nine-hour flight, I should be relieved to be home, but I'm not. I can't help thinking back to the last morning I had with Skyler. She disappeared into the shower during Sophie's surprise visit, then beat feet out of the hotel room, stating she had to catch her flight. I knew her flight was early, but not that early. And I had wanted to drop her off at the airport. She refused with a lame excuse.

"Where's the fire!" I laugh, trying to grab hold of Skyler as she flutters past me.

"Gotta go catch my plane. Get back to New York." She says this as if it were news to me, but I already know she has to leave on the first flight out. Still, by my clock it's only five thirty, and her flight doesn't leave until nine. She's got a little time. Enough to slow down a bit.

"Peaches, relax." I hook an arm around her from behind and hold her back against my front. "You're not going to be late. I wouldn't let you miss your flight." I lay a line of kisses, starting behind her ear, down her neck to the sweet spot where her neck and shoulder meet.

Her body goes rigid in my arms before she shrugs out of my hold and jets to her suitcase, tossing things in willy-nilly. "No, I've got to get there early, read through my lines. You know how it is." She waves her hands around a bit frantically.

I firm my spine, cross my arms, and lean against the dresser. "Is something wrong? I'm getting a strange vibe off you."

She pushes a lock of blonde hair behind her ear. "No, of course not. Just got a lot on my mind. Fun's over. Back to reality."

I watch her shove the last few things of hers into her bag. She turns around, saying, "I've already had Nate call a car service."

"Sky . . . baby, I wanted to take you. Drop you off."

She shakes her head. "Not a good idea. The paps are everywhere after the wedding and are dying for another shot of us. It would be wise to have a little space."

I frown, thinking space from Skyler is the absolute last thing I want. Ever. Still, it's her life too, and I don't have any real claim. Sure, we've agreed to be exclusive—at least I'm pretty sure we confirmed that last night in bed. Then again, we did a lot in bed.

"Okay, I understand. Come here. At least let me give you a proper goodbye. I'm not sure when I'm going to see you next. We need to make this goodbye last." I grin.

She closes her eyes, purses her lips, and nods.

Not at all the response I'd expect from her.

Sky enters my embrace and plants her forehead against my chest. She wraps her arms around my back and inhales deeply. Her hands are locked around me so tight I can barely catch my own breath.

"Hey, this isn't goodbye forever. It's goodbye for now. When I get back to Boston and get settled, we'll touch base. See what our schedules are like and plan our next rendezvous."

"Rendezvous. Right. Sex." Her tone is flat.

I curl my hand around her nape and lift her chin with my thumb. "Yes, incredible sex. Like what we've been having. You. Me. Great sex. Good food. Awesome times. Fun."

She nods. "Fun."

I frown and place my forehead against hers. "What's wrong, baby?"

Skyler shakes her head. "Nothing. I'm tired. We were up . . . late last night."

I grin at the memory of all the things we did last night. Things I'd like to repeat soon. Very soon. God willing.

"Okay. Sleep on the plane. Get some rest. I'll be thinking about you." A lump of emotion builds in my throat, but I push it down, trying to play things cool. I'll be seeing her soon. It's not goodbye forever. Looks like I need the reminder as much as she does.

"Mm-hmm," she offers noncommittally.

Weird. Sky's got her wall up, the one I pushed through and knocked down our first week together. Maybe it's because she's sad we have to separate. That has to be it. I wouldn't know one way or the other. Ever since Kayla, I've not dated a woman long enough to have an inkling what missing her would be like and vice versa.

"I gotta go, Park," she whispers, her breath feathering delectably across my lips.

Leaning forward, I press my lips to hers. She eases her body against me, her breasts smashed to my chest, before she slants her head and opens her mouth. Just the invitation I need. I dip my tongue in and . . . Christ! She's like biting into a minty piece of gum for the first time. I can't get enough. I don't think I'll ever get enough.

For long moments our tongues dance and our arms tighten, bringing the other as close as possible. Ripples of arousal shoot to my cock, reminding me he'd like to say goodbye as well. She must feel my excitement because she moans into my mouth and rubs her lower half against my hard shaft like a cat in heat.

I tunnel my hand into her hair, pull at her roots until she cries out, gasping for breath, and grips my ass with a force I've grown to appreciate when Sky goes wild for it. Since day one, she's been uninhibited and unapologetic about her ravenous sex drive. She matches my desires and libido to a tee. No woman has ever shared my sex drive, but this firecracker explodes with it.

"Ah!" she moans, head tipping back, chin to the ceiling as I grind against her, running my lips down her swanlike neck, nipping as I go.

"You sure you don't have a little extra time . . . ," I prompt with a thrust of my hips.

One of her hands wiggles between us, and she palms my erection through the dress slacks I haphazardly put on when Sophie came knocking.

"Mmm . . ." She rubs up and down. "Would love to, but . . ."

I groan with heartfelt irritation. "You gotta go. I know, I know. One more kiss."

I kiss her so hard and so long my tongue hurts and our lips are swollen and bruised. I plant my forehead against hers. "I don't want to let you go." For the first time in a long time, I admit weakness to a woman. The back of my neck tingles, and I grind my teeth.

"Then don't," she whispers, and for some reason, a niggling thought hammers at the back of my skull. Something important is happening, but I can't quite put my finger on it.

"You have to go back to your life in New York. I have to go back to mine in Boston." I hold her tighter.

She inhales deeply, her shoulders dropping before she nods and moves away. "It's been real, Parker."

I grin. "A real blast." The cheesy joke slips out.

A flash of hurt crosses her gaze, but she quickly covers it up with one of her fake smiles. The ones she gives the paparazzi and people she doesn't really want to talk to but has to, due to her status as a celebrity.

"Yep." All she says before she turns around and hefts her bags. I follow her through the suite where Rachel and Nate Van Dyken, her bodyguards,

are waiting. Fully dressed. All black. Aviators dangling from their shirts. Nate looks like he is about to go to war in a pair of black cargoes and matching combat boots. The dude is a brick house, but he dotes on his wife and treats Skyler like a lady, even when they aren't out. I like them for Sky. They're a great addition to her team.

"Ready?" Nate asks Sky, and she nods rather solemnly. If I didn't know any better, I'd think she'd been given some bad news. Nate grabs both of her bags in one hand. Total stud. He holds out his free hand to me. "Good seeing you, Ellis." Even though I've told him my name many times, he continues to call me by my last name.

"Nate. You as well, man. Take care of my girl."

Skyler's head immediately jerks up from where she's going through her purse, and I swear a wounded expression takes over her features before she masks it.

Her last expression kept hitting me throughout the flight home, like a commercial stuck on repeat. Even when she finally took her leave and I embraced her for the last time, her body didn't envelop me with warmth as I'd come to expect when holding her. I don't know if it was something I said during the night or in the morning, but if I had to guess, I'd say the woman is spooked. Something has scared her off, and I need to get to the bottom of it.

I pull out my phone and turn it on. I powered down on the long flight to save my battery. The second the display lights up, a myriad of dings goes off instantly.

"Jesus. You weren't kidding." I curse, scanning the notifications. Ignoring the messages and texts, half of them from the IG offices, I dial Wendy direct at headquarters.

"Parker . . . I'm so, so, so sorry. You can't know how sorry I am. I didn't mean for this to happen. I didn't realize. I forwarded the file on, and now it's everywhere. *Everywhere!*" Wendy's voice is pained and emotionally charged.

"Wendy, calm down. I don't know what you're talking about." I press the phone closer to my ear to drown out the sounds of the airport around me.

"How can you not know?" she gasps. "Crap, you've been on the plane for nine hours. Parker, I'm sorry. The file Bo sent over to me with the pictures from the photo shoot with Skyler Paige . . ."

"Yeah? You sent them over to *People*, right?"

"I did, but I didn't open the entire file, and inside was a file labeled 'Parker Confidential.' God, I'm so stupid! The pictures of you and Skyler Paige, they're all over the media. The ones of you in the pool together, hanging out at her house . . ."

"What!" I clench my teeth and wait for her to explain.

"Some of you carrying Skyler out of a pool, her half-naked, you kissing her like crazy, and it's so freakin' hot, everyone is talking about it. There's some of you kissing in the bath—"

"Oh my God! Fuck! This cannot be happening." I rub at my temples with my thumb and forefinger.

Bo breaks in. "What's the matter, brother?"

"The pictures you sent Wendy to deliver to *People* . . ."

"Yeah?" He sets down his suitcase closer to our huddle.

"Apparently you added a confidential file of the private photos you took of Skyler and me?"

His eyes widen. "No . . ."

I nod.

"Fuck."

"'Bout sums it up." I inhale slow and deep, trying to calm my immediate anger at the potential ramifications this could have for Skyler and International Guy.

"I'm sorry, Parker," Wendy says. "I'm so sorry. I didn't know. I should have . . . It doesn't matter. I'll pack up my desk." Even though she tries to muffle it, a choked sob sounds through the phone.

"You will do no such thing. We're on our way there. We need to do damage control, see how far this has reached . . ."

"Okay, okay, okay. I'll be ready." She hangs up, and I press into my temples once more, knowing this is going to be a shit show.

"We need to get to the papers now." I lift my chin in the direction of a store across the concourse with all the local and national news.

"On it, brother." Bo strides off while I wait for my luggage to come out.

I pull up Google and type in Skyler's name. A deluge of images of me and her in a variety of settings immediately pops up. I scan through the pictures, and my temperature rises. The pictures are mostly tame. Besides the bathroom picture, where you can see the outline of Skyler's bare breasts plastered against my bare chest when she was taking the bubble bath and I'd attacked her in between takes, the rest show a normal, happy couple. Snuggling on the couch, talking. Standing off to the side, having a cup of coffee. Her trying to teach me a yoga pose and my failing miserably. I chuckle at several of the images, remembering how much fun we'd had together. Then I stop on the image of us in the pool.

"Jesus . . ." I rub at my mouth and enlarge the image. It's stunning and fuckhot. I remember the moment clear as day. I was holding her, the water lapping around our waists, her legs locked around me. She wore a tiny bikini, which left little to the imagination. She was gripping my bicep as I had a hand on her ass. Bo told me to whisper something into her ear. I did and took it one step further. I'd whispered all the sexy things I was going to do to her when she was done shooting. It obviously had her responding positively, because he captured her looking exactly like a lust-driven sex goddess I was about to ravish. After that I lifted her right out of the pool and took her straight to bed, fucking her until we both couldn't walk.

Damn. I save the image to my photos because I can't not. I need that sucker enlarged and placed on a wall in my bedroom for the nights I don't get to see Skyler.

Skyler.

Shit. She's probably losing her mind. I check my phone and see several voice mails from her agent, Tracey, but nothing from her. I take a full breath and finally see my luggage.

Grabbing it and Bo's as quick as I can, I meet up with him while he's leaving the store. His arms are filled with a stack of magazines and newspapers.

"So . . . about this confidential file . . . ," he starts.

I shake my head, grab the stack, and shove what I can into my briefcase and the rest into the front of my suitcase. "Save it. We've got to get to IG and do damage control."

His lips flatten, and a muscle ticks in his jaw. "Right. Just know . . . those were for you." His voice is rough when he adds, "A gift."

I stop and place a hand on his shoulder. "Brother, I know. And in other circumstances, I'd be thanking you. And one day, I'm sure I will. For now, we deal with the fallout. Yeah?"

His chin dip is succinct, but I can tell this is hitting him in the feelers. Bo may be a man's man, a brother from another mother, but he feels things deep. His relationship with Royce and me is right up there with his mom and sisters. We're family, and family doesn't fuck over one another. It wasn't Bo's intention. And the pictures are freaking amazing. It's really unfortunate they got into the wrong hands.

Bo and I make our way to the exit to meet the car Wendy hired for us. Only we barely make it two steps outside when we are bombarded by a barrage of lenses, an eruption of flashes, and a horde of paparazzi screaming my name.

"Parker, where's Skyler?"

"How does it feel to have nailed the hottest chick in Hollywood?"

"Is Skyler pregnant with your baby?"

"When's the wedding?"

"Is Skyler cheating on you with her on-and-off-again boyfriend and costar, Rick Pettington?"

This last question has me grinding my teeth as I push through the mayhem to get to where the hired drivers are standing. One of them has a sign that says "International Guy."

"Who's the guy with you? Is he your bodyguard?" one of the paps yells.

"Yeah, motherfucker, and if you so much as touch him, you'll see a world of hurt. Back off!" Bo yells back as he grabs my arm and pushes with his other arm. We leave our luggage at the exit door in order to push through the bodies.

I can barely see through the explosion of camera flashes, but Bo leads the way.

He gets me into the car, then slams the door and pushes back through the paps. After a few minutes he returns with both of our suitcases, passing them off to the driver to put in the trunk.

As Bo opens the door, the flashes start up again as the paps try to get any image they can.

When he finally gets in, he flops against the seat. "Holy fuck, man. Is this the shit Skyler goes through?"

I nod. "Worse when she's expected. This is tame compared to what I've seen her experience. The crowd at the castle for the wedding was her normal fanfare."

"Jesus. Poor thing." He runs a hand through his tousled dark hair. "You calling her?"

I take a deep breath. "Yeah, I want to be at the office in private."

"She tried to call you?"

I purse my lips and shake my head.

"Say what?"

"Not sure what's going on with her. It was weird when I left Copenhagen. After Sophie woke me up—"

"Wait, Sophie came by your room before Sky left?"

"Yeah. Wanted to say goodbye since I'm not going to see her for a while."

"And you say Skyler got wiggy that same morning?" Bo cants his head.

I shrug. "I guess so, yeah."

"Brother, you can't be this dense."

"Excuse me?" I jerk my head to the side and focus on my friend.

"Sophie's hot and confident, man. We made sure of it."

"So?"

Bo lets out a long breath. "And you've slept with her."

"Not saying anything I don't already know." I grind my teeth together, wishing he'd get to the point.

"And you're sleeping with Skyler."

"Once again . . ."

"She's weirded out about your relationship with Sophie, man. Jesus, you're dumb." Bo shakes his head.

I sigh. "Nah, we talked about Sophie."

"When?"

"After the wedding. It's all good. She knows Sophie's just a friend."

Bo snorts obnoxiously. "Yeah, a friend you were fucking not too long ago."

I frown and rub the back of my neck. "You think she's trippin' about Sophie even after we talked?"

"Uh . . . yeah. I think she's all twisted up about it. And then Sophie wakes you up, pulling you out of bed to say goodbye? Girl probably eavesdropped on your convo, dude. I know I would if I were all gaga over a chick and she was shooting the shit with her girl, and I wanted to know where I stood."

"Huh. I mean, makes sense. And now this . . . Fuck. She's never going to talk to me again."

Bo frowns. "You that much of a dickwad in the sack?"

10

Instinct overrides my common sense, and I automatically punch him in the chest, but not as hard as I can. "Fuck you!"

He rubs at the spot, wincing. "Ugh . . ."

"I take care of my woman," I snarl.

He fires back his response. "Does she *know* she's your woman, or does she think she's your good-time gal?"

"We have fun together, man. We both agree it's casual."

Bo widens his legs and leans back into the leather of the limo seat, making himself more comfortable. "Never met a woman in my life who touches base daily by phone, spends three full weeks with a guy, flies across the world to attend a wedding with him, only sees him and no one else since you hooked up, and still considers herself in a"—he makes air quotes—"'casual relationship.'"

The man has a point. A huge one.

"Brother, why are you so set that this thing with Skyler is casual? If casual were the case, you'd be banging chicklets. Since I know you're not, and you're hung up on a sexy blonde actress with a great rack and a smokin' hot ass—"

"Easy, brother . . ."

He grins cheekily and winks. "Point is, you're already in a romantic relationship with her. Now your shit has hit the public eye, and you need to figure out how the two of you are going to handle it. You feel me?"

Crap. I'm in a romantic relationship with Skyler Paige.

I need to talk to her. Immediately.

The only problem is . . . What could I ever possibly say to make this situation any better?

2

Wendy bum-rushes the door to the IG offices the second Bo and I walk in dragging our luggage behind us.

"Parker, I'm so sorry. I honestly can't believe I didn't look at the file before sending. I . . . I . . . don't know what else to say." Her crystal-blue eyes are glassy, and her nose is tinged with red, but she swallows and firms her spine, showing she's trying her best to keep it together.

I hold out my arms wide in response. Without waiting a moment, feisty, ball-busting Wendy throws herself into my embrace. I hug her tight, her spindly body trembling slightly.

"Park . . . I messed up." Her words are but a whisper as she looks up at me. "It won't happen again."

I cup her cheek and give it a little pat. "See that it doesn't, minxy." I wink and hug her tight once more.

She rests her face against my chest and sighs before clearing her throat and pulling back. "Okay. I'm assuming damage control is step one?"

"Yeah. First, I have a very important call to make. And I can't be disturbed until I'm done." I cock a brow for emphasis.

She points her finger toward my chest. "Got it. And so you know, I've already been on several calls with Skyler's agent and BFF, Tracey. She has a pretty good plan, if I do say so myself, but it's totally up to you. Not sure what the four one one is on you and Skyler since you've not been in the office lately, and there's only so much you can get from cyberstalking . . ."

I frown. "You've been cyberstalking me?"

She crinkles her nose. "Uh, yeah. I'd be a shitty hacker if I didn't keep tabs on all three of you. Though this scoundrel"—she hooks her thumb over her shoulder toward Bo—"has me going in circles over the number of women he enters into his phone, not to mention the ones he sleeps with, and then I have to interface with them when they call, stop by, and just plain physically stalk him." She shakes her head. "Serves you right, man whore."

Bo chuckles. "Jealous, Tink?"

She huffs. "As if. I'm so far out of your league, you're still batting at balls on a stick while Sir Mick is hitting home runs at every turn."

"One day . . . you just wait. I'll have you under me," Bo teases.

"Only if I'm dead and you're into that sort of thing."

I shake my head and leave them to their bickering. It's all in good fun, but honestly, I wish they'd give it a rest once in a while. I swear they need a referee.

As I enter my office, I find Royce placing something on my desk.

"Yo! Long time no see, brother!" Roy pulls me to his chest and gives me a few slaps on the back. "Brother. Missed your ugly mug around here. Though I don't foresee you being home long unless you want to punt the next gig to me."

I go around to the front of my desk and sit in my cushy chair. The leather molds to my ass instantly, and I sigh at the goodness of being home. "What's on next?"

"Fashion designer in Milan. Needs you and Bo to work your magic on their lineup of models. Apparently, they booked women who've never modeled before because their look fit the campaign."

I clap my hands and put my elbows on my desk. "They want us to teach women how to model? Doesn't really sound much like our gig."

He smiles wide, his bright, even teeth shining. "'S'what I said. Then they told me the campaign is for erotic lingerie. Shit changes color when the lights go out. Glows in the dark, has flashing lights. All kinds of kinkiness. So, what they're looking for is someone to teach them how to be sexy and flaunt their goods . . . big time. They have women of all types, and apparently, it's a cutting-edge new thing."

"When do they need us?"

"Couple of weeks from now, ten days would be better."

Ten days.

I just got back from being in Copenhagen for the better part of three weeks, New York for the same, and now it looks as though I'm heading to Milan. Sweet Jesus. I'm going to need a break.

"Can't score any clients in the States, eh?"

Roy laughs full and deep, his head tipping back with the effort. "Got one in the hopper for San Francisco."

I run my hand through my hair and tug at the roots. "Roy, that's still three thousand miles away. It might as well be Paris!"

He shrugs. "Business is business, right? We're a hot commodity right now. We have so many clients on the waiting list, I'm only taking the top-dollar ones for full travel and the ones we can work from here in between."

I nod. "All right. We'll talk about it more later. For now, I gotta call Sky. She's probably shitting a brick about the media shit storm since those pics went live."

Royce sucks in a breath through his teeth. "Shee-it. I saw them pics, brother. Hot as hell. Happy you're with Skyler." He shakes his head. "A high-profile actress. Who would've thought you'd nail down an A-lister?"

"Sure as hell not me." I pick up my landline, signaling I need to use the phone and Roy needs to head out.

"Don't fuck it up," he cautions.

I disconnect the line, still holding the receiver. "What's that supposed to mean?"

He shrugs. "I've known you a long time. You're good at self-sabotage. If she's a good woman, a woman who deserves your undivided attention, give it to her. We're not getting any younger. Every day I notice it more and more."

I tilt my head. "You wanting to settle down?" I'm not able to hold back the shocked tone in my voice.

"If the right woman came along . . . sassy, smart mouth, can handle my brand of control, great dresser, loves her family, loyal, knows how to eat, how to treat a man, intelligent, with a side dose of bootylicious junk in the trunk . . . shoot. Magic. I'd drop to my knees and propose in a second."

I'm pretty sure my eyes are as wide as Frisbees. "Seriously?"

"Absolutely."

"Respect."

He gives me a chin dip. "I'll leave you to it."

When Royce hits the door, I call out to him. "Roy." He turns around, his navy suit pristine, the fine-striped white-and-blue collared shirt starched to perfection. I smirk. "Missed your face too."

He grins wide. "Don't I know it. There's an awful lot of good to miss."

He waves over his shoulder and, smooth as silk, walks out of my office.

Damn, the brother has some serious fucking swagger. Would make a lesser man jealous, but I've known him forever and love him like my own family. Jealousy isn't something that typically rears its ugly head between me and my chosen brothers. Thank God.

Ready to take the heat, but more than that, ready to hear her voice, I pick up the phone and dial Skyler.

She picks up on the first ring.

"Be honest with me . . . Did I mean anything to you? Anything at all?" Her voice cracks with pain, a splitting of the earth; cutting the building straight down the center would have hurt less.

"Sky . . . fuck. It was an accident. Wendy didn't know—"

"I asked you a simple question, Parker. Just one. Give me an answer." Her words are tight, controlled.

I swallow down the dryness in my throat. "Skyler, you mean more to me than any woman in the past decade. Those pictures getting out were an error. Baby, you have to believe me."

"Why, when every man I've trusted in the past has destroyed me? I opened my soul to you—"

"And I do not take your gift lightly," I fire off instantly, because I don't take it lightly. I know what it cost her.

Her sobs tear through the line and cut me one slice at a time, digging deeper and deeper into my heart. My chest is moving, but I'm not sure I'm breathing.

"Peaches, you know me." I try to reach the place inside her that connects so completely with mine when we're together, but over the phone, it's a stretch. A big one.

"What do I know? I know you gave me *you* . . . for three weeks. Then you took it away. And of course, there's Sophie. The other woman you gave yourself to. Your client. What am I to believe? Is part of your service bedding your clients?" she hisses, anger and blame in her tone.

"That's not fair."

"Isn't it? You admitted to screwing Sophie. How many other clients have you taken to bed, whispered sweet nothings to?"

"Only two," I grit through my teeth, not wanting to have this conversation but knowing if I don't, I could lose her forever. "And Sophie is a friend," I try to remind her.

She laughs, the sound bitter and brittle. "Then what am I?"

"So much more."

"Right. If that's true, then lay it out for me. What am I to you, Parker? I mean, oh mighty Dream Maker!" She throws my marketing title in my face.

I grit my teeth, close my eyes, and lay it the fuck out for my infuriating woman.

"You are the woman who occupies my days and nights with nothing but thoughts of your smile. I dream of being with you, sleeping next to you. I imagine your lips and lick my own wishing for a tiny taste. I anticipate the next time we'll be together and what new adventures we'll undertake. There is no one I'd rather spend time getting lost with. Toss us anywhere in the world, and I know we'll have a blast. The simple memory of your scent makes my mouth water. And don't get me started on your body. It's downright dangerous. I want you constantly. Your mind, your sexy body, your goddamned soul. Is that enough for you, or do you want more?" I growl out, angry she's forcing my hand, making me spill my guts just to keep her in my life.

We both stop speaking for a solid minute, though I can hear her breathing.

"I'm sorry I yelled at you," she says softly.

I close my eyes, relief filling every recess of my mind. I've gotten through. My girl is coming back.

"Skyler . . . fuck. I wish I were there with you right now."

"I do too. Why does everything have to be so hard?"

I smile. "Well, Peaches, you're exceptionally talented, and the world wants a piece of you. Though I can't blame them, because I always want a piece. Hell, I want the whole pie."

She giggles.

Giggles.

"Christ, I miss the sound of your giggle." I sit back in my chair and spin around to my view, enjoying the familiar buildings, the water, and the horizon. It's good to be home.

"I do not giggle."

"You sure as hell do, and it's cute."

"Whatever." She says this as though she's affronted, but I know she's not. Never say die. It's part of her charm.

"Peaches, baby, I hate to bring this back to an uncomfortable place, but what do you want to do about the media and the pictures?"

She groans. "Tracey has been up my ass about it."

"What does she think we should do?"

"Trace wants us to make a combined statement to the press."

"Saying what?"

"We're a couple. We're in a relationship, and we're happy as clams."

"And . . ." I need to hear what she thinks about this plan before I respond. As I'm learning, women are fickle, and any move or word could be the wrong one. I don't want to go backward now that I've got her talking to me.

I can hear rustling and a door opening. "I'm going to need another minute," she says to someone other than me.

"Okay, sweetheart, I can wait on the couch." A man's voice.

On the couch.

Sweetheart.

"Who's that?"

"Hmm?" she mutters distractedly. "Oh, it's Rick. We have to get on set and he was sent to get me."

Rick the Prick.

Perfect timing, buddy.

With my loss of control pushing me forward, Rick the Prick getting to be near my girl when I can't pushes the green-eyed monster within me to blurt out, "Do it."

"Huh? What? Do it?" she repeats with uncertainty.

"Tell the press we're a couple." I clench my teeth, and my heart starts pounding a wild drumbeat against my chest. The phone I'm holding digs into my fist, heat building around my hand and crawling up my forearm.

"Parker . . . you said to keep what we have casual. Fun."

I lick my lips, wishing I could hold her face in my hands while having this conversation. It feels like such a big step to take over the phone. Unfortunately it will have to do—for now.

"Peaches, I know what I said. I meant it. Then. Now, after the way you left, the long flight, seeing our private pictures splashed across the papers and magazines, I don't know. Maybe it woke me up. I'm not sure. All I know is I want to be with you. *Really* be with you."

"I want to be with you too," she whispers, a beautiful note of glee in her tone.

"God, I wish I could kiss you right now. Firsts should always be sealed with a kiss."

She laughs heartily this time, and I love it more than her giggle.

"Honey . . ."

"Ah, there's my honey." I grin, my rapid heartbeat slowing down. I can feel myself relax on hearing her sweet endearment. It's going to be okay. Sky and I will find a way to make it work.

"So, we're doing this. Me and you. A couple. A relationship."

"We're doing this."

"And you want me to announce it to the world . . ."

"I'm not ashamed to have the sexiest woman alive riding my coattails." I crack the joke to lighten the heaviness of the decision.

"Riding your coattails, eh?"

"Hey . . . I'm a catch."

"Are you?"

"Yes."

"Who says so?" she teases.

"My mother. And she's probably about to lose her mind at seeing the pictures that went out. She will be my very next call." I laugh.

"Oh boy. That ought to be interesting." Her tone still carries humor but with a tinge of sadness on the edge. We haven't talked about her parents much, and now isn't the right time either, but eventually I want to know all there is to know about Skyler Paige Lumpkin.

"Yes, it will. She'll want to meet you."

"I'd love to!" Her breath whistles through the line as though the mere thought of meeting my parents is awe-inspiring.

"It's not a big deal. Really. My mom and dad are cool. Blue collar. Family oriented. Down to earth. You'll love them, and they'll love you."

"Please tell your mother I can't wait."

"And I can't wait to see you next. I feel like we need to make up."

"You just want the makeup sex!" she accuses, laughing.

"Like you don't!"

She stifles her laughter. "This is true. Okay, as much as I hate to say it, I've got to go on set. I'll have Tracey send over the statement for your review and approval."

"I'm sure whatever she says will be fine, but go ahead and have her send it to Wendy."

"Okay. I'll call you later?"

"I'd be disappointed if you didn't."

"Is it stupid to say I'm excited?" Her voice is whimsical, now with a lightness to it, which wasn't there when I first called.

I chuckle. "No, it's not stupid. It's a big step. I'm looking forward to where it takes us." And I mean it. This thing with Skyler is new, but it's also a refreshing change I firmly believe I'm ready for.

"Me too. Call you later, pretty boy!"

"You do that. Bye, baby."

Before she hangs up I hear a kiss noise. My woman air-kissed the phone.

Fuckin' cute. And silly.

My woman is a dork . . . and all mine.

I shake my head, put down the phone, and stand up. I give myself a good long stretch, realizing how insanely tired I am. I didn't catch much sleep on the plane what with worrying over the weirdness between Sky and me before she left, and then there was coming back to the media going crazy, my woman being upset, working it out, and taking an emotional leap I once swore I never would do again.

Once I get a hold on my equilibrium as well as my frayed emotions, I walk out to the front office.

Wendy, Bo, and Royce are looking at her computer screen, all three of them with guilty-as-sin expressions on their faces when their gazes reach mine.

I cross my arms over my chest. "What are you three jackals looking at?" I crook an eyebrow. "Hmm? Fess up."

Wendy turns the computer screen around, and front and center is a huge image of Skyler and me.

"Damn, brother . . . ," Royce mutters.

"Lucky son of a bitch. Skyler Paige." Bo shakes his head as if he still can't believe I'm with Skyler.

"I think you look really hot together. This site is rating you against her ex-beau, Johan Karr." Wendy points to the screen. "Look, you're winning by sixteen percent."

"Winning what?" I ask.

"Who's hotter, of course!"

I sigh. "This is only the beginning, folks."

"Why's that?" Wendy grins, her lips twitching knowingly.

"Because Skyler and I agreed we're more than seeing each other. More than casual. We're officially in a relationship."

"Brother, you tellin' me you're off the market?" Roy asks, his dark eyebrows arching with curiosity and fishing for information.

I nod.

"Thank fucking Christ! Hallelujah! More chicklets for me!" Bo opens his arms as if he were about to hug the ceiling.

Roy comes from behind the desk and claps me on the shoulder. "Good for you. She's a knockout for sho'. Just make sure she's treating you right. Lookin' forward to the meet and greet. When she coming to Beantown?" His question comes off as more a command than a request.

My brothers want to vet my woman. It's been a long time since any of us have had to grill a brother's mate. Too long. And with the conversation I had earlier with Roy, another one might be in the wings sooner rather than later. If he's in the market for good woman, all the men of Boston proper better bring their A game; once smooth Royce hits the town, game time will be over for the single fellas.

"Not sure yet," I answer honestly. "She's filming now. I'm going to go home, catch up on some sleep, then chat with her tonight. I'll keep you all posted."

"Cool, cool." Royce squeezes my shoulder. "We got things on lock here."

I grab the suitcase I left in the waiting area. "Give me a few hours before calling, yeah?" I lift my chin toward Wendy.

"No problem, boss man."

I grin, and she smiles, her cheeks pinking up.

"Oh, but don't forget to call your mother. I have lunch with her every Wednesday, and she's really worried about your sleep schedule. Says you travel too much and you can't possibly be getting good sleep. Then of course there's Skyler, who she's dying to know more about."

I hold on to the handle of my suitcase and nod numbly, then turn when her words filter through my foggy, tired brain. "You have lunch with my mother every Wednesday?"

She scrunches up her face. "Uh, yeah. I have lunch with Royce's mom every Tuesday. Sometimes his sisters come. Depends on who's available."

I grin and shake my head. "You slipped right into the family didn't you?"

Wendy winks and shimmies in her chair. "Yep. Got no family besides Sir Mick. Since you call each other brothers, I figured I could earn my way into being an honorary sister."

"Gross. I can't fuck my sister," Bo grumbles, then makes a gagging noise.

"Good thing you're never fucking me. Now get on, go find yourself a clingon, and get some rest. Need you both back in business right away. There's a ton to go over."

"Bye, Wendy." I wave.

"Bye, boss man."

"Bye, Tinker Bell," Bo says with naughty innuendo lacing his tone.

"Bye, pencil dick."

Bo and I enter the elevator.

"Wendy is great, isn't she?" Bo smiles and adjusts his leather jacket.

"She is."

When we exit, my heart lifts at the sight of my cherry-red Tesla. "Hi, pretty girl," I coo, then open the back and toss in my suitcase. Bo chucks his bag next to mine with an "Oomph."

I frown. "Hey . . ."

"Got the bike, brother. Gonna hit the bar next to the apartment, see if I can find me a repeat so I can crash hard tonight. Still too wound up from the plane ride."

I groan. "You are too much, man."

Bo cups his junk. "That's what all the chicklets say."

I laugh at his quip. "Catch you on the flip."

Bo hikes a leg over his bike, revs the engine, and offers me a solitary chin lift before walking the bike backward and speeding off.

Lord help us the day he gets smacked upside the head by a woman he can't live without.

3

I slept the sleep of the dead last night. Barely woke to mumble a sleepy hello to Skyler when she called and then crashed hard until morning. Back at work, I finally have a minute to review the *People* magazine spread. I'm unimpressed. It was supposed to be labeled "Bared to You" like the book Skyler loves, but no. That would be far too much to ask. The heading now reads "Skyler Paige Bares It All" and then goes on to talk about her happy upbringing, her start in acting, and even more information on her parents' untimely demise than is warranted.

All the planning and special photo shoots were all twisted around. There are more pictures of the two of us kissing and being overly friendly than need to be shared. The pictures are all tasteful, which isn't the problem. Bo took them, and the man does damn fine work. If these were private images for us to enjoy, I'd be clapping the guy on the back and thanking him for doing superb work. Only seeing my relationship with Skyler bleed out onto the pages of a top magazine is not part of my life goals.

Frankly I'm surprised at how much they played upon our budding relationship, and I notify my lawyer of my concerns on Skyler's behalf, as well as my own. He informs me that since we sent over the files and left the interview open ended, they could report what they wanted to report. Unfortunately all of it was true. However, the way the story was twisted didn't speak to Skyler's true nature or what she wanted to express to her fandom or the public at large, and that bothered me.

I toss the magazine on the desk and pick up the phone, wanting to hear her voice.

"Hey, you . . ." Her voice is sleepy and muffled.

Sleepy Skyler. Mmm. I love sleepy Skyler. She lets me do anything to her in the morning. Go down on her, lick, nip, and suck on her breasts until she's begging for my cock. One time, I even woke her enough so I could shove my hard dick into her mouth. She took it like a champ, sucking it down while waking up.

I groan and fist my hand, wishing I were touching her in some way. "Morning. How'd you sleep?"

She hums. "Good. I was exhausted. Didn't finish up until late after I talked to you. Rick and I didn't even have dinner until close to midnight. We ended up calling in twenty-four-hour Chinese food. I practically crashed in my kung pao chicken." She yawns loudly.

Rick the Prick having a midnight meal with my girl. I scowl but ignore the comment, not wanting to rile her up again after yesterday's cock-up.

I glance at the clock and note it's eight. Not too early, but my woman sounds wiped. "When do you have to go back in?"

"Noon. They had some problem with the equipment . . ."

"Ah. Well, that's good for you. Gives you some extra time to relax before picking it back up."

"Yeah." She hums again before exhaling long and slow. God, I can so clearly recall the feeling of her waking up against me, her breath feathering out across my bare chest. I miss it more than I should.

"I just read the *People* piece."

Silence greets me.

"I've already contacted my lawyer . . ."

Skyler yawns again. "They can't do anything, honey. Freedom of speech and freedom of the press. Besides, everything they printed is the truth."

I grit my teeth. "Yes, but it wasn't what we discussed with them."

"You'll learn soon enough that nothing the press or media says is ever what they're going to print. They always do what they want in the end. Could have been a lot worse. At least it puts us in a good light."

"All I know is that bridge is fucking burned to the ground," I snarl, and run my hand through my hair, wishing there were more I could do or say.

Sky chuckles. "Okay. Oh, I have good news for you." Her voice takes on a sweet lilt, which acts as a balm to my frayed emotions.

"Really? Please, for the love of God, lay it on me. I could use some good news right about now."

"I have the entire weekend off. Friday included. I thought maybe I could come to Boston. Meet your folks. Spend the weekend with you . . ."

She's not even here and the grin I'm sporting is from ear to ear.

When the fuck did I get so excited about seeing a woman?

Never is the answer.

It's Skyler. My personal game changer.

"Sky, baby, you have made my fucking week." Already I'm imagining all the things I want to do to her, plus the things I want to show her once I let her out of my bedroom. Of course, the guys and Wendy will want to see her. "I want you to meet Wendy and Royce too. He's itching to grill you. Make sure you have nothing but good intentions."

She laughs heartily. "Awesome. I was thinking perhaps I could sneak over alone . . ."

Immediately my hackles rise. "Peaches, I know you want to have freedom, but baby, that's not the life you have. You gotta make sure Rachel and Nate escort you. I'm sorry, but your safety is more important than privacy. Especially since the spread came out. The paps will want a piece of you."

She groans and sighs loudly into the phone. "For once in my life, I'd like to be a no-name. Don't get me wrong, I love my job, and thanks to you, I'm over my slump, but the lack of privacy is—"

"Fucked up. Daunting. Stressful." I can think of a hundred things to label what she must be going through, and I've only had a tiny taste. The paps were out in front of my building when I left for work, taking pictures, and at my office, again taking more pictures. I ignored them and moved on. It had to be a million times worse for my girl.

"That and more."

"I know, Sky, but you have to be safe. There are a lot of wack-jobs out in the world. Promise me you'll bring your crew with you?"

She growls under her breath, sounding like a little fire-breathing dragon. "Fine." She's not happy about it.

"One day we'll figure out a better system, but for now, where you go, they go. Promise me?"

"I promise." She lets out what sounds like a frustrated breath.

"Good. Now what are you wearing?" I say salaciously into the phone line, holding my breath until she gives full details.

***

The knock on the door may as well be pounding against my chest. I've been waiting all afternoon for her to arrive, making sure my place is picked up, dirty clothes in the hamper, dishes in the dishwasher. The cleaning service came yesterday to scrub away any man filth and dust from being away so long.

I can't help smiling as I walk to the door and fling it open.

There she is. My dream girl in all her glory. She's wearing a black halter-style one-piece, which crosses delectably at her tits and flares out at the waist into wide, flowing, belled legs. Her feet are encased in a pair of sexy-as-fuck gold strappy heels. Her blonde hair is parted down the center, the long layers cascading in beachy waves over her shoulders.

"Jesus!" I gasp, losing my cool in one word.

Her brown eyes flare in appreciation as she takes in my dress slacks and light cashmere sweater. "You guys can go to the hotel. I don't believe we'll be leaving tonight," she says, smirking.

I finally notice Nate enter the doorframe and set her suitcase inside. He grins and winks before looping an arm around his wife. "Call if you change your plans."

Skyler doesn't take her eyes off mine when she responds, "Will do."

I hold the door open farther. She doesn't walk through the door, she sways inside, her small juicy ass bouncing against the thin silk fabric a bit with her efforts.

My mouth waters with the desire to bite right into that fleshy surface. I push the door and kick it shut, locking it behind my back. She tosses her coat onto my couch and scans the area before turning around. "Nice place," she quips, before lifting her hand to the back of her neck.

As if in slow motion the swaths of fabric at her neck slip down, uncovering her strapless bra, and slide across her bare abdomen and over her rounded hips and toned thighs to fall straight to the floor. A scrap of black lace in the shape of a triangle is covering her sex.

Skyler places her hands on her hips. "You going to stand there all night, staring with your mouth open, or are you going to kiss your girlfriend hello?"

I blink stupidly a few times, taking in the swell of her breasts being pushed up by her bra, the delicate hourglass shape of her small waistline, the flare of her hips.

"My girlfriend?" I tease. It's the first time either of us has used the standard title people give the woman they've committed to seeing exclusively.

She grins. "Mm-hmm. I read it in a newspaper this morning."

I take one step closer, watching her pupils dilate. "The newspaper, huh? Must be true. You know they only print facts." I grip my sweater and undershirt in one go, pull them over my head, and toss them to the floor.

She licks her lips when my naked chest comes into view.

While her gaze runs up and down my chest, she reaches behind her back and unclips her bra. It falls to the floor, and I'm gifted with pale pink tips already erect due to her obvious excitement.

I swallow around the sudden burst of arousal that hits me. My cock hardens painfully in my pants, and ripples of excitement rush along my nerve endings in every direction, readying for the moment when our skin touches for the first time.

"Peaches, you are the most beautiful thing I've ever seen. I'm one lucky man." I shake my head and fist my hands.

She loops her hands at the tiny line of lace at each hip, pushes the fabric down, and shimmies out of it, baring every inch of her naked body. Her wet center comes into view, and I can no longer hold back my carnal response. Everything in me is straining, reaching for her . . . my dick, my hands, my entire body. In two big strides I cup her cheeks and smash her lips to mine.

My girl opens her mouth immediately, tangling her tongue with mine. She tastes of mint and smells of peaches. I suck on her bottom lip, kissing her hard, harder than I normally would, but I can't help it. I need to *feel* her and be *felt* by this woman.

One of her hands tunnels into the back of my hair, holding my head to hers; the other locks around my shoulders, nails digging in for purchase. The heels she's wearing help her stand closer to my height, making it easy to devour her mouth.

I tilt her head and drink deep from her, solidifying everything between us.

Lust.

Desire.

Need.

We're reconnecting in the same way we began. Only now we're familiar. We know what the other likes and wants, making every kiss more intense. Every touch a branding of skin on skin.

With her chest pressed flat against mine, I can finally breathe again. The tension, which weighed so heavily on me from our last day in Copenhagen until right now, is finally lifting.

I rip my mouth from hers, both of us panting, our foreheads resting against one another.

"God, I missed your mouth," she whispers in the quiet space between us.

I grin wickedly and kiss her wet lips hard before falling to my knees in front of her. I clutch her thighs when she teeters off-balance. Her hands flail but then grip my shoulders, finding purchase.

"We can't have you missing my mouth, now can we?" I waggle my eyebrows and inhale her delicious scent only a couple of inches from her center, taking in the familiar, rich essence of her arousal. I lick my lips and stare up at my dream girl.

Her nails bite into my shoulders as she boldly widens her stance, opening herself to me, being vulnerable in a way I know in my heart she's not been with another man. It's a gift I relish and plan to honor with a dozen stellar orgasms this weekend.

I ease my hands along the outside of her thighs from knee to hip, caressing up and down. She trembles under my fingertips, wanting what I'm about to do to her almost as much as I want to drive her insane and hear her scream my name while under my tongue.

"Honey . . ." Her voice is coated in desperation.

I let her need fill me up as I lean forward and open her lower lips with my thumbs so I can reach my goal in the first swipe. The second the flat of my tongue touches her, she ignites, crying out to the ceiling.

Soft. Lush. Heaven.

Her taste covers my tongue, and my hips jut forward on instinct, my body wanting what my mouth is receiving. I run my tongue up and down her slit, licking every inch of her before I spread her wide and hold her firmly so I can fuck her with my tongue.

"Parker," she gasps, one of her hands digging into my shoulder as she gyrates her hips in small circles, greedy for more.

I move my mouth and insert two fingers deep into her wet heat. Her body goes rigid at the invasion, and a heavy moan, which may as well be a hand squeezing my dick, filters through the air. I become so hard in response, I have to undo the button and zipper of my slacks to give "the beast" more room.

Taking my time, I lick around her tight bundle of nerves, alternating between sucking and flicking it with the tip of my tongue. Using a steady, unhurried rhythm with my fingers, I thrust and retract evenly, loving the sensation of her internal muscles gripping my fingers with every plunge.

"Please . . . I need to come." She stirs her hips and grips my hair with one hand, tugging at the roots until I stop licking and look up at her. Her arousal coats my lips deliciously, and I only want more. Honestly, I can't get enough of her taste on my tongue.

"Honey, make me come," she begs, sinking her teeth into her plump bottom lip. As I take in her naked body from my kneeling position, she's absolute beauty personified.

It hits me like a punch to the chest that I'm on my knees, worshipping this woman's body, and there is no place on earth I'd rather be. It's a profound thought, which flares my nostrils as I suck in lungfuls of her honey scent. I flex my fingers to hold her in place and cover her aching bundle of nerves with the heat of my mouth. I lock down on the firm kernel and rub back and forth with as much pressure as I can muster with her constant movement.

Skyler's body jolts against my hold, both of her hands holding my head to her core as she bucks against me wildly.

My dick is seeping at the tip, and I shove my underwear down to wrap its girth in a firm fist to stave off the desire to come. The sound of her losing her mind in ecstasy, her taste on my tongue, and her scent in my nose could have me going off any second.

I lock my lips over her hot bundle of nerves again and suck until she comes in a long stream of *yes*es and profanities.

The second her body starts to shake with aftershocks from one helluva powerful orgasm, I stand up and shift her to the side where I can rest her ass on the back of my couch. Shoving my pants to my ankles and kicking them off, I center myself between her thighs and my raging hard-on at her slippery slit and thrust home.

"Fuck!" I pull out to the tip and slam back in.

Perfection.

Stars race across my vision and relief flickers out of every pore while her tight sheath locks on to my cock. She wraps her arms around my back and sucks on my neck.

"Fuck me hard, honey. We both need it," Skyler pants against my ear, before nibbling on the cartilage.

Shooting star–like tendrils of pleasure surge through my veins, propelling me to take her harder, faster, deeper until I'm powering into her. Every thrust better than the last.

"Perfect," I grind out through my teeth.

Thrust hard.

"Fucking."

Thrust deep.

"Woman!" I growl out.

Before she can respond, I pull out, grab her hips, and spin her around so her pert, juicy ass is pointed at my cock. She grips the couch back and, once again, widens her legs. I can see her glistening sex, swollen and waiting for my entry. It makes me dizzy with lust and greed.

I palm her cheeks with both hands and spread them so I can see everything. Her dark rosette winks, and even though we haven't talked about anal play, I've got to taste her *everywhere*. There will be no inch of Skyler Paige I haven't kissed or licked. I curve my body over her form and kiss a line down her spine, over her tailbone, pucker, and to her center. Skyler's body quivers, and she sighs loudly when I glide over her dark hole, leading me to believe she's not averse to a little ass play.

I want to test her limits a smidgen, so I flatten my tongue back over her center and trail it over her slit and up to the forbidden place I haven't touched yet. I swirl my tongue around the tight rosette, catching a whiff of her peachy bodywash. I groan and flick my tongue against the sensitive muscle until Skyler is wiggling her ass and whimpering for more.

Who am I not to give the woman what she wants, at least a little of what she wants, until I can properly prepare her to take my cock up her tight ass? Using my thumb, I dip it into her wetness and thumb-fuck her for a few lunges, getting the digit nice and soaked with her arousal. Once I've got her moaning consistently, I pull out, stand up behind her pretty ass, and plunge my cock straight into her slit. Her little pucker closes tight as I thrust a few times inside her heat before I feel she's let her inhibitions go enough to circle the muscle teasingly with my thumb.

"How's this, Peaches? I fuck you while playing with your pretty little ass."

"Mmm . . . so good." She pushes her body back against my cock, which sends a bout of euphoria skittering out from my dick, up each nerve ending, and out my lungs in a rough burst of air.

"Jesus!" I hammer her harder in retaliation for her surprise move.

She loves it so much, one of her hands leaves the couch and slides into her curls.

"You playing with yourself, baby? Reach lower, feel me fucking you while I shove my thumb in your ass."

"Oh my God . . ." She gasps as I dip the tip of my thumb into her.

She follows through on my command with her hand. The second her fingers graze the sides of my cock where I'm taking her, I lose it.

Each caress of her fingers against my length and balls is like a jolt of nirvana. I hold on to the feeling as long as I can, wanting her as high as I am. "Come with me . . ." I plunge my thumb in and out of her ass and thrust my hips, battering her swollen sex until her entire body locks down.

"Yes!" She screeches like a banshee, and I redouble my efforts. Pounding into her, holding my thumb deep inside, my other four fingers locked over her tailbone so I can tug her ass and fuck her center at the same time.

Her body is limp as a rag doll while I keep thrusting . . . until she surprises the hell out of me and goes off again. Less intense than the first time, but enough to send me straight over the edge into bliss.

My balls draw up, my mind goes blank, and all I can see, hear, and feel is Skyler. She's all around me as I plant myself flat against her, curve my body over her back, and release deep inside. Shot after shot, I lose all the inhibition, stress, and tension that have crept up this past week until nothing but peace remains. As I come to a few moments later, I'm resting over my woman's naked body, sated and wrung dry.

Firming my stance, I ease out of her, lift her up into my arms in a princess hold, and carry her to my bed. Once there, I lay her down before hitting the bathroom for a warm washcloth. When I come back, I ease open her legs, and she doesn't protest or even stir. I've drained two orgasms out of my girl, leaving her dead to the world. I take care of cleaning her up, toss the rag in the laundry, and go around to the other side of the bed.

Once under the covers, I pull Skyler into my arms and curl my shape entirely around hers. Contentment fills my bones as she nuzzles her ass against my crotch, tugs one of my arms between her breasts, and kisses my fingertips before resting her head on my other bicep, sighing and falling asleep.

I chuckle and burrow my chin into her neck, her peaches-and-cream scent filling my lungs and putting me at perfect peace with my world. Instead of falling asleep, I stare at the beautiful woman in my arms.

Not only is Skyler Paige a stunning beauty, her soul is pure. She could have hated me for the media shit storm, which ensued because of my place in her life and my team screwing up the pictures, but she didn't. Once she got past the hurt and misunderstanding, that was it. No dragging it on and on or throwing it in my face. When a problem arises, we solve it, and then it's done. No bullshit or drama. Nothing like what I dealt with in the relationship with Kayla. That woman put me through the wringer. Now that I have a woman in my life like Skyler, the complete opposite of Kayla and everything she stood for, I'm starting to remember the good part of having a woman. Not just to fuck. Skyler and I have off-the-charts chemistry in the bedroom, but it's more than that.

Having someone to talk to at the end of the day, even if it's a phone call. Knowing someone is thinking about me as much as I'm thinking about her. Planning my world around things that might make her happy and vice versa. I can even see the benefit of thinking about the future, though Sky and I are far from that at this point.

Still, in the past, I couldn't even imagine having children. Especially not with Kayla. And the more I think back, the more I realize how fooled I was by her beauty. She was a bitch to me and a bitch to my friends. Even my mother voiced her concerns about a long-term future with Kayla, which is unusual for Catherine Ellis. While my brother and I were growing up, Ma didn't get involved in our romantic affairs, but she was always there if we wanted to talk. I should have noticed the signs sooner, which is part of why I think I've held off on pursuing the opposite sex for more than a few rolls in the sack. I wasn't sure I could trust a woman again, but with Skyler, I'm willing to try. Take the risk in order to reap the reward.

And Skyler is absolutely my freakin' reward.

4

Skyler flips down the mirror cover in the passenger sun visor of my Tesla for the tenth time. She fluffs her long layers at the roots. For the second time in ten minutes, she reapplies lip gloss. This is followed by a frustrated sigh, which feels like the millionth time.

"Peaches . . . what's going on?" I reach for her hand, clasp it, and rest it on my thigh.

Her palm is warm and comforting, another oddity I didn't expect to enjoy with a woman.

Holding hands. The act seems novel. Probably because I haven't done it much in half a decade. Usually the women I dated in the past would reach for my hand. I'd hold their hands briefly, so as to not make them feel less than, but as soon as I could find a reason to let go . . . I would. With Skyler, I have a constant desire to touch and be touched by her.

Skyler squeezes my hand. "What if they don't like me?"

I practically choke out my laughter. Her head twists toward me, and her eyes narrow into tiny slits. "I'm being serious!" she scolds, her cheeks flushing pink.

I chuckle. "That's what makes it so funny!" I continue to laugh.

"You are *not* helping." She attempts to pull her hand away, but I hold it fast.

"Peaches, they're going to love you. The entire freakin' world already does."

"They don't know me! I want your parents to *know* me. The real me. Not the actress they liked in one of their favorite movies. Just Skyler."

I lift her hand up to my face but watch the road as I kiss the back of her fingers. "Baby, I'm telling you. They are not only going to like you, they will love you. Hell, my mother's probably already planning our wedding and the name of our firstborn with her book group."

I chance a look at her and grin.

Instead of seeing her laughing, I catch her with an expression that telegraphs she's been stunned stupid. I tighten my hold on her hand. "Peaches, relax. I'm kidding. Mostly." I wink, and she finally takes a full breath and lets it out slowly. Her grip loosens, and she slumps back into the leather seat.

"I've never met the parents before. Believe it or not, when I was younger, I was too busy acting to date. And when I was around twenty, I dated a little but not enough to ever reach that point. My first real boyfriend was Johan. And he never introduced me to his parents."

I frown. "Why the hell not? Weren't you with him over a year?"

She sighs and looks out the window as the traffic flows by. Behind us, in a rented blacked-out Range Rover, are Nate and Rachel, Sky's protection team. So far we haven't been followed, at least not as far as I've noticed, but I suspect the paps know what I drive, and a smokin' hot, cherry-red Tesla isn't going to be hard to spot.

"Yeah, eighteen months." She answers my question but doesn't continue. Even though I don't want to push her and ruin any potential mood, I want to know more about her.

"First love?" I ask softly.

She nods. "Yeah, but I was the only one in it. At first, I thought he loved me in his own way. He was busy with his career, as was I. Though looking back, it was all wrong. I ended up being the only one to make any compromises in our lives. I moved in with him, met him at his shoots in between filming or during free times. He rarely came to wherever I was stationed for work."

"Really? That does seem rather one-sided."

She shrugs. "Part of me thinks I held on to him so tightly because he was there when I lost my parents three years ago. We had just started dating, and I was devastated."

Bastard probably took advantage of her. Three years ago, she was only twenty-two. "And they were your only family?"

Skyler sucks in a large breath, which rattles out as I watch her attempt to control her emotions. Still, her eyes turn glassy, and the tip of her nose reddens.

"Hey, you don't have to talk about any of this if you don't want to, or if it hurts too much. I'm trying to get to know you better." I pat her leg, then grip it firmly to solidify my seriousness.

She smiles softly. "I know, and it's good to talk about them. They were amazing. Best parents a girl could ever have. I may not have had siblings growing up, but they gave me so much love and attention, I never felt alone. Until they passed."

I nod and rub my thumb over her hand in what I hope is comforting support. "How'd they die?"

She cants her head and frowns. "You read the *People* piece, and I'm sure Wendy gave you all the information you needed on me."

"This may be true, but I want to hear it from your mouth. The truth. Not what people print in the papers."

She firms her jaw and purses her lips before speaking. "They'd always wanted to travel the world. And with my acting, they did a lot of what they wanted. I made sure of it. Since they dropped everything for me and my acting career growing up, I made sure they had plenty of money to do what they desired when I was an adult."

I smile, hold her hand, and kiss it again, only for longer this time. "You're a good daughter."

"They were great parents. Well, they wanted to rent a yacht and sail the ocean, hit a bunch of European locations. It was a dream they'd had ever since I was a little girl."

"And . . ."

"I set them up with the yacht and team. They didn't even make it to their first location when they hit a heavy storm. Capsized the boat. The entire team was lost, including my parents."

I swallow around the sudden lump in my throat. "Jesus. Baby, I'm sorry."

She sucks in a sharp breath. "Yeah, me too. If it weren't for my setting it all up, they'd still be here."

Oh hell no.

"Sky . . ."

She shakes her head. "Enough. Can we change the subject?" Her words are tight, and her mouth has flattened into a thin, harsh line. Not the prettiest look on her.

"Yeah, baby, we can. Especially because we're here."

Skyler looks out the window at my father's bar. The kelly-green awnings, crisp and clean against the old brick facade, look brighter during the daylight hours.

"This is the place? Where they live?"

I chuckle and cup her nape so she's focused on me. "Yeah, this is where they live in a sense. It's where we all hang out, come to gather as friends and family. It's my pops's bar. Lucky's has always been my favorite place in the world. It's where I grew up. Mom wanted you to come to the house, but it's small, and I wanted you, your team, and the guys to feel comfortable."

Skyler leans forward, cups my jaw, and kisses me softly. She pulls away sooner than I'd like but runs her thumb across my bottom lip. "I love it. This is perfect."

I grin. "Then come on, Peaches. Let's get you a beer and one of the cook's famous pulled-pork sammies."

She moans, a sweet sound I feel in my dick. "Sounds heavenly!"

I run around the car and find Nate and Rachel are already outside, scanning the area, as I open Sky's door and reach out a hand.

She extends a fine, jean-clad leg, which she's paired with camel-colored suede boots that go up to the knees. On top she's wearing an off-the-shoulder, slouchy cashmere sweater. Her wrists display a host of tinkling bracelets. A pair of dangling gold hoops adorns her ears, and her hair is down in beachy waves. My favorite look. I like running my fingers through those soft locks, which I have a sneaking suspicion she knows and likes as much as I do.

I lead her to the building and open the door for her. I can hear Royce's deep laughter and Ma's higher-pitched laugh from the entrance.

Pops has closed down the bar for the afternoon and night, which I know is a huge hit to the budget, but one he'd gladly take in order to have a family event with all the guys. Only downside is my brother, Paul, is still off on some secret mission with the government.

The second we enter, my mother stands up from her place at a long line of tables they'd set up so we could all sit together in the center of the bar. Her arms open as she approaches.

"Parker . . ."

I let go of Sky long enough to embrace my ma and take in her familiar Obsession by Calvin Klein scent.

"I'm so glad you're home and safe." She holds me close and then pulls back. "And now introduce me to your *friend*."

I loop my arm around Skyler, and she wraps one of hers around my waist. I can feel her fingers digging into my side.

"Ma, this is Skyler. Skyler, my mother, Cathy."

"It's good to meet you, Cathy." Skyler holds out her hand.

My mother pushes it aside and approaches Sky, so I have to let her go. "Oh, pishposh. We hug around here. Come here, sunshine." She tugs Skyler into her arms.

Skyler's beaming smile over my mother's shoulder melts my heart.

Ma pulls back but cups Skyler's face with one hand. "As golden as the sun. You know, you're even prettier in person." She pats Skyler's cheek, and Sky lifts her hand up to hold my mother's to her face.

"Thank you," she says, emotion coating her tone.

Ma preens under Skyler's look of awe.

My mother has that effect on people. Everyone loves her, and she loves everyone. Unless they prove themselves unworthy. Then she can hold a wicked-mean grudge, but it's hard to get to that place with her.

"And who do we have here?" Ma gestures to Nate and Rachel.

"Ma, this is Skyler's security team and friends. Rachel and Nate Van Dyken."

"So fancy. Your own team." She lifts her hands to her chest in a prayer gesture, smiling like a loon before shaking their hands. "Well, come on in, take a load off. I'll have Randy get your drink orders."

"Thanks for welcoming us, ma'am," Nate says.

Ma turns around and heads to the table. "Such good manners."

"Hey!" the entire IG team, sans Wendy, hollers out to us.

Royce stands, walks over to us, takes Skyler's hand, and brings it up to his lips. "Nice to meet you, little lady." His voice is a deep rumble.

Sky grins wide and fans herself, looking at me. "Are all the people you know hot?"

"No, just me," Roy jokes.

"Hey! I resent that." Bo hops up from where he's straddling a chair backward.

He pulls Sky into a bear hug. "Hi, darlin'."

Sky returns his hug, much to my chagrin, and pats him on the back. "You over your jet lag?" she asks him, having just seen him last week in Copenhagen.

"Nuthin' a few nights' sleep and a couple of rounds with a chicklet didn't fix." He waggles his brows.

"What's a chicklet?" Sky asks, and I place an arm around her shoulders and tug her away from our resident man whore.

"Peaches, you don't want to know."

"Peaches?" my mother gasps, obviously having heard my nickname for my girl. "So cute." Her happiness practically pours off her in waves.

I roll my eyes as I bring Sky over to my father, who's busy lining up drinks for everyone.

Pops wipes his hands on the towel he's thrown over his shoulder and extends a hand out over the counter.

"Skyler, happy to have you here at Lucky's. Thanks for making the trek from New York."

Skyler shakes his hand. "Of course. Thanks for having me. I was looking forward to meeting Parker's family and friends."

"What'll ya have?" he asks.

"Do you have cider?"

"Sure do. Angry Orchard?"

"Perfect, thank you."

My father smacks the bar top. "Comin' right up. Go take a load off."

We sit across from Royce and Bo, Rachel and Nate to the side of Skyler, Ma and Pops at each end, fluttering around.

The moment Pops sets down our drinks, the bar door opens.

Nate and Rachel both stand up. Nate comes around the table, and Rachel stands in front of Skyler instantly. Both of them have serious "don't mess with me" expressions on their faces.

"Whoa, whoa!" I stand and grip Nate's shoulder. "It's Wendy and I'm assuming her boyfriend," I tell him, and his shoulders ease down, but he still stands firm.

"Hey, boss man!" Wendy flounces in, holding the hand of a tall man. He's wearing dress slacks and an impeccably pressed dress shirt, no tie, and a fitted sweater over his shirt. The man has ash-blond hair and light eyes. He has every bit the "rich businessman on the weekend" vibe, though the woman whose hand he's holding is his complete opposite. Wendy's wearing red tights, a black-and-white houndstooth miniskirt, and a men's-style white dress shirt tied at the waist. The front is open, revealing a red lace bra she means to show off. On her feet are black heeled combat boots. Her fiery-red hair is slicked to one side with a black plastic bow you'd see on a child. With Wendy, you never know what you're going to get, but it's always interesting, and she rocks it as though it's the next haute couture.

"Wendy. Glad you could make it." I walk over and stand in front of her and her mate. I put my hand out. "Parker Ellis. I'm the boss."

"Michael Pritchard. Fiancé."

"Wendy . . ." I smile as she holds up her hand, showing me a big, honking ring.

"He asked me to marry him! Can you believe it? Me!" Her entire being looks like she's about to burst with joy.

I chuckle, and she flies into my arms to hug me, bouncing as she does. Over my shoulder I can see her man does not like her hugging other men. His jaw firms, and his eyes narrow. Still, he doesn't scare me. I could take him if we went head to head.

"Of course I can believe it. You're a catch, minxy."

She grins and pulls back. "Now, introduce me to your superstar girlfriend. And punch me if I go all fangirl."

"You put hands on my woman in anger, and you'll be answering to me." Michael wraps an arm around Wendy's waist, bringing her back against his form.

She smacks at his hand around her waist. "Oh, he's kidding." She snickers.

"Not even a little," Michael responds a tad threateningly.

"Oh shush." She kisses his cheek, which seems to appease him. His demeanor softens at the first touch of her lips against his skin. Wendy tries to look past me. "I want to meet Skyler!"

"Come on over and meet the rest of the family, Michael."

We spend a few minutes introducing Wendy and Michael, sharing in their happy news as Pops gets the drinks. Everyone agrees to having pulled-pork sammies and fries along with some appetizers the cook planned for us. Rachel and Nate decline an alcoholic beverage, and my respect for them goes up another degree. They're on the job even though Skyler repeatedly told them this is supposed to be fun time.

Once the food is served and Ma and Pops are at their ends of the table, the real conversation starts.

"Skyler, I'm dying to know what it's like to be a celebrity. Is it awesome or what?" Wendy asks unabashedly while chomping on a fry.

Skyler sips her cider and licks her lips. I want so badly to lick them for her, taste the apple cider on her pretty mouth for myself. Instead, I rub her thigh from hip to knee in a repeated pattern, which is probably soothing me more than her.

"It has its advantages and disadvantages, I suppose, like any job."

"Yeah, like meeting amazing people and going to cool places." Wendy's eyes light up with interest.

Sky smiles. "True and definitely a bonus. Though the lack of privacy is a constant battle."

My mother frowns. "Do you get a lot of people bugging you for autographs and the like?" she asks.

"Sure. I don't mind talking to fans. Usually they're really respectful, want to tell me what their favorite movie of mine is, or get a signature. The paparazzi are the problem."

"Vultures," Nate rumbles under his breath.

"What are you working on now?" Pops asks.

"Another in my Angel series."

"I love those movies! You're such a badass in them!" Wendy gushes.

Sky laughs. "Thank you. It is a lot of fun to do the action shots, and I try to learn the moves so I don't need a stunt double too often."

"Cool . . . ," Wendy gasps, and leans her cheek into her hand, her elbow braced on the table, focusing entirely on Skyler. My assistant is in complete awe of my girl, but she's reining it in and keeping it together. Over time, I'm sure she'll get past Sky's celebrity and think of her as a friend. Hopefully. Sky could use some good friends, Tracey being the only one I know of.

"It is cool." Sky smiles.

"And probably not hard to work with the hottie Rick Pettington." Wendy fans her face. "That boy is *hawt!*"

Michael tightens his arm around his woman's shoulder; instinctively I grip Sky's leg.

Royce laughs into his fist. "Hoo-boy. And the daggers come out."

"He's very nice to look at, yes. And he's a friend," Sky offers diplomatically.

I jolt my head to the side to look more closely at my woman. "A friend? He's upgraded to *friend* status?"

Skyler sighs and pats my chest. "Yes. He's always been a friend, but more so now. You can't work sixteen-hour days with someone and not become close."

I frown. "How close we talkin'?" I growl, and the entire table laughs.

"Put a lid on it, son," Pops warns. "Girl has to work alongside a lot of nice-looking fellas in her business, I imagine."

"Thank you, Mr. Ellis." Sky beams at my dad.

"You can call me Randy, darlin', or Pops. Everyone does."

"I think I'll be taking a visit to this set, make my presence known." I nudge Sky's temple and lay a kiss there.

"Good idea. Keep a lock on what's yours," Michael affirms with a chin nod.

Wendy rolls her eyes but snuggles closer to her man. He kisses the top of her head, runs his hand around her neck, and tugs on the padlock there. Her eyes dilate, and she sighs dreamily.

"Really? You'll come to the set?" Sky sits up, a hopeful, happy expression on her face.

I cup her cheek. "If my coming to your work puts this kind of smile on your face, you bet your ass I'm coming for a visit."

She smiles super wide. "Awesome," she says on a breathy whisper, and my dick is hardening rather painfully in my pants.

I give her a few pecks on the lips, which has Ma, Wendy, and Rachel sighing and Bo and Roy gagging and throwing barbs.

"Shut it! Just because the two of you haven't gotten your heads outta your asses and found yourselves a good woman doesn't mean you get to harp on me," I fire off, not at all angry, just telling it like it is.

"That's exactly what it means, brother," Royce pipes up.

Bo tips his head back and laughs.

"See what I have to put up with?" I pop a fry into my mouth.

"Yeah, you've got it so bad. Great parents, an awesome assistant, brothers for partners. Let me cry you a river," Sky says, pouting.

"You're on their side!" I fire back, laughing and tugging her closer.

She chuckles. "No, pretty boy, I'm always on your side. Unless you're being an ass. Then I'm on your brothers' side."

I open my mouth to say something when Royce cuts me off.

"Marry her, man." He shakes his head. "Woman's perfect."

"Totally, brother," Bo adds.

I nuzzle her neck and lay a few kisses there. "You are pretty perfect . . . for me."

Sky cups my chin and looks me straight in the eyes. Her gaze is piercing with intention and things to come later when we're alone. "Don't you forget it."

I rub her shoulder and bicep and grab for my beer while I stare across the table unseeingly. "Not a chance."

5

"Then I want the models to gyrate their hips and give a little raunch . . ." The designer swirls his massive hips around in a disgusting move that makes me wince.

I rub my hand over the back of my neck.

"Dude . . ." Bo shakes his head. "Not sexy. Not to *anyone.*"

We arrived in Milan two days ago, and since then, it's been a massive exercise in patience. The designer, T-Bone—like the steak, which is exactly how he introduced himself—has been trying, to say the least.

"Mr. T-Bone. You want to sell this line to women all over the world. Career women, stay-at-home moms, women in their twenties . . ."

"Of all shapes and sizes. Yes. Women should be celebrated!" The guy's voice is gratingly high for such a rotund man. Almost feminine. If I didn't see him eyeing the women like his next meal, I'd have pegged him as swinging the other way. He's as short as he is wide, with pale-white skin, a double chin, and receding hair.

For some reason, though, his designs are speaking to women everywhere, making T-Bone one of the top new designers of the year. I will admit, the lingerie is incredibly inventive and considerate of a woman's shape. There're tucks, ruffles, bows, and ruches in all the right places to make every body look spectacular. It's the things he wants the women to do when they're on the runway that have Bo and me up in arms.

"I agree. All women should feel good about themselves. Especially in the bedroom with their man. However, the average woman—hell, any woman—is not going to want to stop at the end of a runway, swirl her hips, turn around, and bend over, giving the audience a view of her lady bits."

T-Bone cringes, flails his hands wildly in the air, and slams them down at his side. "And why the hell not!"

I do my damned best not to roll my eyes and bite out how insufferable his requests are.

Bo jumps in when he notices I'm having a hard time expressing what I need to say without losing my cool.

He loops an arm around the man's shoulders and walks him over to one of the soccer moms, Marta, who's holding her arms across her scantily covered breasts.

"Marta, how do you feel in the lingerie you're wearing?"

She kicks a shoulder up toward her ear, then looks to the side. "A little uncertain. I'm pretty exposed under all these lights."

T-Bone frowns. "You do not feel beautiful? You look absolutely fuckable."

The comment causes Marta to hug herself even more awkwardly.

Bo lets out a long sigh. "Marta, honey, would you feel more comfortable if the lights were low and you were being viewed in candlelight?"

Her eyes light up, and she nods quickly.

"And how about a sexy robe? Perhaps one of the shimmering ones you can slip off at the end of a runway for a quick peekaboo under flashing lights instead of the lights holding bright and steady on your form?"

"Oh my, that sounds lovely. I think I could walk in front of an audience then."

Bo grins widely and walks to the next woman. She's in a cutout bra camisole, which is completely see-through at the nipples and flows down in shimmery multicolored fabric over the belly, hiding any tummy problems. A pair of boy shorts, which are see-through at the ass with matching multicolored fabric over the pubic bone, finishes the outfit. This lavender piece basically shows the parts of a woman she often likes about herself while hiding some of the problem areas for certain women. Especially those with looser skin around the middle who have had children.

"Bianca, is it?"

The woman nods with her arm over her breasts, hiding her nipples. She's biting into her lip so much the damn thing is now swollen. I can clearly see she's terrified.

"How do you feel in what you're wearing, Bianca?"

She swallows and looks at the floor, her eyes glassy. "Exposed."

"Do you like the way your chest and bum look in the outfit, darlin'?"

Bianca shrugs. "I don't know."

"You look absolutely stunning. Though I imagine you're used to wearing this kind of thing in front of your husband and only him?"

She nods, and a tear falls down her face.

"Why are you doing this, sweetheart?" Bo's tone is soothing. He has an uncanny ability in calming women. Part of why he has so many chicklets.

"Because we need the money, and this pays a lot." Bianca's voice shudders and slips away after her admission.

T-Bone gasps. "You're not doing my show because you feel empowered sexually?" His tone is horrified. Apparently he's starting to see he's doing the exact opposite of what he set out to do, which is empower women, not demean them.

Bianca shakes her head but doesn't say anything.

"What if you were led out on stage by your husband, who would be wearing a pair of matching men's pajamas, and he gives you a sultry kiss at the end of the runway?" I suggest.

Her entire face lights up. "That would be so fun! We could do it together!" She beams with sudden excitement.

"Men's matching pajamas. Genius!" T-Bone says.

He looks down the line at the women in various stages of undress, a thoughtful expression marring his features.

"How many of you would like to walk the runway with your partner?" I ask.

All the women with partners raise their hands.

"How many of you would like the stage lights set lower?"

This time, every hand goes up.

T-Bone walks up and down the line, looking at his lingerie and the models he's chosen. None of them have ever modeled before, which is another task Bo and I have this week. These are real women. Skinny, average, above average in weight, all the way to plus-size. They come from all walks of life. Mothers. Teachers. College students. Waitresses. All hand chosen by friends and family of the designer and through word of mouth. Now that they're all here, it's clear this idea needs to be fleshed out even more. These women were frightened to walk a runway wearing sexy lingerie, but after speaking to several of them, the consensus is they couldn't pass up the payout.

I clap T-Bone on the back. "I've got some ideas on how we can still use your lingerie and your concept of making the women feel beautiful and empowered in it, if you're open to hearing it?"

T-Bone rubs at his double chin. "If it sticks with my vision, absolutely."

"Since a lot of your lingerie glows in the dark, what about a show where the lights flicker on and off at different intervals? While the women walk down the long runway, they would be spotlighted at random. At each spotlight, they could reveal a bit more skin. For example, the first spotlight could center on their bare legs and the bottom of the item they're wearing. As they walk, the glow-in-the-dark features will light up until the next spotlight, which could highlight the women's upper bodies, and so on."

T-Bone nods. "Mm-hmm, yes, I see that."

"Some of the women in the more revealing outfits could walk down with their partners, where you can have a simple pair of men's pajamas, underwear, or robes to match the women's outfits. Two designs appealing to the average woman. And believe me, women like to match their men any chance they get. It would also resonate with women getting married or having an anniversary, etc."

"Yes, yes, I can envision it so clearly. It will be done. I can design a few unique, simple items for a man in no time."

He moves over to a drafting table in his workroom and starts sketching, ignoring the lot of us while doing so.

"I think that's enough for now," I say. "I have more ideas, but let's start there and let him work. Ladies? You ready to get into your street clothes and work on the art of walking a runway?"

A bunch of snickers and giggles are heard throughout the room.

"Go get changed and meet us out in the back of the warehouse. We'll practice outside."

The women file out, seeming happier than when we arrived. I chance a glance at T-Bone, but he's lost in his work, flicking from sketching something to picking up a fabric swatch and laying it next to something he sketched.

"Come on, brother. I believe catwalks are your department."

Bo cocks an eyebrow. "My mother being a designer doesn't make me an expert on modeling."

"Don't lie. I know your history. You were walking a runway before you could run. Besides, I believe you've bedded enough models to make you a certifiable expert."

He grins wickedly. "Now that is no lie."

I chuckle and hook an arm over his shoulder. "Come on, we've got work to do."

***

"You're kidding!" Skyler scoffs. "He wanted them to prance around in next to nothing and make lewd movements on the runway? Did you remind him these women are not porn stars?"

I chuckle. "Baby, I know. It was rather disgusting, but he honestly thought he was empowering them by setting them free to express their sexuality."

"Nuh-uh, no way. He was demeaning them in the worst way. Making them objects. Ugh." She sighs.

"I know, but Bo and I have got him back on the right path. His team is already working on some matching looks for some of the women's partners, as well as adding robes and things to make a woman feel more flirty and comfortable in the bedroom."

"That's good."

"I'm flirting with the idea of having standing mirrors put on the stage."

"Really? Why?"

"Well, in my experience, when a woman likes the way she looks, she checks herself out in her mirror. Makes sure every angle looks perfect. I think when you see yourself looking good, you have more confidence and feel sexier."

"This is true. I definitely check the mirror a ton of times before committing to whatever I'm going to wear for the day."

"And I imagine you do the same when you put on lingerie?" It's a leading question, and I can't wait to hear her answer.

Her voice changes into the sultry lilt I love. "Wouldn't you like to know," she teases.

I groan. "Seriously, women do that, right?"

She giggles softly. "Yeah, honey, we do. We always want to look and feel our best, so of course we check out how we look in the mirror, especially when we put on lingerie."

"Excellent. Then I think I'm going to add mirrors to the side of the runway. Not only would it allow the audience and cameras to capture different angles of the designs, it would serve the women in seeing how magical they look under the low, flickering lights."

"It's a great idea, Parker. I wish I could see it for myself."

"Come out," I say instantly without thinking.

She groans. "I wish I could, honey, but I have to work. The long weekend was the last one for a little while. We have to get these scenes right, and we have some difficult ones coming up."

"Oh? What types of scenes?"

"Parker . . . ," she says in warning.

I grind my teeth until I can feel a muscle ticking in my jaw. "Sexual ones."

"You know it's my job, honey. Out of anyone I know, you are the person I'd hope could understand that there are parts of being an actress that put me in precarious and often uncomfortable positions . . ."

"Like it's uncomfortable to kiss and rub your sexy-as-fuck body all over his," I snarl rather immaturely.

"So, we're going there?" Her tone is accusing.

"I don't like it. Knowing another man is kissing you, tasting your lips, your skin. Touching your body."

Images of me doing those very things flash through my mind, and I press my head farther back into the pillow. I'm trying to get ahold of myself when the phone line goes dead.

She hung up on me.

What the *fuck*!

Tingles of dread and aggravation slither up my spine and out my limbs. Until my phone rings showing a FaceTime request from Peaches.

I click the button, and her gorgeous face comes into view.

"I thought it better we have this discussion face-to-face."

"I'm sorry," I blurt, taking in her kind chocolate-brown eyes and pretty pink lips. Her face is devoid of makeup and still unearthly beautiful. "I shouldn't have said that. It was stupid and immature."

She nods. "Yes, but it was real and honest. Parker, I want you to always feel comfortable telling me the truth. If this is going to work between us, we have to promise to be honest with one another in all things. I've had too many people let me down. I can't be worrying about such things with you."

"Sky, baby, I'll never let you down. Not intentionally. And I'm sorry I'm a jealous jerk."

She grins. "Maybe I'll start calling you JJ when you're acting out of hand."

I chuckle. "Could work as a reminder."

A crisis averted. Yet the clawing of the green-eyed monster is real.

"Are you going to be okay, knowing what I have to do in my job? It's not ever going to change. I can promise you, while I take the roles and characters very seriously, it's all pretend. I'm not kissing Rick or any costar and thinking of how it might feel. I'm constantly in my head ensuring the angle of the kiss is good for the camera, my body placement will look ideal on the big screen, and I'm covering parts I don't want an audience to see. Besides, it's very clinical."

"Really?" I guess, in my head, I assumed they were pretending to kiss and fuck and have it be caught on camera.

"Yes really, silly." She chuckles, no further admonishment in her tone. "There's no less than ten to twelve people on set, with the lighting crew, cameras, director, and makeup, and all the while we're attempting to make the scene look real. As though we're genuinely the characters, in love or lust, or whatever it may be at that stage in the movie. A lot of times we shoot all of the sexy scenes at the end when we have more chemistry, so it usually starts to grate on both of our nerves."

"Wow. I hadn't really considered how much went into a scene."

"I promise, it's a lot. Then as the day goes on, your costar starts to stink from being sprayed with mist and makeup and working to hold his arms just right. So halfway through I'm smelling stinky man funk and worse . . ."

My girl has me laughing, and I want to know more. "What?" I chuckle, enjoying her face screwing up into an expression of distaste as she makes a little gagging noise.

"Rick loves onions. On everything." She shivers, and I bust out laughing hard. "You laugh now, but try open-mouth kissing someone whose breath constantly smells and tastes like secondhand, chewed-up onions! It's super nasty."

"You're kidding." I continue laughing into my fist while staring at my beautiful woman.

"I wish I were."

"Baby, give the man a freakin' Tic Tac!" I laugh some more.

She smiles wide. "I couldn't do that! It would be rude, and I have to work with him."

"Better making him uncomfortable than having to suck face with a raw onion."

Her face twists into a grimace. "Blech. You're reminding me I have another scene coming up. I have to go into makeup, and then we're shooting some super-fast action shot where, at the end, he grabs me and kisses me." She frowns. "I don't want to taste onions. I don't even like onions!"

"Aw, I'm sorry, Peaches. Remember what I said . . . offer the man a mint!"

She sits up and moves her arms around in front of her. The way she's got the camera of the phone leaning against something, I can't see what she's doing exactly.

"Eureka!" She pulls out a small blue plastic case. "Listerine strips, baby!"

I chuckle. "Perfect. Now take one right before the scene and offer him one. If he tries to decline, tell him if he wants to kiss you as the scene requires, he needs to man up."

She pouts. "I don't want to do it, but I can't live with onion-face kisses anymore."

I grin. "At least I know my role in your world as best kisser is safe."

"Who said you were the best kisser?"

I'm pretty sure my face pales before she bursts out in laughter. "Just kidding, pretty boy. You're a mighty fine kisser."

"And don't you forget it."

"How's about you come and visit me soon, so I don't have to?" She bites her lip, seeming as if she's afraid to mention what I promised.

"Actually, I have Wendy routing my trip home after the fashion show on Saturday. Should arrive late Sunday night."

"Really?" Her face lights up with her megawatt smile, which reminds me my girlfriend is Skyler freakin' Paige. Dream girl. Most sought-after actress in Hollywood. And she's all mine.

I feel my chest puffing up with pride at making her happy, especially since the reason she's happy is as simple as her wanting to see me.

"Yeah, baby. I want to see how you work, watch you in action. Then I want to take you back to your penthouse and ravish you oh, say, one, two, twenty times."

"I'd like that." Her cheeks pink up prettily, and I hope she's imagining us together.

"Then you shall have it. Though Peaches, I gotta go. It's late here, and I have to teach a bunch of women who've never modeled before how to walk a runway."

Skyler frowns. "Honey, do you even know how to do that?"

I shake my head. "No, but Bogart does, and he's lead tomorrow. I'm there to offer up the best positions for camera angles and what will make them look and feel sexy in garments they wouldn't normally wear except in the privacy of their bedroom."

"You do have a knack for making a woman feel sexy. That's for sure."

"Oh yeah? Tell me more."

She rolls her eyes. "I thought you had to go to bed?"

"I thought you had makeup to put on."

She purses her lips together. "Maybe I want to make sure my man goes to bed happy and thinking of me?"

"Yeah?" I focus a lust-filled gaze on my dream girl.

She licks her lips and bites down on the bottom one.

Fuck, what I wouldn't give to be there right now, sucking on that lip.

"Yeah. What would make you happiest right now?"

"You offering a little FaceTime play, Peaches?"

She glances at something off camera. "I've got about twenty more minutes if you want to use them wisely."

"Perfect fuckin' woman," I murmur.

"Honey . . . I'm not . . ."

She starts to deny her perfection, but I cut her off at the quick.

"Skyler, take your top off and show me your tits."

A huge grin crosses her face, and she cocks a brow but pulls off her top, unclicks her bra, and all I see are sweet, pink-tipped breasts. My mouth waters at the sight, and I groan.

"You've proved it. Perfect." I slide my hand down and under my boxer briefs, taking a firm hold of my raging erection.

"What else do you want to see?" Her tone is whisper soft and needy.

"All of you. Peaches, I want *all* of you."

6

"No, sweetheart, you don't pucker your lips like a blowfish." Bo lets out what looks like a tortured breath as I enter the dance room we've rented from a local ballet studio.

Once we'd established they truly knew absolutely nothing about modeling, showing off lingerie, or anything remotely fashion related, we knew we were going to have to take a more hands-on, one-on-one approach with the women.

"Ladies, how's about we stop for a minute. I'd like you all to set up those chairs in the corner in a line of four across and three deep for all twelve of you. We're going to try something a little different today." I give them my best smile, so they know we're not mad at the lack of progress they've made.

The lingerie show is going to have a wardrobe change for each model for a total of twenty-four looks, so we need to get these ladies showing their sexy side or International Guy could have our first unhappy client.

Bo walks over to me and sighs. "Man, I've been at it all morning. When they aren't nervous, they're acting silly. When they aren't silly, they're looking at me with a deer-in-the-headlights stare. I hope you've got something up your sleeve, because frankly, bro, I'm losing patience."

Instead of speaking, I smile wide, waltz over to the door, and open it.

In sashay three women. All three have hourglass figures with giant knockers, abundant hips, and smallish waists. They're Jessica Rabbit come to life.

Bo's eyes practically bug out of his head. "Jesus Christ . . . a *gift*. Brother, you shouldn't have." He gasps and sucks in a breath through his teeth, making a whistling sound as he does so. "Though I gotta say, I'm glad you did." Bo starts to follow the three moving to the front of the room, full swagger already in place.

I grab his arm and tsk, holding him back. "Nope. The ladies are not here for you. You can hit on them all you want *after* they teach our ladies how to work their curves and bodies in a way that would entice a man and make for an excellent show."

Bo stares at each woman for a long time before nodding. The leader of the pack is tall, around five feet ten or eleven with long black hair down to the swell of her ass. She's wearing a black satin corset and red satin high-cut panties with bows at the side. Her legs are encased in black fishnet stockings in a large diamond pattern. On her feet, red stilettos. The stilettos along with the bold red lips she's rockin' are my absolute kryptonite. Reminds me I gotta get my woman coating those luscious lips of hers in a bold lip color with matching heels. My girl would do it for me too, just to make me insane with lust. This woman, though not my girl, is no slouch. She's a wet dream, standing hand on her hip, lips seeming soft as she purses them prettily.

The two women flanking her are dressed in matching attire: black pushup bras, red lace panties, and black nylons attached to garter belts. Their heels are black patent leather and sexy as fuck. One is a blonde and one a redhead. They're the trifecta of sultriness.

"I get first dibs." Bo breathes loudly, his nostrils flaring like a wild animal. I'd bet every dollar in my bank account he's barely holding on to his control with all this sensuality floating through the room. It's as if the moment the three women walked in they demanded all eyes on them. And every last woman is staring unabashedly at the three bombshells.

"Brother, you get all the dibs. I've got Sky waiting for me back in the States." I nudge his shoulder, but he doesn't take his gaze away from the women at the front of the room.

Bo's eyes light up with unconcealed lust. "Sucks to be you. Well, kind of. Right now, it does. Don't worry, I'll make up for your losses. Fully."

I snort-laugh. "You do that."

"All night long," he whispers, which is more like a promise he's committing to himself.

I chuckle and move to the front of the room.

"Ladies, welcome to Moving Your Body 101," I announce to the models sitting primly in their chairs. "As you can see, I've got three gorgeous women here at the front of the class. These ladies are going to be your teachers today. They are leads from Italy's hottest cabaret show. Meet Martina, Viola, and Francesca."

The three ladies wave and smile.

"Martina, I'm going to sit back here with my partner and let you do your thing."

"Thank you, Mr. Ellis. All right, ladies, we're going to start by sitting in our chairs and moving our bodies. What I want each of you to do is shimmy your chairs until you can see yourself in the mirror in front of you."

The ladies move their chairs according to Martina's directions.

"Now let's start by crossing your legs and making the move look flirty."

The women all follow along with Martina and, as I suspected they would, start getting into it.

Martina goes over to the sound system and starts up some music. The first song that blasts through the speakers is "Don't Cha" by the Pussycat Dolls.

"All right, my lovelies, now it's time to get a little freaky!" She winks at the group and stands behind her chair.

While the music plays, Martina does a subtle but ultrasexy routine using the chair. It's mostly a combination of sitting, spreading her legs out, bending over the back, the side. At one point she puts her foot on the seat and arches her back, then swivels into straddling the chair the reverse direction. She instructs each woman to follow along and repeats the same twelve moves until they've all got it.

"Holy shit," Bo says as we walk around and watch our ladies do the routine, looking more and more confident and, most important, enjoying every minute. They like what they see in the mirror as they move, which is a powerful motive for a woman.

"Don't forget to work your face and hair. Men love a little sway in the hips, a pucker or a pout of the lips, along with some wild hair."

As I watch in awe, many of the girls pull their hair out of their sedate ponytails and roll their necks, running their hands into their hair, shaking it around, getting into the role.

"That's it, ladies, you're playing a role. Exactly as you will on the runway. You're showing the audience a *fantasy*, a beautiful woman wearing cutting-edge, made-to-fit lingerie to empower you as much as excite the special person getting to see it. Embrace your sexy!" I state while the women continue their routine.

Bo smiles watching the women in the chairs do their thing. It's inspiring to see them transform from the sweet girl next door to smokin' hot sex kittens.

"Keep it up, ladies. You're doing amazing. Now give it your all. My girls and I are going to come around and work with you individually in case there's something you need more help with." Martina's voice is strong and direct, which seems to garner the respect and attention of each woman here.

"Damn good idea, brother." Bo claps me on the shoulder. "Saved our asses with these gals. They were having a rough time of it."

"Yeah. I figured if they had a woman to look up to as a role model, she might be able to bring out their sexy side. As you well know, it's all about unlocking that part inside them. These women felt backed into a corner and uncomfortable. Now look at them. Sexy as hell and loving every second of what they see in the mirror."

"Too true." He grins.

"Perception is key. Now we can have these ladies help us work with the models on walking back and forth and striking poses. Instead of learning it from a man, they can get the feedback direct from a woman whose job it is to be sexy. There's something more legit about it, I think."

Bo nods. "Makes sense. Should we leave them and go have a chat with T-Bone about what we discussed for the night of the show?"

"Yeah, sounds good."

As we're heading out, my cell phone rings. The name SoSo pops up on the display, and I smile.

"It's Sophie. Take ten and we'll head over to T-Bone's?" I suggest to Bo.

"Sure, man. Tell Sophie I said hello."

"You got it."

Bo walks out the door and down the street to where I know there's a little café. I follow his direction only a lot slower as I take the call.

"*Bonjour*, SoSo!"

"*Bonjour, mon cher.*"

"How are you? We haven't spoken since Copenhagen, over a week ago."

"*Oui.* I have been quite busy. And you? Where are you now?"

"Milan actually."

"Really? I'm heading there this weekend for a fashion show. What are the gains?" She laughs sweetly.

I chuckle at her misuse of American colloquialisms. "I believe you mean *what are the odds?*"

"Oh yes. I get that one mixed up," she says.

Still, I balk at the fact my Sophie is going to be in Milan. Those are some damn incredible odds. "SoSo, are you going to T-Bone's fashion show by any chance?"

"*Oui*, among others. Rolland Group is partnering with different designers for combined perfume and clothing campaigns to reach women across Europe. How would you know about T-Bone and his designs?"

I grin. "I'm working with the guy and his models."

"*Mon Dieu! C'est merveilleux.* Though I understand he can be quite the pill to eat. Will you still be in Milan on Friday night before the show on Saturday?"

"It's *pill to swallow*, and yes, absolutely we'll be here. Bo is with me too. He sends his love as usual."

"Oh, send the dear my kisses."

I grin. "I think Bo would like that too much, sweetheart."

She hums. "I suspect you are right. Would you have time to meet for dinner on Wednesday evening? I'll set my travel plans accordingly. I know a great place we can eat wonderful Italian food. My father took me there as a girl. The rest of the nights I'll be working until the show on Saturday."

"Sure. Should I invite Bo?"

"Of course. I'm looking forward to catching up with you. We did not have near enough time in Copenhagen, and you had Ms. Paige with you. Have you settled things with her yet?"

Her tone is friendly yet inquisitive, which I'm used to with my Sophie. She's nothing if not direct in all things.

"We have. And you may be surprised to note we've agreed to being in a relationship. A committed, romantic, couple-type relationship." I smile, enjoying the way the admission rolls off my tongue.

Her gasp sounds loud through the phone. "Really? *Mon cher, c'est magnifique.* I hate to say . . . I tell you everything."

I burst out laughing. "SoSo, it's *I told you so.*"

"Yes, I did tell you so. Which is why I am correct, *non?*"

"No . . . uh . . ." I shake my head. "Never mind."

"Are you happy, *mon cher?* She seems very beautiful and kind. I liked her very much."

I think about the question for a minute. Sophie doesn't say anything, giving me the quiet time I need to pull my thoughts together.

"Sophie, I've never been happier. The time you and I were together was probably the closest I'd felt to a woman in what seemed like forever . . . until Skyler. I'm starting to wonder if my time with you helped me see what it could be like to have a beautiful woman in my life."

"I am in your life, *oui?*"

"*Oui*, SoSo, but it's different, and you know what I mean."

She clucks her tongue. "Yes, it is. I will admit I am seeing a man too." She slips the bomb into the conversation, shocking me where I stand.

My eyes widen, and I stop where I am and lean against the building closest to me. "Who, where, what does he do?" I'm a little flabbergasted because she didn't mention anything of the sort in Copenhagen.

Sophie laughs, and it sounds exactly as I remember: lovely. "He's one of our scientists actually. I had not seen him before because I did not usually go down to the lab unless I was working with the scent mixologist. He is a new hire in the last couple of years and has flown under my head space."

"It's *radar*, sweetheart. Flown under your radar."

"*Oui*, he did. And I've since allowed him to take me on two dates. The second one we had sex, and Parker, it was amazing. He did things to me I had never had done. Even by you!"

"TMI, SoSo. TMI." I frown and see Bo walking toward me, a couple of white paper cups in his hands.

"TMI? I do not know this." Her French accent makes the question sound sultry when it's anything but.

"It means too much information. As in, you probably shouldn't discuss your sex life with your past hookup."

Her tone is lilting with her question. "Why not? Sex is a matter of life. The two of us had wonderful relations. Why should we not discuss them?"

I groan and run my hand through my hair as I recall that a lot of Europeans, especially the French in general—Parisians in particular—are far more sexually intellectual, free, and open. Many see sex as a normal, basic human need. Which it definitely is, but Americans only talk freely about it behind closed doors and with their closest confidants. I personally would never talk about my sex life with Skyler to Sophie. It'd be weird and leave me open for all kinds of problems.

"Call it a cultural difference if you will. Americans aren't necessarily shy about bedroom discussions, but we don't have those conversations so open and freely and absolutely *not* with a former bedmate."

"Hmm. This seems like a missed opportunity. The best people to discuss such things with are those you have already experienced it with."

"Maybe for you, sweetheart, but it's weird for a guy."

"Oh, all right. Then I shall take my leave. I have a million things to do today, but I wanted to touch in with you."

"Touch in?" I snicker. "Sophie, it's *touch base* with you. Like in baseball. You touch bases."

"What does baseball have to do with our discussion or friendship?"

I smile and sigh.

"SoSo, we'll talk more over dinner on Wednesday. I've got to go, but I'm looking forward to hearing more about your new guy. Text me the details on where Bo and I should meet you on Wednesday."

"*Oui. Au revoir, mon cher.*"

"*Au revoir*, SoSo."

***

Sophie steps into the restaurant looking like all class and sultriness. Her hair is down in long brown waves over her shoulders. She's wearing a royal-blue cocktail dress with gold strappy sandals. It's one of my favorites Bo picked out during our time in Paris.

Bo and I stand up as she approaches. She air-kisses my cheek twice before moving to Bo.

I hold out her chair for her to sit at the quaint table for three in the packed Italian restaurant. Thank God Sophie made reservations, or we'd have never gotten a table.

"How goes it, beautiful?" Bo asks when the waiter comes over and fills Sophie's wineglass with the wine we'd decided on prior to her arrival.

"I am going very well, Bogart. How is the female population of Milan handling your stay?" She grins and finishes with a saucy wink.

That's my Sophie, cutting him right at the dick.

Bo tilts his head back and laughs heartily. "You know me well. Though I've slowed down this trip. Only banged one of the models on the campaign and one of the cabaret teachers." He waggles his brows.

"A slow spell for you, I take it?" She pauses dramatically.

"I love you, Sophie," Bo states flatly, enjoying every minute of Sophie's quick wit and pinpoint accuracy when it comes to Bo and his debauchery.

"I know, Bogart. I know."

"Sophie, tell me more about this scientist. Which one is it?" I thought I'd met them all, but perhaps I hadn't if Sophie is dating one of them, which would mean he would have to be a bit younger than the other two men, who are in their fifties.

"He's the son of one of our chief scientists. The department hired him a couple of years ago. His name is Gabriel Jeroux. And he is brilliant in and out of the bag."

Bo bursts into raucous laughter. So much so the patrons at the other tables look our way and offer up their best dirty looks. Bo's definitely fitting the brash-and-loud American stereotype I've come to find Europeans think about our culture.

"Sophie, it's in and out of the *sack!*" Bo corrects her before I have a chance.

"*Oui.*" She waves her hand nonchalantly.

I put my hand over hers on top of the table and wait until she focuses her gaze on mine. "Is he treating you right?"

"Yeah, if he's not, I know three Americans who will have your back in a heartbeat, precious," Bo adds.

She closes her eyes and pats my hand in return, then flicks her gaze between Bo and me. "He is. Probably more than I deserve since I've worked them hard after my father passed. Then, of course, you know about the issue with the team using expired products. How do you say . . . I had to smack the whip?"

"Crack the whip," I correct instantly, and her eyes light up.

"Oooh, that sounds even better. And yes, I've been doing this."

I nod. "It had to be done. The department lead could have caused serious problems for your company. I know they were following orders, but there's really no excuse for it to have gone on so long."

"*Oui*, my problem exactly. Therefore, I have been tough on them, but so far, they have all risen to the challenge. I think I'm gaining more respect from them every day."

"Amazing, sweetheart. I want that for you. For your father's legacy to be sound and resonate alongside your leadership."

The waiter comes over and takes our orders while we sip our wine. So far so good.

"*Mon cher*, it is now the time where you bestow upon me the plan with you and Ms. Paige," Sophie prompts, her lips curling into a coy smile.

"First, you can call her Skyler. And second, I don't know. We have no plan, per se."

"Right now, they're bumping uglies with no one but each other," Bo tosses in, grinning.

"I will shoot you if you don't shut up!" I threaten.

"With what gun?" he fires back.

He's got me there. I don't own a gun. Never had the need for one.

"I haven't thought through that part yet, but getting a gun can't be that difficult, can it?" I grit my teeth while Bo nonchalantly sidles closer to Sophie. He'd never go there even if he pretends to be sweet on her. It's one of our firm rules of the brotherhood. Never date or bed a woman your brother has already bedded. Ever. That shit causes problems we don't need or want.

Sophie smiles while we toss barbs and insults left and right.

"My, you are both very much brothers in every sense of the word, aside from blood, *oui?*"

We nod.

"In answer to your question, though, Skyler and I have basically decided to be exclusive to one another. Monogamous."

Sophie sips her drink as her eyes widen. "This is a big step for you, *non?*"

"It is, but there's something about her, SoSo. Something long lasting, and right now, I've got the desire in me to explore it, so I'm going to."

She nods. "I think the two of you will be very happy . . . as long as you can get past your possessive nature when it comes to people you care about."

I sigh. "Yeah, we had a little chat about that. Knowing she's on the set right now sucking face with Rick the Prick Pettington does not have me feeling the warm fuzzies. Though she did admit he has a constant case of onion breath, which makes me feel a little better."

"Onion breath?" Bo shakes his head. "Dude is making the brotherhood look bad. He needs to keep his shit in check. Chew on some gum, pop a mint. Damn, does the guy have no friends or what?"

I chuckle. "I prefer to think about him as not having friends. Or a woman. Or my woman."

"Oh boy," Sophie remarks. "You are jealous of Skyler's acting partner?"

"No!" I say at the same time Bo says, "Yes!"

"Shut up, man!" I growl low from deep within my chest.

"He's gaga over the chick. Can't think straight. Gets possessive and jealous at the smallest things. Which, if you ask me, does not bode well for your long-term goals, brother."

"Who asked you? Sure as hell not me!" I lob his way.

He shrugs. "Just lookin' out."

"Well, how's about you look somewhere else. Say, in a mirror at your own face and lack of relationship in the last decade!" I lay it out for him.

"Touché." He lifts his wineglass and sucks back the entire thing.

"Boys, boys. Let us have a good evening and speak on something else. How is Royce and the new assistant?"

"Roy's great as usual. Talking about finding his own woman to settle down with." I knock on the table, letting the admission fly between the two of them for discussion.

Sophie nods. "This I see. He is the type to commit. Royce will worship a woman forever if she is the right one."

Bo grumbles, "Not sure why all of you are leaving the single life. Man, I can't imagine committing to one woman when there are so many women I haven't yet had." He plucks at his goatee thoughtfully.

I roll my eyes, and Sophie laughs. "Bogart, when you find the one, you will change your mind."

"I don't think so. She'd have to be one in a billion."

"As she should be before you commit to her," Sophie agrees.

And all I can think about while they discuss women is that Skyler Paige could very well be my one in a billion. Or one in seven billion.

7

T-Bone is bent over his writing desk when I enter his workroom the next day.

"Hey, T-Bone." I lift my hand in a wave.

"Just the man I need to see." His words are rushed and spastic. "We have to discuss Anna-Maria. She will not wear the thong that goes with the piece I've assigned her. She has the ideal body for the style, and it has to be her. I saw it in my dream last night. You must speak to her!" He prattles on while moving from one piece he has hanging on a mannequin to another, tweaking things, adding pins, and doing whatever else a designer does to make something fit their vision.

Anna-Maria, a mother of two, is one of the more prim and proper models in the lineup. The epitome of a soccer mom or what everyone in almost every country, aside from the US, calls soccer, which is *football*, or *calcio* here in Italy.

"I'll have a chat with her. It's not uncommon for a woman of her age and station in life to not want to show her ass cheeks in public. I know it doesn't compute for you because you have a vision, but I have to remind you again . . . these are not your everyday fashion models."

T-Bone purses his pudgy lips, making his jowls jiggle unpleasantly. He's wearing a Hugh Hefner–style smoking jacket with loose pants, which scream smarmy porn director. I fear whatever he may or may not be wearing under the pants. I shiver on instinct.

"Look, I came here because I have another idea for the show that could really work with the ladies and show off your lingerie even more."

His furry eyebrows rise toward his hairline. "I am all ears."

If only that were true. I smile and bite back the rude comment sitting on my tongue.

Client. Client. Client.

You're getting paid to be here, and now, Parker, you must do right by the ladies.

"Well, we've been working with the ladies and the local cabaret."

"You want them to do cabaret on the runway?"

I inhale fully and let it out slowly. "No. Though they are doing a great job learning how to use their bodies while watching themselves in the mirror. What if we place two-way mirrors strategically along the runway? The audience will be able to see through the mirrors, but the models will be able to stand in front of them and strike a pose. We can have the cabaret teachers pick poses for each model to best highlight the garment and their bodies in it. This would also give the camera crew and photographers additional angles to capture the clothes. Front and back at the same time. We could even catch some in the dark with the glow-in-the-dark items."

T-Bone's eyes light up, and he opens and closes his mouth. Then, to my horror, he opens his arms wide and slams me into a teddy bear hug. His belly smashes into mine, and he grips me so tight I can barely breathe. He practically screams into my ear so loudly I worry he'll bust my eardrum. "Fantastic! Perfect for the show! Let's do it!"

"Great. I'll talk to Martina, the coach, and get them working on the poses. Do you have the lingerie ready for each woman? I'd like to do a practice run in the outfits, so they get more comfortable. Also, we need the pants for the partners of six of the women."

"Sì, sì, sì!" he answers in Italian. "Right away. I shall have my assistant deliver what is needed, though I'm still working on some of the pants."

"Sounds like you have a lot to do and only two more days before the show on Saturday."

"This is true. Which means you must leave me to it." He flicks a hand over his head as if he's swatting a fly before removing himself from the conversation.

"I'll go chat with Anna-Maria about the lingerie."

I leave his work space and head to the ballet studio, trying to focus on the upcoming show, but all I can think about is flying to New York on Sunday to see Skyler. The FaceTime sex was a blast and a half, but I need to touch her, listen to her laugh, share a meal with her. I know it's only been a few days since she was at my place, spending time with me and my family, but I want more. And it's the first time in a long time I've really wanted more from a woman. I want to know everything about Skyler, but I want to know it from the source, not from reading it online in a smut mag filled with half-truths.

I press the button on my phone to call my girl and see if I can catch her before she leaves for work. With the time difference, it's nine a.m. there.

She picks up on the first ring. "Pretty boy." Her voice is breathy and seductive.

I grin, loving her voice in my ear. I'd prefer a whisper when she's over my body, naked and sated after a round of our epic sexcapades, but I'll take this too. For now.

"Good morning, Peaches."

"Good afternoon to you, right?"

"Yep. You at home or on set?"

She groans. "On set. Been here since six. I'm getting fitted for this full-body suit that records my movements. Then I'm going head-to-head with the bad guy while the computers record everything. Then they can add all kinds of special effects."

"That sounds ridiculously cool."

"It is, but weird because I'm doing it all in front of a green screen. It's easier to act out things when it's more organic. You know, outside in the elements or on a full set. I don't like the green screen, but it's a good challenge for my acting abilities."

"Which I know for a fact are on point!" I compliment her, wanting her to know how I see her abilities.

She laughs, and it's music to my ears. "You're my boyfriend; you have to say that." Her tone is conspiratorial, but I can tell by the inflection on the word *boyfriend* that she likes saying the word in reference to me. Hell, I like hearing it from her too.

"Sure, but it's easier to say when it's true. And I mean it, baby. You're killing it. And I can't wait to see it live. I was telling Sophie about it last night at dinner . . ."

"What?" Skyler cuts me off, a sharpness to her voice that wasn't there before. "Sophie's in Italy? I thought she was in France?"

"Well, yeah, but she's attending the fashion show and a few others while on business here. Had dinner with her last night—"

I was about to add *with Bo*, but she cut me off.

"I can't believe this! The second I leave, you're off having dinner with Sophie! The woman you told I was a bit of fun, essentially a fuck buddy."

"Excuse me. I have never once, *not ever*, inferred or referred to you as my fuck buddy. And I have no idea what you're talking about, so please, if you will, enlighten me regarding what's got you pissed off all of a sudden."

She groans loudly into the phone. "In Copenhagen on the last day, you told Sophie you were not in a relationship with me, nor were you ready for one, and we were just fucking. Having fun."

I think back to the conversation with Sophie in the hotel room. It's hazy at best because I'd been awakened from a dead sleep. It was crack-of-dawn thirty in the morning, and I was itching to get back to Skyler, warm and snuggled up in the bed I'd just vacated. At the time, I'd have said anything to get Sophie to leave so I could get back to my girl.

"Sky . . . you misunderstood. At the time, if you remember, we were still considering what we had as casual. I wasn't about to go into full detail with Sophie about our budding relationship. And yes, even then I was fighting the term *relationship* because it's a foreign concept to me, and the last time I'd been in one was a complete and utter failure. A fucking disaster!" I growl, clenching my teeth hard.

"Oh really? I wouldn't know, because you've never told me about your past."

"And I'm not sure the time is now either . . ." The skin at the back of my neck tingles, and my clothing is suddenly hot as hell.

"I beg to differ. I've told the team I need thirty minutes. Spill, pretty boy."

"Sky . . . ," I warn, but she doesn't heed the edginess in my tone.

"You told your girlfriend you were at dinner with another woman, a woman you were fucking right before me. A woman you say you are *great* friends with. How am I to trust that you are only friends if you can't tell me what's going on with you? I need to know how you tick, Parker, or I'm never going to be able to trust what we have. I told you about Johan. What happened in your past to make you unable to commit to a woman?"

"I've committed to you. What does it matter what came before?" I grit my teeth and hold the phone closer to my ear. The traffic outside is making it hard to hear as I walk back toward the ballet studio.

"Parker, who hurt you?"

I close my eyes and lean against one of the buildings. The sun shines down on me, warming my body from the outside the way Skyler's whispered request is warming the inside. I'd rather have this conversation with her in private and in person, but I'm finding a lot of our relationship will be via phone. It's the nature of our businesses. I should count my lucky stars I have a woman who wants to be with me even though I'm gone more than half the time.

"Her name was Kayla McCormick. We met in college. Dated her, asked her to marry me right off."

Skyler gasps, and it sounds overly loud in my ear.

I swallow down the disgusting taste in my mouth that thoughts of Kayla always bring. "Bo and Royce hated her, though they put up with her for me. I was blinded by what I thought was love. In the end, I think I was in love with the idea of her. She was beautiful. Smart. And she seemed to dote on me. Turns out she doted a lot on my ex–best friend too. Caught him banging the hell out of her one day. I had no idea she was cheating. So I lost a best friend and my fiancée along with my trust of the opposite sex. Now I'm starting to want what I gave up that day. And I want it with you."

"Honey . . ." Her soft tone pierces right through my chest and squeezes my heart.

"You have no idea how much I needed to hear that one word come from your lips. Skyler, please don't be jealous of Sophie. She's the only female friend I have besides Wendy, and I like her in that role. She hasn't made one move on me. And dinner last night was shared with Bo too. I swear Sophie and I ended any sexual relationship we had back in Paris. We're never going there again."

"It's so hard. She's beautiful and funny and . . . and French, which is exotic! I can't help but feel threatened by her." I can hear the insecurity lacing her words, and I wish I could be there to hold her.

"Skyler . . . Peaches, you are the most sought-after actress—hell, *celebrity*—in the entire world. Everyone wants a piece of you. Especially Rick the Prick."

She sighs, and it hurts my heart. "What if we both agree we're going to stop being jealous of Sophie and Rick?"

I smile and lift off the wall and continue to walk. "I think I can agree to that. I don't want you jealous of Sophie, but I absolutely cannot be in a position to choose between the two of you. Because I won't choose either of you. It's not right. People come into our lives for a reason. She's been a great help to me and a good friend."

"I know. And she gave me no reason to believe otherwise when we spent time together in Copenhagen. I . . . we're new, and it's hard being apart when you're new."

"Yes, it is. But I'm going to be there Sunday night."

"I can't wait." She speaks with a hint of need I can easily relate to.

"Me either. And I'll promise to tame my jealousy toward Rick the Prick too."

"Can you start by not referring to him as Rick the Prick?" she deadpans, and I'm not sure if she's being funny or serious. Probably a little of both.

"Eh . . . that I can't commit to." I laugh.

Skyler chuckles. "Fine. Just don't ever let him hear you say that."

"One last thing, which might make you feel even better about Sophie?"

"Yeah?"

"She's seeing a man back in Paris. So far, she's very happy with him. He's a scientist at her company."

"Really? Awesome." Her tone carries a bit of relief with a side of awe thrown in.

"Thought you'd like hearing that." I grin, but she can't see me doing it.

"Yeah, I do," she says softly.

"Baby, I miss you already, and it's only been a few days. How are we ever going to do this?" I ask honestly, sharing my discomfort with her. Usually I'd keep my feelings to myself, but this woman is bringing out an entirely different side to me. An honest, more open side.

"Same way it's working now. I come to you, you come to me. Whenever we're together, we enjoy our time to the fullest. As time progresses, we'll keep talking about it. Who knows, maybe I'll get a place in Boston."

The simple thought of her being closer in between jobs sends a tight feeling of anticipation thumping against my temple. Though I fear giving the idea even the smallest encouragement because of what it would mean for us. It's too soon. Too fast.

"But your work is in New York—"

"And LA, and abroad. Honey, I work everywhere. I can hang my hat wherever I want. I don't have family aside from Tracey, and she's a hop, skip, and a plane ride to New York City from Boston. You have a business and a family in Boston, not to mention your chosen brothers. I'd never ask you to give that up."

"And yet you'd so quickly give up your home in New York?"

"Home isn't always a place. It's a feeling. And right now, where I think this is headed, I'm more at home when I'm with you. How's about you chew on that bomb awhile. I've got to get on set. My thirty minutes are up."

"Sky, baby, you dropped a pretty serious nuke on me."

"Well, it isn't going to happen this month, or even next month. How's about we put it out into the universe and see what happens this year? We've got all the time in the world to make grand overtures to one another," she teases.

"Have I told you lately that I like you?"

"No."

"I *really* like you." I use my sexy bedroom voice, hoping it will make her think of me when she goes back to work with Rick the Prick.

"I really like you too, Parker. Oh, and tonight . . ."

"Yeah, Peaches?"

"Dream of me."

My girl air-kisses the phone and hangs up without waiting for my goodbye. I shake my head and open the door of the dance studio. It's time to help teach some women how to embrace their sexiness while thinking about the sexiest woman alive back in New York who practically offered to move to Boston for me.

What the hell am I supposed to do with that information?

***

"Anna-Maria, I want you to put on the thong and the robe and come into this room with me." I point to the private ballet space, a small, twelve-by-twelve-foot mirrored room. I imagine dancers use this for one-on-one training. Right now, it's going to be me having a heart-to-heart with a skittish mother of two.

The woman nods, goes to the changing room, and comes back out within a few minutes. Her blonde hair is hanging down around her ears, cut barely to her shoulders. Her eyes are blue, and her features rounded nicely. Under the robe I already know she has large breasts, a bit of a tummy, and wide hips. Her legs are long and strong, thighs pretty toned. Overall, she's any man's fantasy. All soft curves and bountiful tits and ass.

I have a single chair in the center of the room. "Go ahead and take a seat, sweetheart," I say in as nonthreatening a tone as I can.

She does what I ask, though she's watching her feet as she approaches, the robe clutched tight in her fists and around her body.

I go over to the door and find the light switch, where I dim the light.

"In the show, the lighting will be even darker. Though it will flash to brighter spotlights, but fleetingly. Not long enough for anyone to scrutinize over anything in particular."

She purses her lips and nods.

"What I want you to do is to show me the routine Martina taught you, while you're wearing your robe."

"Um, okay. What about music?"

I pull out my phone, hit "Play" on the song "Don't Cha" from the Pussycat Dolls, and set it on as high a volume as it will go.

The room fills with the song, and Anna-Maria starts to move while I stay back near the door.

At first, I can see her movements are stilted, but the longer the song goes on and she starts to repeat the twelve moves, she becomes comfortable.

"Okay now, remove the robe."

"But . . ."

"Sweetheart, I know you're self-conscious, but what you don't know is that you look absolutely incredible. Women everywhere are going to look at you and be amazed. A mother of two who looks as beautiful as you do. They'll feel empowered by what you're doing . . . for *them*. This isn't for you. It's to show women like you they too can be and *feel* sexy with the body they have in this lingerie. This line is made to empower all women of all sizes. And I think once you get past the nerves, you're going to see yourself differently, which is why I wanted to bring you in here in your outfit. So you could have some time to assess what you look like in it."

"It's a thong, and my butt isn't what it used to be," she mumbles, her Italian accent thick and wavering with the emotions manifesting as fear inside her.

"Try. Start with taking off the robe. I've already seen you in the outfit and thought you were stunning. As did the designer. Now it's time to see yourself."

I restart the song as she stands up, firms her spine, and nods resolutely. She undoes the robe and lets it drop to the floor. She's wearing a dark-purple number with satin and lace at the cups, which barely hold her large breasts but give them a slight lift, making them even more enticing. The rest of the piece skims down against her belly in a camisole-type shape adjuster that flattens the tummy slightly, which is supposed to make the woman feel more supported. On the bottom is a scrap of a thong, covering what it needs to in front but completely bare at the ass, a saucy purple satin bow right at the tailbone as if highlighting the ass as a gift. Which, from where I'm standing . . . it absolutely is.

Seeing a woman who's all luscious curves has my dick perking up. I can't help it; she's scantily dressed and stunning. I'd have to be dead not to appreciate this image, but thoughts of my Skyler keep the beast at rest.

Anna-Maria works through her routine, her eyes glued to herself in the mirror. I can see the second she sees what we've all seen. Her eyes light up when she brings her arms together, which has the awesome effect of showing off her ample breasts in the mirror. A little smile curves her lips as she twirls her neck, letting her hair fly around wildly. She spins in a circle and moves her ass from side to side, showing off her very spankable cheeks.

"Jesus, girl, you're going to make men lose their minds." I clap as she smiles wide in the mirror and continues to move her body the way she was taught.

When the music ends, she's ass toward the mirror, looking over her shoulder in the pose she was told to hold on the runway under one of the spotlights. Right then, I flick the lights all the way on so she can see her ass and body in all their glory for a mere ten seconds before I flick most of them off.

"So, what do you think?" My breath is lodged in my throat as I wait for her to say whether or not she'll wear the outfit as the designer expects.

"I . . . I . . . I look really good in it. Even my butt. I . . . I can't believe it." She runs her hand over her bare ass.

"Sweetheart, you wouldn't have been picked if the designer didn't think you were the perfect woman for the design. Which you are. I hope you can see that now."

She shrugs, and her cheeks pinken as I move toward her and hand her the robe. She puts it on, covering up her fine ass. Pity.

"Maybe. I mean, I think it looks good."

"So you'll wear the thong and do the show?"

Anna-Maria smiles and nods. "*Sì*. Yes, I'll do it."

"Excellent. You'll be doing a favor for women everywhere, but I think you'll be doing one for yourself too."

She grins and covers her mouth with her hand. "I can't wait for my husband to see me. He wouldn't do the runway, but he's excited for me. Says he's looking forward to the world seeing how beautiful his wife is, knowing I'm still his."

This time, I smile wide and hook an arm appropriately over her shoulder, careful not to grip anything. "Sweetheart, it sounds like you've got a great man at home."

"I do. And you? Is there a Mrs. Ellis?" Her question throws me off guard.

Mrs. Ellis.

I've always attributed that name to my mother. "Married? No. Someone special? Yes."

"I'll bet she considers herself very lucky. You're a kind man, Mr. Ellis. And very good looking." She laughs as we walk back into the studio where all the other ladies are.

Bo raises an eyebrow in question as we enter. "And should we expect you in the show, Anna-Maria?" he asks.

"Yes. I'm doing the show."

The women standing around jump up and down, clapping, before they rush to her side and give her hugs and words of affirmation.

I make my way to Bo.

"I see you were working your magic again. Care to tell me what worked? You were in there a long time with her."

I frown. "Do you think I hit on her or was doing something inappropriate?"

Bo sucks a breath through his teeth. "Well . . . you do have a track record with clients . . ."

I sock him in the arm. "Brother. She's married! And I'm with Sky. I'd never fuck over Sky like Kayla fucked me over. Not ever." I scowl and wish I'd socked my best friend a little harder. Maybe wipe that smug look off his face.

Bo grins. "Dude. I so had you!" He laughs. "I figured you were in there singing 'Kumbaya' or some shit."

I shake my head. "Not quite. I let her do the routine alone in her lingerie. First with the robe on, then without. Gave her the time to assess herself, see what all of us see. Get her more comfortable with revealing her body to an audience."

"Damn, with those titties and that ass, I'm sad I missed the show." Bo plucks at his goatee with his eyes running up and down Anna-Maria, probably trying to see through her robe.

I groan and scrub my hand over my face. "You make me want to punch you again."

He shrugs. "I have that effect on some people."

"Anyway, the results are good. I'll call over to T-Bone and let him know we've worked it out."

"Good work, man."

"Thanks. Pub tonight? I need a freakin' beer. Got into it with Sky earlier today."

"Shit, man, yeah. Course. I'm here for you. Whatever you need. Is it all good between you two?"

I nod and sigh. "Yeah. Had to tell her about Kayla."

Bo visibly shudders. "Yuck. That had to suck. Talking about that bitch."

"Yep. Basically. Though I think we worked out some of our jealousy shit."

He cocks a brow and gets closer. "Yeah? She done bitching about Sophie?"

Bo knows the jealousy over Sophie is grating on my nerves. I understand it's hard for Skyler to see Sophie's just a friend, especially when she was a client and a former bedmate. She doesn't yet see how it all changed the moment I met her. Skyler's the woman I'm with, and I want her to get that in a way where she's not worrying about anyone else. I'd never stray. Especially not after feeling the shit I felt when Kayla cheated on me. No way I'd do that to another person, which is part of the reason why I didn't get into a relationship again until now. Like I've said before, Skyler is a game changer. I need her to see it for herself.

I let out a long breath. "Hope so. We'll talk more later. Over beers, yeah? Just us," I add, not wanting him to invite one of the coaches or the model he bedded.

"Hey, you need me, I'm there, brother. Any day, any hour, any minute."

I clap him on the back of the neck and squeeze. He pats my back in return.

"Thanks, brother."

"No thanks needed. It's what families do."

8

I toss back some of beer number two before biting into a chunk of beef from my giant burger. I balked when the bartender served the two burgers with potato chips. The thing could have its own zip code it's so big. At least a solid six inches high, with a wedge pickle and long strips of bacon sticking out the sides. Definitely a thing of beauty, but finishing the damn thing will be a task and a half. Still, I'm up for the challenge.

Cheers Pub is tucked into a nondescript street in Milan. Half of the street seems to cater to lower-rent apartments or condos, and the other half has been gentrified. If I had to guess, it will only look more modern as time passes. The nicer buildings have new paint, flower boxes in the windows with ornate wrought iron encasements, whereas the apartments directly across the street definitely need a bit of resurfacing.

The bar, however, could easily fit in with an average neighborhood in Anywhere, America. They definitely have their Americanisms down pat. Sure, there are some things in Italian, but most everything seems to cater to the American shtick, even the name of the place, Cheers, like the old TV show my parents used to watch when I was a kid. It feels familiar and comfortable. Exactly what I need after the week we've had and the conversation between Sky and me.

The floors are wooden slats, as are the bar, tables, and stools. Bo and I are sitting at the bar in front of the brass tanks aptly boasting "Tank

Beer" from a brewery called Pilsner Urquell. The beer is a blond lager from the Czech Republic. I find it oddly interesting that the pub's most common beer on tap or tank is a lager from a country other than its own. Then again, what do I know? I like beer. Mostly craft brews. I'm sure if I told my father about the beer he'd know every detail: who made it, what the taste should be like, and what would be best to eat with it. He's kind of a beer snob, though he prefers the term *guru*.

"All right, you've had your beer; you've got your burger and your brother's ear. I think those fill the three-*B*s requirement."

I frown. "What do you mean, the three *B*s?"

Bo smirks. "Dude. Anytime you want to talk about something weighing down your mind, you always ask for one of your brothers to go out and have burgers and beer. Three *B*s."

I chuckle, then take a healthy pull from my pilsner. "Is that right?"

Bo shrugs and turns to the side, resting a hand on his inner thigh as he widens his legs, getting more comfortable. He rests his left elbow on the bar and leans his weight into it. "Come on, tell me what happened with Skyler. Did you screw it up?"

"You're assuming I screwed it up already?" I scoff.

"Man, I don't know. You're surly, and you look like someone snuck up behind you and screamed *boo* in your ear, sending you jumping out of your chair. What am I supposed to think?"

I rub at my temples and look at my enormous burger. We should have halved it, but that isn't manly. Besides, Bo can pack away a lot of food. I think all the fucking he does burns off all the calories. Although he does hit the gym as often as I do.

"Parker, come on. Lay it on me, man, and I'll see if I can help."

I run my thumb up and down the glass, watching the condensation slip away. "As I told you, I gave Skyler the important parts about Kayla and how she screwed me over."

He nods. "And?"

"And nothing. She'd said I was holding back. Not telling her why I was so against the concept of a relationship in the beginning. So I told her."

"And now?"

"I'm all in, brother. Scared as fuck. Giving it my best, but I can't say I'm good at it. I don't know the right things to say half the time. And then of course, her jealousy toward Sophie, mine toward her costar, Rick." I sigh and twist my glass left and right in order to keep my hands busy.

"Onion breath? I'd imagine that alone takes him off any potential attraction lists regardless of how he looks."

"Breath is easy to fix, man."

"True enough, but a woman never forgets that shit."

"I guess." I pop a chip into my mouth and think about what's really bothering me. "Then there's the bit about her mentioning getting a place in Boston."

Bo's eyes widen. "Say what?"

"Yeah." I swallow down another large dose of beer, needing the warmth in my gut.

"Her moving to Beantown is a lot heavier than being exclusive and seeing one another on the fly like you are now." Bo nails it.

I nod. "Don't I know it."

"Shit."

"Yep."

"Fuck."

"You could say that again," I mutter.

"What do you think about her moving to Boston? Gut reaction." His intense gaze is critical, analyzing my every response.

I grin and give him the side-eye. "It would be a whole lot easier to get into her panties more often."

Bo laughs heartily. "I hear that. What's your second thought?"

I purse my lips, mulling it over. "It would be nice. Having her close. Being able to meet up for dinner and shit. Take her out. Dinners with the family. With you guys. It's a life I'd always thought I'd have."

"Is it a life you want?" he says, digging.

"With Sky? Yeah, but she's also a celebrity, man. There's no normal for us. Never will be. The paparazzi are always going to be down our throats."

"But you've got protection for that." He frowns, waiting for my counter excuse like the good friend he is. Helping me work out my shit.

"Yeah, the Van Dykens are great. Still, what happens down the road when we have kids—"

Bo lifts up his hands in front of me, palms facing out. "Whoa, whoa, whoa. Back the truck up. Did you say *kids*?"

I scrub my face and look his way. "Yeah, man. I did. Want 'em someday. Don't you?"

Bo plucks at his goatee and sighs. "Never thought much about it, truthfully. Not sure I have the fatherhood gene inside me. Never had one to compare to except Pops. My father left long before I could walk. Grandfather wasn't in the picture neither."

"Sorry, brother."

"Nuthin' to be sorry about. You can't miss what you never had. And my mother and sisters took good care of me. Taught me everything I need to know about women." He grins salaciously.

I frown, ignoring his quip. "I always imagined one day I'd have the house, picket fence, pretty wife, two kids and a dog, barbecues on the back patio, the whole nine. I turn thirty this year, and time is creeping up on me."

"You're not old, brother. Relax. Give yourself and this thing with Sky a little time. Let it unfold naturally, you feel me?"

I inhale a full breath, then let it out before raising my now-empty glass to the bartender. "When she mentioned uprooting her life, for me . . ." I shake my head. "No woman has ever put me first like that.

And she's Skyler freakin' Paige. My dream girl. The woman I always compared women to. The idea of her, anyway. And then I meet the real thing, and she's so much more. Fuck, man, I don't know. Skyler's the real deal."

Bo lifts his chin. "I feel ya, but remember, you thought that about Kayla, and the bitch fucked you over. This is the first woman you've allowed in since her. How's about you not worry so much about the future and appreciate what you've got right now. You feed this thing with Skyler, and it will grow into something permanent. Maybe she's your picket fence, maybe not. Only time will tell. Did she say she was packing her shit and moving out next week?"

I chuckle at the exasperation in Bo's voice. "Nah, man, she dropped the bomb and then told me to chew on it."

He laughs. "I like her. Funny chick."

"She can be. And beautiful, and fuckhot in the sack, sweet, charming, thoughtful, good with her mouth . . ." I grin.

"Hoo-boy!" Bo fans his face and winks. "Keeper for sure."

"Yeah. Keeper."

"Then I say you stick with that. Give it the time it needs, enjoying the hell out of every minute. If things get heavy again, you talk to me or Royce, and we'll set your ass straight."

I lift my fist, and Bo bumps it with his own. "Another beer?" I say.

"Fuck yes. Dying of thirst over here."

I laugh and lift up my glass and point to Bo's this time. The bartender nods and sets about getting our refills.

"Thanks, Bo."

"I'll put your shit in check anytime. Now . . . let's back up and go into detail on the part you mentioned where Skyler was good with her mouth. I'd like to hear more about that." He waggles his eyebrows suggestively.

He doesn't see the punch to the shoulder coming, but he feels it. I'll bet it's white hot against his bicep too.

"Deserved," I growl as he rubs at his arm.

"Too true," he admits without shame.

***

"Yo, brother!" Royce answers his cell phone in his deep rumble, but it's his smiling face I'm looking forward to. "Since when do you FaceTime?"

I grin into the screen. "Skyler taught me its benefits."

He runs a hand over his bald head and tilts it as if he's checking himself out. "I'll just bet she did."

"Anyway . . . I'm calling because your text said it was urgent. What's going on?"

Royce purses his full lips. "Press been calling day and night, man. Blowin' up the IG offices and pissing our girl off. We need to do something about the statement that went out about you and Skyler last week."

I frown. "I'm sorry it's hitting you guys back home. I'm not sure what the best plan is. I've been focused on this project and, uh, other things. Hadn't realized you guys were taking the heat back home."

"Nuthin' I can't handle, but it would be nice to nip this thing in the bud, sooner rather than later."

"Yeah, I can see that. I'll call Tracey, Sky's agent, and find out what she thinks is best. What have you been saying to them so far?"

He shakes his head. "No comment. Hanging up the second they speak. Still they're like vultures on a carcass. They keep pecking until they get what they want."

I nod. "Okay. I'll call her after we're done. How's everything else?"

"Right as rain. I've consulted on a few more financial things with Sophie, which has given us a nice payout. Closed a couple of easy cases. Even got Wendy looking into some and giving her perspective. However, I think I'll be traveling the next project with you and having Bogey hold down the fort."

"Yeah? What's next? You mentioned something about San Francisco?"

He nods and rests his head against the back of his black leather chair. "Financial company. CEO needs help finding a mate."

"A mate? Does she have someone in mind? Usually when we're matchmaking it's because the woman wants help getting the attention of someone she already has a crush on. Is that the case?"

"Nope." Royce's inflection accentuates the *p* sound in *nope*.

I rub at my eyebrows, running my thumb and forefinger across the building tension I'm feeling. "What am I missing?"

"Not a thing. The woman's beautiful, intelligent, with a wicked-hot body, and wants us to find her a man. Says she's tired of dating narcissistic, gold-digging, wannabe players. I'm helping her set up her profile now. We're going to rock this old school. Like the *Million Dollar Matchmaker* show. You seen it?"

I blink a few times, trying to determine if I'm in a dream or real life. "Did you just ask me if I watch a reality TV program? The only shit I watch on TV is sports, and half the time, even that's on DVR."

"Patti Stanger, she's the shit. She's got her matchmaking on lock."

I close my eyes and open them again, focusing on his smiling face. "I'll take your word for it. What does this have to do with our client?"

He runs a hand down his blue tie, his onyx cufflinks a nice touch against his white dress shirt and black suit. "I want to try my hand at the matchmaking end of things. We haven't done a cold matchup before, and I plan to dig into this one."

I purse my lips and smile as his eyes flit from one side to the other; he's not looking at me directly. He coughs into his hand and clears his throat.

"Why?"

He frowns, his eyebrows black against his dark-chocolate skin. "Last I checked, we owned this business together, and I didn't need a reason to want to work a client." His tone is argumentative and a bit more forceful than he'd normally have reason to use. There's something he's not telling me.

I smile wide. "No reason needed, I just wanted one. Who's the client?" I prod.

He compresses his lips into a flat line. "Rochelle Renner."

"And what does Ms. Renner look like?"

Royce narrows his gaze at the camera. "Does it matter?"

I smile, knowing I'm goading him, and I don't care. He's my brother; it's my job. "Not sure. Just want to know what we'll be working with."

Royce nonchalantly sets the phone down against something so I can see his entire chest from his waist up and flips open a file before pulling out a five-by-seven image. He turns the image to the camera.

I start laughing instantly.

"Brother . . . ," I gasp, staring at one of the hottest black chicks I've seen since I laid eyes on Halle Berry in *Swordfish*, a movie Roy made me watch. And he made me watch it because she was in it, and you get a full view of the woman's rack. Which is sweet.

"Don't you 'brother' me. Just because our client is a fine-ass sister—"

"Uh-huh." I shake my head. "If you want to play it cool and not let on the *real* reason you're interested, I'll leave it at that. However, I'm guessing the next suggestion you're gonna make is you should be matched with her?" I smirk.

Royce's face goes completely blank. "I'm not even going to dignify your question with a response. Finish what you gotta do over in Milan and get your ass back so we can head to Cali."

I shake my head. "No can do. I'm visiting Sky on my way back. At least two days. Need them, man. I'll head back home on Wednesday, but give me two days."

He purses his lips as if he's going to kiss the screen, but I know it's because he's got one helluva pucker. "It's all good. Take your days. Send

Bo back. I've got to load him up on work or he'll be flirting with Wendy the entire time we're on the West Coast."

I chuckle. "True dat. Which means, if he's not busy, Sir Mick will be visiting, and I really don't want to come back to find Bo strung up by his tighty-whities."

"Mm-hmm. You call your girl's agent. Find out what approach we should take. Want this to be easy on you and Sky, but we need to get them to lay off IG."

"I agree. I'll hit'cha back later, yeah?"

Royce offers a chin lift and a thoughtful "Peace" before hanging up.

I hang up and hit the button for Tracey. It rings a few times before an exasperated "Triumph Talent Agency, this is Tracey" comes over the connection.

"Hi, Tracey, it's Parker Ellis."

"Oh hi. Sorry about the rushed intro. I'm down my assistant today, the day the calls go crazy."

"Murphy's Law."

"Yeah. What can I do for you?"

"Actually, I need your advice. The press is hounding IG offices, and it's starting to hurt my team workwise. The release went out, but the media's still rabid, and I'm not there to run interference."

"I see. I told Sky about this, but she didn't listen. Told me you needed your privacy."

"Told her about what?"

"You guys need to do a live interview. Together. Side by side so the press can get their fifteen minutes, screen grabs, video clips, etc. and leave you alone for a while. At least until one of you does something new to grab their attention."

"And Sky didn't want to?"

"No. She said your relationship is new and she didn't want to add to the pressure that goes with dating a celebrity, but frankly, Parker, it's one of the only ways to get them off your back. You want to have some freedom, give them something to run away with."

I mull over her idea. "How would we best go about that? I'm coming there on Sunday night and will be hanging out on her movie set Monday and Tuesday."

"Really? It's easy then. Before you enter through the back of the set, walk to the front and have her meet you. Or enter together. The press will go nuts. They'll get some pictures of the two of you together. I'll set up a quick lunch interview with a few of the ones I trust most. I say *most* because you can never trust any of them completely."

"I learned that after the *People* piece." The words come out jilted and as jaded as I feel.

"I'll meet you guys at the set, run interference, and give you a Speaking to the Press 101 crash course of things to say and not to say, and how to avoid answering questions you don't want to answer. Like, Are you in love with Skyler?" Her voice is flat, devoid of emotion, and it jolts me off balance.

My throat instantly goes dry, and I reach for the bottle of water on my side table. "Are you, um, asking me right now?" I tug at the suddenly too-tight collar of my shirt.

She cackles into the phone, and I almost have to pull it away. "Oh my, it would have been fun to see your face right then. I can tell by your hesitation, that is a question you would like to avoid answering."

"Fuck yes." I clear my throat while she continues to laugh.

"Don't worry, Parker. I take care of Sky. She's my number-one priority. Has been for years and will continue to be for years to come. Now that you're in the picture, I'll be looking out for you as well. I won't let anything happen. Have your assistant tell me when you're planning to visit the set, and I'll coordinate the rest."

"All right. Thank you, Tracey. I appreciate it. And will you talk to Skyler about what we discussed?"

"You mean you don't want to be the bearer of bad news? Sky hates talking to the press about her personal life. It's a pet peeve of hers but a necessary evil in the business."

"Um, no," I state with no shame whatsoever. Sky and I already had a pretty deep conversation earlier. I don't want to add to it by telling her we need to have a heart-to-heart with the press so they leave my business and staff alone.

"Okay, I've got this."

"I owe you one, Tracey."

"No, you don't. Take care of my girl and don't turn out to be a douchebag, and we'll be aces."

Apparently Tracey Wilson, agent extraordinaire, does not pull any punches, going right for the kill.

"I don't intend to hurt Skyler. She means something to me, Tracey. More and more every day."

"Yeah, I see it in the way she talks about you, how her face lights up, and she gets this faraway, dreamy look in her eyes. She used to do the same thing when she spoke of Johan, and he broke her heart. Let's shoot for keeping a happy look on my best friend's face and we'll be good to go. Now, I've got an enormous amount of work with no assistant, so I'm going to let you go."

I chuckle awkwardly, not knowing how to take all the information she's shared. "See you soon. And good luck."

She sighs heavily. "Without her, I'm going to need it. See you Monday, Parker."

"Thanks again."

"No problem. Bye." She hangs up, and I stand up and head to the bathroom to get ready for bed.

Tomorrow's the show, and I'm hoping everything falls into place for our client. T-Bone may be a misguided wannabe pioneer of women's empowerment through body-fitting lingerie, but he genuinely means well. Initially he went about it the wrong way. Bo and I have ironed out the issues, and I'm looking forward to seeing everyone's hard work unfold at the show tomorrow.

I hit the bathroom, brush my teeth, visit the facilities, pull back the comforter, and slide naked into bed. The cool sheets have me shivering for a moment before I grab my phone and pull up the messages screen.

I notice I've got a video text from Skyler. I click on it and see her beautiful face. She's wearing full makeup, her hair hidden by a long black wig. She's wearing some type of weird armor, which reminds me of Wonder Woman's bralike corset, only this one is black and silver.

"Hi, pretty boy. Just wanted to say I won't be able to chat with you tonight, my afternoon. The director is on a tear about us being a day behind schedule on some of the scenes, so we really need to nail them tonight. No breaks all around except to grab a bite in between. Since I don't know when that will be, I wanted to say sleep well, and I can't wait to see you on Sunday! I'm having Rachel pick you up at the airport. She's convinced you'll need coverage in case the paps catch wind of your arrival. I told her she was nutty, but . . ." She shrugs, and it looks like her armor lifts with her. I chuckle under my breath, not wanting to miss a moment of her words to me. ". . . better safe than sorry. I'll see you soon. Dream of me!" She ends the video with an air kiss, only in this one I can see her lips moving into a perfect bow. She smiles wide and winks before the video stops.

Damn, I'm one lucky man.

I roll over onto my stomach and imagine Skyler in that outfit kicking the ass of some pretend, futuristic villain. I fall asleep smiling.

9

The runway is a long, bright, gleaming-white rectangle set in the center of a large room. There's nothing particularly special about it aside from the freestanding mirrors we've strategically placed on each side. Four in total. The surrounding space is charcoal gray to help with any potential distractions around the runway. Chairs are stationed up an incline on each side so every position gets an unobstructed view of the stage. I take the steps up the side of the runway toward the back and stop at the first mirror.

I pull out the tube of red lipstick and smile, thinking back to Sophie, Skyler, and Christina. I'm becoming a bit of a sap. These cases I work are starting to affect me on a personal level I hadn't anticipated. When I set out to create International Guy, I had no idea how big it would become and the clientele we'd encounter. At first, I thought we'd be analysts and consultants, working with businesses to help them thrive. And we do that, but the slant we've taken now bends toward the personal side of life. As such, I'm finding I'm more interested and invested in my job. It's fulfilling me in ways I never dreamed. Meeting and becoming friends with Sophie. Skyler and I entering a relationship together. Hell, I helped two royals work out their differences and become the next king and queen of Denmark. Who does that?

No one.

No one but my team.

I'm proud of the work we've done these past few months, and with our staff expanding and our caseload filling up with a waiting list, I've never been more fulfilled. I'm happy with my life as it is. A great job. A gorgeous girlfriend. Amazing friends. Sky's the limit.

Sky.

My thoughts go to her as I write her mantra on the mirror. It will be the first one people read as each model poses in front of it.

Live your truth.

I smile, thinking about how I'm going to see my girl tomorrow. *My girlfriend.* Who'd have thought I'd be back in a relationship? Definitely not me. I truly believed Kayla had screwed me up for women forever. Guess it proves if you find the right woman, anything can happen.

People change. I've changed. Grown over the past few years. I'm ready to commit to a woman. To Skyler. She's everything I could ever want and more in a significant other. Beautiful. Funny. Kind. Compassionate. Teasing. Cute. Thoughtful. I even adore her jealous streak, probably because it matches my own.

I make my way over to the next mirror and think of my dear friend Sophie. The only woman I've ever been close friends with. Sophie makes it easy. She's patient, considerate, and gives great advice. I enjoy having her friendship in my life, and I want her and Skyler to be friends one day. I can't say I expect them to be "sisters" the way the guys and I are "brothers," but I'm hopeful. Sophie's a force. Once we got her past her timid nature in business, and the grief of losing her father wasn't so fresh, her tenacity and passion in all things came to the surface full throttle. Eventually I have to trust that the women in my life, my mother and assistant included, will find a happy balance.

Imagining Sophie's smile, I write on the second mirror.

You are golden.

The red stain streaks along with each word, giving it a graphic effect I know T-Bone will like. When I approached him about the mirror idea and the mantras, he positively jumped with glee. It was frightening to see T-Bone jumping around like a bullfrog from lily pad to lily pad.

I shake my head. Fashion people are weird. The entire lot of them. You never know what's going to strike their fancy. It's all a crapshoot.

Next, I move to the third mirror, closer to the front, and remember Princess Christina. I imagine she and Sven are gallivanting in some foreign country, celebrating their honeymoon, happily in love. With the two of them and the years of commitment under their belts, they may come back ready to announce Christina's pregnant with the next heir to the throne. I distinctly recall Christina's mother, Princess Mary, pushing for that exact outcome. Though I think her words were, "Don't come home until you're expecting the next king," or something equally ridiculous. She is all about being a royal, all the time. At least now that Christina is queen, she doesn't have to listen to her mother; her mother has to listen to *her*. I'll just bet she loves every minute of the role reversal. I sure as hell would.

I write Christina's mantra for the world to see.

Own your future.

Twisting the lipstick to add more, I make my way to the front of the stage where the last two-way mirror is stationed. This time, I write on both sides of the mirror, wanting not only the models to see the words but the audience as well.

Embrace your sexy.

I smile as I swirl the *y* down to underline the entire word. Hopefully each of these mantras will help the models connect with their image and what they're doing on stage. Given the cabaret teachers, the lessons Bo and I have given them this week, and of course, T-Bone's incredible collection, I hope each and every one of them feels like a million bucks.

Once I've finished the mantras, I head back to where the craziness is. All twelve models are either undergoing a final on-the-spot fitting or getting hair and makeup done.

I find Anna-Maria and lean into the vanity while the hairdresser is curling her hair into ringlets.

"How are we feeling today?" I smile, wanting her to see I'm here for her. I'm here for all of the ladies.

"Actually, really good." She nods. "Last night, I gave my husband a preview of the walk and poses." Her cheeks and neck flush a rosy color.

"Did you, now?" I grin. "And how did it go for you?"

"Um, really well. He told me I was the sexiest woman alive and even more so after having his babies. He loves how my body has changed, because it shows how our lives have grown and changed together. I'm a mother now. It's a new role, a new body. And when I'm an old woman, a grandmother, I'll have a grandmother's body, and he said he'll love me even more then too because I will have given him a legacy."

I smile wide and crouch down to her level, placing my hands on the arms of the chair. "It sounds to me like your husband knows he has a good thing and wants to keep it that way for a long, long time."

She grins. "Yeah. I love him so much."

"Will he be in the crowd?"

She nods and bites her lip. "He says he can't wait to ravish me after the show, after all the audience sees what only *he* gets to touch."

I squeeze the ball of her shoulder. "Your husband rocks. Make sure you reward him well tonight." I wink.

As I'm about to leave she grabs my hand with both of hers. Her pretty eyes are shining with a glassiness that usually means tears. "Mr.

Ellis. Um, Parker. Thank you for helping me see what I couldn't before. I like who I am. I'm happy to have a healthy body regardless of the extra weight and saggy areas I didn't have when I was twenty. I get it now. I need to love the body I'm in and be thankful for it."

I squeeze her hands and pat the tops. "I never said such things, though I'm glad you're seeing what you need to see. You're a beautiful woman. Anyone can see that. I'm happy your blinders finally came off."

"All because of you and Bo."

I shake my head. "Nope. Sweetheart, it was all you. Own it."

On that note, I leave her to finish getting ready for the show.

As I make my way through the throngs of people rushing around backstage, I find Bo with a needle and thread dangling from his mouth. He's holding up the strap of a camisole.

"Not the right fit?" I ask as Bo pinches the fabric together and flips it so he can sew it back together.

"No. Miss Excitement over here pulled it over her head so fast she didn't center her arm in the right place and stretched the strap past its breaking point."

"I said sorry, Bo." She frowns.

He grins and winks at her. "You can make it up to me later, hot pants."

She licks her lips and leers at Bo. "With my mouth or my body?"

Oh shit.

"I'm thinking a little . . . nah . . . *a lot* of both." He leans closer to her breast and bites off the thread in a smooth, if not racy, move.

She gasps, shamelessly pressing her boobs closer to his face.

"Aaaaaaand . . . that's my cue." I turn around and leave them both chuckling at my awkwardness.

I touch base with each of the models before I notice a familiar face in the distance. I'm happy to see Martina is also here coaching the women on-site. She commands all the attention in a room. Her bombshell looks, height, and sparkling personality have people everywhere gravitating toward her. Me included.

I head to where she's speaking with one of the more timid ladies. I think she's a preschool teacher, unmarried, and all of twenty-five, though her innocent look makes her seem barely of age.

"Remember what I told you. Confidence is key. Some say fake it until you make it, but I don't think that's right. You are perfect in the two outfits. You know your poses; do exactly what you've learned, and you'll have accomplished what you set out to do. Won't that feel good?"

She nods. "Yes, thank you, Martina."

"'Tis nothing, sweet angel." She pats the preschool teacher as if she were the model's mother, though she couldn't be more than a couple of years older.

"Hey, you didn't have to be here today. The contract didn't include the show."

She purses her lips. "No, but these are my girls now, and I support my girls. This show is important to them and to me. I want T-Bone's vision of empowering women to be exemplified by women who feel powerful in his clothing." She shrugs. "I'm doing my part for the cause."

I smile and nod. "Yes, you are." I scan her form and notice she's in yet another sexy corset, this time with black leather pants, a low-slung sparkly belt, and her dark hair a wild mane down her back and over her shoulders. Her lips are coated with the bold red lipstick and paired perfectly with smoky eyes. She looks as if she were going for a night on the town, not to sit down and watch a fashion show.

Martina looks at me from the top of my sport coat to my dress shirt open at the collar and down my slacks to my Ferragamos.

"I like your attire," she says, her voice a husky timbre I haven't heard before.

"Yours isn't half bad either." I clear my throat and run my hand over the back of my neck.

She steps closer, placing her hands on my chest. The woman is already five ten, but in the sky-high heels she's wearing, we're at eye level. "I think I'll like what you have under it . . . very much. How about you and I test out my theory after the show?"

Shit. Fuck. *Damn.*

Normally I'd be all over her invitation like sauce over a meaty steak, but I stop cold. This woman is every man's wet dream come to life. Except mine. I've already got my dream girl, and there is no way in hell I'm going to risk losing that for a night with a sinfully hot dancer.

"Martina—" I begin to decline when we're interrupted by a photographer.

"Picture, Martina?" he asks, and she smiles wide, cuddling up to my chest, pressing her breasts close, and cocking a hip.

I barely know what's happening when he says, "Smile." On autopilot I smile, but the second he's got his shot, I back away.

"Martina, your offer is very generous, and a few months ago, I would have gladly taken you up on it. However, I'm in a relationship."

She pouts, her perfect red lips puffing out, making her look like a sexy, sad dominatrix.

Jesus Christ!

Skyler. Skyler. Skyler.

"Are you sure? We could have some serious fun together. Just the two of us. No one would have to know . . ." She starts to reach for me, and I place my hands up and out, keeping her at arm's length.

"I'm sorry. You're beautiful and a wonderful woman. What you did for the ladies in the show was beyond great. Unfortunately, I have to decline. Thank you again, though, for your contribution. We were lucky to have your assistance. It made all the difference."

Without allowing her to say anything more, I smile and back away fast. "I've got to meet up with T-Bone. Enjoy the show!"

As I beat feet to another section, far away from Martina and her offer, I start to realize I turned down a night of wham-bam-thank-you-ma'am sex with a gorgeous woman. And it wasn't even hard. Thoughts of Skyler swirl around in my vision.

Her smile.

Her laugh.

Her teasing.

Her humor.

Her sexy body.

Her talented mouth.

Her *everything*.

She's all I need or want. I grin, pull out my phone, and glance at the picture she sent me the first night after I left. Hair tousled all over from sleep. Face free of makeup. Lips swollen from my kisses. Eyes gentle and sleepy. Breasts pushed up in tantalizing handfuls. And right then and there, I realize, she's it for me. I want to be with her. I want to be what she needs in a man. I want to have all of my ups and downs with her. I want this relationship to work, to see it flourish into something even more permanent.

I think I'm falling for Skyler Paige. Hell, I may have already fallen.

***

The stage lights flash on and off, signaling the show is about to start. I'm sitting next to Sophie, between her and Bo. She grabs my hand and interlaces our fingers. "*Mon cher*, this is so exciting! I love fashion shows!"

I grin, squeeze her hand, and wait for the lights to dim to a candle-light setting. T-Bone appears from the back of the stage and walks about a third of the way up the runway, a mic in his beefy hand.

He speaks in English instead of Italian. "Welcome, everyone! Thank you for coming to my show."

"Why didn't he speak in Italian?" I whisper into Sophie's ear.

"Fashion is a worldwide business. The international language of fashion is English."

T-Bone continues. "I notice in the fashion industry, clothing caters to women who are from size zero to size eight. Only the average size of a woman is somewhere between an American twelve and sixteen. Nowhere near the size of the standard runway or catalog models. Fashion has forgotten women come in all sizes and shapes, and I for one want to share in that beauty."

Wow. T-Bone is finally coming through on his message.

"Besides, no man wants to fuck skin and bones."

And . . . he just lost it.

Undaunted, he takes a couple of steps and stops, assessing the entire crowd with his beady gaze. "Women are sexy whether they are a school teacher, a mother, a librarian, a sales clerk, a soccer mom, or a college student. Sexy comes in all sizes. I hope women everywhere see these women in my designs and find their own version of sexy, no matter what size they are. Thank you." He bows and turns on a shiny loafer, the sheen of his satin pants glinting in the lights. His floral sport coat, sleeves cut at the forearms, is a direct contrast to the simplicity of his pants.

I blow out a long breath and wait as the music pipes in. I smile as I note he changed it to the Pussycat Dolls' "Don't Cha." It's probably the best song for the more scandalous designs.

The lights dim even lower, and the first model walks out. She's the librarian and the thinnest model in the show. I think it's genius he starts with a body type they've all seen before. She makes it to the first mirror and does the standard hunched-back, hands-on-hip pose we've all seen a million times over in the fashion industry. I've never liked that look, but I love the ode to ordinary fashion it gives. Once she starts toward the next mirror, the lights cut out, and everyone gasps. Her bra-and-panty set glows a fluorescent green, like a neon glow stick.

The audience claps wildly as she continues walking, and the next girl comes out. They both stop at a mirror. The second woman is the preschool teacher. Her body type is a little fuller, probably around a woman's size eight or ten. She looks amazing in the high-waisted, high-cut red panties, a bustier, and a robe falling off one shoulder.

She stops at her first mirror and stands like Wonder Woman, the robe falling enticingly to the crook of her elbows. Showing just enough of her body to make her look sensational and yet still leaving a bit to the imagination. The lights go out, and all the straps of her lingerie glow a bright red.

The models repeat the moves. Each one stopping at a mirror and striking a pose. When four of them are out at the same time, the lights go crazy and a disco ball comes out spinning, lighting the women in a dusting of sparkly lights. This time they do a few of their moves, showing off the lingerie in a variety of ways.

Once the four have moved to the back and the lights come up, the audience gets a great view of the back of the lingerie.

The next set of ladies comes out, and Anna-Maria is leading the charge. She looks positively stunning in her lingerie. Her size twelve body looks molded to perfection. As she starts walking, there's a man across the aisle who stands up, shouting, clapping wildly, and screaming, "That's my wife! She's beautiful! You're beautiful, baby!"

Every single member of the audience is eating up his excitement and her showing off for him. The lights go out, and her entire robe glows in the dark. She pulls it off, and the lace of her thong and the sexy bow at the tailbone light up the runway in a bright T of color. This has her husband whistling like a lunatic. I'm loving every minute. She's rocking her design, and based on the smile she's sporting, she's having a blast doing it.

"I am going to hire this T-Bone to do a campaign." Sophie leans into my space and points at Anna-Maria. "I love how he's empowering women of all shapes and sizes to see their beauty. He's doing an excellent job detailing their attributes."

I inhale a deep breath and let it out. "Make sure you're in control. He can edge toward raunchy when he's not being advised, but his desire and intentions are sound."

"I see you added your lipstick to the mirrors." Her pink lips purse into a knowing smirk. "My message is still on my mirror at home. I like it there. Reminds me of you."

I put my arm around her shoulders and nudge her temple with my nose, taking in her sugar-and-spice scent I love so much. It's not peaches and cream, but it's familiar and reminds me of a great couple of weeks in Paris.

"You are golden, Sophie," I whisper near her ear. "I hope your new man understands that and treats you like the gem you are. Otherwise, he's going to have one pissed-off Bostonian on his ass. I'd have to get on a plane just to open up a can."

She jerks her head in my direction. "What can would you be opening? I do not understand this can you want to open."

I sigh heavily. "Ugh, Sophie. You need to watch more Netflix. Open up a can of *whoop ass*."

She tsks. "Whyever would you do such a thing?" Her nose crinkles, and her face is a mask of confusion. "There is no ass needing a whooping."

I laugh hard, squeeze her shoulder, lean back, and enjoy the rest of the show. The models are killing it. The audience seems to be taking in each piece enthusiastically, and I've got my two friends sharing an experience with me.

Life is good.

10

The moment the plane's wheels touch down in New York, I can hardly contain my excitement. Thank God Wendy booked me in first class and I get to deplane first. I'm positively itching to see Skyler.

I grab my two carry-on bags. Since I knew the case would only be a week, I packed rather light.

In mere minutes, I'm pushing through the airport crush to get to the arrivals area. As I approach, I see little Rachel Van Dyken. She looks as if she walked right out of a badass all-chick commando-type film. Her long, platinum-blonde hair is pulled back away from her face in a series of braids, sticking with the warrior vibe. She's wearing black cargo pants, a matching tank, combat boots, and aviators. She's leaning against the wall; one foot pushes off when she sees me. Only she's not the only one drawing my attention.

Out of nowhere, a horde of paparazzi swarm, their camera flashes going at warp speed, blinding me where I stand. I lift my hand to block some of the flashes. My elbow is grabbed, and Rachel is yelling out commands to the photographers clicking away.

"What does Skyler think about your betrayal?" one man says.

"Did you take both women back to your hotel?" another shouts.

"Will Skyler forgive you?" I hear a third yell.

"What the fuck are you talking about?" I toss out, confused, tired, and flustered. I've just arrived after a nine-hour flight, and I'm being slammed by a round of questions I know nothing about.

Rachel yanks on my elbow. "Do. Not. Say. A. Word. Follow me," she grates through her teeth.

"But I don't know what they're going on about this time."

Jesus. Every time I take a continental flight, I come back to chaos.

Growling my frustration, I push out with my suitcases and follow Rachel to the car waiting at the curb. Nate is in it.

"Good Lord!" he roars when he sees the swarm. He's on me like flies on shit.

"Welcome home, Mr. Ellis." He pushes back the crowd with his arms so I can move past him and into the blacked-out SUV. "Give the man his privacy, you vultures!" I hear him yell as I toss the luggage in the back with me and close the door.

Rachel whistles, already in the driver's seat. Her husband jumps into the passenger side and spins around so he can make sure we're not followed.

"Nice to see you guys, but what the hell was that? How did they even know I'd be here?"

Nate shakes his head while Rachel's jaw firms.

"Your little friend, Martina, talks a lot," Rachel responds snidely.

"My friend? She is not a friend. We hired her team to teach the models how to move their bodies."

Rachel nods, her lips in a flat white line. She pushes a button on the car stereo, and the sound of a telephone call being made can be heard through the speakers.

"Do you have him?" Skyler's voice is warm but direct.

"We've got him," Rachel responds, focused on maneuvering the SUV out of the airport and onto the freeway.

"Skyler. What's going on?" I ask openly, not giving a shit who hears me.

"We'll talk when you get here. I'm glad you made it safely." Her voice is now monotone, lacking any feeling. Not exactly the welcome home I expected from her.

Before I can say anything more, she hangs up.

"What is going on, guys? Talk to me. Please." I'm not above begging. Something's wrong with Skyler, the paps are swarming, and I've got the cold shoulder coming from the Van Dykens.

Nate turns around, his face a mask of unconcealed anger. I lean back and lift my hands in a gesture of surrender. "Bro, I have no idea why the press were here or why. You look like you want to tear my head off with your bare hands." He could probably do it too. The guy is ripped.

"Probably because I do!" He frowns, and his voice takes on a serious tone. "You steppin' out on Skyler?"

I jolt up straight in my seat. "Fuck no! What would give you that impression?"

He tosses two smut mags over the seat back to where I sit. On the cover of one is a picture of Skyler in tears. Not sure where the hell that came from or when, but the one next to it has my full attention. It's the picture of Martina and me backstage before the show yesterday. The caption above says "Skyler in Tears. Parker Wooing Exotic Dancer in Italy."

I groan and look at the next one. "Parker Gets Around. Skyler Is Furious." This one has a picture of me with my arm around Sophie, the two of us laughing at something Bo said at the fashion show. Bo, of course, has been conveniently cut out of the picture. Next to the image is one of Skyler angry, which honestly looks like a picture taken years ago. Her hair is a different color now and much longer.

"Where do these bastards get off making this shit up! Martina was a teacher in the show. Sophie is my friend." I press back into the seat and rub at my temples. "Is Sky pissed?" I hold up the two mags. "She believes this shit is real?"

Nate shrugs and turns to the front.

"I wouldn't ever hurt Skyler like this. I care too much about her." A pang hits my heart, and my chest feels tight.

Nate nods. "Yeah, we figured something was up, but we have Sky's back first. You understand."

I nod. "Does she believe this crap?" I toss the smut rags to the floor.

Rachel shakes her head. "I don't think so, but that doesn't mean it doesn't hurt when she sees her boyfriend plastered all over the papers on the arms of two separate but equally beautiful women."

Attempting to cool down right now is impossible. I'm seething. "Fuck, all I wanted to do was come to New York and spend some much-needed one-on-one time with my goddamned girlfriend. Now I've got to explain a completely innocent situation! Fuck me!" I run my fingers through my hair, tugging at the roots until I feel the bite of pain centering my anger.

"Talk to her, man. She's waiting for you in the penthouse," Nate offers. The anger in his voice and demeanor is gone now that he knows the truth.

Rachel pulls up, and Nate walks me into the building and straight into the elevator. I stand in silence, waiting for the numbers to rise to the fortieth floor, where I'm going to have to explain myself regarding a bullshit situation the media and paps created.

The elevator doors open, and Nate unlocks Skyler's door, letting me in. "You guys going out tonight?"

"Fuck no." I grit my teeth and enter the condo, every footfall harsher than the next. Her scent fills the air, and even though I'm pissed, the familiar, welcome scent soothes me.

"Sky!" I holler through the room, wanting to go right to her.

"In here!" she yells somewhere near where the kitchen is centered.

With quick strides, I make it to the kitchen. My girl is bent over the oven, ass in the air, checking something.

"Baby . . . ," I whisper, and she stands up straight, closes the oven door, and spins around.

She's a vision. Blonde hair down in beachy waves, her face with a hint of makeup, but nothing to take away from her natural beauty. She's wearing an olive-green tank, which goes great against her honey skin tone. Her bottom half is encased in a tight, form-fitting pair of skinny jeans, which mold to every curve. Her feet are bare, toes painted a dark wine color.

I grind my teeth for a moment, taking in all that is her before I spew what's on my mind. "Tell me you don't believe any of the shit they printed?" My shoulders seem weighted to the ground, my feet in concrete boots as I wait for the verdict.

Skyler grins, which turns into a sparkling smile. She runs toward me and jumps up. I catch her at the ass, and she locks her legs around my waist and smashes her lips to mine. Her lips are warm and taste of cherry lip balm. I dip my tongue in, not waiting for her invitation. I need a taste, and when our tongues meet, we both groan. I turn around and place her on top of the counter, barely able to hold myself up, let alone her too with the amount of relief crashing over me. Skyler threads her fingers through my hair, tugging on the overlong strands curling at the top. She moans into my mouth, and I kiss her harder, deeper. I run one hand up her thigh, locking on to her hip, the other up her spine and into her hair, where I cradle her head. Our tongues duel for supremacy, both wanting to lead. I win, tipping her head to the side so I can delve deeper, take more, until we're both a mess of wet, bruised lips.

Needing air, I ease back. She follows, and I smile against her lips. "Thank God."

Skyler blinks her eyes open almost sleepily. "I never believe everything I read in the papers. Though the look of real concern on your face when you saw me said it all for you. I'm not sure what happened, but I trust you, Parker. If we can't trust each other, we have nothing. Especially in my business."

I press my forehead against hers. "I had no idea all that crap was printed. Once more, I got off a plane after landing in the States and was bombarded by the paparazzi spilling their lies."

"So the picture of you and that Martina woman was fake?" She leans back enough so I can look her in the eyes.

"No, but they made it look like more than it was. Martina was a dance coach for the models Bo and I were hired to help. She taught them how to move their bodies. She and two others from her dance company. We spent the week working with women who'd never modeled before. It was amazing and exhausting at the same time."

"Then she didn't ask you out?"

Now how do I avoid this topic. Unfortunately I don't think I can. I suck in a long breath and grip Skyler's hips. I run my hands up and down her thighs, soothing my battered soul through touching her. "Actually she did ask me out. Offered me a no-strings-attached night of 'fun,' but I didn't take her up on it. The picture was taken immediately after she asked me out. A random photographer came up and asked for a picture and said *smile*, and baby, I did it on autopilot. I'm sorry."

She shakes her head. "No, it's okay. And of course, I knew Sophie was going to be there. Then again, you looked pretty comfortable sitting there . . ." This time, her voice holds a teasing note.

I grin. "Well, Bo was on my other side, and you can't see my other arm, but it's around his chair too."

Skyler traces my face with her fingertips, running her fingers from my temples down to my lips, where she caresses them with a feather-soft touch. "I believe you. At first, it irked me to see those pictures, but it's going to happen. This isn't the first time, nor will it be the last time one of us has something printed about our relationship that is so far from the truth it's mind-boggling. We need to promise to always talk it out. If I'd spent time speculating which parts were the truth and which were lies, I would have gone crazy."

I run my hands up her thighs and back down. "I'd never hurt you like that. And I promise to always be honest with you."

She smiles, leans forward, and places a soft kiss on my lips. "It's what I've come to expect from you. Part of the reason I like you so much. I always know where you stand."

I nibble on her chin and along her jaw before bringing her into a full-body hug. She tightens her legs around my waist and wraps her arms around my back as I set my nose against the crook of her neck and breathe her in. She's content to sit there while I hug her.

"I missed you, Peaches," I murmur into her hair.

She hums, and I feel it straight through my chest on a path to my dick. "I missed you too. And I have a surprise for you, if you'd turn around and let me go."

"I don't want to ever let you go."

She tightens her hold briefly. "Good answer," she whispers against my cheek, before kissing the edge of my ear and running her teeth along it.

I chuckle and pull back, needing the room, or I'm liable to fuck her on the kitchen counter. Then again, it doesn't sound like a bad idea.

"Turn around, pretty boy." A coy smile spreads across her lips.

I step away as she slides off the counter. I turn around and see her kitchen table is set for two. Candles are burning, place mats set, fine dishware placed perfectly along with cloth napkins. She's even added a bouquet of sunflowers, making her table bright and cheery to coincide with her romantic gesture.

"I'm cooking for you tonight. I've made my mother's famous Tater Tot hot dish, a salad, and warm garlic bread."

I mull over what she said. "You made me dinner, baby?"

She grins and nods. "All by myself."

"You know how to cook?"

She shrugs. "A little. I know some of the dishes my mother taught me, and this one is my favorite."

"Tater Tot hot dish."

"Yeah."

Not rack of lamb. Steak. Linguini, fish, or anything gourmet. My girl sets about making her man a meal and makes her favorite family recipe. Which also happens to be something a mother would make her small child.

"You did say Tater Tots, as in the square little fried potatoes we used to get back in the elementary school cafeteria?"

She looks around the room. "Is there another kind of Tater Tot?"

I cover my stomach, tilt back my head, and laugh to my heart's content. "You are full of surprises."

She snuggles up against my front, lifts her head, and pops up onto her toes. She kisses me firm and fast. "How about you go freshen up, put on some pj's, and come settle in with a beer."

"I didn't bring pj's." I loop an arm around her waist and bring her body flat against my chest so she can feel every inch of me touching every inch of her.

Skyler grins. "Good thing I bought you a few pairs online and had them delivered. They're stacked in a section of my closet. You can hang anything you want in there."

"Moving me in already?" I tease.

She flicks her hair over one shoulder and frowns. "No. I wanted to make my man comfortable when he visits. I want you to feel like you're at home here the same way you made me feel at home with your family at Lucky's and in your apartment. No ulterior motives. I promise." She crosses her finger over her heart.

I grin. "Thank you, baby."

"Go! Get settled and come back. I'll be waiting."

My girlfriend will be waiting. I shake my head and smile while carrying my luggage to her room.

***

The next day, after what I found out is the best hot casserole ever and a fuck-a-thon with my girlfriend, we finally make it to the set. The director knew she was coming in late and planned ahead. Tracey meets us at the gate as Nate and Rachel exit the SUV and escort us to the entrance of the set.

Sky holds my hand, an ease about her I don't feel within myself. The media is everywhere. The cameras are going off like a tornado around us, and my heart is in my throat.

My girl squeezes my hand. "Relax. They won't bite. Much." She winks.

The paparazzi are screaming out requests to Sky. Ever the professional, she turns her body toward mine and loops her arms around my waist.

"Get your pictures now, people. I've got a movie to film." She laughs, and the crowd claps and whistles, some calling out questions.

"Based on your body language, I'm assuming you and Parker are still together?" one asks.

She answers him right away. "Yes. We've been together for a little over two months and are enjoying spending time together when our schedules permit." She lifts her head and smiles at me while I look down at her pretty face. I want to kiss her so badly, but I'm afraid of breaking some type of Hollywood protocol rule I haven't been informed of.

"What do you think about the pictures of the women he was with in Italy?"

"I trust my man." She lifts her hand and places it on my stomach in a possessive gesture that speaks volumes. At least it does to me. I squeeze her shoulder, keeping her closely wrapped in my hold.

"Sophie Rolland is a personal friend of ours, and they attended the fashion show together. Martina was a dance coach hired by Parker to assist the models. You can't believe everything you see in a photo!" She smirks, and the crowd laughs, taking picture after picture.

I stand there practically mute, holding her close, rubbing her shoulder and trying to smile as much as possible.

"Parker, are you excited about visiting Skyler on set?"

Sky nudges me, and I realize I'm supposed to answer the question. "Yeah. It will be great to see my girl in action and meet her coworkers."

"What do you guys think of the media calling you SkyPark?" another calls out.

"Yeah, SkyPark!" another says.

Skyler and I both look at one another and start laughing hysterically.

"I guess I have my answer."

Tracey butts in, an arm held out to each of us. "Sorry, guys, Skyler needs to get on set. Thanks for stopping by." She ushers us through the gates, and Skyler and I both wave.

"Well, that wasn't too bad," Tracey says as we follow her to the huge concrete building a good fifty yards ahead.

I lay my hand on Skyler's nape, and she smiles. "You were amazing as usual. You never miss a beat. I don't know how you do it."

She grins. "Years of practice. Don't worry, you'll be an old pro in no time."

And the best part is her thinking I'll be around long enough to have mastered dealing with the press when it comes to her and our relationship.

I smile and bring her in closer to my side as we walk. "Have I told you today how much I *like* you?"

She licks her lips and pats my ass with her free hand. "I do believe you have, but I sure love hearing it!"

"I like you more than I like my burgers and beer."

Her eyes widen, and she pretends to gasp in surprise. "Not sure I can handle the depth of those words, pretty boy."

I nudge her shoulder playfully. "Hey, don't be knocking my burgers and beers. Before you, they were my one true love."

Oh fuck.

Insert foot right into mouth.

Skyler stops in the middle of the sidewalk and stares at me. She swallows slowly, her eyes searching mine while I suck in a harsh breath.

"Baby, that came out wrong."

She narrows her gaze. "Mm-hmm. I'm going to let it slide, pretty boy." She pokes at my chest. "You better watch it, mister, or I'll start to believe you like me more than . . . your Tesla!" Her mouth opens into a wide O that she covers with her hand.

I shake my head and curl my lips. "You're lucky my cherry-red baby didn't hear you say that. You are a piece of work, Peaches. You know that?"

Skyler shrugs and smirks. "Never been accused of being easy."

"Oh, I don't know about that." I get closer to her and grab her by the hips, slamming her body against mine. "If memory serves, I got in this luscious body pretty easy . . . ," I tease while slipping my hands around to her ass and gripping each cheek firmly.

She whimpers, and I squeeze her bottom again, harder this time, hopefully reminding her of the fun we had this morning. I got those cheeks nice and rosy pink with a handful of well-placed smacks to her heart-shaped ass.

"Guys, you do realize the paparazzi can still see you, which means the pictures of you guys kissing and groping one another will be tonight's Hollywood news," Tracey says. "Congratulations, Parker. Everyone's going to know you're an ass man."

I groan and place my forehead against Sky's. "Nothing's sacred, baby," I complain, pouting.

"It is. Just not when you do it outside of the privacy of our bed-rooms or houses. Now you know, for next time." Tracey responds while Sky snickers.

"I'm already going to have to call my mother about the Martina and Sophie press. Now she's going to scold me for not treating you like the lady you are."

"Aw, your mom thinks I'm a lady. That's so nice. I love Cathy."

"Oh, she loves you. By the way, she thinks Catherine Paige is an excellent name for her future granddaughter." I nail her right in the gut with my innuendo.

With that offhand comment, I let her go and follow Tracey, this time an arm's length from my beautiful girl.

"Excuse me? What have you been telling your mother?" she fires off, a hint of indignation in her tone. "Let's go back to the future-grandchild part of this discussion."

I shake my head. "Nope. Gotta get to the set. Besides, you need to introduce me to Rick the . . ."

Her eyes go wide, and her face takes on a warning expression as her eyes flick to Tracey.

I barely regurgitate something believable. "Rick, the costar of the movie."

She sidles up to me and interlaces our fingers. "Nice save there, SkyPark."

"Ugh. Did they really give us a Hollywood-couple meshed name?"

Skyler grins. "I actually like SkyPark. It sounds pretty cool. Remember Brangelina for Brad Pitt and Angelina Jolie?"

I shiver.

"Or Bennifer for Ben Affleck and Jennifer Lopez."

I suck a breath in through my teeth. "SkyPark works."

"That's what I thought. Come on, I want to introduce you to the team."

"Lead the way, Peaches. I'll follow you anywhere."

"Aw, that was really sweet."

"Was it? Huh." I rub at my chin with the hand not holding hers. "Following you means I get an excellent view of your ass in those jeans."

Skyler tips her face to the sky and groans. "Why me?"

SKYLER

I'm trying my best not to squeal with excitement. He's here. Parker's shooting the breeze with the director of the movie, laughing at her quips and making a friend out of her instantly. I have to admit, my man is smooth. He can charm anyone. He's definitely charmed me.

Before I can introduce him to the camera guys I've become close with over the past few movies in the series, Rick enters the set. He sees me and rushes over, a happy, puppy dog–type bounce to his steps. Without warning, he pulls me into his arms and lays a series of kisses against my neck, making a loud show of it as if I were one of his family members.

"Skyler Bear!" He jostles me around in a bear hug. "How's my best girl!"

I cringe and go stiff in his arms. He eases me back an arm's length. "What's got you down? Your guy not make it here yet?" His eyebrows rise up in question, and I'm about to answer when I'm physically pulled out of Rick's arms by said guy.

Parker's chin moves into my neck, and he loops an arm around my waist, plastering my body flush against his front. Tingles of anxiety prickle against my skin as he growls into my neck. "This does not bode well for you, baby."

Ugh. I slump into his arms. "Rick, this is my boyfriend, Parker. Parker, this is Rick, my costar."

"Yo, man! It's awesome to meet you! Any friend of Skyler Bear is a friend of mine." He smiles wide and holds out his hand.

Parker eases me to his left side, farther away from Rick, and takes his hand. He must squeeze it rather hard, because Rick's eyes go wide, and he pulls his hand away fast.

"Dude! That's one helluva grip you got there." Rick shakes his hand as if he's in pain.

"Sorry." Parker squeezes my hip. "Didn't realize my own strength."

Sure, you didn't. I narrow my gaze at Parker.

"It's cool you're here today. We're shooting one of the racier scenes. Would be righteous to get your feedback on how to best hold and touch her. You know, since you know her *intimately* and all." Rick leans closer to Parker, and a bout of anxiety ratchets up my spine.

Please don't get into it, I silently pray, hoping Parker's jealousy doesn't come out swinging.

I can feel Parker's body grow still, a tick in his jaw flickering like mad. He's grinding his teeth. Shit. This is not going to be good. I have to get him away from Rick somehow.

"Um, guys, maybe we shouldn't talk about this—" I start, but am cut off by Parker.

"Oh no, we *absolutely should*. Tell me, Rick . . ." The inflection on the letter *k* is scathing coming from Parker's mouth. "What kind of feedback were you looking to get about my *girlfriend?*" His tone is filled with malice, and I can see his hold on his emotions is flying away like a flock of birds heading south for the winter. Problem is, Rick doesn't even notice it. He's oblivious to Parker's jealousy because he doesn't think of me in that light.

"Honey . . . ," I try again.

Parker lifts a hand between us. "No, I've got to hear this. Go on, Rick." Again, with the *k* sound thick on his tongue.

"Well, dude, don't spread this around,"—he leans in closer to us— "but Sky and me, we're having trouble showing chemistry on the screen during our romantic scenes. The director is not happy, and I could use whatever tips you've got."

God. Rick is *so sweet*. He genuinely wants Parker's help, and I desperately hope Parker can hear it in Rick's voice and be the bigger man.

Parker backs away a bit from Rick, holds up a finger toward my blissfully ignorant costar, and brings me a few feet away before dipping his head down to my ear. This move curbs my anxiety hundredfold. The farther away Parker is from Rick, the better.

"Peaches, you didn't mention the two of you were having trouble," he whispers.

I purse my lips. "Yes, I did. Remember, I told you we had to reshoot some scenes."

His brows pinch together as if he's mulling over what I'm saying.

"Honestly, I haven't had to do a role like this with intimate scenes since I was in a committed relationship to Johan, and he didn't care one bit about who I was kissing or whether or not I was showing full nudity and such," I whisper conspiratorially against his chest. He cups my cheeks.

"First of all, I'm sorry if I made you nervous when you needed to do your job. I trust you. Do I trust him? Fuck no. I wouldn't trust any man who gets to touch you in any way. That's who I am, baby. I think you get that. We both have a bit of a green monster living inside of us. I don't see that changing anytime soon. It doesn't mean I'm going to interfere in your job in a way that hurts your career. I know you have to do these roles and scenes. I may not like it, but I respect it."

I run my hand down his cheek and rub my thumb against his bottom lip. "Thank you."

"Now what can I do to make this easier on you?"

I shrug. "Frankly, I don't know. Rick and I are going to have to figure something out, though, because he was not lying. The director is unhappy, and I don't need that kind of press spreading throughout the industry. It could affect my future roles."

He firms his chin, leans down, and kisses me softly. "I may have an idea."

I grin, loop my arms around his neck, and pop up onto my toes to touch his nose with my own. "I like your ideas."

He grins. "You might like this one, you might not. I'm going to have a chat with the director if you trust me."

I lick my lips, inhale fully, and let it out. I run my hand through his overly long hair, plucking at one of his curls on top. I love when his hair is overgrown and his curls pop out. It makes him seem younger, more vulnerable. "Parker, I've entrusted you with my heart. Which is far more important than anything you can do to my career."

He smiles wide, and I love seeing his happiness. I want to see it more. I want to be the one who puts those beatific smiles on his handsome face.

"Be right back." He goes over to the director, taps her on the shoulder, and she turns around toward him, giving him her full attention. My guy has that effect on all women. Their eyes always stray to him.

He really is gorgeous. Tall, tan, with light, crystal-blue eyes. A dashing bright-white smile. His chiseled jaw and high cheekbones give him a *GQ* effect that hits me straight through to the heart, and *lower*. I squirm, watching my man make gestures to the bedroom and bathroom set across the way. I leave him be, wanting him to do what he feels he has to do.

Tracey comes up behind me. "What is he doing?" She lifts her chin toward Parker.

I cross my arms over my chest and rub at my biceps. "He's got some idea for the director on how Rick and I can work on our chemistry . . . romantically." I purse my lips and glance at my best friend.

"I'm sorry, Birdie, I don't think I heard you. Your boyfriend is talking to the director on how to best get you and your insanely handsome model costar to have more romantic chemistry on the screen?"

"Yep," I state with absolute pride.

Tracey frowns deeply. "Am I the only one who thinks this is really freakin' weird?"

I shake my head. "Nope."

It is weird. And charming. My man hears I have a problem and sets about helping me fix it, even if it's something that would make any man uncomfortable. Because he cares more for me than the subject matter at hand. He wants me to succeed even at the price of making him uncomfortable.

He's amazing. Wonderful. Sexy. Strong. Intelligent.

And I'm falling for him.

I watch the animated conversation from afar while Rick comes up to my little huddle with Tracey. "Your guy is a little intimidating," Rick admits.

I chuckle. "Yes, he is. And hot as fuck." I smile and take in all of my man while both Tracey and Rick roar with laughter.

Parker comes back, his swagger in full swing. He's wearing a pair of jeans that form to his well-toned thighs to absolute perfection. He's paired them with a tailored, long-sleeved black sweater. The black shows off his strong neck and brings out his sparkling blue eyes. As he walks, his sandy-brown hair is glinting a coppery color off the set lights, making my fingers itch to run through it, preferably while riding on top of him.

"All set!"

"What is?" I go straight into his arms as the director shouts for the actors to get in hair, makeup, and wardrobe. "What in the world did you do?"

"You'll see . . ." He smirks and smacks me on the ass. "Go get ready, I've got to chat with Rick."

I blink a few times and shake my head. "Fine. Like I said, I trust you."

***

There wasn't much to be done for my hair since I'd already styled it this morning. Though I was surprised to be put back into the bra-and-panty set for the beginning of the love scene. It starts in the bathroom while my character is getting ready.

Breathe, Skyler. It's going to be okay. Parker understands.

I take a few yoga breaths as the cameraman gets into position.

"Skyler, you're at the fluffing-your-hair position," the director calls out, and I raise my arms and stand on my mark, watching myself in the mirror.

"Ready . . . set . . . action," she calls out, and the cameras float toward me as I work my hair and assess myself in the mirror. My breasts are pushed up high in the pink lacy bra, the matching bikini bottom edged in the same fine detail.

"Angel . . ." I hear my character called from behind me, but not by Rick, by Parker.

I turn around, my body and my gaze heating instantly at the sight of his bare chest, muscles on full display. He's got his jeans on with one button undone, showing off a bigger slice of his happy trail I adore. The bit of hair leading down to his cock makes my mouth water and has my temperature rising.

I blank out for a mere second, realizing I'm supposed to play along. "Phoenix, you shouldn't be here. They may find you." I whisper the lines, using the hero's name, Rick's character, as Parker moves closer.

Parker reaches me and runs a hand from my shoulder down over my breast, which has me mewling with need and excitement. "Nothing's going to happen to you when we're together. We're magic, Angel. Don't you know that by now?" He mimics my costar's lines.

"Phoenix . . . ," I gasp as Parker's head falls to my neck and he runs a line of kisses from the crook of my shoulder to up behind my ear. He lets his lips drag across my ear.

Ripples of pleasure soar through my body as Parker cups my chin and throat, commanding, unrelenting, putting me where he wants me. His lips come down to mine, and I sink into his kiss. He ravishes me with his mouth, deep plunges of his tongue swirling with mine. I wrap my arms around his neck while his hands fly to my ass. He grinds his denim-clad crotch against my flimsy lace, and I moan, sighing into his kiss and movements. He lifts me up and plants me on the vanity.

I forget where I am, who's watching, and what we're doing. He makes me forget everything else but him.

His lips.

His minty taste.

His thick erection pressing against me.

His warm skin all around me.

His breath between each plunge of his tongue.

I'm losing my mind. He's stealing my heart. I've got nothing left, I've already given him my body.

"Parker . . . ," I whisper when his mouth drags down my neck to the tops of my breasts.

"Cut!" I hear screamed through the bullhorn.

I grip my man, digging my nails into his shoulder blades. "Fuck," I whisper, and Parker's body starts to shake against mine. He runs his hands up my back and cups my cheeks.

He's laughing, his entire body moving with each guffaw. "Baby, you forgot where you were. I get my mouth on you, and you light up. Fuckin' love it." He kisses me once, hard.

"Duuuuude! That. Was. The. Shit!" Rick claps. "Skyler Bear, we have to do exactly that for the cameras!"

I slide off the vanity and hide most of my body against Parker's front until my stage assistant hands me my fluffy robe. Parker pulls it around my back, covering me up first so I can shimmy my arms into each hole and keep a modicum of my privacy.

"It's not easy, Rick," I mumble, my cheeks heating with the embarrassment of losing myself on set.

"Why the heck not! You're an amazing actress!" he gushes.

"Yeah, why not, Peaches?" Parker kisses the top of my forehead.

"Because you're not my man!" I want to stomp my foot and cross my arms like a child who isn't getting her way.

Before anyone can respond, the director approaches. "Mr. Ellis, that was exactly what I want to see on screen! If you ever decide to enter the acting business, let me know. I'd film you in a second. You look good on camera."

Parker chuckles. "That's kind of you, but this was a one-time cameo. Now, Rick, did you see how I approached Skyler with confidence? Baby, will you humor me and stand right here like he's going to approach you in the scene?"

I do what he asks.

Rick immediately steps to Parker's side, pulls off his own T-shirt, showing his muscular body and getting into character. It's not as good as Parker's chest, but then again, I've tasted and touched Parker's intimately. It's mine and I love it.

"Use your swagger, and when you approach her, don't be timid. You have to show through each finger impression on her skin, every kiss you bestow, that you are *into* her."

Rick licks his lips and bites the bottom one as if he's really focusing. Poor thing. This is his first big role and romantic scene with an A-list actress. I'm not tooting my own horn, just stating a fact. I remember back when I was in his very position. It's not an easy battle to overcome.

"Now, approach her, and grip her body as though she's your woman and you can't wait to get her under you."

I wait while Rick approaches. "Phoenix . . . ," I whisper, stating my line so he can get into character. "You shouldn't be here. They may find you."

Rick hooks his arm around my waist, and his eyes pierce mine with an aggressive grit he didn't have before. He says his line while running his hands up and down my arms before cupping my jaw and throat the same way Parker did. He kisses me, and I'm happy to taste mint. The same minty taste my guy chews between meals. I close my eyes and try to imagine I'm kissing my man, getting into it the same way I did with Parker.

The director calls out, "Cut!" We both pull away from one another. Rick is grinning like a loon.

"Exactly what I was looking for," the director calls out. "Sky, lose the robe. Makeup, freshen her up. Everyone get into position, we're shooting this right now while it's smokin' hot! And Parker, you're with me behind the camera. Want your thoughts on the scene and the ones following. And, I owe you a bottle of your favorite liquor for making it happen." She points to Rick and me.

Yes, my man is quite the charmer. And a genius.

"I love your boyfriend, Skyler. He's the shit!" Rick gushes, looking at Parker as though the sun rose and set on him.

I think I'm falling in love with him too.

"He absolutely is," I say, instead of admitting my deepest, wildest thoughts.

Parker follows the director but glances over his shoulder back my way.

"Have I told you today how much *I like you*," I call out, and bite into my bottom lip, cocking an eyebrow for his benefit.

"You don't have to tell me. I felt it in your kiss." He tosses his sweater over his shoulder like he walks through a movie set half-naked all the time and continues chatting with the director.

I shake my head and let makeup tend to me while I think about Parker.

The man really can do anything.

How will I ever measure up?

The end . . . for now.

SAN FRANCISCO: INTERNATIONAL GUY BOOK 5

To my bossy beta, Tracey Wilson Vuolo.
San Francisco is for you.

I feel it's the place where soul sisters were made . . .
brought together from different coasts . . .
united through the love of books.

I'm honored to have borne witness to it.

1

"Whiskey neat. Two fingers." Royce's voice sounds like rolling thunder off in the distance as I push my way through the other first-class patrons to the empty seat next to my partner. "Look who finally made his appearance." He cocks a questioning eyebrow.

I smile at the flight attendant who took his drink order. "Beer. Sierra Nevada if you have it."

"We do. I'll be back shortly." The thin, pretty woman smiles before heading to the galley.

"Yeah, yeah. I know I cut it close, but I'm here." I shove my briefcase into the overhead bin, remove my sport coat, and set it on the hanger in front of my seat.

Royce lays his hands over his stomach, fingers interlaced. "Was worried you might pull a skip, seeing as you were supposed to be back two days ago." His lips have a slight curl to them, proving he's not angry but giving me shit on purpose.

I turn a bit in my seat. "Couldn't be helped. Once Sky and I did the lunch interview on set a few days ago, the crowds went crazy. Tracey suggested we go out around town, give them something more to capture, which, as you know, took the heat off the IG offices."

Royce nods. "True. Gotta be rough, dating an A-list celebrity. Imagine everyone wants a piece of your girl and you . . . by default."

By default.

His words zip through me like an approaching storm, rumbling and growling with the promise of a full downpour. Being with someone like Skyler is unimaginable for a regular guy like me. It's the shit they make movies about. Hell, a movie she'd play a starring role in. Then where would I be? The hero who won the girl, or the one that got passed over for someone better suited to her lifestyle?

I push those irritating thoughts aside and focus on the here and now. "Yeah well, all the pieces are mine. At least the pieces that count." I smirk, and he shakes his head. "Besides, I'm here, and we're heading to Cali right on time. Now, bring me up to date on our client. You said her name is Rochelle?"

When I pose the question, Royce smiles, and his face takes on a dreamy, serene quality. *Shit.* As I suspected from our chat last week, he's already gonzo for the woman.

This is not good. Especially since we've been hired to find her a man.

"Top-notch businesswoman, beautiful, intelligent. The shit she pulls with numbers, the logical analytic approach she takes is second to none, man. And I know numbers. They never lie. This woman has an uncanny ability to anticipate market fluctuations and profit and losses, making her one of the all-time best financiers in the business."

"Sounds like you'd trust her to manage your money." I toss out the carrot to see if he bites.

Royce sits up and fluffs his suit coat. "I have mad respect for her skills. It's an art form the way she works."

"Really? An art form?" I grin and lean back into the comfortable seat.

"Yeah. Not a lot of people can do what she can do, especially at her age."

"Oh yeah? How old is Ms. Renner?"

He doesn't even have to look at her file before answering.

"Twenty-eight."

"And you happened to memorize her age."

Royce frowns. "I did my homework, which is much more than I can say about you, I might add."

"You could say that, but I did read through her file on the plane from New York. I wouldn't necessarily have remembered her exact age. When does she turn twenty-nine?"

"December 1 . . . ," he says automatically, then realizes his error and firms his lips into a flat line before glancing out the window as if the airport tarmac is the most interesting thing he's seen all day.

"Brother . . ."

Royce lifts a hand. "I have a good memory. Don't read anything into it."

I shake my head and am about to dig into how much he knows about Ms. Renner when the flight attendant approaches with our drinks.

"Here you go," she says to Royce and me. "Please buckle up, the captain is going to prepare for takeoff now."

"Thank you." I smile at the efficient woman. She's nice looking, tall, a little on the thin side. Not much for curves. I'd put her at about a six to a seven on my sexy scale, which means she could score herself a man who's around a five in the looks department and he'd worship the ground she walks on.

I sip on my beer and let the cool taste of the hops settle in my gut as I mull over how to best approach what I think is going on in Royce's head.

"Look, Roy . . ."

"Park, respect, brother, but you have no business telling me *anything* when you're currently bedded down with a client, and not for the first time. Frankly, I don't want to hear it." He puts his drink to his lips, his shoulders shifting toward the window.

I know better than to push Roy when he feels he's being backed into a corner. The bruiser inside will come out fighting if provoked.

Still, I wouldn't be a good friend if I didn't put out there what my intuition is telling me.

I try a different approach. "It's cool, man. Happy to be here with you. Mind showing me what the two of you have discussed with her profile?"

Royce nods succinctly, sets his drink on the armrest between us, and leans over to retrieve his briefcase. He pulls out a blue file and opens it on his lap.

"Here, we've filled in the particulars about her. Educated, wealthy, city girl. Doesn't have much in the way of family. Work is her life. Looking to have a child, lay down a legacy to leave her business to one day."

"I know a guy like that." I chuckle, and Roy's gaze lifts to mine, the happy sparkle I'm used to seeing in his eyes now present . . . thank fuck. I'd much rather be on his good side. No one wants to be on his bad side.

Roy continues with a smirk. "Lives alone, penthouse in the heart of the city."

Opposite of Royce. He has a three-bedroom, two-bath home, complete with front and back yards he mows every weekend without fail. Says he wants to keep the neighbors off his back, but I think he likes things looking pristine. He's proud of what he has achieved against all the odds.

"Penthouse . . . wow. Far cry from the family life you've always mentioned wanting," I state, needing to see if Royce's attraction is truly an *attraction* and nothing more.

"What are you gettin' at, Park?" His face becomes a blank mask.

I clench my teeth and hold my breath, wondering if I've tweaked his temper. "Not much, just pointing out an observation."

He grabs his drink and takes a healthy sip, pointing a finger at me around his glass. "And your girl, where does she live again?" His voice is deeper, a touch of indignation fluttering along the edges.

Dammit! I was trying so hard not to back Roy in a corner, I did it to myself.

"Not only a plane ride away, but in a swank penthouse, if I remember correctly," he adds accurately, making one helluva point.

I lift my hands in surrender. "I get it. You win. You're right. Skyler and I *do* currently have a long-distance relationship, but it's not across three thousand miles."

Royce moves to interject, but I cut him off.

"And . . . she loves Boston. With her job, she can live anywhere in the world. I won't leave my family or business behind. Would you?"

For some reason, his nonanswer feels weighted, like a heavy burden placed around my shoulders. Here we are, two men looking at our futures, women who—on the surface—seem absolutely perfect, and yet we both have some major hurdles to jump. I couldn't be happier in my relationship with Skyler. As much as our seeing one another is limited, those times are filled with connection, laughter, incredible sex, and talk of the future. She's a woman I can share my day with, my hopes and dreams, as well as bring home to my mother and my team. Skyler fits into my world in a way I never thought possible.

What happened in my past destroyed my idea of having a loving relationship built on trust and mutual care for one another. Skyler single-handedly rebuilt that desire.

One kiss at a time.

One hug.

One whispered promise.

She has filled my heart with unending possibilities, ones I can't wait to explore further. I want that for Royce. He deserves to have the world, and as his brother, I feel as though it's my role to help keep an eye out. Make sure he's not making a shit decision based on mere lust, but on genuine connection and compatibility. Since my time with Skyler, I know what that looks like now, how to spot it more clearly than ever before.

Royce leans farther into his seat and glances out the window. Without looking at me he responds, "For the right woman, anything is possible."

***

Rochelle Renner's outer office has clean lines and tasteful pops of color. The reception desk is white and chrome, rather sleek. Purple orchids in full bloom sit at the end of each corner as we approach.

We're greeted by a painfully thin, rather petite African American woman wearing a perfectly fitted navy pencil skirt and white silk blouse with a pair of nude pumps. Her black hair is pulled back into a low ponytail.

"Hello, little lady," Royce purrs, putting on his charm.

"You are?" she asks with banality.

I flick my gaze to Royce's and hold out my hand. "Mr. Ellis and my partner, Mr. Sterling, with International Guy. We're here to see Rochelle."

"She's on the phone right now . . ." She starts to answer with a bored tone, and then her eyes suddenly light up like candles on a birthday cake. "You're the team that's going to find her a man! Praise Jesus. Hallelujah!" Her excitement is palpable and instantaneous as she comes around the desk and shakes our hands. "Oh, I didn't think she was going to go through with it, but she is. How long are you planning to be here? I'm heading out on vacation tomorrow, because if I don't use my vacation, I'll lose it, according to her *highness*."

Royce whispers under his breath, "Ouch."

Her babble is constant and unusually candid for a personal assistant. If Wendy blabbed about one of us, she'd see the back of the door.

"This is perfect. Just perfect. Now there will be nothing in my way." The woman beams.

Royce frowns and takes a seat in the small waiting area. "May I ask who you are?"

She waves a hand. "I'm *nobody*, but once Rochelle is off the market, I'm bound to be a somebody. An *available* somebody who will definitely get *his* attention." The woman practically gushes, her face alight with joy.

Instead of sitting I walk over to where she's now straightening papers on her desk and lean against the side. "You're her receptionist, I take it?"

"Yes, sir. Helen Humphrey."

"And how long have you worked for Ms. Renner?" I offer her an easy smile, but I'm getting a strange feeling from the slight woman. Her body language is wired, her word choices and inflections erratic.

"Ages." Her eyes widen as if she realizes she's forgotten something she left burning on a stove and is in desperate need to leave and tend to it. "Can I get you some coffee? I'm sure you have a lot to discuss about setting Ms. Renner up with a man," she says while wagging her finger. "Even when the perfect man is right in front of her face. Not that she'd notice. Work, work, work, work, work." She tsks and shakes her head.

"You think your boss works too much, Ms. Humphrey?"

"Mm-hmm. Taskmaster too." She dips her chin definitively. "This will be great. Having some days off, fun in the sun . . ." Her voice lowers as she moves around the space, stopping in front of a corner bar where a gleaming silver coffeepot and espresso machine sit. She puts coffee grounds in and pours water from a freestanding pitcher into the machine. As she does so, I can hear her mumbling, "And then I'll come back to find the dragon lady is out of the picture. Poof!" She spins around on her spiked heels.

Dragon lady? Wow. This woman does not care for her boss.

"If you need anything, and I mean *anything*, you just come on out and call on me. You hear? I'll take care of you. VIP *all the way*." Helen smiles wide and practically dances her way back to her desk. "She's off the phone. Come on."

She leads us down a hall past numerous offices with people milling about in sharp suits and professional attire. Once we reach a large white door with windows on each side, she knocks sharply and opens the door without waiting for permission to enter.

She introduces us while holding the door open for us to enter. "Ms. Renner, your eleven o'clock. Mr. Sterling and Mr. Ellis from International Guy Inc."

I enter first as the face of the company, but before I can reach our client, Royce comes up from my side, hand extended to Ms. Renner. I watch the interaction take place, knowing exactly what this is.

The woman is gorgeous. Tall, at least five feet ten, maybe closer to six feet in her stiletto boots that come to just under her knees. Her black leather skirt is skintight with royal-blue stitching, which runs down the side of each hip to the hem. She's wearing a royal-blue sleeveless blouse, the collar tied into a flirty bow. It accentuates her figure but leaves enough to the imagination to instill intrigue and mystery at what is hiding underneath.

"Ms. Renner, so good to finally make your acquaintance in person." Royce pours on the charm, smiling wide to show off his even white teeth. I'm told his smile makes the ladies gaga with one glance.

Ms. Renner offers him one of her own pearly-white grins, her eyes never leaving his face. "And you, Mr. Sterling. I recognize the deep timbre from our phone conversations." A blush dots her cheeks.

Oh boy.

I wonder if this is how Bo felt when I first had eyes for Sophie? Maybe we need a new rule. No hanky-panky with clients. A prickle of irritation at myself needles me at the temples. Hypocrisy is running rampant through my mind, and I'm at a loss for how to stop this train from leaving the station when I've already taken two trains myself. One that led me to the woman of my dreams. Who am I to tell Roy to back off?

Royce continues to shake her hand, showing no intention of letting her go anytime soon, which leaves me to introduce myself.

"And I'm Parker Ellis. We're happy to be here and help you with your . . . situation." I roll the word around my tongue, but it still doesn't sound right.

Finally she pulls her hand away, takes mine for a brief shake, and sits back in her chair, gesturing for us to sit in the two chairs opposite her. She steeples her fingers, elbows on her glass desk, and rests her chin on the tips.

"I guess calling it a situation fits." She grins and becomes even more lovely. "Let's just put it this way, Mr. Ellis: mostly I'm tired of being alone. Tired of dating losers who, on the surface, seem perfect but always have something wrong with them. And without sounding like a whimpering woman in a cheesy romance novel, my biological clock is ticking. Like a bass drum. Maybe some bongos."

Royce chuckles and covers his mouth. "I heard that."

Her gaze flicks over to his, and a sultry smile crosses her lips. "Basically, I don't have the time or desire to keep hunting in a sea of goldfish. It's why I've hired your team. To find me a great white."

"Since I'm being brought up to speed, I'd like to hear your thoughts on the last three men you dated and why they were wrong for you."

She tilts her head, and her eyes dart to Royce. I can see her tracing his body from the tips of his Hermés shoes up his pitch-black Tom Ford–clothed form to his bald head and goateed jaw. I'm sure she clocked his fancy watch, trimmed nails, and large hands. A woman like her doesn't get into her position by not being able to read people. And if nothing else, Royce dresses to impress. Watching her take him in, I get the feeling she is as taken with him as he is with her. The fact that they have barely looked away from one another since we entered her office says it all.

Eventually she sighs and sits back in her chair, seemingly put out. She lifts a hand and hooks the first finger. "Last man was Jamal. Built,

NBA player. God in the sack. The problem there was he wasn't just fucking me. He was screwing half the cheerleaders on the team."

I shake my head, my mind instantly flicking back to when Kayla did the same to me. Except Kayla did it with my best friend. At least now with Skyler I don't have to worry about cheating girlfriends ever again.

She hooks another finger. "Before him was Trey. Perfect on paper. Actually, met him through a friend of a friend. She'd given me his resume." She furrows her eyebrows and purses her lips, a bit of attitude coming out in her tone. "Brother played me for a song. Turns out he was broke, practically homeless, and wanted to move into my house within the first two weeks of dating. We'd only gone on four dates. When I asked why he was so eager to move in with me, jumping several hurdles in our relationship, he said he'd spent all his money on our dates and was stone broke. I get that a man comes up on some hard times, but to spend your cash on a woman and then expect her to take you in from the cold?" She shakes her head. "What kind of crazy fool did he take me for?"

"I couldn't say," I respond, when, in my head, I'm cursing the brother out. This is the type of man ruining the playing field for all our kind.

Royce groans. "Ruining it for brothers everywhere."

I grin, wanting to fist-bump my friend but remembering to keep it professional. "And the one before that?" I ask.

She huffs, her chest jerking with the effort. "Worst one yet. I thought I loved him and he loved me in return. We talked about marriage and babies. He was the perfect man."

I cross my leg, resting my ankle on my knee. "What happened? He lied about wanting marriage and children?" I surmise.

"If only. Lord . . ."

"What'd he do?" Royce sits up, a machismo in his tone we do not need right now. Like the man could up and find the guy and beat the shit out of him for playing a pretty woman.

"Oh, he was honest about the marriage and children . . . he already had both. A wife and two children. Was living two lives. I was with him for close to a year before I found out the truth. He gave me a promise ring and everything."

"Say what?" Royce growls.

"Damn" slips through my teeth as I grind my molars so I won't convey what I really think of the scumbag. She doesn't need me to commiserate with her; she needs me to help her out of her funk when it comes to finding a good man.

I know exactly what she's going through. Kayla played me for the ultimate fool. Studied with me. Slept in my bed at night, talked about how many kids we were going to have and what we'd name them . . . all to get me to put a ring on her finger. And I did. Schmuck of the century. She had me wrapped around her golden lies as she was banging Greg and planning to break it off with me. Apparently Greg wanted her to wait until we'd set up the business before announcing she was leaving me. So while she openly planned our wedding and I prepared for the brightest future with what I thought was the ideal woman, she was actually living a lie.

I push all thoughts of Kayla aside. She's no longer part of my life. Kayla can't hurt me, and Skyler never would. Her soul is pure and her intentions sound. I believe she very well could be the woman that changes my life forever.

"Mm-hmm, except I got him back in the end. Told his wife all about his lies. She's taking his ass to the cleaners in divorce court right now."

"As she should." Royce sneers. "Man like that should have his balls cut off, even if I can see why he'd do it."

Rochelle and I focus our gazes on him. "Excuse me?" she says at the same time I give a baffled "What?"

Royce rubs at his chin. "I said, I can understand why he'd do it. Risk living two lives." His voice is clear and concise.

Rochelle sucks in a breath, obviously about to interrupt, when Royce keeps going.

"He probably took one look at you, all you had to offer, and wished he had a different life, was a different kind of man. Instead of doing the right thing by you and his wife, breaking it off with her or never going there with you, he took the lazy man's route and did nothing. Man probably looked over his shoulder all the time, which means he never got to fully experience the beauty that is you."

Rochelle's eyes are coal black and piercing as she stares at Royce. "No, I don't suppose he did. What would you have done, if you were in a similar circumstance?"

He purses his lips but doesn't move an inch otherwise when he responds. "I mean no disrespect, Rochelle. You're a mighty-fine woman, and any man, including *me*, would be lucky to have you as his own, but I hold the commitment of marriage in the highest regard. I wouldn't have strayed. If I were lucky enough to have a wife and kids, they would be my everything. Nuthin' could break that bond."

The tension in the room thickens so much I swear I could karate chop that shit as Royce and Rochelle have a stare-off. I've seen staring competitions between pro wrestlers last for a shorter length of time, and they're paid to build the intensity. Finally she cuts the tension and speaks first.

"Good answer."

"It's who I am," he says automatically.

"I think I like who you are, Mr. Sterling." Her tone is unmistakably flirty.

"Feelin's mutual, Chellie." He licks his lips and smirks.

Chellie? A fucking nickname? He's known her all of five minutes. This is going to hell in a handbasket real quick.

I clear my throat until the client looks at me. "Now that we've established what you *don't* want, let's get to what you're looking for and how International Guy can help."

She sighs as if the entire thing is draining, even though she's the one who approached us.

"For starters, I need a man who's confident in who he is. Not a liar. Had enough of those."

I nod. "Any ethnic preferences we should know about?"

She clucks her tongue a bit suggestively as she eyes Royce once more. He's a tall, six-foot-four African American who undoubtedly could grace the cover of any magazine with his good looks.

"I've always preferred black men, but I'm not going to cut my nose off to spite my face by reducing the pool of prospects because they are white, Latino, or otherwise."

"Noted. Work, career?" I nudge her because her entire focus is on Royce. Hell, maybe I should let them have a go at it and tell her to call me when it falls flat. I'm not getting a match here other than intense attraction. If this woman wants her forever, as Royce recently stated he's in the market for, she's knocking at the wrong door. He's not going to leave Boston or his mother and sisters. As the sole male in the Sterling family, he watches over his women like it's his second job. He's a family man, regardless of his success with IG. The difference between us and other corporations is we make the rules to enhance the lives of our employees rather than regulate those lives. If he wants to build a family and work from home a couple of days a week, he can do that. If he wants to travel less, he can make the choice. Still, it does not mean he's going to move three thousand miles away for a woman, and by the looks of this woman's office and her success on the West Coast, I don't see her moving either. And those are not the only red flags.

"White-collar career would be preferred, because a lot of times I need to attend black-tie events and hobnob with the big dogs in my industry. I need a man comfortable enough in his own skin and around other businessmen to shoot the breeze when required, not just talk beer and baseball."

I choke down a laugh. I personally can talk beer and baseball all night, and so can Royce. It's one of the many things we brothers have in common. Although you wouldn't know it from our business acumen, which leads me to believe she may have preconceived notions about men in general.

"Again, Ms. Renner, it would help tremendously for you to give me your top-tier desires as they pertain to finding the perfect mate. If we're even capable of such a thing. Love is tricky; it doesn't follow rules and regulations, and people don't wear signs over their heads saying 'compatible.'" I speak straight from the heart, because every word is true. Love is the most complex thing I've ever experienced. From being destroyed by Kayla to being lifted higher than the galaxy by Skyler, I know how extreme the differences can be. Especially if one has been burned, which Rochelle and I have in common.

Rochelle tips her head back and laughs heartily before placing her hand on her chest as if to catch her breath. "Oh, Mr. Ellis. You misunderstood my request. I want you to find me the perfect mate. No one ever said anything about *love*, though it would be a huge bonus. Hiring a service to find me love would be preposterous, don't you think?"

"You'd be surprised what we're hired to do." I grin and clasp my hands, thankful that Rochelle's expectations of finding a love match are realistic. It took me several years to be open to love again, and finding it even longer. I don't know if I would have even come this close if Skyler hadn't come along.

"Fair enough." She sits back in her chair, where she crosses her long-ass legs, her skirt riding up her shimmery mocha-colored thigh. I glance at Royce, who's clocked the move, nostrils flaring as he swallows slowly.

"If you're not looking for a love match, lay out your parameters. What is it you want in the perfect mate?"

"Like a laundry list?" She chuckles.

"More like your absolute must-haves. Don't pretend you don't have a list already going in your head. You're an intelligent woman, and you didn't call us in for nothing. What is it you desire, Ms. Renner?"

"For starters, tall, black, and beautiful."

"Got it. Next?" I urge.

"Has a job but doesn't need to make a lot of money. I make plenty to provide. Doesn't have a lot of bad habits, like expecting me to cook his meals and be home every night at six."

"Working and independent. Next?"

"Can stand by my side at functions without complaining. Contribute to conversations eloquently or be silent as needed."

I have to grin at that last one, because Royce is not the type to sit back and watch his woman work a room without participating. Hopefully he's seeing some of the differences between them and isn't too blinded by her looks.

"Well-spoken but not intimidated by his woman's success. Anything else?"

She nods. "Doesn't have an overbearing mother. Ugh. I can't stand dealing with momma's boys."

I glance at Royce. He's tugging at the collar of his shirt and readjusting his tie.

Score one for my superior instincts. Royce is the biggest momma's boy known to mankind.

Maybe this client won't be an issue after all.

2

The bar is barely filled with patrons when I pull out a stool and place my tired ass in a seat. We picked a spot right in front of the big screen at the bar so we could catch the Giants playing the Brewers without our view impeded. These days, it feels like I never catch a game as it's happening. My DVR is practically maxed out. I need to spend a weekend at home burning through nothing but the games I've missed. My mind immediately adds a fuckhot blonde curled against my front while we lie on my leather sofa and take in the game.

I think Skyler would appreciate the serenity of sitting around and loafing on the couch. Eating hot dogs, chips, and nacho cheese followed by some rowdy sex. Yep, I'm certain my girl would be up for it.

"Hey, man, you know what the end score was for the Red Sox by any chance?" I ask the bartender as he approaches.

He nods and wipes his hands on a towel. "It was awesome, man. They won eight to five against the Orioles."

I lift my hand and high-five the guy. Man code. I could tell by the enthusiasm in his tone he was happy the Red Sox won. "Sweet! Can I have a pint of the Almanac IPA? Gotta drink the local brew while I can."

"Same for me." Royce lifts his chin and maneuvers his big body onto a stool. He's obviously taking a break from his normal whiskey neat, which isn't unusual when he's having a meal. Though I wouldn't be surprised if he switched after dinner.

"Two Almanacs coming right up. You want a menu?"

"Sure do. Thanks," Royce says.

When the bartender leaves, Royce doesn't hesitate before turning toward me and leaning against the bar. Almost the same exact body positioning Bo took in Copenhagen when I was spewing my fears about Sky and me.

"What?" I frown.

"Wasn't Rochelle the shit?"

I'm pretty sure I look like one of those stress dolls with the bulbous eyes that bug out when you squeeze it really hard. "Dude, seriously? What was with the nickname?"

Royce rubs at his chin. "Man, what you talkin' about?"

"*Chellie.* When did she become Chellie and not Rochelle, or hell, even Ms. Renner, since she's a *client.*" There's no hiding the irritation in my tone; it's like a live wire running through me.

"Says the man who fucked not one, but *two* clients in the past few months." He holds up two fingers to emphasize his point.

I wince and suck in a large breath, planning to let out what I've got to say quickly and, I hope, painlessly for us both. Still, he's nailed me to the wall. He's got me stuck, at war between needing him to see the truth in this scenario—how it's going to turn out all kinds of bad—and acknowledging what I did. "I get this is a pot-and-kettle vibe you're feeling, but man, this woman, she is *not* for you."

He scowls. "Not that I want to go there, but I'd sure as fuck like to know why you think you've got a lock on why she's not the woman for me? Seeing as I met her, have been talking to her for the past three weeks, and got to know her pretty fuckin' well. What, just because I grew up with a shit-drunk father in a shit-hole two-bedroom house, working at the age of fifteen to help pay bills, does that mean I'm not good enough for a woman who's living the high life? You don't think I can play ball with the bigwigs or somethin'?"

A sledgehammer to the face would have hurt less. My entire body locks down, preparing for battle. "Fuck no! Jesus, Roy. Your upbringing, brother, it's something to be proud of. Taking care of your sisters and mother when you were only a teenager. Helping make ends meet any way you could while still pulling in the grades? I have more respect for you than any man I know."

Royce seems to firm his jaw as he focuses his gaze straight ahead. Him not making eye contact burns like a white-hot poker to the heart.

"I know what you went through growing up. Father who put you in the hospital, mother who worked till her fingers bled, taking care of four kids." I shake my head. "Mad respect. Though part of your history is what makes me see that Rochelle is not like you. She has zero interest in settling down for the long haul." I note the obvious from our conversations with her.

"So? What does that have to do with anything? Besides, she said she wanted a kid."

I nod. "Yeah, to set her legacy in place, to hand over her company one day. I do not see that chick taking time off work or even being a typical working mother. Nannies will be raising any child she has. There's nothing wrong with that, but it's not you. You come from a tight-knit family. The loyal, get-in-your-face type, like mine. You gonna tell me that's not the type of woman you want for the future?"

He shrugs. "Not sure what I want. All I know is there's something between us. I can feel it in the air."

"It's lust, Roy. Believe me, I know it when I see it. You're hot for her. As you should be. Every man in his right mind would be bending over backward to get in there."

Royce rubs at his bottom lip with his thumb. "The woman sure is fiiiine."

I sigh. "Yeah, she is. She also wants to find the perfect man to play housemate with her so she's not lonely at night. Wants to look good at events with a trophy on her arm. Roy, she doesn't want an alpha-male type like yourself, even if you push one another's hot buttons. She wants a submissive man. Someone who worships her and caters to her every need."

"What makes you so sure? Just because you're in good with Skyler, for the first time in fuckin' forever, you think you're the expert on love now?" He scowls. "'Sides, I didn't get that from her feedback." He grabs one of the pints the bartender sets down in front of us.

I try to ignore the jab he threw, and continue undaunted. He needs to see what I see. Open his freakin' eyes to the obvious. "You weren't reading between the lines. Part of what I do in my role is figure out what the client *really* wants, even if they don't know it, or think they know it, and I have a pretty good track record, as you know."

He shrugs.

"Roy, I'm telling you, she wants a submissive male. Mark my words. You go there with her, not only will we lose a client, which I can handle—risked that myself, as you pointed out—but I don't want to see you losing your heart in the process."

The bartender interrupts by handing us both menus.

"Do you have a pulled-pork sandwich?" I ask without looking at the menu.

"Course."

"I'll have that with fries." I hand back the folded piece of paper.

"Same for me." Royce passes his menu too.

When the bartender leaves, I watch the big screen, allowing Royce a few moments to collect his thoughts. The Giants score a run with a runner on second base.

Royce sips his beer and then rubs his bald head with his free hand. "Not sure how I can avoid the heat between us, Park. Not sure I even want to," he admits, concern coating his words.

I nod. "Feel ya, brother. Still, I think it's in your best interest to fight it."

He purses his lips and nods succinctly. The two of us continue our evening watching baseball, drinking beer, and eating a helluva good pulled-pork sandwich. The silence isn't as comfortable as it usually is, but it's my cross to bear. One I will willingly take on for what I believe is the greater outcome.

***

Back at the hotel, my cell rings, and I see "Peaches" on the display.

"Hey, baby, you're done early tonight." I grin and flop onto the bed in my underwear.

"Not really, it's midnight here, but we did have a good day. With your chemistry tips, we were able to shoot all the sexy scenes the last few days. The director didn't want to risk waiting." She chuckles.

I clench down on my molars, not wanting the jealousy monster to claw its way to the surface, especially since I'm the one who gave her costar the tips he needed. Instead of asking for details, I change the subject. "That's good. What are you filming next?"

"My action scenes! I'm super excited about them too. I've been taking *krav maga* training, which is helping give me a more realistic approach to my combat scenes."

"And probably a killer workout too." I imagine her body moving across the floor, punching mightily, getting all slicked up with sweat. A flicker of arousal glimmers at the edges of my subconscious as I attempt to focus on the conversation.

"Well, you're not here, so I've got to burn off the restless energy somehow." Skyler's voice lowers to the sultry timbre I recognize as her bedroom voice.

Well, there goes the hold I had on my arousal. Time to kick it up a notch. I want to *see* my girl. I smile and click the "FaceTime" button on my phone. She accepts it pretty quick because, in mere seconds, I'm gifted with her pretty face and soulful brown eyes.

"Peaches, you are so beautiful."

She smiles huge, which makes her more magnificent.

"Have I told you I *like* you today?" she responds.

I shake my head. "Nah, but I sure as fuck like you. A lot." I waggle my eyebrows to get her giggling.

"Me too, honey." I watch as she enters her kitchen. I can see the cabinets in the background and her movements telling me she's opening the fridge.

Boo. I was hoping for some sexy FaceTime. Still, I'll settle for conversation.

"What are you doing over there?" I ask, watching her move around her space.

"Haven't had dinner yet."

I frown. "I thought you usually got something with Rick."

She crinkles her nose and pouts. "I spent all day kissing and touching him."

Kill. Me. Now.

It doesn't matter that Rick presented himself as a brother-type figure to Sky when I met him—I don't want any man touching what's mine. And Skyler is *mine*. I'm going to hold on to her with both hands and never let go.

Sky crinkles her nose and continues. "The last thing I want to do is have a meal with him. I mean, Rick's cool, and the things you taught him are definitely helping, especially the chewing gum before a scene." She runs a hand through her hair and blows on the loose bangs hanging over her forehead. "Thank you, by the way. No more onion breath." She raises her hand as if she's fist-bumping me.

I laugh and watch my girl as she sets about making herself a PB&J, one of her favorites. God, now that I have her in my life, I wouldn't know what to do if I didn't have this. Her telling me about her day, looking absolutely tousled and gut-wrenchingly fantastic at the same time.

"What did you do tonight?" she asks, and this incredible feeling warms my body from the inside out. Being able to share with someone who cares what I was up to, how my day went, and whether I was happy or sad. It's nice. Not a luxury I've ever had before.

"Visited a pub with Roy. Watched the game."

"Oh yeah? Which teams?"

"Giants versus Brewers. Giants won."

Her eyes light up. "Oh, that reminds me. I heard the Red Sox won today. One of the camera guys was talking about it. Bet that made you happy."

Even at work she's thinking of me, as I do about her. It's amazing how thoughts of your significant other can weave into your day. Lately I find that there's always something I want to tell her about or think she might find funny or interesting. Then again, knowing I have someone to vent to if I have a rough day or one of the guys pisses me off is a surprising blessing. The only thing better would be coming home each night to a warm bed with her in it.

"Peaches, do you like baseball?"

She shrugs and sets the phone down on the counter so I can see her upper body. She opens the peanut butter and slathers on a heaping serving. I'm glad to see she's eating a bit more lately. In my opinion, she was far too slight. This man likes a little meat on his woman's bones.

"I don't *not* like baseball, or sports for that matter. My dad used to love baseball, so I know more about that sport than any other. I haven't been to a live game, though. Maybe you can take me."

Exactly what I was thinking. "Oh, baby, it's a date. I'll have Wendy check the Sox schedule and book us a couple of seats."

"Really?" Her eyes light up at the prospect.

"Long as you can get away for a couple of nights, hell yeah."

"I think I can manage it. The director feels like she owes you. I'll use her words as my 'get out of jail free' card if needed."

I chuckle at her savagery. "Good idea."

She continues to make her sandwich as I think back to the meeting earlier today with Rochelle and Royce. It's weighing on my mind, and I can't shake the bad vibe I have.

"Honey . . . I can see something is bothering you. Do you want to talk about it?" Her concern is soothing, breaking through the tension nudging at my temples.

I bring her up to date on the meeting we had today and my concerns about Royce falling for the client.

"Park, you did exactly what you're telling him not to do." She smirks.

Letting out a deep breath, I nod. "Yeah, I know. Still, I have this gnawing sensation in my gut that if either one of them makes a play for the other, it's not going to be pretty."

Skyler takes a big bite of her sandwich and chews thoughtfully before swallowing and adding her two cents. "Royce is a big boy. He's got to make his own mistakes. If this is indeed one of them. You have to let him choose his own path, and if it goes to hell, be there for him as his brother in life and partner in business."

This woman blows me away. Her logic, compassionate soul—it all comes so effortlessly with her. "You're so wise. Must be why I'm falling for you." And I realize what I've admitted.

My girl licks her lips and sets down her sandwich before picking up the phone, bringing it closer so I can see more details of her face. "Now why did you have to go and say something so freakin' sweet when I can't be there to show you my response properly?" She pouts.

I laugh, so damn thankful she didn't backtrack or slow down where this is moving. Not wanting to make too much of it, yet eager to hear what she'd do if I were there, I smile and ask, "Oh, and what would your response be?"

Her face lights up with joy, and the sensation of relief turns into a simmering excitement, anticipation of all this woman could bring to my future settling nicely in my heart.

"To tell you I feel the same, and I'm falling for you too." She cocks an eyebrow.

"Oh yeah?" I grin ear to ear. This is a major step for me, for us. Not a scenario I ever thought I'd be in after the shit show with Kayla back in college. Skyler and I may have jumped into the sack lightning fast, but we've taken our time getting to know each other these past months. It feels good to admit she's more to me than any other woman from my past.

"Yeah," she murmurs sweetly, and I wish with my whole being I could be there to kiss her lips and make slow, passionate love to her, sealing this new phase in our relationship.

"What would you do afterward?" I prompt, trying to get her to play along.

She taps at her lips. "After? Hmm . . . I'd likely jump your bones."

I bite down on my bottom lip, trying to hold back the wide grin her words bring. "Let's speed forward to the part where you jump my bones. How exactly would you go about doing such a thing?"

Skyler glances off to the side, taps at her beautiful pink lips again as if she's deep in thought about the best way to achieve her desired outcome. "I'd start by straddling your lap."

"Mmm. Good start. And . . ."

"I'd get really close to your face, hands on your shoulders."

My dick perks up at the visual she presents in my mind. Having her soft naked body in my lap, rubbing against my hardening erection. I'd run my hands up her back and down the silky skin of her arms. That simple touch would have her nipples hardening, and she would arch forward to offer me a succulent pink tip.

I suck in a harsh breath and run my hand down the bricks of my abdomen toward my dick. "Would I have clothes on or off?"

She shrugs nonchalantly. "Could be either. I'd take you how you came."

"How I *come* . . . this gets better and better," I snicker, even though my boxer briefs suddenly feel an entire size too small over my rapidly growing erection.

Sky rolls her eyes.

"Then what? Baby, don't leave me hanging." I run a hand over the stiff ridge of my shaft and give it a firm squeeze.

She crinkles her nose in the cute way I've come to adore. "No, you're going to make fun of me."

I shake my head avidly. "No, Peaches, baby, I won't make fun of you. Tell me," I urge, lust filling my tone, the heat of my arousal suffusing my skin.

Skyler licks her lips and sets the phone down and away so I can see her body. She's wearing one of her tanks, but I can see the erect tips through the thin cotton.

In a second flat, she reaches down for the hem of her tank and whips it over her head, leaving her upper body completely bared to me.

"Fuck!"

I grip my dick harder than before, pleasure spiking from my pelvis and out.

Skyler runs her hands up her belly to her pillowy mounds. Her breasts are perfection. I could look at a hundred Playboy bunny photos and not find a more fantastic pair of tits. They are a full C cup, and the right size for my hands. Her nipples and areolae are the palest pink. Sky cups her breasts as I stare at the magic before me.

Her wicked grin proves she knows what she's doing to me. I jerk my length once in response and let a groan slip past my lips.

"Do you have a hand wrapped around your cock yet?" she teases.

"You know I do." My voice is rough, like I swallowed a box of jagged rocks.

One of her eyebrows rises. "Show me yours. I showed you mine."

"Oh, you want to play that game, huh?"

Instead of speaking, she nods. I shimmy my hips and, with one hand, rid myself of my underwear. Then I wrap one hand around my eager length once more. With the other hand, I point the phone down my body, so she can see my dick standing at attention. All for her.

"Jesus, honey. You're so hard you could drive nails into the wall with that thing."

I turn the phone to look at her once more. She's cupping her breasts with both hands, her thumbs swiping back and forth along the tight nipples, which I'd like to wrap my lips around and tug with my teeth.

"Pinch them hard, baby. Enough to hurt a little, like I would if I were there. See if you can make yourself come from just playing with your tits, imagining it's me doing the playing."

She moans and closes her eyes but continues to do what I've asked. "Are you stroking yourself?"

"Fuck yeah. Watching you touch yourself . . . God, I wish I were there. I'd suck each tip so hard, baby. Until it burned and you cried out for more!"

She drops her head back, her hair falling down behind her. God, I love that look the best. When she's succumbing to the moment, to her passion. My mouth waters at the sight of her tugging at her pretty flesh.

"That's it, tweak those little tips for me. Do you like plucking your pretty titties while I watch and jack my dick? Hmm?" I arch my hips into my hand, imagining I'm sinking my cock into her wet heat . . . no, between those soft-as-fuck breasts.

A shiver of excitement ripples up my spine, and I arch into the pleasurable sensation. "You know what I'd do if I were there right now?" I continue.

She shakes her head. "Tell me . . ." It comes out as a whimper.

Her nipples and areolae are dark, a deep crimson. "I'd lay you down on the kitchen floor . . ."

"Yeah," she moans, her lips falling open as she gasps for air. The sound ping-pongs through my chest, making me feel alive, warm, my body tightening, knowing what those little puffs of air and moans mean.

My balls ache, feeling full and heavy, ready to blow. I grind my teeth, and a fine sheen of sweat mists along my hairline, torso, and abdomen as I stave off my pending orgasm for a little bit longer.

"I'd straddle your chest, wedge my hard fat cock between those perfect tits . . ."

"Oh my God, Parker . . ." She gasps and licks her lips, fingers still moving over her breasts in a whirl of motion.

"And I'd press those babies together tight around my dick. Then I'd fuck your tits, allowing the wetness at my tip to graze your lips, and you could suck the head." The visual alone causes tremors to erupt all through my body. "Jesus! You make me so hard . . ." I moan and thrust faster into my firm grip.

"Parker . . . ," Skyler croons, and rapid gasps leave her mouth as her body jerks.

Watching her go off from hearing my voice and playing with her breasts sends me over the edge. I cup my balls and thrust up into my hand one, two, three times until I'm gone. Shooting straight into bliss. "Sky . . . baby!" I cry out as my release coats my hand and abs in a sticky mess.

Both of us spend a minute or two coming back to ourselves, our breathing labored as if we've been running and are now trying to catch our breath.

When I open my eyes, Skyler is leaning on the counter, her head down, hair falling in waves around her face. "Wow. Remind me to FaceTime you more often." She smirks. Her cheeks are a lovely pink, and the rest of her has a healthy glow I love seeing on her skin.

"That will not be a problem." I laugh and stretch the rest of my body, letting the pleasure twist around every ounce of my being for a few more blessed moments.

"I wish you were here," she admits before I can say the same damn thing. She swallows and dips down behind the counter, I assume to grab her tank. "How long do you think you'll be in San Francisco?"

I sigh, letting all the air out of my lungs before sucking in another weighted breath. "Not sure. Depends on how quickly we can set up the client with a pool of prospective men we've vetted."

"Assuming Royce is not leading the pack." She grins and tugs on her tank, her beautiful body covered once more.

I pout at the missing visual and at the comment. "Not funny, Peaches."

She tips her head. "I don't know. I found it kind of funny, pretty boy!"

"Well, as much as I'd like to talk to you all night . . . I've got quite the mess to take care of here."

Her eyes heat up with a renewed lust. "If you were here, I'd take care of that for you. Actually, you wouldn't have had a mess at all. Think about that and see how long it takes you to make it home." She winks at me, picks up her sandwich, and takes a bite, chewing while gloating.

"You are bad."

"You like bad. As a matter of fact, I believe you said you were falling for bad." She gifts me a smug smile.

"I am. Get some rest, eh?"

"Okay, honey. You too. Talk to you tomorrow?"

"Yeah, baby."

"Dream of me." And then she blows me a peanut butter kiss before ending the call.

I shake my head and get up to head to the bathroom.

Dream of her.

With a body like hers, a face angels would sing to, and she comes like a goddess . . . it's safe to say Skyler is always in my dreams.

3

"Ms. Renner, good morning." I hold out my hand to our client.

She barely nods at me while shaking my hand before taking both of Royce's between hers. "And good morning to you, handsome." Rochelle smiles at Royce.

He grins wide, looks her up and down, and pours on the charm with a "You're looking lovely this morning, Chellie."

I nudge his shoulder . . . hard.

He clears his throat, and the smile slides off his face. "I mean, Ms. Renner."

Her lips quirk, and she murmurs an "Mm-hmm" as she walks around her desk and sits in her chair.

Both Royce and I take a seat across from her.

"I've cleared the morning for the two of you so we can get right to business, or should I say *play*?" She leans back in her chair, the red of her silk blouse popping against the supple-looking leather. Her hair is flat ironed into a sleek, glossy sheet, parted down the center, leaving the longer lengths to fall prettily over her shoulders. There is no denying Rochelle Renner is a stunning woman.

Royce removes the first set of folders we have to show her. He stands, moves around the desk to her side, and lays one of them out and hands me my copy.

"First and foremost, we connected with the biggest online dating/ relationship site, I-Bliss. For a fee, we were able to work with them to secure their top ten suggestions for men who fit the criteria we set. We have since contacted all of them, and eight are interested."

Instead of keeping her distance, Rochelle places her hand on Roy's forearm and cocks one perfectly shaped eyebrow. "Is that so? Eight?"

"Indeed, it is. You're a very desirable woman." Royce's voice flows into a deep rumble that sounds like Barry White reincarnated. I want to lash out, but instead I dig deep and keep my shit in check, trying to remember that Royce is his own man, and as Sky recommended, he can make his own choices.

I do, however, jump into the fray before things get more complicated. "Ms. Renner, aside from the eight prospects we've secured, we have also contacted our long-standing matchmaker. She has reviewed your criteria and was able to locate five additional prospects."

"Thirteen . . ." She sucks in air between her teeth. "An unlucky number—" She starts to interject her thoughts, but we're interrupted by the door flying open.

"Chelle, I'm sorry to interrupt, but this is too important to wait!" A tall, built black man in a bespoke suit enters. He's wearing thick black-framed glasses, the kind Superman wears when he's disguised as Clark Kent. The overall impression is marred by the heavy frown he's sporting. He has close-cropped black hair, shaved at the sides, giving him a Tyson Beckford appeal. Unlike Royce, whose skin is a darker ebony, this man's skin tone is lighter by quite a few degrees. More of a milk chocolate to Royce's dark. Rochelle is right in the middle.

Her gaze tracks the man across the room until he's standing before her. "Gentlemen, this is Keehan Williams, head of information technology and analytics and overall Mr. Universe. Best man I know."

Keehan stops in his tracks for a second and smiles at Rochelle. The smile seems far more personal, as if the two of them share some type of secret code.

"Keehan, this is Royce Sterling and Parker Ellis of International Guy."

Keehan's eyes flash from the tablet he's holding to the two of us, his mouth tightening at the corners. "You went through with it, then?"

She grins, completely ignoring the clip in his tone. "I told you I would."

His shoulders rise with what I can sense is irritation. "It was supposed to be a joke, Chelle. Lord Almighty. What have you gotten yourself into?" He rubs a hand over his short hair as an unease settles in the air around the room.

Her gaze narrows on him, Royce and I disappearing from the space as they hash it out. "What do you mean? I told you I needed a man in my life."

Keehan winces when she says *man in my life*, which to me is beyond telling. This dude is hung up on his boss. Big-time. Huge.

"Kee, I'm tired of spending my evenings alone. Holidays . . ."

He visibly bristles. "With me?" he blurts, offense coating his tone.

Her gaze softens, and she lays a hand over his wrist, petting the top of his hand with her thumb. "You know I enjoy our time together, but a woman has needs, Keehan. How the hell you go about your celibate lifestyle is beyond me." She shakes her head and laughs before sitting back in her chair, putting distance between herself and the man who's 100 percent focused on her. A herd of galloping broncos could ram through the wall, and he'd have eyes only for her.

I glance at Royce to see if he's catching what I'm seeing. His jaw is hard, his lips tightly pressed together into a flat line.

He sees it. And he doesn't like it.

I bite back the laughter wanting to spew out of me and follow Keehan's hand gestures and body language while he communicates with his boss. His very *attractive* boss. One he seems to know on a rather personal if not *intimate* level.

Keehan lays the tablet in front of her. "While you've been planning to become a happy homemaker—"

Rochelle bursts out laughing. "Homemaker? As if. You're funny, Keehan. I may want a kid one day, but I will not be doing the child-rearing full time. Man, Kee, you always make me laugh."

Oh snap! She's basically just confirmed everything I'm thinking about how wrong she is for Roy. If we were back in Boston and I were behind my desk, I'd stand up and take a long bow.

"And you have such a beautiful one," he says with a smile, reaching out a hand to touch a lock of her hair. "Like your hair straight, Chelle. It's silky smooth."

She beams at him.

Holy smokes! It's like they're experiencing foreplay right in front of us, but neither of them realizes there's an audience. And one of them has *no idea* it's foreplay.

Royce finally glances over to me, his brows furrowed. He lifts a thumb toward the desk and mouths, "This guy?"

I nod and grin wide. He can finally see that Rochelle doesn't plan on falling in love with a man, because she's already carrying on an intimate relationship with Keehan. Hell, she may be in love with him and not even know it.

The memory of me telling Skyler I was falling for her flutters through my mind. My heart squeezes, and I swallow against the dryness in my throat. *Am I in love with Skyler, but haven't admitted it to myself?* The wild thought has me gripping the arms of the chair, digging my nails in. I take a few deep breaths and do my damnedest to focus on the craziness playing out in front of me instead of the potential revelation I just had about my own life.

"You're too good to me, Kee." She pats his hand affectionately, and the truth smacks me in the face. Rochelle doesn't need a man at home; she already has one at work. Her two loves in one place. Work and Keehan. Although from the body language, it seems Rochelle hasn't crossed the barrier from boss to girlfriend. Unlike me, she seems to have a different version of professional etiquette I somehow missed in my training at Harvard.

I cough, rather unsubtly breaking through their intimate chatter.

Keehan blinks slowly and turns his head in our direction, almost as if he's just remembered there are two strange men sitting in front of his boss's desk. "I'm sorry, I'm being rude. Keehan Williams." He holds out his hand to me and then Royce. We both take him up on his offer and shake his hand.

"I'm sorry to interrupt, but this simply could not wait. Chelle, look at these numbers here from last quarter." He points down at information I can't see from here and then swipes left. "Then here, the quarter before." Swipes left again. "And the one before that."

"They're dropping, which happens when interest goes up and down. You know this." Her gaze runs over the information in front of her.

Keehan shakes his head. "You see, that's the thing. These stocks have gone up in the past two years, and the interest rates are fixed. The quarterly figures should be steadily going up, not incrementally going down."

Royce stands up and walks around the desk. "May I? I'm a numbers man myself."

Keehan looks Royce up and down and clenches his teeth. "I'll bet you are. Just her type too," he says under his breath while moving off to the side so Roy can take a gander at the work.

Dang, if I didn't sense a threat before, I absolutely can now. Keehan is not pleased with the fact that we're here or the fact that she's looking for a man. To me, it's plain as day from one meeting that he wants to be the man in Rochelle's life.

Royce scans the information on the tablet. "And the profit-and-loss statements?"

"At least five here. Just click on each tab," Keehan mumbles.

Royce and Rochelle scan the documents.

"Hoo-boy, this is not good." Royce rubs at his chin. A move he does when he's uncomfortable with a piece of information.

"You can say that again." Rochelle crosses her arms defensively and inhales loudly. Frustration oozes from her pores as she silently takes in whatever unsettling information is in front of her.

I, unfortunately, or rather fortunately, am not a numbers man. I can get by with standard profit-and-loss checks and balances and generic accounts payable stuff, but nothing deep in the nitty-gritty. It's the reason why Royce manages IG's money as well as Bo's and my personal investments. He's made all of us very rich men by using his Midas touch when it pertains to the stock market. He's a genius at knowing where and what to buy and when to sell.

"Then, it's what I think it is?" Keehan directs his question at Rochelle.

Her voice is laced with a tinge of anger when she responds. "If you think someone is stealing from me, then yes, it's what you think."

I cringe but stay silent. This is not my territory. In sensitive situations such as this, it's best if I keep my opinions to myself and let the experts figure out the proper course of action. My job in San Francisco is to find a suitable mate for our client. And watching Keehan offer his support and undivided attention to Rochelle has proven my job is going to be far easier now that my top candidate has unintentionally jumped into the pool of prospects. While they worry about an embezzler in the firm, I'm quietly planning how I'm going to work this scenario to the best advantage.

"Finding the culprit will be interesting." Rochelle bites her bottom lip and taps at her chin, seemingly lost in thought. "At least forty of my staff have access to those accounts."

Royce starts to pace as Keehan walks around the desk and places his hand on Rochelle's shoulder, a show of support if I ever saw one. She pats his hand and looks up at him with a somber smile. "Thank you for looking out for me, as usual."

"It's my job in more ways than one, Chelle. We've been in this together since the beginning." He says it loud enough for the entire room to hear his meaning.

Lay off my girl, big, bad Royce.

I smile, enjoying the pissing match. "You've worked for Rochelle a long time?" I inquire.

Keehan nods, then squeezes Rochelle's shoulder. "Since the very first day she opened the doors of Renner Financial Services."

Rochelle nods and grabs Keehan's hand. "He's my rock. I couldn't do what I do without him."

I smirk. Maybe this will be a walk in the park.

***

While Rochelle and Royce put their heads together, requesting documents, reports, and a variety of other things, I follow Keehan out the door.

"Um, can I help you with something?" he asks.

I shrug but match his stride, even though I'm a couple of inches shorter. "Figure while they're busy, I could tag along with you, get to know more about your boss."

He frowns.

"You two seem close." I let the statement hang out there in the wind and hope he picks it up.

"We are. She's an amazing woman." His words carry a sense of awe and devotion one wouldn't usually hear from a mere employee.

"Gathered that in one meeting. Not to mention her business profile is superb."

He nods. "She's the best in her field."

"And what about you?"

"What about me?" He nudges his glasses higher on his nose.

"What's your take on your career? Your position with RFS?"

He frowns but keeps up his pace. We steadily move past employees busily working in their offices. It appears the entire place is set up with nothing but offices and meeting rooms. No cubicles, which I imagine is ideal for people working with confidential information such as a person's or business's money.

"My position is solid. Like I said before, Chelle and I have been together since the very beginning. We've been through a lot. People may come and go, but one thing is always the same."

I grin. "And that would be?"

"Me." He smiles. "I'm here for the long haul."

"What about settling down? You're hitting the age most guys find a woman, have a coupla kids. The whole nine."

Keehan clasps his hands in front of him as we walk. "I don't know. Sometimes I imagine having a child. But a woman would have to understand my work comes first. Rochelle has been screwed over by countless men in her personal and professional life. I'm never going to be added to that list."

"Wow. You make it sound like Rochelle is the most important person in *your* life." I chuckle but continue to lead him to what I want him to at the very least see, or even better, admit to.

He shrugs a little. "She is. We both have very little family and none in the area. We spend holidays together, long nights in the office working the numbers, setting goals. I wouldn't know what to do with myself if I didn't have her."

"Interesting."

He turns a corner, and I follow him down a long hallway. As we pass a wall of windows, the hum of the giant servers within makes the air pulsate against the back of my neck, hands, and face.

"Why interesting?" Keehan inquires.

"Doesn't matter. You didn't seem happy Rochelle called us in to find her a mate. Why is that?"

His eyes harden, and I can see a muscle in his cheek flicker. "No reason. If she wants to find herself a toy, it's her business. They never last. I'm not worried." ·

Um, he doesn't know my man Royce. If Royce wants Rochelle, he'll be relentless in his pursuit. Besides, I have confidence in my abilities to find her the right man.

"Oh, this one will last. I'm getting paid to find her the proper mate. Someone to share her life with, have a child with."

He stops as if he's been jolted by a lightning bolt. "You have got to be kidding me." He growls, turns, and starts to pace in the hallway like a caged animal. "This is insane. She can't seriously be planning on settling down with whomever you find for her." He grits his teeth and practically snarls like a pit bull ready to attack an intruder.

"Why?"

"Because she can't marry someone and have a child!" He runs his hands over the back of his head, his elbows parallel to the floor. Anger swirls around his form like a physical tornado. I can almost see his fury about what I've stated.

"Why not?" I ask again with the same easy tone, not letting his irritation affect my attitude.

"Because she's supposed to be *mine*! *Marry me*. Have *my* child! Fuck!" He groans, turns on a heel, and slams open the door at the end of the hall. It shakes in its frame as he storms through. "I cannot freakin' believe she's doing this." His shoulders slump. "Why can't she see?" He turns around and stares at me, his eyes black as night. "Tell me, please, you're the expert. Why can't she see what's right in front of her face?"

I shake my head and clasp my hands in front of me, being the epitome of calm. "Based on what I've witnessed so far, the two of you are close."

He nods. "Absolutely."

"You count on one another," I hint.

"Implicitly."

"Have worked together for a long time."

"Yes. All of that," Keehan says, exasperated at my not getting to the point.

"Yet I get the feeling you have never made a move on her."

Keehan's entire body seems to slump right before my eyes. His broad shoulders curve forward, his chin dipping down toward his chest, and his face displays a sullen expression. "You can't just hit on a woman like Rochelle. Especially not after the history we have. She'd laugh in my face."

"Why?"

He half laughs. "Rochelle is way out of my league."

The man is insane. I look him up and down, taking in his large form, fit, well dressed. I see no reason for him to think he's not in her league, and I set about making sure he knows it too. "Not true. You're handsome, career minded, intelligent. Seems to me, you fit pretty well."

He huffs and looks away, resting a hand on his waist, the other rubbing over his chin. "You wouldn't understand."

I jerk my head back. "Excuse me? Actually, you'd be surprised. I know exactly what you're going through. Wanting someone you think is so far out of your stratosphere you're in another universe completely."

"Yeah right."

I put my hand on his shoulder. "Man, my girlfriend is Skyler Paige."

His entire body seems to go stiff as a board, and his eyes widen. "The actress?"

I nod.

"The hottest woman in Hollywood . . ."

I squeeze his shoulder with a little extra force. "Watch it." Without even trying, my voice turns into a warning. Like a dog circling its territory. Even mention my woman's name in a sexual manner and I'll bite your head off.

Keehan whistles through his teeth. "Damn. You do know what I'm going through. Only to the hundredth degree. Still, when it comes to Chelle, I become a total loser."

"So, you're admitting to not having given her a reason to think of you as more than a friend and confidant. A colleague."

"We're more than colleagues," he sneers.

I raise my eyebrows. "Could've fooled me."

"It's never been the right time."

"At the rate you're going, bro, it never will be. I've seen snails move faster than you. Ninety-year-old men chasing tail in a nursing home move faster. Be real with me. What's holding you back? She's beautiful; you're a handsome man. The two of you seem to care for one another, if what I saw back there in her office was any indication."

"I guess that's the problem. I care too much," he admits with a note of defeat.

I wager a guess. "You don't want to risk a good thing?"

His gaze is tortured. "If it goes south, we lose it all. Our working relationship would be impossible. And as sappy as it sounds, man, she's my best friend. Work has been our combined goal. It's what makes us who we are."

"And yet you want more."

"Yeah." He rubs at the back of his neck.

"She sure as hell wants more, or she wouldn't have called us."

Keehan walks over to his desk and sits behind three matching monitors all lined up in a row.

"What is this? The command center? Wow." I scan the room, noting more desks with stacks of monitors lined up. A couple of flat-screen TVs are against one wall, showing the stock market and Nasdaq numbers in real time.

Keehan grins, finally showing a bit more of his natural exuberance. "You could call it that. I run a variety of the company's reports, keep track of the financial shifts, track different stocks and markets, all while sending real-time reports to the team and Chelle. I also manage all the rest of the networks, developers, help-desk guys, and the like."

"So, tell me . . . With running such a tight ship, how could someone steal from RFS? Wouldn't red flags be flying?"

He nods while his fingers tap the keys, flying into a blur of activity. "I know Rochelle said there were forty people who could access those accounts, but they can't without leaving an electronic trail. Royce told me to look for an unusual person accessing that account. And the system logs everything people do."

"Then it shouldn't be too hard to figure out who's accessed the accounts and made withdrawals or moved money in a pattern of some sort, right?"

"In a perfect world, yes. From what I was able to surmise over the last six quarters, the person has been doing it for at least eighteen months, maybe more. I'd have to go back further to find out for sure."

"If I were you, I'd get on it immediately. Take your results to the boss lady." I grin and wink suggestively.

Keehan's cheeks seem to darken a bit. "Yeah, I'll do that. What are you going to do while we deal with this storm?"

"About this situation?"

He jerks his chin up in agreement.

"Nothing. I'm not here to find out who's embezzling from her company, although I'm certain Royce is making it his personal mission. Regardless of how you feel, I'm here to find her a mate."

Keehan scowls and clacks away at his keyboard. "And how do you propose to do that, if I may ask?"

This is too freakin' easy. Like shooting fish in a barrel. "Why? You going to throw your hat into the ring, finally?"

"Maybe." He centers his gaze on me and doesn't move a muscle, his fingers hovering over the keys in front of him.

"I have thirteen prospects to present."

He huffs. "Including me?"

"You'd make fourteen," I add dryly, as if the number isn't high. Technically it really isn't, but to a man who's in love with a woman, been hiding it for years, that's thirteen competitors vying for the heart of the woman he wants.

"Good Lord. This is a nightmare." He presses his fingers to the bridge of his nose.

"Sorry to hear you feel that way. I can say I'm glad this scenario is pushing you out of your comfort zone. Something tells me Rochelle is not a woman who waits around. She'll want a man to be assertive. Show her he's interested. Not sit twiddling his thumbs while she goes to bed alone every night."

"Oh, she's not alone unless she wants to be. Have you seen her?" He smirks.

I cant my head to the side. "How does that make you feel?"

The smirk dies on his face. "Like scum on the bottom of her Louboutins. Like a loser who's pining away for a woman, living a rather celibate lifestyle because no other woman will do it for him. I see her, and my entire being comes alive. Other women, and my lower half flatlines." He shakes his head. "Nothing."

I whistle. "Harsh."

"Truth," he rebuts.

"Sounds to me like you need to make some serious changes and fast, if not for you, then for your friend." I flick my gaze to below his desk and back to his eyes, so he catches my meaning loud and clear.

"And how do you propose I do that?"

I grin, pull up a chair, and sit my ass down in it. The plan I hatched while they talked embezzlers is falling right into place.

4

The next morning, it's business as usual as I make my way through the halls of Renner Financial Services, or RFS as the employees call it. I know Royce worked late with Rochelle trying to nail down the schmuck who's stealing from the company, but I haven't been briefed. I went to bed before he made it back to his hotel room, which, if I think about it, concerns me, but as Skyler reminded me again last night, Royce is a big boy and can handle himself.

Still, I'm not certain I shouldn't ask him to jump ship and fly home, take on another client he's not so affected by. It would be the wise thing to do for sure. His desire for her is messing up the flow.

Kind of like when you were falling all over yourself for Skyler, or falling into bed with Sophie for that matter.

I'm such a hypocrite. A knot forms in my gut. I know I need to let this play out, but it's gnawing at my insides to fix it. Fix Royce's problem. Help my brother find what will soothe his soul, like I've found what soothes mine. How can wanting to see someone you care about get what they truly desire in life be so wrong?

When I reach Rochelle's office, I'm still debating with myself on how to best broach the issue again with Royce when I hear laughter through the door. A very distinctive laugh to be exact. I open the door slowly and grind my teeth at the tableau I encounter.

Rochelle is sitting on her desk, skirt hiked up to her waist, Royce cradled between her opened thighs. Her head is tipped back, more laughter coming from her throat as Royce lays a line of kisses up her neck to her lips. His hand curls around her smooth thigh and hikes it up higher around his waist.

Sweet baby Jesus, this is bad.

"You want me to nail you right here in your office like I did last night?" His voice is a wicked promise.

"God, yes." Her hands move around his form to his ass, and she pulls him even closer.

I can't tell if he's dressed, but he seems put together from behind, his pants not sagging around his knees; I guess I can thank the good Lord for small favors.

"It's very unprofessional . . . ," he taunts.

"Yes, it is. *Very* unprofessional," I state loudly.

One bald head and one dark one jerk out of the sex trance they were in and both turn to me. Royce, still in front of Rochelle, lets her leg fall back to her desk. Rochelle pushes him back so she can slide off the desk, gripping her skirt and tugging it down as she does so.

"Brother." Royce's tone is flat and devoid of emotion when he faces me. As I suspected, his pants are still done up, not much out of place besides his tie dangling around his neck and a few of the shirt buttons undone.

"I see someone is working hard." I clasp my hands in front of me, one holding the tablet with the information about the men I was planning to go over with them.

Royce closes his eyes momentarily and sighs.

"Mr. Ellis, this is not what it looks like . . . ," Rochelle starts.

"Really? It looks like my partner was about to pound you into next week on your desk, and from what I heard, it wouldn't be the first time." All of this I state flatly.

Rochelle smiles coyly. "Okay, so it *is* what it looks like, but no harm, no foul. It's not serious. We're having a bit of fun."

A bit of fun.

The phrase spins around in my mind back to a time where I thought I was having a *bit of fun* with a fuckhot blonde. A bit of fun turned into a committed relationship. Which would mean, if I believed that Rochelle was Royce's one in seven billion, I'd back off. The confirmation from her mouth that Roy means nothing to her but a little fun in the sack proves my point.

I shake my head, turn around, and close the door to avoid any onlookers who might happen by. "Look, if the two of you want to go *there* with one another, far be it from me to get involved. However, you hired us to find you a mate. Has that changed in light of recent events?" I gesture to Roy and the desk he's leaning against.

Before Royce can respond, Rochelle immediately replies, "No."

Royce's mouth opens and closes tight. His professional mask slips over his face. Having known this man for a decade, I can tell her response is not what he was expecting to hear. Royce may have his fun and games, but he definitely wouldn't risk something at work if he weren't at least a little taken with the woman, more than for a quick fuck on her desk.

"No? Are you sure?" I ask again to be certain she's not hung up on a certain brother of mine.

Rochelle smooths her hair down on each side before responding. "Roy and I are compatible physically, but his life is in Massachusetts; mine is in California. A few fantastic fucks is all either of us can offer one another. Right, handsome?" She smiles and winks in his direction.

Royce licks his kiss-swollen lips and jerks his chin up at her. "Right, Chellie. And you're one fantastic *fuck*." His voice is guarded, but the choice of words is meant to pierce the woman's steely veneer.

The barb hits and rolls right off her chest. No wound can be found. "See, no issue here. Parker, I understand you want to go over the list of men?" she asks me, her eyes lighting up in the process. "I admit, I am excited. It's kind of like Christmas, but instead of unwrapping a present, I'm unwrapping my future husband." She brings her hands to her chest in a little show of cheer.

My God, was I this callous about sexual relations in the past? I mean, I had my man whore days for sure, especially after Kayla screwed me over, but I'm convinced any woman I bedded since those days knew the score. Sophie definitely knew the parameters; hell, she helped set them. Royce does not. My gaze flickers to Roy, and my heart beats hard. He's standing tall and seemingly unaffected, but I know better. He likes Rochelle. Likes her for more than what she is offering. This has to be a blow to his manhood. Silently, I chastise myself for being so careless toward women in the past. No more. Sky's it for me. She's changed me for the long haul. Now if I could only help my brother find *the one*.

I remind Rochelle of our commitment while watching Royce brood silently. "We can't promise marriage. Our goal is to set you up with the best possible match. It's up to you to take any relationship further."

She waves her hand in the air. "I understand."

While I try to figure out how to smooth this situation over—one Rochelle is obviously not seeing as a situation at all—Royce adjusts his jacket and attitude, becoming the perfectly poised professional, and heads over to the door.

"If you two will excuse me, I'm going to meet with Keehan and go over some of the things we found last night. Give him the list of the five people we need to investigate further regarding the missing funds."

Rochelle smiles wide. "Excellent idea. Thanks, Roy." She bats her eyelashes as if nothing's happened. She really is a smooth operator and a hard-and-fast workaholic, treating her request for a mate as a business transaction and nothing more. And I thought I was bad. Rochelle puts the entire IG team to shame when it comes to work ethic. Morals, however, may be an entirely different story. The woman can blatantly bang a business associate on her desk, try for more in the morning, and brush it off as though she's dismissing a second cup of coffee.

I don't think I could be so brash, but I search my memory bank, pretty sure I've been rather douche-like in my past. When Kayla ruined what we had, I definitely dipped my wick in a lot of women. Many whose names I can't recall. Again, these were club and bar hookups. They got out of me what I got out of them. Royce wants more. Keehan wants more.

It makes me wonder if I'm going to be able to make her see the truth. Help her figure out that what she truly needs is something she's had all along.

On top of my budding concern about whether or not I'll be able to fully help this client with what we've been tasked to do, I'm worried about my brother. He hasn't put himself out there in a long time. This might be a huge blow to his confidence he doesn't need. At least with me, Royce can be honest and let his displeasure show, but having to hold it back because of the job . . . I don't know how that's going to go over long term. I hope he sees the situation for what it is. A hookup.

Royce bails before I can say anything to him, which is probably best. We'll catch up later once the burn cools.

"Ready?" Rochelle asks, the excitement she mentioned before coming off her in waves of electric energy.

"As I'll ever be." I smile tiredly as I sit on the couch near her desk, and with a few taps on my tablet to mirror it on her monitor, a picture of a black man in his early thirties appears on the screen. Rochelle sits up, brings her knees together, and sets her chin on her propped hands.

"Michael Conway. Software developer in Silicon Valley. Freelance. Has created successful apps that work with the emergency response network in the area. Income annually is in the low six figures, but has solid investments."

"Family?"

"Divorced. No kids."

"Really? He's either been hurt before or was the one doing the hurting."

"Is that important? Do you have a preference either way?" I go right for the jugular, wanting her to feel a twinge of remorse, especially after the shenanigans she inadvertently pulled on Roy. *Inadvertent* may be too generous of a word, because I don't think it's possible that Rochelle does anything without thinking through every possible outcome. It's definitely the way I would and *did* handle a business hookup. Except with Sophie—I respected and cared enough about the woman to form a platonic relationship after the fact.

"Just taking this seriously. My future depends on it. If he's been hurt, he'll be more likely to not hurt me. Right?"

It's sad, but she's right, and I'm not surprised to see her taking this seriously, asking the questions that are truly important to her, regardless of any potential judgment. I respect the ballsy approach. It's obviously gotten her far in her professional life, but less so in her personal. Hopefully I can fix that.

I click my tongue and pull up his file to scan it once more. Once I find the nugget I'm looking for—thank you, Wendy, world's greatest assistant—I offer it up. "According to the county recorder's office, his wife filed for a marriage license a week after their divorce was finalized three years ago."

She makes a sour face and pouts. "Poor, sexy man."

I flick to the next image. "Sean White. Recently retired from professional baseball. Already secured a job as coach of the San Francisco State University team."

"Pass. I have zero desire to go to college baseball games or any sports-related events of any kind. Ever."

"You sure? His mother has passed, which means no annoying mother-in-law, and he was cheated on by his last two groupie girlfriends, which means he'll be loyal to you."

She shakes her head. "Again, Parker, I have no desire to watch, talk, or deal with a jock in any shape or form. I'm not trying to be difficult, but I dated a professional ballplayer. They are angry when you don't want to go to games, angry when you want them to shut it off and spend time with you, angry when you know very little of the sport or don't root for a team. Jocks need to be off the list."

Angry when you don't spend time with them.

Flashes of midnight studying spells where Kayla would walk out in a sexy nightie, wanting me to stop prepping for finals and, instead, spend time making her feel good come to mind. Those nights would kill me. It seemed every time I had something crucial to prep for, she'd pull her "you're not paying any attention to me" bullshit. I'd spend half the evening making her feel worshipped, and the other half pouring coffee down my throat and going to class bleary eyed and sleep deprived. All for what? A woman who was getting herself some from not one but two different men. Making sure her future was shiny and bright with at least one of us to take care of her.

With a scowl, I bring up the next image. "Done. What about a man in finance?" I ask, even though the next candidate is not in finance but a firefighter.

She looks at the monitor. "He's hot."

"He's a fireman." I point to him. He has cornrows tightly braided to his scalp in what seems to be a perfect quarter inch apart. His smile is wide, and based on his bio and evaluation, he's the most down-to-earth gentleman of the bunch. Still, I need to get her to think about someone a bit closer to home. Someone who is already ass-over-dick in love with her. "What about a man who shares your profession?"

She shrugs. "Would make things a lot easier at functions and work events."

"This guy has a big family, but they're on the East Coast, so you'd likely have to visit only on holidays, anniversaries, etc."

"Nice. Keep him in the mix for sure."

I flick the button to bring the next image on the screen.

"Damn . . . you've got some striking men. Kudos to you." Her dark eyes light up at the image before her.

I grin. The man is wearing glasses similar to what Keehan wears and looks a lot like the guy. Similar skin tone and close-cropped black hair, except Keehan is usually clean shaven and this man has a goatee and thin mustache. The image is his professional headshot Wendy pulled off the UC Davis website, so he's in his standard white coat and wearing a hospital badge. She can't be visually attracted to this man and not be attracted to Keehan. It's aesthetically impossible.

"Doctor. Head of emergency medicine at UC Davis."

"Nice. Busy guy. Wouldn't have a problem with me working all the time because he'd be working all the time. We could meet at home long enough to share a meal, take a roll between the sheets, and sleep. Having a doctor on my arm would be lovely at parties."

"If he doesn't have an emergency. Apparently, that's his reason for not having a mate. He goes on plenty of dates, but most of the time, he's also on call and has to leave the woman hanging."

She tips her head. "Not a big deal for me. I'd likely never have the time for the date in the first place." Her corresponding laughter rings out.

Hell, that reminds me. When was the last time I took Skyler on a bona fide date? The Italian restaurant and show. Unless you count the royal wedding we attended together. Skyler deserves some romance. A candlelit dinner, a walk along the beach . . . something that will make my girl feel as special as she makes me feel. I make a mental note to have Wendy send her some flowers, which has me wondering what her favorite flower is.

I'm a shit boyfriend. I see my woman enough to eat, sleep, and fuck her most of the time. We need a change. The idea of her moving to Boston sends a little thrill up my spine, weaves its way around my neck and face until I'm sporting a huge smile. My mother and Wendy would love getting to know Skyler better.

Rochelle's voice cuts into my thoughts. "Uh, hello? Next guy." Rochelle laughs.

Instead of changing the screen, I lean forward and make a show of scrutinizing the photo. "Man, this guy reminds me of someone . . ." I put the carrot out and hope she takes a bite.

Her eyes narrow, and then, out of nowhere, a huge smile spreads across her cheeks. "Oh my God! You're right. He looks like Keehan! Down to the glasses and all." She laughs.

This is my chance to plant a seed.

"Keehan said you guys have been together since the beginning?" I ask.

She nods and looks wistfully at the image on the screen, but somehow, I know she's not seeing the doctor but Keehan's face. "Yeah, he's like family to me. Committed. Best employee and friend I've ever had."

"Really? You two hang out?" Damn, I'm good at my job.

She grins. "When our schedules permit. Nice thing, we almost always have the same schedule, so it's natural to eat a lot of our meals together, spend holidays with one another, and the like. I've met his family, he's met mine. We are both single children of overachievers. My parents live in New York and run their own company. His parents are in Seattle, big in the shipping industry."

"And the two of you have never hooked up?" I toss out the golden coin, hoping she reaches for it.

Her face contorts into a confused expression. "What? No. We're colleagues. Friends."

"Oh, so you don't find him attractive." I state it matter-of-factly in order to urge her to consider his physical attributes.

She frowns. "I never said that."

"Well, do you?"

"Keehan is one of the most attractive men I know. Women everywhere drool when we enter a restaurant or walk down the street. And you can't see his body behind his suits, but we often hit the gym together, and the man is a brick house."

"And yet you don't drool over him?"

She chuckles. "When he's got his shirt off, I will admit to the possibility of a little drool."

I laugh to keep the comradery and light conversation going. "Huh, I guess it's weird."

"What's weird?"

"You and he, two attractive people, working closely together all these years, spending your free time together. Just seems, I don't know . . . a little strange you haven't fallen into a relationship."

"I never said we didn't have a relationship. My relationship with Keehan is the most important in my life. He means the world to me. He's the one man in the world besides my father I trust to always tell me the truth and treat me with respect. Keehan has my back in all things, as I have his."

"Oh, so it will be a little strange when you have to give up a lot of your time together for your future husband."

"Excuse me? What are you saying?" She frowns, pushes into the seat, straightening her body in a more defensive posture.

I lean back into the couch and stretch my arm out. "Rochelle, any man who secures you as his woman is not going to be okay with the tight relationship you have with Keehan. He'll have to take a bit of a step back in order to let your man be the one you count on, go to for things. Be there for you at night, on holidays, if you've had a hard day. Take you out for your birthday . . ."

Her response sounds strained as she replies. "But Keehan takes me out every year. We have a tradition. On my birthday we fly to a new place we've never been. We stay the weekend and take in all the sights. We do the same on his birthday. It's kind of our way of taking a small vacation and decompressing. It's sacred, and we've done it since we were in college together."

"And you think your new man is going to be okay with you gallivanting away for a weekend with your 'friend' and employee, while he sits back at home?" I cock an eyebrow so she realizes the gravity of what I'm saying.

She shakes her head and puts her hand over her mouth. For a long time, she doesn't say anything. "Show me the next picture, please." Her voice is tight, no longer expressing any excitement in the task at hand.

"You're the boss."

Mission accomplished. I smile smugly as I bring up the next photo. "Harkin Elba. Engineer. Never been married. Parents are deceased. Has a sister and a brother he's close to—" I'm about to say more when she cuts me off.

"Fine. Next." She waves her hand at the screen, barely giving the man a glance, she's so lost in her thoughts. Which I hope all lead back to one man.

Keehan Williams.

***

"Hey, Peaches." I answer the phone and plop into the armchair in my suite. "I'm about to meet up with Royce for dinner, so we have to be quick."

A sob tears through the connection, and my hackles rise.

"Skyler, baby, what's the matter?" I stand abruptly, looking around the room, not knowing what to do when I hear her cry.

"H-he, he's going to show the w-world . . ." Her voice shatters into another bout of loud sobs.

I clench my teeth and roll my shoulders. "Skyler . . . baby, you gotta stop crying so I can understand what's got you so upset. I want you to breathe with me, okay? In . . ." I suck in a long breath. ". . . out." I let the air out loud enough for her to hear me. I do this several more times until her crying subsides.

"Now talk to me. You're scaring me. Who's going to show the world, and what are they going to show?"

"Johan. He . . . Oh my God, Parker, it's so bad." Every word seems painful.

"What is, Peaches? What is so bad? Tell me."

"You'll hate me. They're all going to hate me!" The tears start back up.

"Skyler, stop crying right now and speak to me!" I scold with the harshest tone I can muster, hoping it shocks her out of her crying jag.

"Johan is my ex." Her voice cracks.

"Yes, I know. You were with him almost two years. We haven't talked much about him, though I know he was important to you and he hurt you."

"Yeah, but not like he's about to." Her words come out in a breathy whimper, each one apparently requiring extreme effort.

My heart pounds a furious beat in my chest as my worry for her increases. "Baby, what is going on?"

"He has pictures of me, Parker. Scandalous ones. And he . . . he . . ." She swallows loudly and lets out a breath. "He says he's going to write a tell-all book and include the pictures. Show everyone! And I . . . That's not who I am! I only . . . God . . . I did it for him!" She starts crying again.

"Okay, okay, sweetheart. I think I've got the gist of this. He's going to write some type of bullshit book about your relationship with him and share some pictures you don't want shared? Am I following?"

"Yeah." Her voice is broken, and I can hear the devastation in every word she utters.

"What are these pictures of?"

"Me!" she chokes out.

"I gathered that, baby, but be more specific so I understand why you are so upset."

"Doing things. Posed in compromising positions." Her breath comes out ragged, and I wish I were looking into her face right now, ready to help take on this burden by her side.

Based on how much this is hurting her, I'm guessing the man took naked photos of her. I grind my back molars, walk over to the bar, pour two fingers of scotch, and slam the liquor back in one go.

"I'm assuming you're naked in these photos?"

She sniffles. "Yeah, honey. But it's more than that. He was into kinky things and made me do things to him . . . wear things he wanted."

Visions of my Skyler in a variety of seriously debauched positions fly through my mind. "Such as?"

"Well . . . in one of them, I was tied up to a cross on the wall. You can see e-everything. I was blindfolded. I didn't even know he took them!" Her voice rises and falls with her fury.

"Fuck!"

"Parker . . . ," she whimpers. "Please don't hate me."

"Baby, I could never hate you. I'm not so innocent. We've both tried some kink in our past. As long as you were a consenting adult, there's no problem. The problem is him taking photos without your knowledge."

"In another one, I've got a ball gag in my mouth, and I'm wearing nipple clamps and nothing else. Again blindfolded, but you can tell it's me. Anyone could!"

The ball gag doesn't do a thing for me, but the nipple clamps would have my dick firing at attention if my girl weren't so distraught and I ready to commit bloody murder on her ex.

"He says he's going to tell the world about how kinky I am and how I liked to whip him and I left scars on his back the makeup artists have to cover up in his photo shoots. But I never did that! The most I did was flog him, and it wasn't much fun. He always wanted it harder than I could do, and we'd get in a huge fight, and he'd tell me I was a terrible lover, and . . . and . . ." Her breath starts coming in labored pants, leading to a whopper of a meltdown.

"I know, baby, and he's dead wrong. You're the best lover I've ever had. Ever. You're so hot in the sack, baby, I never get enough. Don't listen to him. He's pissed he doesn't have a chance with you ever again. He's a piece of shit who wants to make money off your good fortune."

"But what am I going to do? He'll ruin my reputation in the industry. Kill my career."

I shake my head, though she can't see it. "I highly doubt that, Skyler. Have you talked to Tracey?"

"No. I called you first." Her tone is soft and needy.

"Oh, baby . . ." My girl is being threatened, and she calls me first. I'm the first person in the world she goes to. Nothing could make me feel stronger, bigger, and more of a man than I do in this moment. Now I need to figure out how the hell I can help her through this. Flying to wherever this Johan is and beating the shit out of him sounds like the perfect idea right about now.

I pour myself another two fingers of scotch right as there are a couple of knocks on my door.

"Sky, listen to me . . ." I wait for her crying to stop again as I open the door and wave Royce in. "You're going to breathe through this. You're going to go and take a long hot shower. Then you're going to call Tracey and tell her everything this schmuck threatened you with and what you think he plans to do with those pictures and his bullshit story. Then you're going to pour yourself a nice stiff drink and order a pizza. Turn on the fire and watch the romance streaming app you like. Passionflix, is it?"

"Yeah . . ." She sniffs and lets out a shuddery breath.

"You're going to be okay. Repeat it for me, Peaches."

"I-I'm going to be o-okay."

"Good. Real good. Now hang up with me and call Tracey. I want you to call me back later when you've gotten more information and heard from Tracey. Okay?"

"Okay." A beat of silence greets me before she says, "Park?"

"Right here, baby."

"You don't think any differently of me? You know, because I did that stuff?"

My poor girl. I close my eyes and run a hand through my hair, pulling at the roots until I feel the prick of pain. "No, Skyler. I don't feel any differently about you. You're my woman. I like you a lot, remember? And besides . . . I'm falling for you."

"I like you *so much*." Her voice cracks on a little sob. "I might even love you a little bit. Especially now."

I smile huge, because I feel the spear of her words hit my heart and burst my chest open with pride. "Save that type of talk until we're face-to-face and I can hold you . . . and do other things to you. Okay?" I try to use my most suggestive tone so she'll calm down.

"Promise?"

"Peaches, very little could keep me away from you for very long. I wish more than anything I were there with you now, so you could cry on my shoulder and I could hold you close. I swear this will pass. We'll figure it out. You, me, Tracey, whatever it takes."

"I'll do what you said and call Tracey after my shower."

"And order a pizza, and turn on your Passionflix. Remember when you told me they made one of your favorite author's books into a movie? Sylvia Day, right?"

"Yeah, but it's not the Crossfire series."

"No?"

"No. It's *Afterburn Aftershock*."

I frown. I have no reference for that title, but it doesn't matter. It's a distraction. I hope a good one. "Have you watched it yet?"

She sighs. "No, I've been filming."

"Then treat yourself."

"Okay."

"Okay, shower, Tracey, pizza, movie. Got it?"

"Got it."

"Call me later," I remind her.

"I will."

"In the meantime, I'll be thinking of you."

"Me too."

She hangs up, and I hold up a hand to Royce, who is on instant alert. I'm sure he's figured out my girl is in a bad place and wants the details. I pull up my contacts, find Tracey Wilson, and type out a text.

To: Tracey Wilson
From: Parker Ellis

After you speak to Sky, please go stay with her. I don't want her alone tonight.

She responds in two seconds flat.

From: Tracey Wilson
To: Parker Ellis

What's going on?

I text back as fast as my fingers can move.

To: Tracey Wilson
From: Parker Ellis

Let her tell you. Please go there tonight. She needs her best friend.

I turn to the table with the scotch and pour Royce a drink. My phone dings as I hand the tumbler to him.

From: Tracey Wilson
To: Parker Ellis

Done.

"Now tell me what the fuck is up with your girl," Royce demands, holding his drink level at his knee.

I shake my head. "It's a shit show, brother, and it's about to blow up in a big way."

5

The scotch burns as I sip the fiery liquid, letting it mellow the rage inside my soul. I bring Royce up to date on what Skyler told me. His body becomes more rigid, like a jaguar ready to pounce, with each new piece I reveal.

"This chump is going down . . ." Royce's words are a shrewd, lethal promise.

"Damn straight."

"We need to find out who his friends are, what's going on with his finances. Something is riling him up. He didn't wake up one day and decide to do this to a woman he hasn't been with in years. There's got to be a reason, Park."

I nibble on my bottom lip and pace the room until I realize there's one person besides Tracey who can help. I grab my phone and pull up her name.

It rings a couple of times before a man picks up. "To what do we owe the pleasure of your call at . . . eleven in the evening, Mr. Ellis?" He addresses me formally, as he knows this wouldn't be a call I'd be making at this hour if it weren't business or extremely important.

"Michael, I need to speak to Wendy. I need her help with something immediately." I form my request as a demand, leaving not even a hint of wiggle room for him to deny me if he wants his woman to keep her job. I wouldn't fire her, but he doesn't know me well enough to come to that conclusion.

Wendy has become part of our extended family in the short months she's worked for us. She's irreplaceable.

"I see." His tone is direct, businesslike. "Please hold a moment."

There's a rustle of sound, and then as if from far away, I can hear him speak.

"Cherry, you may put on your robe for the length of time you speak to your boss. Do you understand?"

"Yes, sir." I hear her voice but just barely.

"The moment you end the call, you will remove the robe and come kneel at my side."

"Yes, sir. Thank you, sir." I hear Wendy's answer, much softer than her usual go-getting nature.

I grind down on the back of my teeth, wishing I hadn't heard all that, but I'm intrigued nonetheless. I'd already figured out their D/s dynamic prior to this call. But if I hadn't, overhearing what I did definitely confirms they are deeply into a lifestyle I know very little about. Unfortunately, with the pictures likely to be released to the public, I may have to become a lot more knowledgeable once my girlfriend's photos hit the stratosphere.

"Parker? What's up?" she asks, all chirpy Wendy. I'm not sure what I expected, but she sounds normal as usual.

"Wendy, look, I'm really sorry to bother you." I rub at my temples with thumb and forefinger and start to pace once more. "Skyler's in trouble. Her ex, Johan Karr, is threatening to share some kinky naked photos of her and write a tell-all book about her sexual proclivities, which actually aren't hers but his, and I need to figure out why. Or at the very least, come up with something that can go up against what he's threatening."

"Oh my God! What a creep!" She yells into the phone so loud I have to pull it away from my ear for a second.

"You can say that again."

"I'll um . . . talk to Mick and get right on it."

"I want you to go deep. We need to know his finances, what, if anything, he owes, who his friends are, where he frequents, anything and everything. If he's threatening to ruin my woman's career and good name, I want to fight fire with fire."

"Oh, I'll find everything," she promises.

I lick my lips and lower my voice, not wanting to put myself or IG on the line, but knowing I'd do anything for Sky. "Even if you have to use some questionable means to do it . . . I . . ."

"Parker, this is family. When one of us gets hurt, all of us get hurt." Her words make my chest constrict and my heart feel like it's going to pound its way right through bone and muscle and burst to the surface.

She continues, "We may not have known one another for long, but besides Mick, you three guys are all I have. I'll dig deep. *Real deep.* There will be no stone left unturned. Feel me?"

My mouth goes dry, and it's hard to speak around the sudden catch in my throat. "Yeah, Wendy, I feel you. Thank you."

"I'll hit you back when I've got something."

"Anything," I whisper, but it comes out as a plea.

"You got it, boss man." She hangs up before I can thank her again.

"Good idea, calling in Wendy. She's a freakin' genius, man. If there's anything to find on him, she'll uncover it. For sure."

I nod numbly and stare out the window at the San Francisco sky-scrapers, wishing I were seeing a different view. The one from Skyler's penthouse would be ideal right about now.

Royce claps me on the back. "We're going to figure out how to help your girl. Let Wendy and Tracey do their jobs. There's nothing more we can do from here 'cept wait."

I agree with a short chin lift, then tug at my tie, yank the offending thing off, and toss it at my suitcase.

Royce pours me another drink, picks up the hotel phone, and orders from room service. "Yeah, we'd like a couple of steaks, medium, with a side of potatoes and greens sent up, along with another bottle of scotch. Put it on our room. Thirty minutes? Great."

I kick off my shoes, and after hanging up the phone, Royce follows. He undoes his tie and the first two buttons on his collar, then folds his tie nicely and sets it on the table. He removes his jacket, folds it in half, and places it over the back of a chair. Once he's more comfortable, he sits down on the large sofa in the suite's living room, grabs the remote, and finds the latest baseball game. I bring my drink over to where he's sitting and stretch out, phone in one hand, drink in the other. Silently, but in absolute solidarity, we watch baseball and wait to hear something back from either Wendy or Skyler.

***

Two hours fly by and no news. I've texted Skyler and called. She's not answering, but I do get a text from Tracey stating she is with Skyler and has some ideas.

I groan when the baseball game ends late. It's ten in the evening here, with no word from either female. I sigh and move around the room, needing to release some of this pent-up energy. A distraction right now would be nice—then I remember what happened earlier in the day. Since Royce is here keeping me company, there's no reason not to dig into what went down at Renner Financial Services.

"You gonna talk to me about what happened with Rochelle?" I lift a leg up on the couch and turn toward the big man.

Royce shakes his head resolutely. "Nope."

I grind my teeth, trying to figure out a way to get him to open up. I know he's miffed about her blowing him off. Any man would be. Then again, maybe he doesn't want to talk about it because it proves I was right about her all along. He needs to get this out, for the sole reason of moving on.

"Brother . . . you banged her, were about to do it again until I walked in, and then she dismissed your time together as a fling. Knowing you're not a 'hit it and quit it' man, that had to burn you up inside. At least a little."

"Not really." He attempts to lie, but I can hear the scratch of disappointment in his tone. "Who's to say there still won't be anything between us? We had something last night. It was intense, filled with passion, and felt as if it could last awhile if given half the chance."

He's insane! The man still thinks he has a chance. "Roy, she's not available to you. Not to mention she spent hours with me looking at suitable future husbands. She's also eagerly anticipating the party we're throwing at the end of the week where she can meet the top candidates. She's probably going through their profiles now."

He shrugs and leans his bulk back against the couch, putting his feet up on the coffee table. "Don't care. There was something there . . ."

"Yeah! A whole lot of lust. Believe me when I say I know exactly what that looks like. I had it with Sophie. Now she's one of my closest friends. But it's nothing compared to what I feel for Skyler. She turns my insides into molten lava when I see her. The shit about butterflies in your stomach and stars in your eyes . . . yeah, that sums it up. I'm batshit crazy over the woman."

"You're in love with her, man," Royce says resolutely.

"Yes!" I admit out loud for the first time since Kayla. I'm in love. Holy shit. "Fuck!" I brace my weight against the back of the couch and take several deep breaths.

I'm in love with Skyler.

Skyler freakin' Paige.

My dream girl.

Mine. All mine.

And she's hurting. Dealing with this shit storm without me by her side. We can't go on being this far apart from one another all the time. They say absence makes the heart grow fonder, but right now, I want to throat punch the guy who came up with that shit. I need her. I *need* to be there for her when life throws her a curveball and vice versa.

"We need to get through this case, but in the meantime, you can't be fucking around with the client. No more. I mean it." The words leave my mouth, and I hardly recognize them. It's the first time I've ever made a demand of one of my business partners. Suggestions, yes. Idea sharing? Absolutely.

Demands? Never.

"Say what? I think you better get off your high love horse and think about what you just said to me . . . *part-ner*." He emphasizes the single word that means the world to all three of us. "I'm your *partner*, not your employee. And I am your brother . . . by choice. Don't you dare try and tell me how I'm going to act with a woman I'm interested in. I would never intervene if a woman meant something to you."

"Roy . . . I'm sorry. I . . . She's not for you." It's a lame statement if I ever heard one, but I'm at a loss to figure out how to get through to him.

"What? Now that you're in love with your woman, have found your one in seven billion, you think you're the expert on love? The love guru or some shit? Let's not forget the last woman you loved jacked you over with your best friend. I'd never jack you over like they did. I'm not him. I'm also intelligent enough and capable enough to make my own fuckin' decision about who I choose to be with and who I don't. You hear me . . . *brother*?"

"Roy, she may have taken you for a ride, but the woman is in love with someone else . . ."

His head jerks back. "Now you're making shit up."

I shake my head furiously and stand up. "No, I'm not."

"Who?"

"Keehan."

"The black Clark Kent?"

I roll my eyes, because even though we're having a heated conversation, I made the same comparison he did. "Yeah."

"Shee-it. She doesn't have eyes for him. He may have them for her, but she didn't so much as blink when he put his hands on her the other day in support. She patted his hand like he was a good friend and nothing more."

I disagree and make it known. "She didn't act that way when I showed her pictures of other guys. One in particular looked like him, and she was all over it like white on rice. She's pushed the idea of them so far out in left field, it's never surfaced as an option, but if it's thrown in front of her face, I believe she'll bite."

Royce gets up off the couch, walks over to his shoes, and sits on the chair to put them on. "I don't see it. Rochelle is a strong woman. She needs a strong man by her side. Someone who can bear some of the burdens for her."

I shake my head. "No. She needs a man who can stand by her side and be there to lean on when things get tough, someone who will help lift her up, not take the spotlight from her. Mark my words, Royce, she wants a submissive male. Someone who lives to be with her, whose every decision is based on how to make her happiest. Keehan is that man. He has already devoted his entire life to her. She needs to open her eyes and see what's in front of her face. It's time for Rochelle to want what she already has."

"This is ridiculous. You're shooting out in left field, and I'm warning you . . . there's something between Chellie and me, and I'm going to find out what it is."

I sigh and place my hands on my hips. "I'm afraid you're sorely mistaken, and the last thing I want is to see you get hurt."

Royce's eyes are sparkling with white-hot fire, and he raises a finger to me. "You need to trust that I know what's right for me."

"I can't do that when I know she's all kinds of wrong for you. I'm going to continue with the contract and find her the right man for *her*. Mark my words, Roy . . . it's not you."

"Well, I guess we'll have to agree to disagree now, won't we. And may the best man win." He positively sneers his venom.

I raise my hands and let them fall to my sides in defeat. "It's not a game!" I holler, and race for the door in time to see his long strides eating up the hallway alongside his ire.

"No, it's not." This time he points at his chest, puffed up with pride. "It's my fuckin' *life*. Stay out of it!" he roars, then shoves his key card into the door of the suite at the end of the hall and disappears inside.

"Fuck!" I grumble as my phone buzzes on the coffee table.

I stalk over to it and see "Peaches" on the screen.

"Sky?"

"No, it's Tracey." Her best friend's voice comes through the connection.

"Where's Sky?" My heart is pounding a million beats a minute. Between my fight with Royce and the anxiety over what's happening with my woman, I'm a goddamned mess.

"Sleeping. My phone died from all the calls I made while she watched her movie and drank a few glasses of beer."

"Is she okay?" I rub at my temples and close my eyes tightly, rivers of anger washing over my skin. I wish I were in her bed, holding her protectively in my arms where nothing could harm her.

"No. Johan means business. His lawyer already called me with an offer."

Knife straight to the gut. "An offer? Like he's selling something to the highest bidder?" I scowl. "What's his offer?"

"Fifty million and the problem goes away," she states flatly with zero emotion.

He wants $50 million.

"Jesus Christ! She's not going to pay that, is she? Does she even have that much money?" I muse absentmindedly, not realizing I've said it out loud.

"Parker, she's the highest-paid actress in Hollywood and has been for the last few years. Of course she has the money. Her last film alone netted her that much."

My entire body feels heavy, and I sink down into the nearest armchair and rub furious circles over my temples to ease the pounding in my head. "Oh," I say lamely. I guess it never dawned on me how loaded my girlfriend is. Not that I care. I love her, not her millions.

"The lawyer is pulling together the agreement. We're going to see about meeting up with them next week."

"She's going to meet with the bastard?"

"It was part of the agreement. Sky's choice. She wants to look him in the eyes."

I run my hand through my hair and clench my teeth, practically spitting through them when I respond. "This is fucked up, Tracey. Can't you or one of her lawyers get her out of it?"

She sighs deeply. "I don't think so. The pictures are real. Sky confirms it. They are in his possession to do with what he wants."

"But she says she didn't agree to them." I slam my closed fist on the tabletop nearest me. The light flickers at the onslaught, and Roy's empty whiskey glass rattles, almost falling over.

"She agreed to be gagged. She agreed to be blindfolded and tied up. Now that the pictures could hurt her, she's saying she didn't agree to those. It's hearsay. We don't want this taken to a judge and have a media storm of the century on our hands. If she pays the money, we get the pictures back."

"And the book?"

"I don't know. At this time, they're negotiating for use of the pictures. He doesn't want to agree to a full NDA. We may have to offer more to secure his silence."

I close my eyes and let the powerful punch of this information hit me fully. Pain oozes from my heart through my veins and out every pore. Disgust coats my nerve endings as I tighten my hands and try my damnedest to control the urge to go ballistic and destroy this hotel room in a blind rage.

I want to hurt him.

I want to smash his face in so many times he'll never model again.

I want him *dead*.

I've never wanted a person dead before. Never had enough hate in my heart to wish death upon someone. Even Kayla. Sure, I might wish her an STD, or a punishment equally fair to how she broke my heart, but never death.

I wish Johan Karr would fall off the face of the earth and never be heard from again. Disappear so he will never be able to hurt the woman I love, or anyone else for that matter, again.

Those tears she shed over him on our call tonight were torturous enough. Now to find out she's going to pay this pig $50 million for pictures he wasn't supposed to have taken and another whatever amount to keep him from lying through his teeth in a tell-all book? It's not right. The world cannot possibly be this lopsided in doling out justice.

"Parker . . . Parker, are you there? Did you hear me?"

I shake off the image of Johan, handcuffed behind his back, being led into a jail cell wearing an orange jumpsuit. If only . . .

"Yeah, yeah, I'm here." I clear my throat and take a deep breath.

"I said, I'm going to have her call you tomorrow, but I'll be here with her. I won't leave her side."

"Thank you, Tracey. You're a good friend."

"After all that's happened . . . I'm trying to be. Sky deserves to be happy, and she's changed since she met you. She's different. There's a lightness in her steps, an excitement in her eyes all the time. Especially when she's talking to you or about you. I haven't seen her this happy since before her parents died. You've done that for her."

"Yeah, well, she's opened my eyes to a lot of new things too." One being falling in love. Not something I ever had a hope of finding again, but I wouldn't admit that to Sky's friend. No, those truths are all for my girl. "Take care of her."

"I will. When are you planning to come home? I know she mentioned something about a baseball game. Was all giddy about going to one with you. Would likely take her mind off this garbage, if only for a few hours."

I smile at the idea of enjoying a baseball game with my woman. Eating hot dogs, yelling at umpires, kissing for the kiss cam, sharing something I love with someone I love. Nothing sounds better.

"Not sure when I'll be home. Hopefully in a few more days. However, if Sky needs me, I'll head out and leave Roy to handle the rest of the job." Usually what I said would be accurate, but this time, I don't mean it. I'll have to call in Bo. Royce is 100 percent off his rocker on this one and can't see the forest through the trees. Maybe I should call Bo, get his opinion on what to do in the meantime.

"All right, well, it's close to two in the morning here. I need to get some shut-eye if I'm going to be any use to Sky in the morning."

"Thanks again, Tracey. For being there when I can't."

"Parker, I don't want to be rude when I say this, but she was mine first. She'll always be mine in some way." Her voice takes on a twinge of humor, but I can't help reading through it to the fact that she considers Sky more important than just a friend.

"I know you're her family, Tracey. And I know you feel responsible for not doing more when she lost her will to act and you thought you pushed her to her breaking point. I think you learned a little more of what was most important during the experience. Now you're stronger for it. And besides, if it hadn't happened, I wouldn't have met the love of my life."

Tracey gasps. "I knew it. You're in love with my best friend."

"Not going to answer one way or another, because the first time I tell my woman I love her will not be through her best friend. Got it?"

"Loud and clear. Lips sealed. But, Parker?"

I sigh. "Yes, Tracey."

"You hurt her, and I'll kill you. She's been hurt enough by people claiming to love her, and she's about to undergo a new battle with another one. She wouldn't survive being hurt by you. Especially now."

I close my eyes and let the statement seep deep into my bones. "I know, and I don't intend on hurting her. Have her call me in the morning, okay?"

"Sure will. Good night."

"Good night, Tracey."

With the end of this shit day, I pull off my clothes and fall into bed. Hopefully Wendy will provide more information about what this Johan character is up to. There has to be a reason he's going after his ex for such a large sum of money. None of it makes sense. He leaves her alone for two years and then—*whammo*—decides to threaten her reputation and livelihood? Why did he wait a couple of years? It would have made more sense to go after her when they were still linked. Now, it seems desperate.

A man doesn't go after a woman from his past unless he's being backed into a corner.

It makes me wonder, Who's doing the pushing, and what do they have on him?

6

To: Peaches
From: Parker Ellis

You okay? Call me when you're free.

I pinch my lips and read the text again. I've already tried to call once with no answer. She probably woke up and jetted to the set. I know they're close to wrapping this film, and the director was going to do as many reshoots as possible with the little time they had allotted. Still, it doesn't calm the worry swirling around my mind like a vortex, sucking up all the energy in its wake.

A twisting sensation fills my gut as I make my way into Renner Financial Services. As much as I want to be on the next plane to New York, there's still a job to be done. Before I left the hotel, I checked Royce's room. He didn't answer, leading me to believe he'd already left for RFS.

As I make my way to Rochelle's office, my phone buzzes.

I stop in my tracks and grin at the display. I have no idea how she did it, but at some point, Wendy accessed my phone and changed her name in my directory from her given name to the title of her choosing.

The smile on my face also digs into my heart, making me feel a moment's reprieve from the heaviness of the past twenty-four hours.

From: World's Greatest Assistant
To: Parker Ellis

Compiling information. Was at it all night. Will have more tonight. Lots more. Someone has been a very bad boy . . .

I read and reread the text. A bad boy. That could mean anything, but knowing Wendy, she means Johan Karr has some skeletons in his closet, and she's unearthing them. I smile, knowing whatever she's found could very well help my woman not have to pay a red cent. God willing.

Pushing through the door to Rochelle's office, I spy her sitting at her desk, head back, laughing openly at something Royce must have said. A smug grin sits on his face as I enter the fray.

He dips his chin in greeting, not showing any hint of the battle we had last night; however, I know it's not fully resolved, simply held back for the sake of our client and business relations. The last thing I would ever want is bad blood between me and one of my brothers, especially over a woman. I've got to find a way to fix what I've broken.

"Good morning, Mr. Ellis."

"Morning, Ms. Renner . . . Royce." I focus my gaze on the client. "I trust you slept well?"

She smirks. "Not as well as I could have if *someone* here hadn't turned down my offer of dinner and drinks."

I slide my gaze back to Royce. He turned her down last night? I don't have time to fully digest her comment before he cuts in.

"Yeah, well, *family* needed me, and as sweet as the thought of having dinner with you is . . . when family calls, I answer." His response digs a hole into the meaty muscle of my heart, right where he intended the blow to fall.

Rochelle clucks her tongue. "Pity. We could have had a little more fun before I zero in on one of the delectable specimens Parker has set up for me."

A dark shadow passes behind Royce's eyes before he blinks it away and is all business. I want to call Rochelle out on her bullshit, but Royce reminded me last night that it isn't my business. Made it very clear I need to back off.

"Yes, well, we can't always have *fun*, now can we. There's also work to be done." Royce's irritated tone cannot be denied. "Speaking of, I worked with Keehan to narrow down the list of potential employees who may be stealing from you. I added one more to the list you may not like, but it has to be considered . . ."

I'm proud of him for tossing her a grenade. The woman needs to see she's playing with fire. Curious, I walk over to her desk to see the name he added. I'd already gotten the list from Keehan and had Wendy working on it.

While Rochelle reads it, I note her entire body goes ramrod straight, and she pushes back from her desk until her fingertips are barely holding on to the glass edge.

"It's not possible." Her voice is tight, irritated.

I scan the list and note the single familiar name scrawled on the bottom in Royce's penmanship. Damn it all to hell. The single name has me working hard to put myself in check. He's trying to push her, and it's not cool. I tilt back my head and sigh at the sky.

Fuck.

This will not go over well, and worse, I have to wonder if Royce is suggesting it to get Keehan out of the running as a possible man for Rochelle. Only he doesn't know we already went there, at Keehan's insistence.

As I shake my head and assess the way Rochelle is shooting daggers at Royce, it's hard for me to swallow against the thought that Roy might be putting his desire for the client over the truth staring us all in the face. Keehan Williams is in love with Rochelle. He'd never in a million years steal from the woman he's devoted his life to. The problem is, Royce is too blinded by lust and the thought of his own picket fences to see the truth staring him in the face.

"Brother . . . ," I say in a harsh whisper.

"Had to be said. There's one man in this entire company with full access to everything and the ability to cover his tracks completely." If I didn't know him better, I'd swear he's gloating.

Rochelle shakes her head, her crimson lips compressed into a thin, flat line. "Not possible."

"Chellie, it's very possible," Royce encourages.

She continues to push herself back before she stands and faces us both. Rochelle crosses her arms over one another and cocks out a hip. "No. It. Isn't."

Royce's facial expression softens, making him look less imposing in his dark-gray suit. "Just because you're friends doesn't mean he couldn't hurt you. He has the means and ability, Chellie . . . I've seen it before. Too many times, in fact."

Rochelle huffs obstinately, blatantly not appreciating where Royce is taking this conversation. "He's the one who brought the concern to my attention. Why would he do that if he were stealing from me?" Rochelle grinds out through clenched teeth, anger coating every last word.

I'm about to tell her that's a very good point when Royce leans against the desk, resting the flat of his palms on the glass surface. "To throw you off the scent."

She lifts her hand in a "stop" gesture. "No more. I will not hear any further suggestion that Keehan could be stealing from me. It's simply not possible."

"No, it isn't. I'd never hurt you or what I helped you build." Keehan projects his thundering voice into the conversation from where he stands, having just entered the office.

Perfect timing, Keehan.

Royce stands up and places his hands in his pockets. "It had to be said. No offense, brother, but it's our job to make sure she has all the evidence," he states mechanically.

Keehan shakes his head. "I'm not your *brother*, I'm your client's veteran employee and longtime friend. If you were doing your job, you'd have already scoured my bank accounts, which I gave to your partner yesterday, looking for additional money."

Jesus, this situation is deteriorating quickly. My desire to protect Royce and his suggestion is overpowering.

Royce's eyes shift up so his gaze meets mine. "Park?"

I nod. "Keehan mentioned his concerns, and I asked Wendy to run the names of the employees on your list and run their financial histories for the last two years. He had me include his own for the record. Full disclosure. Wendy emailed them last night before I called her about the other thing." I allude to the Johan issue, having no desire to share my personal dealings with our clients.

Royce nods. "I wish you had mentioned that to me." His statement is accusatory and uncalled for.

"Was planning to this morning. Emailed over Wendy's findings to the three of you not an hour ago when I had a chance. As you well know, I was a little busy last night."

He closes his eyes and briefly dips his chin. "And what did you find?"

Keehan lays out the sheets in his hands. "None of the people on this list have any unusual fluctuations in their bank accounts or investment portfolios."

Royce scans the documents and nods. "It's true. These staff members are clean."

"Well, that's a small relief. All of these names are people I've worked with a long time," Rochelle says. "Each of them has their own stake in the company doing well. Stock shares, the whole nine. But where does that leave us in narrowing down the search for who is doing the stealing?"

"At this point, we'll have to run every name in the company, which is going to take some time." Royce picks up his phone and lifts it to his ear. "Wendy, yeah, we got the information for RFS. Unfortunately, we're going to need to broaden the search to the rest of the staff." He nods silently and glances out the window. "We understand that could take some time. Send over the ones you get completed as you get them."

I inhale sharply, instantly aware that if Wendy is doing the work for the client, she's not doing the funky poaching on Johan.

Royce's gaze flickers to me, and his voice turns hard when he asks Wendy, "Did you, uh, finish with the other thing? Okay, I'll let him know. Get on those names, yeah?"

Wendy must ring off, because Royce hits a button on his phone and shoves it into his pocket. "She's going to run the rest of the staff's names and financials and see if she can come up with anything. Said it will take a couple of days for that many people."

Rochelle sighs. "So, we're back to square one."

"I'm afraid so." Royce knocks two knuckles on the glass top of her desk. His chin dips, and his dark gaze reaches mine. "Parker, I need to speak to you . . . privately." He gestures to the doorway.

Both Rochelle and Keehan frown.

"We'll be right back," I say.

"While you're gone, I'll call HR to have the employee list sent over in Helen's absence."

"Thanks, Chellie." Royce smiles.

Rochelle nods, and Keehan looks at Royce with fire in his gaze. Accusing Keehan is not going over well with Rochelle's right-hand man or Rochelle, especially when Keehan offered up his information freely.

Royce didn't have any nefarious intentions when he added Keehan's name; nevertheless, even if he did it because he was jealous and wanted to get a leg up on the man, I would still back him. He wasn't wrong about the need to run Keehan's information, if one takes in the bigger picture, which I did at Keehan's suggestion. However, Roy could have been more tactful.

What it comes down to is he's letting his lust get in the way of the job. Been there, done that. Got the hot blonde to prove it. And the job didn't suffer in any way when I hooked up with Sophie and later with Skyler.

Once Royce steps outside the client's office and into the hallway, he takes a few long strides to the right, giving us more privacy.

"Wendy said she's got the information ready for you and is emailing it now. I wanted to make sure you had the time to go over it, and see about us taking a couple of hours to review it, put our heads together . . ." He licks his full lips, prepping for a team huddle.

I put my hand on Royce's arm. "Brother, one of us has to deal with the client, but it means the world to me that you're willing to drop it all and step up to the plate for me, and more importantly for Sky. Means you're not still angry about last night—"

His head jolts back. "The fuck? You are not getting off that easy." He places a beefy finger against my breastbone. "You said some things that were completely uncalled for . . ."

I shake my head, glance around the space, and see an empty conference room. I nudge Royce into the room and shut the door. "You've got to be kidding me. Royce, you were out of line."

His eyes widen so much those black orbs are nearly bulging out of their sockets. "Oh, so you can fuck two clients, fall in love with one, but I can't?" His black eyebrows are dark arrowheads arching over his eyes.

"This isn't about me!" I blurt.

"It sure as fuck is!" he growls. "Regardless of what's going on with Rochelle and me, I should be able to explore what's between us in whatever way I deem appropriate, without worrying my *brother* is going to be up in arms." His words are scathing.

I sigh and run my hand through my overly long hair. "What do you expect me to do? Cut and run? Let you woo the client who's hired us to match her with prospective husbands? You want that role, Roy? You going to jump ship and move across coasts to be with her?"

Royce's jaw firms before my eyes, and a muscle in his cheek jumps while he grinds his teeth.

I continue, knowing I'm poking an already angry bear. "You going to leave your momma and three sisters behind in Boston? Alone?"

This time Roy's lips flatten, and he sucks in a harsh breath through his teeth.

"It's my decision, not yours." Each word is clipped.

"You going to bail on IG?" The mere suggestion sends a lightning bolt through my mind. Fear. Anxiety. Grief. All batter at my fight-or-flight instinct, making me want to grab Royce and blow this Popsicle stand. Get the hell out of Dodge and leave Rochelle and all her drama behind.

Royce rises up to his full imposing height of six feet four. "I could run a West Coast office, if I so desired. Wouldn't be a bad idea . . ." His nostrils flare as the magnitude of what he's suggesting has me reeling.

An invisible claw wraps around my neck. The concept of not having Roy in my life every day is far too much to swallow. "You're willing to leave us? Your *brothers*, when shit just got good?" I gasp, shocked nearly stupid at what I'm hearing.

He closes his eyes and backs up a step before rubbing his bald head with both hands.

"No. I'm not. None of those things are going to happen. I couldn't leave my mother and sisters. I'd never leave what we built for a woman I just met, unless it was dead serious. Marriage, kids, all of that. And I sure as shee-it wouldn't leave my brothers from another mother!"

"Thank Christ. Then why the hell are we fighting?" I let my shoulders fall and put my hands in my pockets, tipping my face down to make sure my shoes are still on my feet for how heavy my head feels.

"It ain't about that. It's about it being my choice. Park, you're gettin' in my way. You've made demands you never should have."

"Because I can see the writing on the wall . . ." I raise my hand and point to the side of the conference room in the direction of Rochelle's office. "She is not going to settle down, go to family dinners with her man and his mother and sisters. She may be beautiful, intelligent, and all kinds of hot in the sack, but she is *not* for you, brother." I rub at the back of my neck and lift my head to lock my gaze with his. "You deserve it all." The words leave soft and sincere from my suddenly dry lips. "A woman who will worship the ground you walk on right alongside the foundation you're laying for your future with her."

"Park . . ." Roy's voice is thick, but I don't let him get a word in edgewise. Not yet. Not until he understands.

"Rochelle is great; she's amazing, but she's not made for *you*. She's made for a man like Keehan. A man who already worships her. She needs to see what's on offer right in front of her face. It's everything she needs and wants. She consumes him. Now it's my job, *our job*, to make them see that. You are getting in the way with your big dark-chocolate awesomesauce. The right woman will present herself, and the day she does, I'll be her biggest fan. Today is not that day. Maybe not tomorrow either, but soon. Mark my words. You are not meant to be alone, but you are not meant to be with her either."

I stop my rant and take a few moments to *breathe*, feeling like I just ran a fuckin' marathon.

"Brother, you called me dark-chocolate awesomesauce."

I cringe and run my hand down my face. "Yeah. Sky's lingo is rubbing off on me."

Royce smiles wide and claps me on the back, pulling me into a hard hug. "Love you, man. Love that you want to watch out for me.

Love that you care. Do *not* love you telling me what to do." I can hear the slightest quaver in his voice, but he's staying strong, just the way I'd expect him to.

I hit him a couple of times on the back. "Couldn't stand by and let my brother wade too far into a bad deal. I'd have done the same for Bo, or my brother Paul. Blood or not, doesn't make a difference. I don't have it in me to sit and watch you fall when I can do something to help."

Royce backs up, rests both hands on my shoulders, and leans down so we're eye to eye. "I get you, but you need to get me. When I want your opinion, when I *need* your opinion—and there will come a time when I'm ready to have it—I'll *ask* for it. You may be right on this one, but it does not change one fucking thing."

I nod, letting his words soak in. I got lucky on this one, but for the foreseeable future, I'm going to have to watch how I wade into Royce's dealings with women. He's testy about it, and part of me wonders if it's because I've found Skyler and he wants to find his own forever. Be that as it may, I need to respect his wishes and stay the fuck out of it.

"Brother, I'm sorry I pushed so hard regarding Rochelle—"

Royce cuts in. "No. You were right . . . about *this* one. She has little feeling about our connection other than the physical. And possibly it's because she's gone for Keehan. That remains to be seen. You were wrong to push so hard, especially in light of your own past with clients, but . . ." He sighs and shakes his head. "I'm not used to having my decisions questioned, especially by you. We support one another. It's who we are and the brotherhood we've created between the three of us. However, there's a line . . . You crossed it. Big-time."

I close my eyes, concerned this is going to be a huge thing between us. Right now, with the worry over Skyler, it seems as though everything is falling apart one brick at a time.

Until Roy brings me peace with his next comment.

"Park, I accept your apology. We move on from here, more knowledgeable about where we stand with one another, and wait for the other brother to give the go-ahead to wade in. Truce?" He lifts his fist.

"Truce." I knock his fist with my own. A wave of relief fills the room, acting as a balm on my fraying nerves. "Now are you going to help me hook Rochelle up with Keehan?"

He purses his lips and sighs. "Jeez-us, Park. I just barely decide I'm pulling my hat out of the ring, and you want me to hook her up with the geek?"

I grin. "Hell yeah, I do. I'll get you up to date on the plan I've made while you've been pining away despite my advice."

"Watch it." Royce inhales sharply but doesn't deny it. He wouldn't have a leg to stand on if he did.

I spend the next ten minutes giving him the plan while he listens intently, nodding and smiling.

"I like it. Sneaky," he admits.

"You cool to handle the next phase while I head to the hotel and review the information Wendy sent over regarding Johan?"

"You can count on me."

I grin wide. "I know."

Royce lifts his hand in a fist, and I bump it with my own again. He nods. "Get out of here. Go find out how you're going to kick the fool in his family jewels without having to do it in person and have charges pressed against you. Then again, if he's ever in Boston in a dark alley . . ."

I chuckle. "Uh-huh. Don't be planning evil ways to get back at my woman's ex without me. I want in on all the action."

He grins. "We'll see. Go review the information and hit your girl up. See how we can best destroy this chump without her having to pay a dime of her hard-earned cash."

I wave over my head. "Will do." I stop at the door and turn to my friend. "Royce?"

"Yeah?" He straightens his tie and presses it down flat against the wall of muscle he's hiding under it.

"Thanks, man." All of the frustration, hurt, and anxiety start to seep out of my body one breath at a time. At least for now, Royce and I are back on the same page.

"Back atcha, brother."

Without a second glance, I'm out of the office and pulling out my phone.

I hail a cab at the same time I press "Call" for Wendy on my phone.

"Boss man."

"Lay it on me, Wendy."

7

Jesus! Johan Karr is the biggest douchebag in the known universe. The more I read from the documents Wendy emailed over, the more disgusted and angry I get.

"How has none of this come out in the press?" I glare down at Wendy on the phone. We're FaceTiming one another while going over the documents on the computer.

Her red hair is shiny and slicked back on the sides, leaving a large pouf at the front. She's wearing bright-red lipstick, which makes her skin look pearlescent. Between the skin tone and the red hair and lips, her blue eyes pop wildly.

"I don't know, boss man. I'm pretty surprised some of this information hasn't leaked to the press. Which, of course, I have zero problem making happen." She grins wickedly.

I shake my head and hold up a finger. "Not yet. We need to think about the best way to approach him. The goal is not to ruin him, although after his despicable history, I'd like nothing more than to string him up by his toes and let the paparazzi have a go at him, but the priority is Skyler."

Wendy nods and taps at her lips while I scour another document and read out loud.

"Repeated DUIs, four stints in and out of juvie for thievery before the age of eighteen. As a kid, Johan was no better. Besides the two sexual assault charges his family settled out of court with his high school girlfriend and a woman his first year in college, did you find any others?"

She shakes her head. "No, just those two. Family paid off both girls handsomely, and the reports were dropped with the police. I had to dig deep to even find anything on Johan from before he dropped out of college and started modeling his way through life. Lot of reports of him dating Sky, though."

I grind my teeth, wishing my girl had never gotten mixed up with this scum. "Yeah, don't remind me." I cringe.

Wendy smiles. "Check out his finances. He's in the hole big-time. Apparently invested most of his money in some company that folded and went bankrupt a couple of months ago. His bank accounts are not only dwindling, they are practically destitute. And with how he's been partying, jetting all over Europe, snorting things up his nose, I'm getting reports of some shady dealings with loan sharks, who he owes a pretty penny. As in hundreds of thousands. Not to mention, he's in the hole huge with his credit cards. All maxed out. He needs money and fast."

"And what about his parents? They bailed him out several times before. Had his juvie records sealed; otherwise, the press would have dredged up his past long ago."

"Yep, and there's nothing on them having any type of relationship after that point. It seems he wore out his welcome with the Karr clan through those two settlements. I haven't seen anything in the past five years to indicate they have any relationship. No phone calls listed from his phones. No social media posts of family gatherings of any kind. It's as if they wrote him off after the last screwup in college."

I groan. "I don't blame them. Mess up once, shame on you, mess up twice, shame on me. My mother would hold on until the bitter end, but my father would never let the two of them get taken over and over by me or my brother. With his history and record as a kid, my guess is they got to the point where they realized they were enabling his bad behavior by bailing him out all the time. When you don't suffer the consequences of your actions, you tend to repeat them. Johan has been repeating his offenses in different, more despicable ways."

Wendy nods while scanning the computer and typing furiously.

"Even with all of the strikes against him, do you think the two assault charges will be enough to get him to leave Skyler alone?"

"You mean if we release the charges and the names of the women and what they endured at his hands . . ." Her voice cracks, disappointment and uncertainty slipping along her pixie-like features.

"Hell no! I'd never do that to those women. They are survivors of whatever he did to them. We can't dredge up their past in order to hurt Johan or save Skyler's future. It wouldn't be right."

Wendy beams, and her gaze says something she's not. Pride, perhaps. Pride that I wouldn't risk another to save my own woman's ass.

"No, it wouldn't. However, there's something beyond bad in the last document. I think that will be your ace in the hole. Definitely something so hideous it will get him off Sky's case. If the information in that report gets out, he'll be destroyed. His career. His name. Everything. No hope for curing his dire circumstances."

I frown and open the last document, scanning it.

"What am I looking at?"

"It's a private accident report. One for which I had to use personal contacts and Michael had to promise favors to secure. This one is very serious, Parker."

"Wendy . . . I'm sorry. I wouldn't have asked had I known you were going to include Michael in this." My voice quavers, and tension builds at the base of my skull.

Wendy waves a hand in front of the screen. "No problem. You care about Skyler. I care about my new bestie. I don't want anyone hurting my new family. We have to stick together and do what it takes to protect one another, right?"

I close my eyes and take a single calming breath. "Yeah, Wendy, we do. Thank you."

"No worries. Michael will enjoy every second of cashing in his rewards with me." She winks. "And regardless of what you might think, he may be arrogant and growly around all of you, but he loves me to distraction. He wants me to have an extended family. Men and women I can count on. He knows all I've ever wanted in life is a family. Marrying him, working here, is giving me everything I ever dreamed of. I want to help, and he wants to help in order to make me happy."

Wendy's words are a sledgehammer to my pride. This woman is honest, straightforward, with no bullshit. If my parents had ever given me a sister, Wendy would be perfect. Even so, she's digging her way into my heart and the hearts of Bo and Royce as well.

Before I can say anything, she starts talking, speaking low into the phone.

"Apparently, Johan is a regular member of a sex club. A heavy-duty, *underground*, membership-required type of *torture* club."

The word *torture* rings like an alarm in my mind.

"I would disgrace the practice and the lifestyle by implying it's a BDSM club, because what they do there is not part of the lifestyle, nor is it always safe or possibly even consensual. This particular establishment caters to twisted, dark pleasures. Bloodletting, bestiality, burning, branding, whipping to scar, and so much more I can't even stomach to tell you."

"Jesus, Wendy." The sour taste hits my mouth again.

Bestiality?

Whipping to scar?

What the fuck.

"And Johan's a member?" I ask, knowing the answer already.

"Card carrying. Used to send a hundred thousand a month to an account I was able to track down through a bunch of shell companies and corporations."

I grind my teeth.

"Apparently, one night six months ago, Johan and two women had a bad accident."

"Accident?" I'm almost afraid to ask.

"One of the women ended up dead, the other so messed up in the head she still regularly sees a shrink."

"What happened?"

Wendy's jaw tightens, and her lips curl into a sneer.

I watch as she gets ahold of whatever response is plaguing her and emotionally detaches herself from it. She takes a slow breath and swallows. "According to the police statements, Johan and two women got high on cocaine. So high, the women agreed to allow Johan to tie them back-to-back to a spinning Saint Andrew's cross. The crosses are usually used so two Masters can access their subs at the same time or spin it around and trade, make the subs a little dizzy, off-kilter, that type of thing."

"Okay, I'm following . . ." The image of Skyler tied to one of those, blindfolded, forms in my mind's eye, and a foreboding shiver races up my spine.

"Well, Johan gagged one of them with his boxer briefs and blindfolded her. Usually the practice is when you gag a sub in any way, they have a signal, or something they hold that they can drop, a button they can push that makes noise. Basically, something to alert the Dom to the sub's distress. While high, they didn't put any of those safety precautions in place." She takes a deep breath and lets it out slowly. I can see by the lines around her mouth and the tired look in her eyes this story is hard to tell.

"It's okay, breathe through it and finish up when you're ready."

She takes another calming breath and then rushes what she says next. "So, while he was having sex with one woman, the other had gotten nauseous from the spinning and drugs, and he didn't realize she was vomiting behind her gag. She drowned in her own vomit. By the time he made his way to the other woman and pulled the gag out of her mouth, she was gone."

"Holy hell." My gut clenches, and my palms become sweaty.

"Yeah. It shouldn't have happened."

"And how did he not go to jail for this?"

Wendy shrugs. "The woman signed her life away in explicit consent forms. Also, you could see from the videotapes he didn't intend to hurt her. The club paid off the family, and used its ties to the judges they had in their pockets and kicked Johan to the curb. It was all swept under the rug as if nothing happened. I will say, if this gets out to the press . . . I may have to go into the witness protection program. The people who run the club are notoriously bad guys, and Michael and I want nothing to do with them."

"Christ! This is insanity. This man is disgusting, and he's got his clutches on Sky." I slam my fist down on the desk and push my hand through my hair so hard, the curls on top get tangled in my fingers, sending bouts of pain sliding along the surface of my scalp.

"Well, I'm pretty sure if you threaten him with this information, he'll back off instantly. He used up all his 'get out of jail free' cards on this one, which is probably why he's doing this to Skyler. He needs the money . . . *now*. Loan sharks are after him. He's got a drug addiction, and there's little interest from the industry for him to model now that his body is looking haggard."

This definitely explains why he's coming after Skyler. He's a man with nothing to lose, which puts Skyler in a very dangerous predicament. Johan is unstable. Thank God she's working and not scheduled to meet him and his lawyer for another few days.

"Thank you, Wendy. I need to try to call Sky again. Please, give my appreciation to Michael and let him know I owe him one. Same goes for you."

Her face lights up, and the earlier distress flickers out of sight. "Oh, I know you do. And I've already chosen what I want."

I furrow my brow and focus on my coy assistant.

"Which would be?" I tap my fingers against the wood surface of the desk in my suite.

She grins wide. "Three things, actually."

"Three?" I chuckle, enjoying her happiness, the darkness leaving her eyes. I decide to play along, needing to let go of the garbage we've uncovered. And I do owe her huge for this info. I don't know what she and Michael had to do to secure it, and frankly, I don't want to know. It would likely piss me off and make me want to tie her to her office chair, where we could keep an eye on her and make sure she doesn't get herself into any trouble.

"Number one . . ." She holds up her index finger. "Two weeks' paid vacation at the end of the year so Michael can whisk me away on our honeymoon."

"Done." That was painless.

She claps her hands with unhindered glee. My goodness, this woman is easy to please.

"Next?" I encourage her to continue.

"Double date with you and Sky, when she's in town, and me and Michael. I kinda sorta already bought four tickets to the Red Sox game next month so we could all go together."

I shake my head and laugh out loud. "Meaning you already planned to trample my baseball date with Sky."

She pouts. "Michael loves baseball as much as you do, and I want you two to be friends. Plus, I want to get to know Sky better."

I think about Michael and his cold, stoic nature. How he secured a fireball like Wendy is beyond me, but there's nothing wrong with the guy. Seems nice enough based on the one time we all met up at Lucky's. I actually know very little about him and am intrigued by their relationship and lifestyle choices. A double date isn't a bad idea. And Sky would love that it's a very normal, couple-like thing to do. My girl is always looking for ways to live outside of the limelight. Still, it's not likely she wouldn't garner any attention.

I focus my gaze on Wendy. "You know what going out on a date with Skyler could mean, Wendy? The paparazzi are relentless."

She shrugs. "Believe me when I say there's nothing to find on me except my picture on the IG website and only professional stuff to find about my man. I've made sure that's the only info anyone would find, even good hackers. Besides, I already told Michael, and he was ecstatic," she says with a flourish.

I snort, thinking of the extremely self-possessed man. "I highly doubt that."

"He was!" She pouts.

I narrow my gaze.

"Okay, maybe *ecstatic* is the wrong word to use, but he definitely didn't hate the idea, and I was able to use your contacts to score us seats behind the dugout. Which means we won't be bothered by other fans. It's where all the celebrities sit. Cost you a mint, by the way. I'm figuring out a way to make it 'entertaining staff and a client,' so we can write it off on IG's business expenses."

"Of course you are. What's the third?" I offer a crooked smile and wait for her to lay it on me. The next thing could be as crazy as a pajama party at the IG offices for all I know. With Wendy, anything is possible.

She frowns. "Third?"

"Minxy, you wanted three things from me for your sleuthing services." I cock an eyebrow and lean back in my chair to hear what crazy thing she's come up with.

"Oh yeah." Her eyes widen, and she twists her lips into an expression that leads me to believe she's uncomfortable . . . no, nervous.

"Wendy . . . you can ask me anything." I dip my voice to a tone that's calm and hopefully kind, especially in light of the harsh information we've burned through about Johan.

She licks her lips, a bit of anxiety set in her body language. "I was hoping, um, thinking maybe you could, you know . . ." Her head tips from side to side. "I mean, if it wouldn't be too much trouble, and you wanted to . . ." She twists her fingers in front of her.

"Spit it out . . . ," I laugh, trying to relieve some of the tension that seems to be rattling my usually unflappable assistant. The only other time I saw her uncomfortable or anything but in control was when the confidential pictures of Sky and me got out to the press. Other than that, she's solid as a rock and can be as hard if she wants to be.

"You see, I don't have anyone to, you know . . . um, at the wedding . . ."

"Wendy." I voice the single word as a command to get this show on the road already. She's beat around the bush long enough.

She lets out a fast breath. "Would you walk me down the aisle?" She lets out the request as if it was painful for her to say and she had to get it out as fast as possible.

I frown. "You want me to walk you down the aisle at your wedding? You mean . . . as in giving away the bride?"

She locks her fingers together and nods.

"Why?" My surprise is obvious.

"There's no one else. I don't have a father or brother to do the job, and I know you're technically my boss, but I look up to you, and respect you so much, and . . ." Her face crumbles for a brief moment. "Oh, forget it. Never mind." She shakes her head, and I can see her shutting down.

"Wendy, look at me."

She doesn't and looks everywhere but at me. "It's okay, it was stupid, and I . . . uh, I'm sorry I asked. It's too soon. You haven't known me that long, and—"

"And . . . shut the hell up and let me speak, woman!" I fire off hotly. Her head lifts, and her eyes darken.

"Jeez, woman, you'd tire a priest in the confessional! Let me speak." I lighten my tone but still put enough force into my demand for her to truly listen.

Wendy bites her bottom lip and nods.

"First and foremost, I'm honored you'd think of me. Second, it doesn't matter how long you've known someone. When they are a part of your life, it's not up to anyone but each individual to decide the value of a person has in their lives. I hold you in the highest regard, Wendy. I'd be very pleased to walk you down the aisle, if you wish."

She grins huge. "I wish. I mean, it would be *awesome*." The last word is said with a note of awe and excitement.

"Then I believe we are even." I smirk so she knows nothing she's requested is out of left field.

"Even Stephen, boss man!" She salutes me in a ridiculous imitation of a soldier signing off. "Let me know if there's anything else you need. I'm going to get back to checking out the staff at Renner Financial Services. What are you looking for in their financials anyway?"

"A thief," I state flatly.

She grimaces. "Bummer. Righto! Back to it." Wendy finishes and hits the button, and my iPhone reverts to the home screen.

I scan through the documents she sent once more. Johan Karr is a disgusting individual with some pretty twisted tastes. It looks like his family may have disowned him. His career is going downhill, and he's a druggie with very little to lose. My blood boils inside my veins.

How can this disgusting piece of shit have held the beauty that is Skyler in his hands?

Swallowing down the urge to break every last one of Johan's fingers, I count my lucky stars that I have Skyler now. I'm in her corner. Me and my team will do anything and everything to get her out of this mess he's created. I need to move carefully, plan out how I'm going to hit him with this information, so he'll back off Sky for good.

Without realizing it, I'm already tapping Sky's number on my phone. I need to hear her voice. Let her breathy timbre calm me down before I do something stupid. More than anything, I need to make sure she's okay. After finding out more information, seeing and hearing how dangerous Johan is, I need to know she's all right.

She answers breathlessly on the second ring. "Hey, honey . . ."

"Sky, baby." I let out the breath I was holding until I heard her beautiful voice. The burning anger licking at the edges of my nerves starts to ease, shifting into a simmer. "How are you?"

"I'm okay. Throwing myself into work today, trying to get my mind off everything. Tracey is doing some research about how to best drop this type of bomb to the press and how to deal with the backlash if he does release the pictures and write the book."

My entire body tightens like a live wire, and I breathe through the madness I feel weaving its way through my system. Regardless, Wendy's supersleuthing is the answer to the problem, and I make a promise to my girl, believing every word. "It's not going to happen."

Her voice is weak when she replies. "You say that, but you don't know Johan. When he sets his mind to do something, he does it, and if I don't pay him off . . ."

"You're not paying that piece of shit a penny. I've had Wendy looking into his past. He's got some nasty skeletons in his closet, ones we can use to get you out of this predicament."

Her tone lifts. "Really?"

The speck of hope in her voice fills my chest, pride swelling in my mind as I assure her, "Yeah, baby, really. I'm going to take care of this. When can we go over what I've got on your ex? Preferably when you're safe and sound, sitting within the privacy of your own home."

"As much as I want to know everything right now, I have to stay focused. We're shooting late tonight and early tomorrow. Later tomorrow, after we wrap and I'm home, I'll call you."

A ten-foot-tall pine tree isn't as high as I am knowing I can give her some relief. "Okay, honey." I use her endearment.

Her voice is calm when she says, "You really think whatever you got on him will get me off the hook?" I can hear the contentment in her tone, and I'm overjoyed to be the one to give her a modicum of comfort.

"Not think . . . *know.*"

Her voice teeters on the edge of tearful emotion. "Parker . . ." She sniffs, and I know she's trying to hold back the tears.

I press the phone closer to my ear, wanting to hear every inhalation, every word more clearly. "I'll always take care of you. As long as I'm alive, no one is ever going to hurt you. Not ever." It's a vow I intend to keep.

"Honey . . . I love . . ." She starts to make the most important admission in our relationship yet, one I've recently made myself, but I want to say it when I'm looking into her eyes, sitting next to her, preferably naked and in bed.

It kills me to make her wait. I too want to shout it from the rooftops. "Peaches, hold that thought until we can be together. I have some admissions of my own." My voice comes out rough, as though sandpaper scratched up my vocal cords.

"Yeah? Ones starting with *I love* . . . ," she teases, and the weight of the world slips away. This woman is all I need. Everything I could ever want.

I grin wide, tip my head back, and laugh at the ceiling. This woman is all mine. All freakin' mine, and I can't wait to tell her to her face how very much I adore her.

"Maybe," I admit softly.

"Then I'll look forward to when you're back from the West Coast and firmly planted in the best coast."

I chuckle at my silly girl. "Call me tomorrow, and we'll go over what Wendy found on Johan. Does that work for you?"

"Yeah, honey, it works perfect. And . . ." Her voice shakes a little. "Tell Wendy I appreciate whatever she did for me."

"You'll be able to tell her in person. When you come up next month for our baseball date, we'll be doing it as a foursome with Wendy and Michael."

Skyler giggles, and the sound fills my heart and wraps my body in all things good and right. The blackness, which slid all over my skin from reading through Johan's past, is falling away with every word my woman says.

"Sounds like fun! I enjoyed spending time with Wendy and her guy. He seems pretty serious; maybe a baseball game double date will lighten him up."

"Maybe. If anyone could do it, it would be the two of you wild women together."

She laughs heartily. "Beer and baseball won't hurt either."

My mouth waters at the idea of a ballpark hot dog in one hand, my arm around Skyler, that hand holding a cold beer while watching my favorite team play. It honestly sounds like the perfect day. "No, it wouldn't hurt. As long as you're there, I'll be golden."

"I can't wait," Skyler says happily.

"Me either. But first, we have to get through this case, your movie demands, and your scum bucket of an ex and his threats."

She groans. "Ugh. I just want to live my life. Why can't it all be easy, run smoothly?"

No truer words have ever been said. We all wish for ease but live with drama. "Nothing in life is smooth sailing. Sometimes we have to make our own waves in order to move forward."

"I guess so," she says distractedly, and I hear a voice in the distance calling to her. "I've gotta go. Break time is over."

"Okay, Peaches, remember to call me tomorrow after shooting, and we'll figure out the Johan situation together."

"Okay. Tonight, when you're done with your evening and you're back in your room . . ." She lets the rest of what she was going to say float away.

"Yeah?"

"Will you dream of me?"

"I always dream of you, Skyler. Always."

8

"Everything in place?" I call out to Royce as he maneuvers his big body through the crowd of club goers.

I'm sitting in the VIP section of a rooftop club in San Francisco called Skyline. According to a business contact who owns the joint and my googling, it's the premier hot spot for those who can afford the hefty entrance fee of two hundred a pop. Since I'm acquainted with the owner, I scored VIP for a song.

"Yep."

"And Rochelle?" I glance around him but don't see her.

"Touching up her makeup in the bathroom. The five finalists?" he adds, making his way up the five steps to the VIP section.

I hook a thumb over my shoulder behind me to where the men are sitting on the black velvet benches scattered throughout the posh area. "Settling in with drinks and talking to the couple of fill-in women we vetted and hired from the agency to make things not seem so focused on Rochelle but more of a party atmosphere."

He rubs at his chin and watches while our client finally makes her appearance. It's as if the crowd is parting like the Red Sea for her. She is quite the vision, wearing a silver swath of fabric that swishes around her body like shimmery water flowing over her curves. The dress has a deep V with a slip of fabric between her breasts to prevent the garment from showing her unmentionables. There's a slice up her thigh that leaves very little to the imagination about how long and toned her sexy legs are. I bite down on my lip and chance a glance at Roy.

"Jeez-us," Royce rumbles, his gaze all over our client. Knowing him as well as I do, I'm sure he's likely remembering the one time he got in *there* and wishing he could get in there again.

I clap a hand on his shoulder and squeeze. "For the greater good, brother."

He grits his teeth. "Got it. Don't like it, but I've got it. Where's Keehan?"

This time I grin and lift my chin. "At the bar, getting a cocktail."

Royce scans the area and then finds him. He also notices what I notice. One of the women we vetted is carrying on a conversation with the tall, geeky, buff, black Clark Kent. She flings her hair over her shoulder and touches his forearm. Keehan laughs at something she says and then looks down and back up, flirting with her.

I still as Rochelle grabs the banister and approaches us. "Are we ready for some fun tonight?" she says, all smiles and confidence.

"We are. Looks like your friend has already started without us." I nod to where Keehan is talking to the buxom brunette, setting the plan into motion.

Rochelle's gaze flashes to where Keehan is, and a frown slips across her face. "Who's he talking to?"

I shrug nonchalantly. I didn't hire her to be in the VIP section, but I did hire her to hit on Keehan mercilessly, mostly because she's beautiful and looks a fuck-of-a-lot like Rochelle. What's more entertaining is Keehan is none the wiser. He's genuinely putting a little mack daddy action on the model. I'm proud of him.

"Not one of the women I hired for the VIP." I fudge the truth.

"Shouldn't Keehan be over here, with us?" Her tone is agitated.

"Why?" Royce asks flatly, still probably miffed she had the goods, as in *him*, and could so easily move on to the prospects we've chosen.

Apparently when Rochelle says something is fun, she means it. When it's over, she doesn't look back. It's her nature. If it weren't Royce she's blowing off, I wouldn't have a problem with it. People are who they are. Plus, she did make it clear to him, regardless of whether he might have been feeling differently.

Her gaze narrows. "Because he should be checking out these guys, helping me pick the right one." Her tone is put out, and I have to hold back my own laughter at the haughtiness she's expressing.

"And why would he do that?" I query lightly, making sure not to lead her horse to water so quickly.

She huffs. "He's my best friend. My right hand in all things. I would assume he wouldn't want me making a bad choice. This is the rest of my life."

I nod, agreeing. "True, but maybe he doesn't want to see you commit to another man the way you've committed to him all these years."

She frowns and leans a hand on the banister, seeming to need the balance. "What do you mean?" She wraps one arm around her waist but doesn't so much as glance my way. Her eyes are glued to the spectacle before us.

Keehan leans in, brushing the woman's hair off her shoulder. She preens beautifully and smiles away at his gentle affection.

"Well, he's always been the constant man in your life in all ways except physically, right? Maybe he's tired of the celibate lifestyle you were hinting he had earlier in the week."

Her brow furrows. "I . . . I guess so."

"And with you offering up all that is you, maybe he realized he better find his own replacement." I intentionally dig the knife in a little.

"That's absurd. I'd never replace Keehan. He's everything to me." She grips the banister with both hands, fingers blanching with how tight she's holding on.

I set my hand on her shoulder, and she finally looks at me. "Is he?"

"Yes." She shrugs off my hand.

"Then why are we here?" Royce questions rather dramatically.

Her nose crinkles, and she purses her lips. "I need a man in my life and my bed. Eventually I want to have a child. A legacy to carry on what I've built. What we've built." Her eyes flash with heat, but they don't stray from Keehan.

"And you want to do that without Keehan?" I push.

"No! He'll always be a part of my life . . ."

"In what way?" I push harder.

"All ways," she fires back.

I shake my head. "Not if you don't find him attractive. That's why all of these men are here and he's about to score with a hot brunette."

"This is ridiculous." She spins on her heels and practically storms to the VIP section.

"Not what I had hoped would happen." I sigh and massage the back of my neck.

Royce smiles away, hands in the pockets of his tailored-to-perfection suit, and rocks back on his heels.

"What do you know that I don't? The situation feels pretty out of hand right now. I'd expected her to see him with Gloria over there and get so jealous lasers would spew from her eyes, causing her to dramatically intervene and claim her man. Only she's now in the VIP section about to chat up her prospects."

"Oh, she's jealous. Look at her." He lifts his chin in our client's direction.

I turn around and watch Rochelle politely introduce herself to the firefighter, whose gaze slides up and down her form and then back to her face. She offers him a tight smile, not appreciating his assessment. However, as she speaks to him, her gaze keeps flitting to the bar where Keehan and his companion are carrying on. Her lips seem to tighten, and her jaw firms in what I now know, after having been around her for the past week, is pure irritation.

"I think we should turn this up a notch. What do you say?" Royce grins wickedly.

"How so?"

"I'm going to go over and invite Keehan and his lady companion to have a drink in our section." He grins some more.

"You're ruthless." I cover my smirk with my hand.

"Perhaps, but you've got a woman to get back to, I've got a life back in Boston, and I'm tired of being in Cali. It's time to turn this motha out."

"Brother, I couldn't agree with you more." The desire to get the hell out of California and back to the East Coast and Skyler is burning through my veins.

Royce nods and heads over to where Keehan and his friend are at the bar. I see him order a drink from the bartender and then speak to the couple. Once he has his drink, the two of them follow him back to the VIP section, all smiles and soft touches.

"Keehan." I offer my hand in greeting.

"Parker." He shakes my hand. "This where all the excitement is happening?" His word choices encourage the party vibe, but they come across solemn. He is definitely affected by what we've set in motion for Rochelle, regardless of spending time with the beautiful woman next to him.

"Yep. And who is this lovely lady?" I pretend not to know the woman I hired from the modeling service where I found the other women.

"Gloria," she states without missing a beat, following along.

"Pretty name for a pretty lady." Royce lifts her hand and kisses her knuckles. It's one of his signature moves when meeting someone he thinks is sexy.

I nudge Roy's shoulder, and Keehan's eyes narrow at the spectacle of Rochelle laughing at one of the men's jokes, slapping his shoulder playfully.

"Come, Gloria," Keehan says. "I want to introduce you to my friend Rochelle."

I grin and watch as the two approach the crowd we've assembled in the private section of the club.

"Man, I wish I'd brought popcorn. This shit is about to get interesting," Royce says, chuckling, as I watch Rochelle's eyes turn to ice shards and her bitch face come out at the introduction of Keehan's companion.

***

As the night wears on, the dance Rochelle and Keehan do around one another is comical at best, annoying at worst.

"Why the hell hasn't he made his move?" I growl into my gin and tonic as the two couples square off on the dance floor. Rochelle has chosen the doctor, who is essentially the Keehan look-alike. Keehan has stuck to Gloria like glue, even if his eyes have followed Rochelle all over this club.

Royce shakes his head. "I will admit to this being exhausting. Why the hell did we agree to do this?"

I cock an eyebrow and point a finger at him around my drink. "You chose this client and this job because you fell for a pretty face."

He inhales so deep his nostrils flare. "I will admit to being taken by her looks. The woman is fiiiiine."

I nod because he is not wrong. Rochelle is an absolute knockout. Legs for days. A tight body. High cheekbones. Bright smile. Long dark hair. Intelligent. Driven. An absolute catch. She just needs the right fisherman to throw his net over her.

"True." I watch as her body undulates suggestively around the doctor.

Keehan's gaze is glacial as he watches her seductive dance.

Silently I root for the man. *Come on, Keehan. Take charge.*

It happens when the doctor puts a possessive hand on Rochelle's hip and grinds his crotch into her backside. His other hand runs up her rib cage and over her breast. Rochelle goes still in his arms, and her face contorts into an expression of discomfort. In the doctor's defense, she was grinding up on him, but she was the one in control. She touched what she wanted, not the other way around. This gave the impression to me, and likely to him, she'd appreciate a little more handsy behavior from her dance partner, but his bullishness has absolutely gone too far.

Royce and I stand up abruptly from where we're sitting and head to the dance floor to intervene. When we make it to the duo, Keehan is right there. He grabs the doctor by the wrist, yanks the offending hand away from Rochelle, and twists it behind the man's back. The doc hollers in pain.

"Watch it! I'm a doctor!" he yells pitifully and rather drunkenly.

Rochelle crosses her arms over herself defensively. "Then you shouldn't have been grabbing my boob with it!"

Keehan twists the guy's hand higher. "Apologize to the lady."

"But she started with her grinding . . ."

Keehan roars into his ear and yanks his arm up higher until he cries out once more. "I said, apologize."

"Sorry. Shit, I'm sorry. Let me go!" he pleads.

Keehan keeps the man's arm twisted but puts his other hand around the guy's neck and grasps his chin, forcing him to look at Rochelle while Keehan grates angrily into his ear. "I'll let you go, but you will turn around and get the hell out of this club and never look back at my woman again. You see her . . ."

"Yeah, man, I see her. I see her!" he screeches painfully.

"No. You. Fucking. Don't. See. Her. Ever again. You hear me?" He pinches the man's face and hurls him toward the exit. "Now get the fuck out of here."

The doctor catches himself before falling to the ground. He rolls his shoulders and shakes out his arms. "You're nuts! And the two of you"—he points to Rochelle and Keehan—"can have each other. You're both a mess!" he snarls, and cuts his way through the crowd and out of the club.

I come up around Gloria, who is standing there with wide eyes watching it all go down. I lean down near her ear and slip an extra couple of hundred dollars into her hand. "Now's the time for you to disappear. A tip for a job well done." I wink, and she grins, waving as she slinks through the patrons to head home. She's already been paid handsomely by the agency, but extra cash never hurt anyone, and she did do an excellent job making Rochelle jealous and Keehan feel like the strong man he is. Though the Hercules he became when the doctor touched Rochelle inappropriately was not something I expected he had hidden inside of him.

Rochelle throws her arms around Keehan, planting her face against his neck. He wraps his arms around her and runs his hands up her bare back until her rapid-fire breathing slows and his own temper gentles.

"If you weren't here . . . Ugh, I can't believe I was so stupid. Rubbing up on him like that," she admits.

"Why the hell were you doing that? I've never seen you act so wanton." His words are a fiery brand on her ego, and she pulls back but doesn't take her arms from around his neck, nor does he let her go.

"I was trying to make you as jealous as you were making me!" Her voice rises with her agitation. "Although I'm not sure you could see anything with Gloria all over you like a wet freakin' blanket."

"She was not all over me. We were dancing. Unlike you, grindin' all over the blubbering idiot I kicked out."

"Are you saying it was my fault he grabbed me inappropriately?" She flings herself back again, her face losing its calm and composure.

Keehan locks his hands around her waist above her ample ass so she can't move away. "Absolutely not. No woman is asking to be groped unless that man is her man."

She places a hand on his chest. "And what was that about you calling me *your woman?*"

"You are," he grinds out.

Her gaze narrows, the lights of the club making specks of color dance across her face. "Am not! Says who?" she demands angrily.

"Says me. I'm tired of this dance, Chelle. I've been your man for the last decade, and it's high time I be your man in *all the ways* that count." He runs both of his hands down to her ass and squeezes her against him.

"What are you doing?" she cries out in surprise, but holds on to his neck, bringing her body closer, instead of pushing away like she did with the doctor.

"Groping *my woman,*" he states honestly.

Her mouth opens and her eyes blaze, but before she can fire off a saucy retort, he slams his lips over hers.

I want to applaud as the two go at it on the dance floor, mouths fused, hands groping.

"Damn. I thought she was hot for me. Shee-it. It was nothing compared to the way she's lightin' up for him."

Keehan holds Rochelle close, one of his hands firmly on her ass, lifting her up against him, the other tunneled into her hair, holding her face to his so he can devour her. And devour he does.

"Um, I'm wondering if I should stop this before they tear one another's clothes off in the middle of the club."

Royce chuckles and nods. "Yeah, that kiss is . . . still going."

"Like the Energizer Bunny. Jesus Christ. I'll break it up." I head over to the couple sucking face, giving the entire club one helluva show, and tap Keehan on the shoulder.

He shrugs off my touch, focused solely on the woman he's kissing.

"Keehan, man, you gotta let up. Take your girl and get out of here," I suggest loud enough to break through their lust.

"Huh?" He pulls away, and his unfocused gaze centers on mine before he looks around the club. "Shit. Chelle, sweetheart, we gotta take this elsewhere." He hooks a hand around her waist, and she looks dazedly around her before she starts giggling.

Rochelle, giggling. Not something I expected I'd ever witness with the fiery female.

"'K, your place or mine?"

"Mine's closer," he rumbles, and clears his throat.

She laughs. "You're on the tenth floor, and I'm the penthouse."

"Like I said, my place is closer." He nips at her lips, and she melts against his side. "Come on. I think we've got some life-altering things to discuss."

"Oh, we're not talking." Her statement is more of a suggestion of what they'll be doing, which probably doesn't include conversation.

Keehan looks down at the woman he's gone for and smiles. "All right, making love until you fall asleep exhausted in my arms, then talking over breakfast."

She hums against his neck and nuzzles him there. Keehan's smile, when he looks up at me, is a moment I'll never forget. Seeing a man with his arms full of the one thing he wanted more than anything else in life, something he never thought he'd have . . . powerful. The joy and relief at securing the love of his life is an incredible moment to witness.

Keehan leads Rochelle toward the door.

Royce calls out to them, and the couple stop and look back. Keehan, none too pleased with being interrupted in his goal of getting the woman of his dreams home and in his bed, has an angry expression plastered across his face. Rochelle is happily dazed as she tilts her head.

"Tomorrow afternoon we meet up to go over the staff findings. Then we're off to Boston tomorrow night."

"Royce is right. Once we've nailed down the issue of who's embezzling from Renner Financial Services, I don't think we're needed here anymore . . . unless of course Rochelle wants us to continue finding her a mate," I add to ensure Rochelle steps up and fights for her man the way he fought for her.

Keehan's body stiffens next to her. She sidles up to him, gluing her body to his side. "No, I agree. I most certainly will not be needing your services after we figure out the embezzlement. I've finally got the man I want to be with, the right man for me."

I smile even when Royce's body language goes from easygoing to solid rock. He's putting up his walls and applying his armor. I want to extend a friendly word or a gesture of some sort, one that says I know what he's going through, that I've felt the sting of rejection in the past myself, but now is not the time, and he wouldn't welcome it. He's not that type of guy. He'll deal with the burn of what wasn't meant to be in his own way, and I have to let him have that. I'm not his mother—most certainly not his father. All I can do is stay back and be his friend. His brother in this disappointment.

"We'll see you two around ten," I state, making sure they know we're not expecting them to come in early.

Rochelle runs her hand up Keehan's chest. "Take me home."

"Better make it noon, fellas. We're going to be very, very busy." He licks his lips and looks like he's about to devour Rochelle right here.

Before he can dip his head, I clap my hands loudly. Both of them jerk and must realize they're still standing in the club. I smile. "Carry on, then. Be safe."

Rochelle offers a little wave, and I head to the VIP section to release the men and tell them Rochelle has made her decision. When I get to the section, they've all paired off with the models and are enjoying themselves, so I leave them be.

Royce takes the steps behind me and glances around the area. "Damn, we're good. Matchmaking motherfuckers." He shakes his head, and I laugh.

I clap Roy on the shoulder. "Come on. Drinks on me, brother."

He nods and follows me to the bar silently. When we get a seat, the bartender puts a whiskey in front of him and a fresh gin and tonic in front of me, and I lift my glass to his.

"To another successful job."

He clinks his glass against mine. "Cheers."

We both sip our drinks, and then I stare at his big dark form, the lights making his normally kind face look a bit more sinister. "You upset she chose Keehan?" I ask.

He shakes his head. "Nah. Wasn't meant to be, like you said."

"Still, you liked her," I note softly, not wanting to rub it in.

"Yeah, I did, but I think I liked the *idea* of her more."

I frown and set my drink on the napkin in front of me. "How so?"

"It's time, man." He's dead serious.

I cock an eyebrow. "Time?"

"For me to settle down. Feel it in my bones." He lifts his shoulders as if he's feeling something right this very second in his body.

"Momma Sterling pressuring you?" I know his mother is one meddling woman.

He laughs and sips his drink. "Always, but not more than usual. She wants me to be happy, so of course she brings up the benefits of a good woman." He sighs. "Want to have something to look forward to at home. Something waiting for me. A warm body to sleep next to. A woman I can love and dote on, put my babies in her and watch them grow. It's time," he says again matter-of-factly.

I nod.

"Do you feel that yourself with Skyler?"

I shrug. "I know I love her and can't wait to tell her. I have a feeling she loves me and is waiting to tell me too. She's mentioned moving to Boston, and I'm all for it. Mostly because, like a lot of the things you said, I want to come home to her. I see Sky, and I want to tell her everything that happened in my day and am genuinely interested in what happened in hers. I want to shove my fist in the face of every costar she has but glory in the fact that they may get to pretend with her, but I get the real thing. I get all of Sky's morning smiles and sleepy *hellos*. I get all of her *good nights*. And her beautiful body is mine to worship. If that's what you mean by feel it, then hell yeah, man, I *feel* it with Sky."

Royce chuckles and claps my back. "Happy for you. I can imagine it's not easy being in a relationship with a celebrity, but the two of you seem to be handling it A-OK."

"I'd do anything to be with Skyler. Now that I've had her, all of her, I'll never want for anything else. Her fame is an inconvenience and nothing more."

"Good man. Now update me on the ex and his threats. What all did Wendy find?"

I sneer and suck back the rest of my gin and tonic in one go.

"Shee-it. That bad?" His eyebrows rise up on his forehead.

I raise the glass to the bartender. "Another round, please."

He nods, and Royce finishes his whiskey.

"Yeah, it's that bad." I grit my teeth and hold my hands in fists until the bartender brings our refreshers.

"Lay it on me, brother."

9

The next morning, Royce and I walk through the offices of Renner Financial Services to find Helen back from her vacation and making coffee. The woman is painfully thin, but when she turns around, I'm shocked at how much she looks like Rochelle. Similar hair, makeup application, and attire. Pencil skirt, stilettos, and a silk blouse. What she's wearing honestly could have come direct from Rochelle's closet.

I frown and glance at Roy. "You seeing what I'm seeing?"

He runs his gaze over the slight woman. "Has no booty, but damn. Girl could be Rochelle's sister."

I nod. "Weird," I whisper, before Helen smiles and greets us.

"Gentlemen. I'm back and ready to find out the goods. Did you find Rochelle a match?" Her eyes are more excited than should warrant for a simple employee. Then again, she did say she'd worked here for ages.

"Client came to her own conclusions about the opposite sex and the individual's contribution to her life," Royce offers vaguely.

She grins wide and squeals. "Eek. I can read between the lines. She's got a man, but you can't say one way or another because you're all professional and smooth operators!"

"We're just going to go on in and wait for Rochelle, if you don't mind."

Obviously excited, she waves a hand and leads us into her boss's office. "Have a seat. I can get you some coffee . . ."

Before either of us can accept, Rochelle and Keehan enter the room, both with dazzling smiles and a bounce to their steps. A lot of sex will do that for you. It's exactly how I feel after a weekend with Skyler.

Helen's head lifts and turns to the door, but her eyes are not on welcoming her boss; they are focused solely on Keehan. "Hi, Keehan," she whispers throatily.

"Hey, Helen!" He greets her warmly, hooks an arm around her shoulders, and squeezes, giving her a side hug. "Long time no see. How was the time off?"

She shrugs and pouts like a woman flirting and trying to get a man to look at her mouth. "It would have been better if I'd had a man like you to share it with." Her eye color changes from a deep brown to coal black, and I can practically see the animated cartoon hearts floating around her head.

Keehan nods. "Now that I understand." He rubs her arm, and she sighs.

Then Keehan continues, not realizing the effect his touch and words are having on Helen. "If I didn't have Chelle to be with on my vacations, they'd be boring as all get-out too!"

Helen's nostrils flare at the mention of Rochelle, and her expression falters into one of irritation. As quickly as it crosses her face, it's gone and a fake smile in its place.

I am not getting a good vibe about this interaction.

"Glad to have you back, Helen. It's been rough without you," Rochelle states over her shoulder, going to her desk and sitting down.

"I doubt that," Helen whispers under her breath, but it's loud enough for me to hear.

"What's that?" Keehan asks.

"Don't doubt that." She blinks up at Keehan prettily.

"You remember the team from International Guy?" Rochelle asks.

Helen's lips twitch into a scowl for a nanosecond until she turns around and places the fake smile back on her face. "Yes, Ms. Renner. Introductions were made prior to me leaving. I was delighted to see you'd moved forward with your plan."

"I have," Rochelle confirms, happiness filling the air in the office with positive energy.

Helen twists her fingers together. "Any sparkling, noteworthy prospects?" Her voice wavers, almost as if everything in her existence is hinging on Rochelle's answer.

Rochelle's entire face lights up. "Turns out, I didn't need IG to find me a match." Her eyes land on Keehan's, and he moves from Helen's side to Rochelle's.

Helen's face goes completely blank as she takes in how close Keehan stands to Rochelle. "What do you mean?"

I cant my head and watch her body language and the microexpressions as they flit across her face when Rochelle wraps a possessive arm around Keehan's waist with her right arm and rests her other hand low on his belly above his belt. A very telling location. Rochelle's body language telegraphs loud and clear the intimacy she and Keehan have shared.

Helen inhales dramatically, and her hands clench into fists at her side. "I'm not sure I understand."

"Isn't it obvious?" Rochelle rubs Keehan's belly up to his chest and stands by his side, bringing her body closer.

Helen stands stiffly, her eyes blazing white-hot fire. "Not to me, it isn't," she grates through clenched teeth.

"Rochelle finally saw what was in front of her all along . . . ," I add, watching this woman silently fume. If smoke came out of her ears, I wouldn't be surprised.

"Which is what?" She scowls.

"That Keehan is the man I've always desired, and I was too afraid to risk what we already had, of course." Rochelle laughs, tipping her head up, and Keehan lays a big, fat smacker on her lips in front of all of us.

Helen's expression contorts into one of shock, then rage. "What!" she screeches unusually loud, almost as if it is ripped right from her very lungs.

"You know, you were right all along, Helen. Apparently, Rochelle was hot for me," Keehan jokes, nipping Rochelle's lips. "We're together now. Isn't it fantastic!" He's gazing into Rochelle's face. He's a man with the entire world in his arms, and he knows it.

"No! All the conversations we've had. You said . . . you said you were only friends, and she'd never see you that way!" Helen's response is one of a scorned lover, not a friendly employee.

Keehan and Rochelle both cut their gazes to Helen, but it's Keehan who speaks first. "I thought you'd be happy for us. You were always saying how I needed to get out, find a woman of my own. Someone I could take care of, who could take care of me." He eases his woman's chest to his front. "Rochelle has always been that, and we finally realized what we had was more than friendship."

The woman digs her hands into her hair and pulls at the waves, screeching, "This can't be happening!" She shakes her head back and forth, her entire face darkens, and her pupils are completely black.

I feel like I'm having an out-of-body experience while watching a demon take over the petite body of Helen Humphrey.

"You said she was your friend. You said you weren't like that with her!" she yells at the top of her lungs.

"Damn, girl, relax." Royce raises a hand, but she continues in a storm of anger and begins pacing the floor.

"Helen, what's the matter with you?" Rochelle asks softly. "You're acting strange. Are you feeling all right?" Rochelle moves out of Keehan's arms and is set to approach the woman.

I shake my head, and Royce stands up, creating a wall between Helen and the couple. Keehan pulls Rochelle back into his arms protectively.

Helen points a finger at Rochelle. "You get everything! Everything you want. It's all yours. The job. Money. The man! I'm so tired of being your little pushover doormat! I'm tired of watching you treat men like playthings. I'm tired of watching Keehan pine away for you, year after year, and never once look at me!" Her mouth twists into an ugly sneer. "I'm as good as you. No, better! Because I'm not a stuck-up bitch! My God, Keehan, you can't possibly want to be with this trick!" Her body jolts with the effort of expelling so much fury, and she stands with her chest heaving and a nasty snarl about her lips.

Keehan lets Rochelle go and walks around the desk toward Helen.

Royce puts out a hand. "I wouldn't if I were you. She's unstable, man."

"Unstable!" she screams. "I'll show you unstable." She grabs a crystal vase filled with flowers and chucks it at Rochelle. It falls short, crashing through Rochelle's glass desk, shards flying everywhere.

Before Royce can finagle his arms around the spastic woman, she lunges for Rochelle with the strength and speed of a puma. Her little body lurches past Royce and Keehan and tackles the client. Rochelle falls to the floor, and she cries out.

"Fuck!" I roar, and enter the fray, trying to step around glacier-shaped pointy desk pieces and get any kind of grip on the two women tussling, rolling around over glass, punching, kicking, and pulling hair. At one point, a black length of hair flies through the air, and I notice it's one half of Helen's extensions.

"Bitch! Those cost a fortune!" Helen tugs at Rochelle's hair, but nothing happens. Either Rochelle has awesome extensions, or her hair is real. My bet would be the latter.

Rochelle rolls on top of Helen, grabs the other side of her hair, and rips that one out too, holding it up triumphantly.

Helen screeches in pain and runs her pointed nails down the sides of Rochelle's arms, leaving nasty red welts.

"Bitch." Rochelle reiterates what Helen called her. "Oh, hell no! I'm far worse, you triflin' ho! I'm your worst fucking nightmare! You're fired, and I'm pressing charges!" She grabs Helen by the head and smashes her skull down against the carpet. The woman's eyes roll, and the fight leaves her body momentarily.

I shove a piece of desk aside and kick at her office chair. "No . . . no . . . no!" I rush to grab Helen's arms right as Royce loops one of his own arms around Rochelle's waist and pulls her up into the air, where she kicks wildly. He twists and deposits her in front of Keehan's chest. Her man wraps his arms around her immediately, locking her in place.

"Hoo-boy! I can't remember the last time I saw two women fight it out over a man." Roy's grinning while straightening his bespoke suit.

I chuckle, because it's impossible not to at this juncture.

Royce picks up the phone off the floor and presses a button. "I'm going to need security in Rochelle Renner's office. We have a woman who needs to be detained, and please call the police."

He nods and sets the phone in its cradle on the floor near the shattered desk. Large shards of glass point every which way, making her office a dangerous place for the two of them to have been rolling around fighting, but neither of them seems to need more than a first aid kit.

While Keehan speaks to Rochelle in hushed tones in the corner of her office, I tend to Helen. Royce gets me a wet washcloth, and I wipe away the blood from her head and nose. She's mumbling under her breath, and her gaze is unfocused. It's as if she's completely left the building altogether.

I dip my head and try to hear what she's saying.

"Was supposed to be mine. I got the money now. He was supposed to be mine. I got the money now."

She keeps repeating the two sentences over and over, and it hits me what she's referring to. The embezzled funds.

"Roy, can you keep an eye on her? I have a call to make."

I glance down at the woman, who's rocking back and forth, knees to her chest and chanting.

I leave the office and walk down the hall, pull out my phone, and call Wendy.

"Hey, boss man, did you get your girl?"

"Girl?" I frown, thinking she's referring to Skyler.

"She's been stealing from RFS. I sent over the report ten minutes ago. I narrowed it down to a Helen Humphrey. She's the only employee who's had majorly fluctuating finances with tens of thousands of dollars deposited every two to three weeks. Plus, when I dug a little deeper, she was doing it using Rochelle's access code. Technically, it looks like Rochelle is stealing from herself."

"Wow."

"Yeah, according to what I gathered, she's stolen over six hundred thousand dollars in the last two years. The woman needs to be in a jail cell."

I look over my shoulder at the open office door and can barely see the slight speck of a woman who lost it this morning. "Or a psych ward."

"Uh, something tells me there's a serious story behind that reply. One I'm eager to hear!" Wendy chuckles.

"I'll let Royce update you. I'm planning to visit Sky on my way home."

"Figured. Which is why I already have your flight taking you direct to the Big Apple tonight on the red-eye, instead of back home."

I grin. "You are the best."

"I know. Don't forget it!"

"Please, you'd never let me."

She laughs loudly. "True. True!" Her voice gentles. "Have you, uh, talked to Sky about the information I found?"

I lower my voice. "Not yet. She knows I've got information to share and it's not pleasant. Since we're going home tonight, I'll save it for when I see her."

"Face-to-face. Probably a good idea. Let me know if there's anything else you need from me, and hopefully, you'll come home soon. I'm tired of having the Flirt Master Two Thousand as my only company. Or better yet, next time you and Royce feel the need to flee, take him with you."

I'm laughing out loud and shaking my head. "Giving you a run for your money, eh?" I imagine Bo hitting on Wendy nonstop, barbs flying across the office, her verbal retaliation.

"Nah, I can handle him."

"God willing!" I hear Bo's instant quip, and then suddenly I've got his familiar voice in my ear as he continues. "Brother. Read through what Wendy sent over. I'm here for you. Whatever you need. If you want me to get on a plane and meet you somewhere to beat some ass, I'm right there with you. The shit he's pulling with Sky . . . fuck no. Nuh-uh. Not one of ours." He growls into the line.

I close my eyes and press my fist against my forehead. "Thanks, Bo. For now, I'm going to head to New York, hash it out with Sky, and plan our next steps."

"I can meet you there. Hell, I can beat you there, with you being on the West Coast."

I grin. "'Preciate it, brother. More than you know, but I'm going to go solo on this one. Will let you know if any further action is needed."

"All right. You know I'm a phone call away."

"I do."

"Get back to it, then, and tell Roy I'll be seeing him at the office. Sophie's been calling about some document she needs him to look over immediately."

"Have her email it to him."

"She did. Apparently since he's been so focused on you and the client, he hasn't picked up his emails for the last couple of days."

I sigh. "We've been busy. Between this shit with Sky, the embezzlement, and finding the client a mate, it's been one thing after another."

"Yeah, that's what I figured. Also had Wendy look into Sophie's new boyfriend." Bo's tone is neutral, not betraying anything.

My heart starts pounding, and I'm worried Bo's going to impart additional shitty information that will make me lose my mind. Skyler's man issue is already running rampant in my head. I don't need my best female friend's new beau added to the list.

"Please tell me he's clean . . ."

He chuckles. "Checks out. Wendy said she did her worst, and the dude is positively squeaky. And get this . . . apparently he recently visited a jewelry store and bought a very expensive item."

"You think he's going to pop the question? Already? It's been what, a month or so?"

"Brother, I don't know. You've seen Sophie . . . all of Sophie. Not to mention she's smart, rich, and full of life. No reason to wait when you've got something like that on the hook."

"Says the man whose dick shrivels up and dies at the mere thought of commitment." I rub at the back of my neck, trying to work out the tension. "Fuck. He's going to pop the question."

Bo howls with laughter. "Suspect it."

"I'll give her a call. Check in on her."

"Probably a good idea. Make sure she's not jumping into her rebound man after you."

I instantly take offense. "I wasn't her man in order for her to have a rebound, punk ass!" My voice sounds scathing even to my own ears.

"If you say so. Woman seemed pretty hung up on you when we were in France," he says with a nonchalance his comment doesn't carry.

"A lot happened when we were in France. Then everything, my whole freakin' life, changed when I was in New York. And that's forever, brother."

"Figured that too."

"Then why are you bringing this up?" I frown and tap against the wall of the hallway outside Rochelle's office. I turn around and lean my back against it.

"Because I know how much you care for Sophie. How much we all do. Just want you to know, things are progressing in her love life at warp speed. The train has left the station, and it is not stopping."

I swallow down the instant worry I have about my friend being screwed over. Not every person is Kayla. Skyler's not Kayla, and Sophie's man isn't either. Not everyone is out to burn another's heart. "As long as she's happy, I'm happy. The bastard better worship her."

"No joke."

No sooner do I finish my call with Bo than the elevator doors open and a pair of security guards leading a police officer walk up.

"In there." I point to Rochelle's open door.

The three of them enter, and I follow closely behind.

***

I'm bone weary as I slouch into the comfort of one of Rochelle's office couches. She's lying longways on the opposite one, her forearm over her eyes. The cops have taken Helen for processing, and a team of janitors came and cleaned up the mess, carting away the giant shards of broken glass. Her office looks far too open and bare without the large glass desk taking up the bulk of the space.

"We got lucky, you know," I mutter to her prone form. Keehan and Royce are pulling together the final reports to give to the cops. Rochelle's going to hire a forensic accounting firm to do a full audit of the company's books to determine the extent of Helen's damage.

Eventually she'll probably get back some of the money the woman stole, but these things take a long time when the legal system gets involved.

"How you figure?"

"Helen wanted Keehan. You had Keehan this whole time without even knowing it. She was doing everything she could to secure him. Used your access code to steal from you. Dressed like you. Did her hair and makeup the same. Never a good combination. Then she throws a vase at you, busts up your desk, and the two of you go at it."

She sighs. "I shouldn't have been so stupid. He's always been in my life. My right hand, the man I go to for everything. I compare all others to him and have always found them lacking."

I snort-laugh. "I guess sometimes it takes an expensive business agreement to find what's been in front of your face all along."

She smiles, lifts her arm, and winks. "Worth every penny."

"Glad to hear it. Do you mind if I give you another bit of advice?"

"Would I be able to stop you?" One of her dark eyebrows rises in question.

I grin, appreciating the banter with Rochelle. I can see why Royce went for her. Besides the outer package, which is nice, she's got a quick wit and a smart mouth. All of which can be a lot of fun for any man, especially a man like Royce. In a lot of ways, Rochelle Renner is the perfect package for Royce. Still you can't change that the woman is going to work herself into the ground and doesn't want to deal with familial distractions. Royce's mother and sisters are so deeply enmeshed in who he is, there is only room for a woman to be added to his heart, not replace the women already there.

"Shoot." She turns on her side and rests her head in her hand, giving me her undivided attention.

"It's not always about seeing what's right in front of your face, although it was very important in your case. Sometimes that part can be managed by opening your eyes."

"Then what is it about? I'm on pins and needles here." She smirks.

I take a deep breath and hope I'm not about to offend her. We've ended this case with her falling for her man and weeding out an embezzler; the last thing I want to do is piss her off when she's already got a lot on her plate. Still, I wouldn't be doing her justice if I didn't put the truth out there for her to chew on.

"I firmly believe the answer to what you've been seeking is not as simple as finding a mate, or being the best in your field. It's about wanting what you already have. Keehan's always been there. Fear got in the way. Don't let fear control your life . . . and for the love of God, live a little!" I scold playfully. "If you spend all of your time working, you spend none of your time living."

The door opens. Keehan goes right to Rochelle's side and sits in the curve her bent hips leave available on the couch.

I stand up. "I'm going to use the restroom before we head to the hotel and airport."

I move to leave the room, and she calls out, "Parker," and points to the closed door in her office.

"Thanks." I open the door and find a perfectly white bathroom. Everything is white. The floor, the walls, the towels, the sink, even the faucet.

"Strange woman," I mumble under my breath, and take care of business. As I'm washing my hands I notice the vanity mirror runs all the way across the sink and the area behind the toilet. I grin and think back to the four times I've written a message on a mirror. In a split second I decide if there's a lipstick tube in the first drawer, I'll do it. If not, I won't.

I open the drawer and find it filled to the brim with makeup and beauty products. Three tubes of lipstick practically gleam in the right-hand corner of the drawer. I pull one out and find a deep crimson color just itching to be used.

"Must be fate." I take in the cocky expression on my face as I lift the tip to the corner of the mirror and write Rochelle a little reminder.

Want what you have.
Love, Me

I cap the lipstick and toss it back into the drawer. Time to catch a plane and get to my girl, because I am one man who absolutely wants what I have.

10

The town car Rochelle hired pulls up to San Francisco International Airport at the curb for departures. Royce and I pour out of the vehicle and secure our luggage from the driver.

Once we've both checked into our flights, we head to the closest bar. "Drink first, food after?"

"Hell yeah," Royce rumbles on an exhausted sigh, his big form trudging through the airport crowd in the direction of the nearest flashing neon sign. We find a sports bar, if you can really call it that, in the dead center of the airport; it will do for our purposes. The top-shelf liquor in gleaming bottles along the back of the bar makes it a good choice for us.

"What can I get you?" a ginger-haired brute of a man asks. With his red flannel shirt and the curly rust-colored beard and mustache, he looks like he'd be more suited in the Sierras, chopping down trees and yelling *timber* than behind the bar serving drinks to folks rushing to catch a plane.

"Whiskey neat, three fingers. Macallan Eighteen if you have it." Royce tucks his jacket over the back of his chair.

The bartender glances over his shoulder at the array of whiskies displayed. "We do."

He goes for the bottle as I call out, "The same for me." I crack my neck from side to side, attempting to relieve some of the built-up tension this case and the worry for Skyler have brought upon my shoulders. At the rate things are going, I'm going to need a full-body massage to get through this stress. Instantly the visual enters my mind of Skyler's toned thighs straddling my ass, her silky hands running up and down my back. The pleasant image has my dick stirring, reminding me of what's to come when I get done with the five-hour flight to JFK. Jesus, I can't wait to see her. Get my hands all over her tanned skin.

Royce's gaze flicks to mine, a thick black eyebrow cocked in question, which kills the vision in my head.

I answer the only way I can. "Need to feel the burn tonight." There is so much clouding my brain right now, a veritable tornado of information flying dizzyingly around.

"I heard that." Royce offers a tight-lipped smile, drops his head low, and runs a big paw over his neck and the back of his scalp a couple of times.

The bartender sets two tumblers in front of us and fills them a touch higher than three fingers. "You boys need some food?"

"Eventually," Royce says tiredly, lifting his glass to offer a toast.

I lift my own and clink it against his tumbler.

"Thank fuck this one's done!" he says tiredly.

I chuckle with the hilarity the toast brings. This case wore big, badass Royce out. "Glad it's over." I let the whisky slide down my throat, settling like liquid warmth in my gut.

Royce sucks in his bottom lip and runs his teeth over it. I can tell he's chewing on something he wants to talk about.

Taking a guess, I wade in where I know I shouldn't. "You thinkin' about Rochelle?"

He eyes me sideways but doesn't turn his head before he takes a slow sip of his drink, hissing softly upon completion.

"I'm man enough to admit I was wrong about her. She wasn't meant for me. Got that. You and I came to an understanding. Got that too. Doesn't change the fact that I'm heading home to an empty fuckin' house ready to be filled with a family I don't have, now does it?"

The weight of Royce's current situation is hitting my brother hard. The waves of his unhappiness swirl around us, and I reach out a hand and clap him on the back between the shoulder blades while leaning closer. He stays solid, looking straight ahead when I speak.

"What can I do?"

He shakes his head once. "Not a thing. Unless you've got a beautiful sista who's ready to settle down and deal with my overbearing momma and crazy-ass sisters"—he flicks a finger out past his glass—"and who's willing to handle a man who travels a lot, has two brothers from another mother who are always around, and a business that needs attention . . . there's not a thing you can do."

I breathe deep and let it out slowly. "She's out there."

He nods, but I don't get the impression he believes it. Rochelle was a bigger blow to his ego than I initially realized.

"Think of it this way. Skyler came into my world out of nowhere. Woman opened the door in a camisole and the tiniest pair of panties, thinking I was her best friend who'd forgotten her key."

Royce blinks slowly and shakes his head, about to interrupt, but I forge on.

"I spent too long fighting my instincts with her but eventually caved in to the best thing that ever happened to me. And believe me, brother, it is *not* easy. She lives a plane ride away. She's a fuckin' celebrity everyone wants a piece of, including me. Only the piece I want is *huge*. The whole damn pie." I take a breath and dip my head in his direction. "What we've got is special. And you know, anything worth having is worth working for. Now you're going to have to put in the work. Put your feelers out there. Find your soul mate."

Finally Royce turns his head to me, and I drop my hand to my knee but stay close so as to not share our conversation with anyone in hearing distance.

"She your soul mate?" His tone is filled to the brim with emotion I most certainly was not expecting to hear from him, especially in a crowded sports bar in the middle of a bustling airport.

I think about Skyler's blonde hair falling down her shoulders. Her nose crinkling cutely. The way she calls me *honey* and how it makes me light up. How she loses herself completely when I'm inside her, giving me *everything* that is her. Remembering Skyler's excitement and nervousness about meeting my family and brothers, wanting to be liked by them. How she lets her entire self go when she's laughing. There's a lot to Skyler; every day I'm finding out more, and it's only been a few months. I couldn't imagine the possibility of another woman being my soul mate. Loving someone more than I do her.

"I want to believe she is. How's about I tell you when I'm certain?"

"Fair enough." Royce purses his lips and lifts his drink. "Gonna hit the dating scene hard back home, but don't tell my momma. She finds out, and she'll have every one of her friends' available daughters lined up with numbers on their backs like in an auction."

Laughter bubbles up with no stopping it at the visual. "She'd absolutely do it too!" I chuckle and sip my drink.

"Yes, she would. You eager to get to New York?"

I run my finger over the rim of my glass. "More than I can express. I'm worried about her. This Johan is a real piece of work."

"You think he's going to hurt her? Physically?"

I shrug. "Don't know. All I do know is he's hurting her mentally and emotionally, and I'm about to lay the ration of shit on him Wendy found, which is not going to be pleasant one way or the other." Chills ripple down my spine, and unease sets up a beat in my stomach.

"You in touch with Sky's security team?" he asks thoughtfully.

"Yeah, sent a message to Nate about keeping a close eye on her and that I'd update him on the new threat when I get there."

Royce chuckles. "How'd it go? Don't suspect a man like Nate Van Dyken or his pistol of a wife would be okay with you butting in on how they take care of their charge."

Once again, I laugh out loud. "Too true. He responded with a single word: *Done*."

Royce smiles wide, the first time since we left Renner Financial Services. "They picking you up at the airport?"

I shake my head. "Nah, I haven't even told Skyler I'm coming to see her, plus it's the red-eye. Want it to be a surprise. I know she's working late tonight. We were supposed to talk later this evening, but I sent her a text telling her I'd touch base tomorrow when I'm home."

God. All I want to do is fall into her bed, wrap my arms around her warmth, and let her peaches-and-cream scent fill my lungs and ease my soul.

"Good man."

I nod. "Since it will be late, and Skyler is on set, the paps won't be hounding me. I should be able to slip through the airport, catch a taxi, and be at her place with no one but her doorman being the wiser. Unless, of course, they're watching her door, which could be possible. Either way, it's worth the trouble."

He takes another swallow of his whisky. "Oh, wanted to let you know I reviewed the documents Sophie sent over and sent her my response. She's nervous about some board meeting coming up and wants everything to be in place, but she's got it all. She didn't need to be so worried."

"Good. Did Bo tell you he had Wendy looking into her new boyfriend?"

Royce grins. "Find anything on him?"

I shake my head. "Nope. Clean as a whistle. Wendy did find out he made a sizable purchase at a jewelry store recently. Very sizable."

Royce frowns.

"Bo thinks he might propose."

Royce's eyes widen with the comment. "Shut the fuck up. I mean, Sophie's all of that, but it's been, what . . ." He flicks a few fingers out as if he's ticking something off in his mind. ". . . a few weeks?"

"Something like that," I mutter, and suck back the rest of my whisky.

The bartender lifts his chin in a silent request to see if I need another.

"Beer. Sierra Nevada." I switch my drink. Unlike Royce, I can't hammer back the whisky and not get shit faced fast. As it is, I can already feel the liquor swimming in my empty gut.

"I'll take a refill." Royce lifts his glass, and the bartender nods. Royce eases his body against the chairback and crosses his arms over his chest. "You okay with this new development in Sophie's world?"

I lean back and put my arm on the bar. "How so?"

"Know you're protective of her. Had your physical moment, but more than that, she's important to you. Hell, she's important to me and Bo too."

"Yes, she is. More than anything, if this is the man she wants, I'm happy for her. Do I think it's too soon? Fuck yeah. Gonna reach out, make sure she's doing all right and not jumping with both feet into something because she's still grieving over her father. Plus, she's got a lot on her small shoulders running that company. I won't tell her not to marry someone if she's in love with the guy and thinks he's her future, but I will warn her to slow down and take a breath."

Royce runs his thumb over his bottom lip. "Agreed. Sophie's young and sweet. And with no one to look after her, it's on us to make sure she's being smart."

"Truth." I make a mental note to check in with Sophie as soon as I can. "Where to next?" I ask, since he was running the show before I came back from Milan and we headed out on this trip.

"Montreal. A cyber-tech company CEO wants us to ferret out a rat in her company. Someone selling trade secrets, and something about bugs in the system."

Thank God it's not another case involving romance of any kind. Corporate espionage. Sounds downright mellow compared to the emotional shit show we've been dealing with as of late.

"Gonna take a few days off. Get past the shit with Sky and Johan."

Royce nods. "Figured. We'll discuss next steps back home, yeah?"

"Yeah. Catch you on the flip?" I stand up and pull on my jacket. Royce does the same before clapping me on the back and squeezing my shoulder.

"See you back home, brother," he says.

I drop three twenties on the bar to cover our bill. "You got it."

"Call us if you need us in on this Johan issue."

"Will do."

Royce lifts two fingers. "Peace."

***

Skyler's penthouse is deadly quiet when I enter at two a.m. Not wanting to wake her, I place my suitcase quietly on the floor near the front door. Since it's so late, the paparazzi weren't out hovering like vultures at her door for a speck of meat, as I suspected. The doorman waved me through as if he'd known me for ages.

I untie my dress shoes and step out of them, not wanting to make too much noise by clomping through her home. Once I've removed my jacket and tossed it over the couch back, I set the single white rose, which was waiting for me on the plane in first class, down on top of it. Seeing it reminded me of Skyler, so I saved it for her, knowing it would make her smile. Since I live for each smile, I had the stewardess wrap it in a wet napkin and a baggie and brought it with me here. I let out a long weary sigh before heading through the dark halls to Skyler's bedroom.

When I get there, I'm surprised to see her bed is still made and she's not in it. I frown and glance at the clock on the bedside table. Two fifteen. My shoulders fall as if they've had a ton of cement added to each side.

Bone weary, I make my way into her bathroom, strip off my clothes, and get in the shower. Her scent assaults me the second I enter the steamy space.

I groan. "Where the fuck are you?" I let my head hang and the water glide over my muscles. Needing to be with her, feeling her all around me but not here, I pour her bodywash into my palm and wrap a tired hand around my cock. I find it's already semihard merely being in her home, surrounded by her peaches-and-cream smell. With a firm grip around the base, I tug up to the very tip, imagining it's Skyler with her petite hand wrapped around me instead, running her slippery thumb around the bulbous crown.

"God, baby, I miss you." I let my forehead rest against the chilled shower tile. My mind fills in the blanks for me as I slide a soapy hand up and down my length.

My dream Skyler plants her naked breasts against my wet back, one hand on my waist, the other wrapped around my cock, jerking me to beautiful oblivion. Her lips fall to my shoulder, where she scrapes her teeth along the ridge up to my neck. There she lays an openmouthed sucking kiss, driving me wild.

My dick hardens painfully in my hand as my ass cheeks clench and thighs tighten, holding my weary weight up. I slam my other hand against the tile wall and arch into each pull.

"Peaches . . . ," I whisper, my balls becoming heavy with the need to burst.

I close my eyes as dream Skyler wraps both of her hands around my cock, jacking me magnificently with all her might. Her soft pants are lost against the noise of the shower beating down over us and my loud grunts.

"Give it to me, honey. Give it all to me." She rests her face against my bicep so she can watch the power she has over me.

"Fuck!" I growl out, tightening my hand into a fist against the tile. I squeeze my dick hard, needing the firm grip as dream Skyler talks dirty to me.

And then it hits me: the base of my spine tingles, and I go up on my toes and arch into the pleasure ripping through my body as jet after jet of my essence spills out over my hand to the watery floor below. The orgasm goes on and on as I imagine Skyler pumping away, greedy in her desire to get every last drop of my pleasure.

I hang my head but keep a tight hold of my cock as I come down from my one-handed pleasure escapade, wishing it were my girl and not my own hand. I figure she'll be home soon. She has to be. They often go late at the set, and I know they were wrapping today, but this is ridiculous.

Maybe they had to reshoot some scenes.

Taking hold of my bodywash—the last time I was here, my girl had stocked up on all of my preferred products—I pour some into my palm and quickly wash the grime of the day along with any remnants of my hand job from my body.

Tired as fuck, I dry myself off with one of her fluffy towels and drop it into the hamper on my way out of the bathroom. I walk naked through her home and find my phone in my jacket pocket. Uncaring about my nudity, knowing Skyler won't give one flying fuck, I head back to her bed, pull the covers back, and roll onto my side. I go to my favorites, press her number, and let it ring. Instead of a tired "Hey, honey," as I would expect, it goes to voice mail.

"You've reached Skyler. Leave a message after the beep, and I'll give you a ring when I'm available." Her chipper voice mail greeting finishes.

"Peaches, it's me. Wanted to surprise you, but you're not home. I'm naked in your bed, waiting for you. Come and get me." I dip my voice seductively at the end and grin before hanging up. I set the phone ringer for high volume and toss it on the bed beside me in case she calls back.

I'm dead to the world in a second flat.

***

My standard alarm on my phone goes off at six a.m. on the dot, and I pat the bed, looking for my phone. Shit, I should have turned it off before falling asleep. I knife up, find it blaring in the empty space next to me. Skyler's side of the bed is still empty. She didn't come home. I rub the grit and sleep from my eyes and realize I've had less than four hours of sleep, but she should have been home.

I tap the display on my phone and note she hasn't called me back. No text, no voice mail, nothing. Since I left a voice mail for her, I can't tell whether or not she's even had a chance to listen to it.

What the fucking fuck?

A knot of tension pounds against my tired brain, and I rub at my temples. I frown and punch her number. It rings several times before her voice mail picks up again.

"Call me ASAP. I'm at your house, and you're not here. I'm worried." Then I bring up the text feature and text her.

To: Peaches
From: Parker Ellis

Left you messages. You didn't come home last night. I'm at your house. Call me soon as you get this.

I sigh and flop back on the bed before I go to the display once more and pull up Nate Van Dyken.

To: Nate Van Dyken
From: Parker Ellis

Sky still on set? I'm at her house.

I get out of bed, pad out to my suitcase, and get a clean pair of underwear and slip it on. Next, I pull on a pair of jeans, grab a Red Sox T-shirt, and tug it on. My phone buzzes when I'm on my way into the kitchen to start the coffee. Only it's not Skyler; it's Nate.

"Ellis, it's Nate." He speaks gruffly into the phone. "We saw Skyler home last night at five p.m. She stated she would not be going anywhere and would not need our services."

My heart starts pounding in my chest. "Five yesterday? I got here at two this morning, and she wasn't here. Bed unmade, house quiet. She's not been home."

"Fuck! I'm tracking her cell phone now." His voice is firm yet controlled.

Not capable of any normal brain function, worried out of my gourd about Skyler, I lean against the kitchen counter, gripping the bullnose edge and listening to Nate's breathing as he does his thing.

"Says here she's at St. Regis Hotel right here in New York."

The pounding at my temples presses in, and I frown. "Why the fuck would she be at a hotel when she lives in the city?"

"I don't know. I'll head down there, see what I can find out. Scare a few people."

"I'm coming with . . . ," I grate through my teeth, heading to my suitcase to get my socks and shoes.

"No, you're going to keep calling her and wait at home in case she shows up. Rach and I are on this. We'll get your girl. Stay put."

I grind my molars down so hard they might turn to sawdust in my mouth. "You have no idea what you're asking me to do. I can't just sit here," I growl, making my intent perfectly clear.

"You're not. Call her phone again in ten minutes. We'll be at the hotel in twenty. If I think something nefarious is going down, I'll have the cops on it and call you immediately."

Swallowing down the sour taste in my mouth, I close my eyes tight. "Fine. Get there." I hang up the phone and start to pace. When the clock reads seven minutes later, I say, "Fuck it," and dial her number. It rings almost as many times as it would if the voice mail were going to pick up when a man's deep voice answers.

"Hello?" he says sleepily.

"Who the fuck is this?" My voice is harsh and brooking no argument.

"Johan. Who the fuck is this?" he responds in kind.

My heart leaps into my throat at the man's name. "Where's Skyler?"

The man chuckles. Actually. Laughs. In. My. Ear. "Taking a quick shower. What's it to you? You the boyfriend?"

"Yes," I grind out, my heart pounding, sweat prickling at my hairline. "Put her on the phone."

"Man, she's washing off a rather fun-filled evening, and if I were going to bother her in the shower, I wouldn't have answered the phone. Besides, girl needs a break from me, if you know what I mean." Sexual innuendo drips from his words, and an overwhelming rage plows into my chest.

She cheated on me.

With her scumbag douche of an ex who's blackmailing her.

She's a liar and a cheat.

I love her, but she *never* loved me.

Horror and self-doubt shred my heart and mind, making it hard for me to focus on the here and now. Except, regardless of what she did, I can't let her go without making sure she's safe. It's not in me to walk away from the woman I love when I know she's still in danger.

"Look, Johan, I know what you did. How you let a girl die in that club. How loan sharks are all over you for hundreds of thousands. I even know about the two women you assaulted and your family paid off. Now I'm thinking the people from the club who tossed you to the side wouldn't take too kindly to this information getting out to the public. I'm assuming neither would your modeling agency or your family for that matter."

"You son of a bitch!" he roars into the phone. "You say a fucking word—"

"And what? What are you going to do? I've got nothing to lose, motherfucker!" *You've already taken all I hold dear* is what I want to say, the ice pick going straight through my heart, but I won't ever give him the satisfaction of knowing what he's doing, what she has done to me.

I can hear his labored breathing through the line and take the opportunity to continue my own threats, which are more like promises. "Here's how this is going to go down. You're going to leave Skyler alone—"

"Not thinking she'll like that much, now that, you know, we've rekindled our connection."

I clench my teeth so hard I could crack rocks with them. My heart is ready to explode, and I want to break everything in my line of sight, but I breathe through the pain and anger and speak as clearly and as directly as possible.

"Leave her alone. Let her walk out of that hotel room. Do not contact her ever again. You destroy those images, or I will make sure every media outlet from here to Timbuktu spreads the disgusting truth of how you let a woman die under your care in a filthy underground torture club. Also, I'll let it be known you're a drug addict, and I'll take your parents down for paying your way out of jail on two separate sexual assault charges. You think your mommy and daddy dearest deserve to get thrown to the wolves after having your back? Hmm?"

"You say I'm scum, but you're no better," Johan sneers, his accent becoming thicker the angrier he gets.

"That may be. Regardless, you don't have a choice. Let her go, and stay the fuck out of her life." I grind out each word as if I'm stabbing him in the chest the same way the knowledge Skyler cheated on me is digging into my soul.

"Johan? What are you doing with my phone?" I hear her sweet but guarded voice in the background.

"You've got fifteen minutes to get her out of your room and into the lobby, where her security team will be waiting, or I press 'Send' on the email I've written to the *New York Times*. Among others." I end the call and slam the phone down on the counter.

Picking it back up, I call Nate. "She'll be in the lobby in fifteen minutes."

"I'll bring her back home to you, man," he assures me.

"No need. I'll be gone when she arrives. It's over between us." On that note, I end the call and chuck the phone at the tiled wall so hard it shatters into pieces, metal bits flying everywhere. Stomping over to my suitcase, I pull on my socks and shoes and close my case.

It's over. Sky and me. Done. I can't fathom that she'd rip my heart in half this way. She was supposed to be the one. My one in seven fuckin' billion. Now what?

Acute rage slithers through my entire body, building like gas contained in a small space, expanding, needing to get out. I grab the first photo I see on the table near the couch. It's the one of Skyler and me in the pool. She framed it. Put it on the table with all the people she cares about.

A lie.

It's all a fuckin' lie.

On a roar, I slam the frame to the ground and stomp it into pieces, the glass and wood splintering. It's not enough. Without even thinking, I glance at the table of pictures.

All lies! She's a liar. A liar and a two-bit cheat! On another animal-istic cry, I slide my arms down the table, pictures falling to the floor, shattering on impact.

It's not enough. It will never be enough. Nothing feels this bad. Kayla's betrayal didn't destroy me like this. I've got to get out of here. I look around and notice the mess. Fuck her! I don't care. I need a car. I spy my destroyed phone. I didn't think that through. Picking through the rubble I find the SIM card and tuck it in my pocket. It's the last lucid thought I have before the black of everything that just happened fills my mind and soul.

Without looking back, I leave Skyler's penthouse in the sky, planning never to return.

SKYLER

Twelve hours earlier . . .

I glance down at my phone for what feels like the millionth time and read Parker's message again. He'll call me tomorrow. Ugh. I'm tired of waiting to talk to him. He said he had some information to give me about Johan and his threats, but I'm *still* waiting. Tracey is on my case to approve the press releases she's written regarding the pictures coming out, and I don't want to do that until I've spoken with him. He seems so convinced that whatever Wendy's found will take this problem off my hands, and the pictures will be safely destroyed with the public none the wiser about my stupidity.

Except Wendy and Parker don't know Johan. He'd never do something like this without a reason. I may have been young and infatuated when we were together, but that's not who I am now. I'm stronger. More capable of handling the problems I'm faced with. And I know Johan. Regardless of what Parker might think or suggest, Johan isn't dangerous.

Nevertheless, something major is happening in his life that's making him strike out at me.

He wants $50 million.

I've known Johan for a long time, and he was never that cruel. He may have been aloof, cheated on me repeatedly, and used me for my money, but cruel wasn't his gig. And when my parents died, he was there for me. Held me close every day through the months when I cried myself into oblivion. Went to the funeral with me and sat with me while I clutched his hand, a tether to the real world when everything felt so surreal. He helped me during my lowest point. Without him in my life, I might have done something worse than drown my sorrows in booze and pills. When I couldn't function and saw nothing but darkness, Johan lifted me up. Made me better. Helped me to see the light at the end of the tunnel, which, at the time, was my career.

It's hard to believe he'd blackmail me like this. The sensation I've been dreading tugs at my mind, and I purse my lips. I *need* to talk to him. Face-to-face. Find out why he's hurting me like this. I walked away from him eighteen months ago and never looked back. He didn't care. Practically urged me to go. Of course, all of that was after he'd cleaned out our shared house account of every dime it had in it. Thankfully I'd transferred only monthly payments into our combined account and not the money I made from working or I fear he'd have cleaned me out too.

Which is kind of what he's doing now. He doesn't know I'm worth several hundred million, more money than I'd ever know what to do with. All I've ever wanted was to act in great films, tell beautiful stories with my craft, find a man to love who would love me, and build a life. Have a couple of kids one day and give them all my parents gave me and more.

I sigh at the vision of Parker with a toddler on his shoulders as he touches my pregnant belly with happiness. One day. But I'm afraid the day will never come if I don't get this situation with Johan settled and him out of my life.

I was so close to telling Parker I'm in love with him. And I know he feels the same about me. I believe it in every breath I hear through the phone, each one of his whispered "*Peaches*" in my ear, and the way he worships me and my body when we're making love. He's everything I want in this world, and I'm not going to let a pissant like Johan and his attempt at extortion ruin that. I don't want Parker's lovely mother and happy-go-lucky father to see those tawdry pictures of me and think ill of me. Those pics shouldn't have been taken. Johan talked me into doing those kinky things because he's into it, and at the time, I wanted to please him. I don't have any problems with the kink lifestyle, but after a few forays into it, I know it's not for me. What Parker and I have when our bodies come together with one another *is*. It's everything I need and more. I can't let anything get in the way of what we have. I'll pay any dollar amount.

Decision made, I pick up the phone and dial Johan's cell, feeling confident I can handle this myself. Shockingly he hasn't changed the number and answers it on the third ring.

"Hello, Skyler. I was expecting you'd call at some point. How are you?" His tone is that of a long-lost friend, not someone who is blackmailing me for more money than most people will ever see in their lifetimes.

I grit my teeth and take a huge breath. "I want to meet you. Now. No lawyers."

"You going to bring the money? If so, I'll bring the pictures," he says nonchalantly, as if he blackmails women every day.

"I want to *talk*, Johan. Where can I meet you?"

"The St. Regis Hotel. Room two four two." He hangs up the phone, apparently without a care in the world.

Instead of turning around and calling the Van Dykens to get me there, I call down to the front desk and have a taxi booked.

***

Johan holds his hotel room door open wearing a pair of jeans and a blue dress shirt unbuttoned at the collar. His eyes have dark circles around them, and his normally thick dark hair is a lackluster mess atop his head. Even his cheeks are sunken in, making him seem gaunt, skinny even.

"You look like shit," I observe, storming into the room and tossing my purse and jacket on the couch.

"You, however, do not. Always beautiful, all golden sunshine with great tits, ass, and legs. I'm sure your new beau is enjoying your attributes very much. I know I always did."

"Really?" I huff. "If you enjoyed them so much, you wouldn't have been banging half of the models you worked with."

He tuts. "Water under the bridge. Besides, you're not here to fluff my ego, and I'm not here to sample your extraordinary wares. Nevertheless, I could very easily be persuaded, as you well know."

I roll my eyes and gag. "Why are you doing this to me? Blackmailing me?"

He ignores the question. "*Blackmail* is such an ugly word, don't you think?"

"I believe it accurately describes what you're doing to me. Threatening to show inappropriate pictures of me, ones I didn't know you were taking, in a moment where I was very vulnerable. I trusted you, Johan." My voice cracks, and he has to know what this is doing to me. If he cared for me at all, he must know.

"And I took care of you, many times if my memory serves. You were always such a hair trigger in the bedroom. Easy to please," he muses, as if this is a game, ignoring the hurt he's causing.

Furious, I hold my fists at my sides and let him have it. "Because I loved you!" I holler, wanting to stomp my foot and throw a full-on tantrum the likes of which the world has never seen. However, for my own pride, I barely rein it in.

He frowns. "That is unfortunate, because I'm not capable of love. You figured that out."

"The hard way. Yes. Yes, I did. Even so, I never thought you were cruel. I know you cared for me. Took care of me through my parents' deaths . . ."

"I still care for you. It does not, however, change the predicament I'm in. I *need* money. A lot of it, or my life is in danger. I've made some very bad decisions in the past and with some horrible people who plan to hurt me. Take my life if I don't pay. I have no choice," he grits out through clenched teeth, and I'm finally putting two and two together. The worry in his eyes, the fear in every word he utters even as he's trying to hide it. He's scared. Afraid for his life.

"Johan . . ." I clutch at my chest. "Everyone has a choice," I gasp, allowing the hurt he's causing me to filter through my words.

"Not if I want to live. You're my last resort." He swallows and clears his throat.

Making a rash decision, I do what my mother would have done. She'd never let someone she cared for live in fear. Even if they hurt her. When she loved someone, she loved them unconditionally. I do as well. With her in my thoughts, I offer something I know I shouldn't. "Then I'll help you, because you were there for me when my world went dark. Because at one point I loved you more than anything on this earth. And because I could never live with myself if I walked away and your life was in danger."

His gaze flies to mine and softens, his shoulders falling in what I imagine is relief. "Skyler . . ." His voice shakes, and he rushes to me and pulls me into a full-body hug. Memories of the time he held me when I was numb to the world after my parents' deaths come rushing to the surface. His cold nose dips to my shoulder, and beyond my comprehension—for I've never, not ever, experienced this type of emotion from Johan—I feel his tears wet my skin.

"I'm sorry, I'm sorry I hurt you. Thank you. Thank you, Skyler."

As much as I loathe what he did to me when we were in a relation-ship and what he's threatened to do to me now, I feel his agony. He's lost and scared and going about it the wrong way. It's up to me to show him real kindness. The same he showed me. "We'll figure this out. I'll help you. Let's start with you telling me who you owe and how much."

***

By the time we called for room service last night, we'd already gone through the extraordinarily long list of individuals he owed and who he referred to as *very bad guys*. It was well after one in the morning, and I was exhausted when we were done. With the press hounding the entrance of the hotel, Johan encouraged me to spend the night in his room, saying he'd take the couch. After compiling the list and working with my broker to pay off each debt—to the tune of $20 million, not $50 million—he handed me the flash drive of pictures, which I pock-eted, planning to use a hammer on it when I got home.

He still didn't tell me what the extra $30 million he'd originally demanded was supposed to be for, but I had a feeling it was to put him in a cushy position because he'd lost his status completely in the mod-eling and acting industries. When all was said and done, he admitted to me he had a serious drug problem, and I once again agreed to help him by paying for him to be in a drug rehab facility that catered to the rich and famous and kept things anonymous and quiet, so the clients could get clean in peace without worrying about losing their status in the industry. Eventually he agreed to this and thanked me profusely. He also apologized repeatedly for what he had been planning to do.

This morning, my entire body feels as if it's coated in grime. I didn't have a chance to shower after a full day at the set before I rushed over here. Knowing Johan won't mind, I double-check the lock is still in place on the bedroom door, slip into the bathroom, and take a long shower, letting the entire week flow out of my fingertips as the water heats up and eases my tight muscles. When I'm done, I dry off and put my grubby clothes back on, not about to walk out of here in another man's attire. As it is, the press is going to go crazy when they see me leave a hotel in the same clothes I wore last night.

Grabbing my shoes, I head to the bedroom door and hear Johan on the phone. I eavesdrop, not believing for a second that he'll be perfectly honest with me about his dealings, but knowing I have the pictures ultimately puts me in the clear—for now. I also know I will have helped someone I once cared very much for. My mother would be proud. Hell, I'm proud of myself. Besides, he was there for me when I needed him, and I feel as though this has returned the favor hundredfold. Now I can go about my life with Parker, knowing I did right by Johan, and in the end, I hope to be able to say he did right by our friendship.

"You son of a bitch!" I hear him yell into the phone. "You say a fucking word—"

I cringe, thinking he's likely talking to yet another one of his dangerous "very bad guys," trying to work out the debts with the money I've given him.

"Not thinking she'll like that much, now that, you know, we've rekindled our connection," he says in a tone I recognize as his sexy voice. It does absolutely nothing for me now, but it's an odd thing to say to a man you owe money to. So much so that I open the door and pad into the area where he's standing, phone pressed to his ear.

"You say I'm scum, but you're no better," he sneers into the phone, and turns around. That's when I realize he's holding my phone, not his own.

"Johan? What are you doing with my phone?"

He ignores me, listens intently, and then presses it off, tossing it back onto my purse.

"Who were you talking to?" I demand, knowing instinctually, my heart starting to pound a foreboding beat in my chest.

"Your so-called boyfriend, but I don't think he's your man anymore. You're welcome." He shivers and makes a gagging sound. "Skyler, you sure know how to pick 'em. First me, then that guy? You're downgrading, not upgrading. You deserve better."

I rush over to him and push at his chest with both of my hands, knocking him off his feet to the couch behind him. He falls in a pile of limbs.

"What the fuck have you done?" I screech so loud I hurt my own ears.

"Skyler, the guy is a dick. Threatened me with some shit in my past that would end up getting me killed if it got out."

My entire body begins to shake uncontrollably. "Oh my God . . . ohmygod! He thinks . . . Jesus!" I grab my phone and notice the texts and the voice mails. Before dialing Parker back, I listen to his messages and slump to the couch, tears in my eyes. Each message strikes a blow to my heart so deep I don't know how I'm ever going to heal from it.

"He thinks . . . oh no." My world is crumbling all around me, piece by piece, as my stomach clenches and bile works its way up my throat. I'm barely capable of breathing through it.

"Skyler, what I did was a favor. A thank-you for helping me out. The guy isn't good enough for you. But you have to go, because he said your security team is down in the lobby waiting."

I choke out a sob and stand up, grabbing my things. "Johan, never, *ever* contact me again. I wish you the best, but you've ruined my life for the last time. Please, please consider the money I've given you as the gift it is and get your life back together."

"Skyler, no, let's be friends. We helped each other out, like old times . . ." He follows me to the door of his suite.

I shake my head and spin around, tears falling down my cheeks faster than I can wipe them away. "No. Move on with your life. I already have, although I don't know how I'm going to clean up this mess with Parker."

"Fuck him. He's not worthy," he states snidely.

"You're wrong." My voice is shredded as though I've swallowed razor blades. "I'm the one who's not worthy of him. I love him, and now he thinks I've done the worst possible thing a person could do. Cheat." I gulp down the pain that single word brings to my heart.

I spin around and thank my lucky stars the elevator doors open right away when I press the button.

I've hurt the man I love, and I don't know how to repair it.

He thinks I cheated.

Mom, Dad, if you're up there in heaven, please help me reach Parker before he ends it all.

I need to tell him I love him, and I'd never in a million years be unfaithful to that love.

The elevator dings, and I rush out of it and right into Rachel's arms. She catches me easily. "Hey now, I've got you."

"I have to get home! Now!" I state emphatically, terror and anxiety ripping along the frayed edges of my consciousness.

"Okay, okay, we'll get you home, but you have to calm down. There's an entire mess of paparazzi outside."

"I don't care! I need to get to Parker!" I yell hysterically.

Rachel nods, grabs the baseball cap off Nate's head, and tugs it down over mine, shielding my sodden face from view. She removes her long jacket and wraps it around me protectively. "Keep your head low. They don't need to see your tears. Don't give them that."

I nod and wrap my arm around her familiar weight as they lead me through the throngs of people screaming my name and taking pictures. I jump into the SUV and slam my back against the leather. "Did you talk to him?" I put my arm on Nate's shoulder.

"Yeah."

"And . . ."

"He said he'd be gone before you ever stepped foot out of the hotel."

I smash my hand against the back of the seat and scream my frustration. "No! No! No! This can't be happening. I love him. Don't you understand!"

"Yeah, Sky, we do. You love him. We know that. He knows that. It will be okay. We'll get through this together. Right now, we need to get you home and safe." Rachel's voice is controlled and completely in charge.

I shake my head and slump into the seat. "I'll never feel at home again. The only safe place I've ever been since losing my parents is in his arms. And he's gone. I don't know how I'm going to get him back, make him understand what happened."

Rachel rubs my arms and tucks me lovingly against her chest, the way I imagine a sister would. "It will all work out," she promises. I fear that promise is empty before she ends with, "When love is involved, there's always a way."

The end . . . for now.

MONTREAL: INTERNATIONAL GUY BOOK 6

To Pierre Bourdon.

You shared your love of Canada
and the French-Canadian ways
with me and my soul sister.

These two California girls will never forget
standing in the snow, in the spring . . .
the busted tire in Old Quebec . . .
dazzling vistas, snow-covered relics . . .
and a church light show that
will live in our hearts forever.

Merci, *kindred spirit.*

1

Hollow, inside and out. Everything I am, everything I thought I could be, I left in the hands of a woman. A beautiful, effervescent, sexy, and in the end . . . *manipulative* cheat. I should have known it would never, *could* never work between us. She's famous. A celebrity. I'm nobody when compared to all that is Skyler Paige.

My fuckin' dream girl.

Why would the likes of her settle for a businessman, a beer-and-baseball-type guy living in Beantown, when she could have anyone in the entire world? It makes no sense. *We* made no sense, even though for a while, I thought she was mine. I held all of her beauty and what I believed was her soul in my heart.

Somehow, I lost it, lost *everything*.

I have no idea how to move forward. What my next steps should be. I've honestly not felt this low in . . . forever. Even when Kayla burned me, it didn't feel like this. Like I've been gutted, skewered beyond repair.

There's also the issue of my brothers. Once Bo and Royce find out, they are going to be all over me. Forcing me to talk about her, get over it, move on. How does one get over or move on from the love of their life? Sure, I've been hurt in the past. Which means I knew exactly what I was getting into when I signed on for a relationship with Skyler. Yet I still waded in. Blinded by her sweet *honeys*, her self-doubt, and the way she seemed to need me.

Having Skyler count on me made me feel ten feet tall. Being her man, hearing her voice in my ear on the phone each night, having her body in my bed every chance we got, was living a dream. And like all dreams can do, mine so easily turned into a nightmare.

With her, I guess it just wasn't meant to last. I've found a lot of things in life are like that. Not meant to last. My mother even warned me about such things when I was a boy.

"Sometimes beautiful moments are like sand slipping through your fingers one granule at a time. When you're experiencing it, it's the biggest, brightest sensation in the world. And then, as quickly as it came, it slips away. We're left with only the memory of that moment, of the feeling of having something so soft and glittery within our grasp. That's part of its beauty. Knowing you had a hold on it for a brief time is a blessing. Remember that, son. Not everything in life is meant to last."

I walk to the kitchen to get another beer, planning to add it to the other four empty bottles on the table. I took the flight back from New York in a complete daze. I only recall going to the first phone store I saw, buying a new phone, downloading my most recent backup from the cloud, and shutting it off. I've since locked myself in my apartment. The landline rings at random—caller ID shows the calls are probably from Wendy—but I ignore it and let the calls go to voice mail. I numbly move around. I'd told Royce I was going to take a few days, touch base with them sometime today. He probably thinks I'm balls deep in my woman right now, which is exactly where I should be!

Intense anger screeches up my spine and surrounds me like a living, breathing evil. "Goddamn it!" I roar as the claws of betrayal slither all over my skin, digging into any bit of meaty flesh they find. The hair on the back of my neck stands straight up, and I clutch the empty beer bottle in my fist and look up at the ceiling.

White. Flat. Nothingness.

Images of her flood my vision.

Skyler in Johan's arms . . .

Spending the night in his bed . . .

Those delicate hands on his body . . .

His lips on hers . . .

It's like a demented waterwheel, dropping the next load of horrible pictures, each one worse than the last. My skin is awash with violent tremors as though a bucket of spiders has been dropped over my head and they're skittering across my skin.

"Why, Skyler? Why would you do this to me? To us!" I holler into my empty apartment, the fire inside me building to epic proportions, burning flesh and muscle from the inside out. I can't fucking take it. The despair. The ugliness I feel about the one woman I gave my god-damned heart to!

Another image of her blowing me a kiss enters my mind, and I clench my teeth, close my eyes as tight as I can, and impulsively pull my arm back and smash my fist and the beer bottle into the kitchen wall. Not only does the glass shatter and cut into my hand on impact, my fist goes straight through the drywall.

A searing pain ricochets up from my hand, through my forearm, and to my shoulder. A guttural scream tears through the room as I fall to my knees, clutching my bloody hand. I barely catch myself on the counter as I go down, breaking my fall. My knees hit the tile violently, and I jerk, my body shuddering as the agony of my hand and knees filters into my consciousness.

The door to my apartment slams open, and I barely glance up. A pair of dirty black motorcycle boots come into my view.

"Brother . . . fuck!" Bo's tortured voice penetrates my consciousness as the man leans down and grips my shoulders. "Jesus Christ . . . what did she do to you?"

I close my eyes, shame flowing out every one of my pores.

Bo lifts my arm. "Shit, Park, you're gonna need stitches. You might have even broken your hand. What did you do?" He glances at the smashed section of wall above the counter where I'm kneeling. "You hit the wall?" He snatches a towel from the counter and wraps my hand. "And how the fuck did you cut your palm? Dude . . . it's deep, and you're bleeding like crazy. We have to go to the emergency room."

I shake my head. "No way. Not going."

"Yes, you are. Unless you want me to call Mrs. Ellis to talk some sense into you? I think that might be a bit more painful than swallowing your pride and letting your brother take you, eh? Now come on, you're soaking the towel through, and blood freaks me out."

Blood freaks Bo out.

I stifle a chuckle as the four beers I finished in the last hour twist and turn in my gut. The woman I love cheated on me. Just like Kayla. My past rushes to the surface along with the heartache. Haunting me. Digging the vile knife of betrayal deeper into my heart.

My mouth salivates, and a sour taste flows over my tongue. "Oh no." I make a gagging sound and clutch at my stomach with my good hand.

Bo hauls me up and over to the sink just as my liquid lunch pours out of me. When I think I've got it all out and the heaving stops, I turn on the faucet and rinse out my mouth. The acid in my throat burns like I've swallowed razor blades.

"Bottle of water, please." I point to the fridge.

Bo gets a bottle, puts it on the counter in front of me, and leaves the kitchen without a word. I've barely taken a handful of calming breaths before he's crouching at my feet with my Nikes in place. I shove my feet in one at a time while he ties them for me in silence, taking care of me when I can't do the same for myself. He snags my gray hoodie from where it lies on the counter and eases me into the garment, helping me carefully push my wounded hand through the armhole as gently as possible without adding any pain and suffering.

Christ, I have the best friends.

He leads me toward my front door and grabs the keys to the Tesla on the way out. Bo drives a motorcycle, and he knows I won't ride bitch. Injured or not. No way, nohow.

The car is quiet as we motor down the road to the closest hospital. "You gonna tell me what happened?" he finally asks.

I sigh and rub at my forehead with my free hand. "Not much to say."

He chuckles and gives me the side-eye. "In my experience, there are always very good reasons a man puts his fist through a wall, and all of them center around one thing . . ."

"Oh yeah? Do bestow your worldly wisdom on me," I crack numbly.

"A woman."

I grind my teeth and focus my gaze out the window.

"Your woman is probably the hottest woman alive, and a beauty like that can also be hard to hold on to." He glances at me with an expression of pity plastered across his face. "Then there was this morning's top sleazy magazine report, which has her leaving last night from her home and going to the St. Regis Hotel in New York. That same report states she left this morning from the same hotel, which also happens to be the exact hotel her ex-dickhole is staying at. There's no way it's a coincidence," he surmises.

"Not a coincidence." I sigh and clench my teeth, trying to hold back the boiling frustration the admission causes.

"Why'd she go there?" His question is more a gasp of surprise.

I shrug. "Fuck if I know."

"And you haven't talked to her?" His head jolts back in his seat as if he's offended by the absurdity.

I huff. "I called this morning after three hours' sleep in an empty bed at her house. Worried about her safety. Guess who answered her cell, boasting about the fun they had last night?"

Bo's entire expression turns into one of extreme disgust. "I don't believe it."

I wish I didn't either.

"Believe it. She was there. I heard her voice after I'd nailed him with all the shit Wendy has on him."

"He's going to leave her alone?" He passes a couple of cars and moves into the fast lane.

I keep my arm at a right angle with my hand pointing up. "One can only hope. Except I'm guessing that point is moot, because she was there with him all night."

Visions of her rolling around in a bed with Johan cause my chest to tighten so much I can barely breathe. I gasp for air and roll the window down to let the cool breeze ease the nausea.

"Has she tried to call you? Tell you what happened?" His tone is one of anger and disbelief.

The fire I'd put out by ralphing into the sink comes back like a raging inferno in my gut and chest. "Doesn't matter. She cheated on me. With her fucktard ex who was blackmailing her."

Bo frowns and plucks at his goatee. "I don't know, man. The woman I saw at Lucky's was doing cartwheels over being with you. And don't try and pretend you weren't gonzo over her, because we all could see it."

"I fucking love her, Bo. *Love her.* And she cheated. Just like Kayla. You're smart to have your chicklets, have your fun. Fuck love and fuck her!" I grate out between clenched teeth, the pain in my hand making my entire body hot. Sweat tingles against my hairline, and my vision swims before I shake it off and open the window farther, the wind taking the blackness away with it.

Bo shakes his head. "Man, I know you're hurting and shit's eating you up inside, but there's got to be an explanation. Skyler's not the cheating kind."

I slam my head back into the leather seat. "And who is the cheating kind?"

"Me?" He grins.

I let out a slow breath and swallow down the lump in my throat. "Bullshit. Your chicklets know the score. All I know, man, is that she was there, with him, all night. She didn't answer my calls or texts. I slept in an empty bed while she reconnected with her ex."

"Is that what she said? That she was getting back together with her ex?" His tone might as well be dipped in shit for how vile he thinks that would be.

I cringe. "No! That's what *he* said!"

"And you believe him?" His words are ones of outright shock.

"She was in his room and spent the night in his bed. A man who threatened to distribute disgusting pictures of her . . . that he'd taken without her consent. Someone who wanted fifty million dollars to keep it out of the press. And she went to his hotel room. Left her security team at home."

Bo sucks in a sharp breath. "That's dangerous as it is."

"Yeah, it is. For her, it could be lethal. And she took that chance to meet up with him at his hotel, and stayed the night. When I called at six in the morning and threatened him, he was all too keen to share how he'd gone there with my woman . . ." I choke out the words as ice fills my veins and chills my soul. "Fuck!" I feel like I'm about to come out of my skin or alternately punch another hole in something. The dashboard looks inviting.

"Relax, we'll figure this out. I just find it hard to believe, that's all," he offers in a soothing tone.

Sometimes I wonder if Bo has ever cared enough about a woman to let her get close enough to burn him the way I've been burned. Since I've known him, he's had many women. None he's given an inch of himself to outside of the inches in his pants. He wouldn't understand.

"I don't find it hard at all. I loved Kayla, and she cheated on me with our best friend. I love Skyler, and she betrays me by opening her legs for her ex. See a pattern here?"

Bo inhales low and deep, taking the off-ramp that will lead us to the hospital. "Regardless of how messed up this all is—and I agree, it's fucked up—give her at least one chance to settle things with you. Yeah? Can you do that?"

The desire at the prospect of hearing her voice lifts my heart but is quickly followed by revulsion with the memory of what she's done. "I can't make you any promises."

Bo nods resolutely. "Well, let's get you stitched up for now. The rest can come later."

***

Two broken fingers, now splinted, twenty stitches in my palm, a fully wrapped hand, and I'm back home, feet up on my coffee table, a fresh beer and prescription painkillers at the ready. Bo, sitting on the couch, arm stretched along the back with his own beer dangling from his fingers, has his booted feet up on the table next to me. Across from Bo is Royce, sitting in the single chair, socked feet up on the ottoman. Man would never disgrace another man's furniture by putting his shoes on it. Even if his shoes cost more than the chair and ottoman put together. On the floor with a bowl of popcorn in her lap is Wendy, eyes glued to the flat screen, where a game is playing. She's wearing skinny jeans, Converses, and a Red Sox T-shirt that I have a feeling belongs to her man, because it's about four sizes too big on her slight frame.

While I was being seen at the hospital, Bo called IG to update them on the developments and let them know where we were and why. The call resulted in the team being at my place when Bo brought me back and the IG offices closed for the rest of the day.

The doorbell rings, and Wendy bolts up as though she has pogo stick springs for legs. "Pizza! I'll get it. Charging it to the company, FYI." She bobs over to the door, signs the receipt, and brings the two large pies into the kitchen.

She hollers from the kitchen, "Bo, want to get up off your ass and come help me serve our bros?"

Royce covers his grin by sipping his whiskey.

Bo rolls his eyes, drops his feet from the table, and stands. "Tink, you know it's the woman's job to serve her man! I think I'm going to have to teach you a lesson!" he warns playfully, but heads into the kitchen to assist.

"How you doin', brother?" Royce interrupts my thoughts on the inner workings of the friendship between Crazy Number One and Crazy Number Two.

I lift my hand and turn it from side to side. "Between the painkillers and the beer, I'd say just about right."

Royce chuckles, leans forward, splays his legs out wide with feet on the floor, and rests his elbows on his knees. He looks up at me from under dark eyebrows, his eyes laser beams of truth. "Not talkin' about the war wound, though I can't say I'm happy 'bout that either. Bo updated us. It's why we're here."

"Got that. 'Preciate it too."

He nods and purses his lips. "Still doesn't change why we're here. Your girl fuckin' you over. How are you dealing with that?"

I close my eyes and inhale full and deep, trying to squash any visions of her with Johan before they ever enter my mind. It works, thank fuck. I shrug. "Not sure what I feel. Anger is at the top of the list."

His lips flatten into a thin line. "You talk to her yet?"

I shake my head. "Got nuthin' to say to that woman. It's over."

"Brother . . ." His words are left dangling.

"It's over."

"Park . . ." He continues undaunted. "Know you fell hard for her. Know she fell hard for you. Could see it in every line in her face and body when we met her at Lucky's. You don't just give that up and walk away."

"She did," I sneer, tightening my grip on my beer.

Royce nods slowly and runs a hand over his knee. "With the way you were feeling in San Francisco, maybe you ought to give her a little time to explain."

I jerk my gaze to his. "You think anything she says is going to make it okay that she betrayed me? She fucked that piece of shit the same night I was sleeping alone in her bed."

Royce lifts a hand. "Now, hold up. You don't know what happened in that hotel room."

"Don't I? Woman jumped me the first fuckin' night I was in her penthouse. She was with Johan for close to two years."

"Doesn't change the fact that he was blackmailing her, she was scared, and you were out of town."

"So that gives her the excuse she needs to betray me?" I counter, my voice laced with fury.

His head jolts back, and he groans. "Fuck no! It means shit was swirling around in her head. Bad shit. Her man wasn't there. Maybe she thought because of their time together, she could handle the chump herself. Stupid, I admit, but knowing Skyler, that's more likely than her going there and offerin' her goods up on a silver platter. You need to look deep inside yourself, inside that heart of yours that made you fall for her, and *tell me* . . . do you think she could betray you? Really?"

I grind my teeth and let his words sink in. "What do you think?" I ask right as Bo and Wendy walk in with two plates apiece, each loaded with pizza.

"I think there's got to be more to this story than what a filthy manipulator spews out his trap." His tone is resolute and convincing.

"Oh, are we talking about what happened with Sky? I'm all over that. Ran her credit cards, her phone records, everything before I came over." Wendy hops into action, digging into the satchel she set near the entertainment center. Once she has a hold on her thin laptop, she opens it and sets it on the table.

"Tink, not sure Park wants the comings and goings of his woman right this second." Bo sets a hand on her shoulder.

I sit up and put my feet on the floor, cradling my hand. My heart starts pounding hard at the mention of finding out anything about Skyler. "Actually, I do. What do you have?"

She nibbles on her pizza, then sets it indelicately on her plate, licks her fingers, wipes them on her napkin, and takes to the keys. Once she swallows her bite, she lays it out. "Yesterday she was at the set. I have her phone tracker on. Made sure to do that when she visited us last time. Keep tabs on all of you"—she twirls a finger around all of us—"just in case something goes down—"

"Seriously, Wendy? What the fuck you think is going to happen to us, girl?" Royce interjects, shaking his head tiredly. "Woman is too damn smart for her own good. Brothers better watch yo'selves."

She ignores him completely. "Looks like she got to her house yesterday, then made a call to a number I found out was Johan's. They had a very short—as in two minutes—conversation, and then she used her credit card in a taxi that took her to the St. Regis, which is where she stayed the night, though she didn't pay for a room."

I clench my teeth and toss my plate of pizza on the table, no longer hungry. "That's enough—" I start, when Wendy waves her hands and shakes her head frantically.

"No, no, it's not. That's when things with her finances get crazy."

I frown, and Royce stands and walks around to crouch where Wendy's got her computer set up on the coffee table. The word *finance* to Roy is like waving a juicy steak in front of a dog.

"How so, girl?"

Her eyes light up with excitement. I swear if Wendy were a cartoon she'd be a part of the Scooby-Doo crew. She looks more like Daphne, but she's definitely got Velma's intellect.

"Here and here." She points at something I can't see on her screen. "Bank transfers to the tune of a lot of zeros. I've traced one to a Miguel

Fuentes, who's some highfalutin businessman, but in reality, the guy's a top-notch loan shark. The kind that looks all rich and professional, but word on the web is that he has no leniency with people who go for a long time owing him. They end up missing. Never found again."

"Come on, this isn't *The Godfather* . . ." Bo eases back in his seat, his brows furrowed.

"Kind of is. Miguel Fuentes is known for being connected to the Mexican mob," Royce adds flatly. "I know a lot about the money market, and there is word that Miguel has some shady attachments. Hence the reason only the rich, powerful, and unlawful tend to do business with him. Problem is, cops have been trying to get a lock on Miguel and his backdoor dealings for ages but can never pin him down."

"Shut the fuck up!" I growl. "And he's got Sky into this?"

Wendy's fingers clack against the keys faster than before. "Only in that her account wired money to his account. A lot of money. Ten million to be exact."

"Jesus Christ." I run my hand over my sweaty forehead. The meds and the beer are kicking in, and not only am I starting to feel woozy, my train of thought is slowing down.

"Also, she sent at least fifteen other wire transfers. Credit cards. Bank loans. Mortgages, and a few other payments to shady individuals."

"Fuckin' hell, woman!" Royce rubs at his mouth and chin.

"Goddamn it!" Bo grits through his teeth.

I don't say anything. My heart, mind, and body have lost all will to move, exhaustion lying heavily in my bones.

"With all of those, the strangest one is the last payment she made last night."

I frown. "W-what, ish it?" I slur, even my tongue feeling heavy.

All three of them look up at me, different worried expressions flitting across their faces. "Just finish." I wave my good hand in a hurry-up motion.

Wendy licks her lips and bites down on the bottom one. "According to this . . ." She points it out to Royce and Bo, who can see her screen.

Bo's eyes widen, and he closes his eyes.

Royce shakes his head. "Shee-it. What kind of play is he making?" he murmurs, still looking at the computer.

"What?" I blink away the sleep trying to invade my mind.

"Skyler paid for what looks like a three-month stay in a rehabilitation facility for one Johan Karr." Her voice is steady, but her eyes are huge and bright blue against her pale-white skin.

That seals it. She's paying for him to be rehabilitated so they can get back together.

Fuck my life.

"On that note, I'm-I'm-I'm gonna g-go lie down." I stand, and my knees start to weaken. I catch myself against the arm of the couch as Bo jumps up from his seat and wraps an arm around my waist.

"Lean on me, brother."

I smile and make a kissy face at him. "Aw, Bogey, who'da thought you cared." I start to close my eyes, but Bo moves me around the couch toward my room. When we get there, he leads me to the bed and pulls back the covers. I fall to my ass and back, curling to my side, where I tuck my bad hand against my chest.

"Dude, sleep it off. I'll be here when you wake up."

"Go-shh home. 'S okay. I cool," I mumble as sleep starts to invade.

"Sweet dreams, punk ass."

It's the last thing I hear before I see nothing but black.

2

I wake later that night to find Bo in the kitchen making pasta. I cradle my hand, which feels as though it's getting repeatedly slammed into a car door. I swear it aches and throbs along with every single heartbeat and every shaking breath I take.

Breathing.

Breathing without her is unthinkable. Except I have to, so here I am, holding my hand at a ninety-degree angle, fingertips to the sky as I shuffle onto a stool in the kitchen.

Bo spins on a heel, gets a bottle of water, opens it, and sets it in front of me. "You need to hydrate on those meds, bud," he informs me while motioning to the bottle.

I slam the bottle back, draining half of it in one go. The cool liquid eases my dry throat and perks up my sluggish brain.

"Turned your phone on after the charge. Seems as though you have a dozen texts and calls. Pretty much from the same person." Bo gestures to the phone that's connected to the charger about two feet from where I'm sitting.

For a moment, I take in a deep breath and try desperately to calm my instincts to rush for the phone. Whatever lies she plans to say aren't going to work. They don't matter. The deed has been done.

"Not sure there's anything she could say that would fix where I'm at right now."

Bo frowns while stirring the mixture he's got going in a skillet. It looks like a light red sauce, bordering on white. Frankly I don't care what it is, because the scent of tomatoes and garlic bread is entering my nostrils, and my mouth salivates. I didn't get down much of the pizza before the conversation took a turn to Skyler and her finances, which had the added effect of me losing my appetite. At this point, nothing could make me lose my hunger. I'm freakin' starving.

"Is it possible, brother, the shit that went down with Kayla is coloring your version of events, which may or may not have happened with Skyler?" Bo eases into the fray, voicing what I'm sure Royce thinks as well.

I run my hand through my messy hair and sigh. "Honestly, I don't know. All I know is I'm fucking hurt. It's as though there's a hole in my gut that won't mend, and she's the cause. I don't remember feeling this jacked up over Kayla."

Bo snorts. "You were a goner back in the day, although it could have also been losing Greg at the same time as your fiancée."

My phone buzzes where it sits charging, and I can't hold out any longer. I'm curious, and if I'm being straight with myself, there's a shred of hope the situation can be explained, but my subconscious is not letting that part of me come to the surface.

I unhook the cord and pull up the text. Bo was wrong. There are actually fifteen texts since this morning. Six voice mails. Four from Skyler, one from Sophie. Another from Ma. I ignore the voice mails and go right to the texts. For a single moment I close my eyes and take a breath, and then I start to read.

From: Peaches
To: Parker Ellis

Baby, please pick up. You've got it all wrong.

The next one:

Parker, please. I'm begging you. Answer your phone.

Another text:

I need to explain. You don't understand.

Again:

Call me when you get off the plane.

And another:

It's not what you think! I swear.

Again:

I wouldn't hurt you like that. Never. Not ever.

The messages keep going on in that similar vein . . .

Fine. You're not going to respond to my texts. CALL ME!

This is insane! I know what you're thinking, but you have it all wrong.

Baby, please. Trust me. Trust in us.

Each text digs deeper and deeper into the wound that she's made in my heart. She wants me to trust her, but how can I? She spent the night in that bastard's hotel room. The entire world knows she was with him overnight, or at the very least suspects it. She didn't take her security team, putting herself in grave danger. Johan Karr is unstable. That much I could easily glean from our discussion. The fact that she put herself in such a perilous position . . . For what? What did she think she could get out of it? I keep reading the rest of her messages.

Parker, call me. I can't make this right until you do.

Why are you ignoring my calls? You're hurting me, and you don't even know the truth!

I tried the IG offices and got voice mail. Wendy isn't returning my calls either. Please, please, call me!

I cringe at the need I can feel pulling at my brain with each of her requests.

Honey, I know you're mad. I'm sorry. I was stupid. So stupid, but I had to try and fix it myself.

I run my good hand over my stubbled chin and lips as I read the last two.

Parker, I need you to trust me. If there is any hope for us, you have to believe I would never betray you. Never ruin what we have.

The last message guts me, and I have to bite down on the inside of my cheek in order to not let the overwhelming emotion building inside of me pour out like I were a weak, pansy-assed wuss. I'd have to give up my man card if I let the feelings that are making my nose drip and my tear ducts sting have their way. I read it again and let the full force of her words slam into my chest and heart, right down into my soul.

> You are the best thing that's ever happened to me, Parker. If nothing else, believe that. Please give me the opportunity to explain what happened. I'll give you some time, a few days, to think about everything. Call me when you're ready to talk.

I rub at my tired face and set the phone down. Bo turns off the stove and dishes out a fusilli pasta with a creamy reddish-white sauce over the top and fresh-cut shreds of basil.

"Dude, when did you learn to cook?" I stare at the food as if it materialized from magic fairy dust, not because my best friend just slaved over the stove to make it for us.

He grins. "Momma Sterling has been teaching me."

"No joke?"

He smiles and pulls out a sizzling half loaf of buttery garlic bread from the oven. "Nope. She said if I wasn't going to have a steady woman in my life, and I couldn't always get to her house to eat a real meal, she was going to teach me a few staples to keep me fit and fed." He snickers, putting two thick slices of bread on the side of the plate next to the pasta.

Once he's plated the meal for both of us, he comes around the bar, gets situated in his seat, and pokes away at his food, forking up a giant bite.

I sample my own and am happily surprised at how good it is. "Bo, this is the shit." I chew and swallow it down, forking up more eagerly.

"True dat." He smiles. "So . . . about those texts?" He gestures to my phone. "Anything interesting?"

"Fishing for info?" I smirk.

"Absolutely. I want to know if this woman played you. Hell, brother, I want to know if she played us all. See, cuz the woman I met, the one I took pictures of back in New York, the one that sat in my brother's lap while we broke bread together at Lucky's, a spot that's fuckin' sacred to all of us . . . that woman is who we all started to care about."

I shake my head. "She seems upset. Begging to talk to me. Wants to explain. Says whatever I'm thinking I've got it all wrong. Doesn't change the facts. She skirted her security team and stayed the night in a hotel with a man who was blackmailing her. Not only that, according to Wendy's super sleuthing, she paid off all of his debts and set him up in rehab, for Christ's sake! What am I supposed to think about all of that?"

Bo chews thoughtfully before responding. "All true. However, those facts do not mean she slept in a bed with him or fucked him. Do you think you could forgive her for the other as long as she didn't sleep with him?"

I spend a solid five minutes mulling over his question. Bo knows when I need the space to think, and he doesn't push for an answer. Instead, we sit in companionable silence, eating the dinner he's made.

Can I forgive her if she didn't betray me physically?

Yes. I believe I can. It doesn't fix what happened, and I still don't know the details, but the real hurt, the betrayal, would be her cheating. The hows and whys of that wouldn't matter.

I set down my fork and hold my chin up with my hand, elbow to the counter. "Yeah, I could forgive her for going to him when she should have waited for me. In my opinion, she should have avoided the bastard at all costs. Regardless of the reasons, it was a stupid thing to do."

Bo nods. "So what are you going to do about it?"

I shrug and run my good hand over my arm. "I don't know yet."

"You need to talk to her. She's the only person who's going to be able to give you the answers you seek, brother. This you know."

"Yeah, I'm just . . . fuck. Straight up, the thought of her going there, spending the night, even if he was on the couch or vice versa. The entire thing is . . . man, it's eating at me." I punch my chest, needing to feel something, anything, other than the hurt in my mind and heart.

"Heard that. Can see it all over you. Proof is staring me in the face. The hole in the wall, the stitches in your hand, your broken bones. You're *bleeding* for her, inside and out. Only way to stop that flow is to find out the truth. You're not going to be able to rest until you do."

I rub at my head, my hand pounding a violent, painful rhythm as I consider his words. I grip my wrist and hold it tight, trying to stave off the unbelievable ache.

"Hurt?" he asks.

"Fuck yes!" I growl.

Bo gets up off his stool, goes into the living room, and comes back with a pill bottle. He opens it and shakes out two pain pills. "Doc said you can have two at night before bed but only on a full stomach and with plenty of water. Drink up, eat up, wash those down, and we'll get you back to bed. I'm going to sleep on the couch, as I mentioned before, in case you need me."

I clap Bo on the back. "You don't have to do that. I can call you. You're only down the breezeway."

He shakes his head. "Would feel more comfortable if I were here in case you have a bad reaction or some shit."

Picking my fork back up, I prod and poke at the pasta. I shrug and shove the tasty morsel into my mouth. "Suit yourself."

"Don't mind if I do."

After I wash down most of the rest of the water, I glance at Bo, who's sweeping up the sauce on his plate with a wedge of garlic bread.

"Thank you," I mutter, my voice thick and dry at the same time. "Would do the same if the situation were reversed. You know that, right?"

He nods without saying anything. It's our way. Brother watching over another brother. Keeping an eye out. Being there when shit goes down.

I wish romantic relationships were as easy to maneuver. What I'm dealing with is like walking through a freakin' minefield. I don't know where to step or stand. The only thing I do have solid footing on is the need to flee. Get back to work as soon as possible and put some serious space between me and this entire mind fuck of Johan and Skyler. More than anything I need some perspective.

"Regarding the Montreal job, I'm going to the office tomorrow. Have the CEO come in and give us the lowdown about her company in secret. From what I understand, she's been waiting for us to get back in town and situated. I'm thinking this job might be an entire-IG-team approach. What do you say?"

Bo grins. "Been needing to get the hell out of Dodge. Canada should be great this time of year."

And far, far away from my personal problems.

***

Alexis Stanton is not at all what I expected when Wendy leads her into my office two days later. She's tall with a killer body and bangin' curves. The woman is a walking, talking Playboy bunny in person. However, based on the file Wendy provided on her, she's a savant-level genius in her field.

Trying to ignore my aching hand, even after a dose of painkillers, I take my time evaluating the woman while she sits across from me. Her blonde hair comes to her shoulders, full-bodied and in big curls that look to be made of spun gold. Unlike my blue eyes, hers are a bright cerulean that could match the color of any crystal-clear Caribbean waters on a sunny day. She has a pert little nose and high, rounded cheekbones. Her lips are full and glossy pink, the color so tempting any warm-blooded male would kill to have a taste.

I clear my throat and try not to look down at her form-fitting white dress. The sleeves are long, coming a tad past her wrists, though they're the only long thing on the item of clothing. The hem of the dress hits just above the knee but climbs all the way up a lean, toned thigh when she sits and crosses her legs. She's paired the dress with nude strappy stilettos, the kind that make a woman's legs look a mile long. Problem is, on this woman, they are *lethal* since her genetics are such that her legs already go on for days.

I press against my temples and sit back in my chair, then adjust my tie awkwardly with one hand since the other is bandaged. Outside of the bandage I have the two broken fingers splinted and taped together.

"Mr. Ellis, thank you for seeing me. I'm happy you're back early. The situation with my company is becoming dire. There's not a moment to lose."

"Why don't you start at the beginning and give me an idea of what we're facing? Royce tells me you're concerned that someone is stealing trade secrets and selling them to your competitors. Is that correct?"

She nods. "Yes, but it's more complex than that."

I frown and lean forward to cross my forearms on my desk. "How so?"

"Not only have the last three products been stolen and released by my direct competitor two to three weeks earlier than our planned releases"—her mouth twists into a scowl—"but someone is sabotaging our work processes in the meantime."

"In what way?" My interest is piqued.

"Software corrupted by viruses, files lost or deleted, seemingly out of nowhere. It's as if the programs are under siege by a ghost in the system."

I dig back into my memory bank from my days at Harvard. "I've heard of this term, *ghost in the system* or *ghost in the machine*. Has to do with computer artificial intelligence or bugs of some sort coming about through errors in coding, right?"

She nods and bites down on her bottom lip. "I'm not sure you can help with that threat. I've got the greatest minds in the industry working on the technology issues. Besides, my brother and I have written all the original code, but I do need to figure out the *very real* threat. Someone is sharing our product information, and after endless research and scrutiny of my team, I'm at a loss to figure out who it is."

I sit back and curl a finger around my chin. "The simplest explanation would be that both problems are being perpetrated by the same person, no?"

She sighs and winces, following it up by arching her back. The move is designed to ease tension, but the shape her body takes is electrifying, especially in light of her jutting out her very large chest like a white flag waving in surrender. She eases back into the chair and crosses her legs to the other side. I swear I can hear the swish and glide of the fabric along her tanned thighs. The move sets my teeth on edge, and I mentally chastise myself. It's only been three full days since I ended things with Skyler. *Ended* being rather questionable, since technically she's still waiting for me to call her.

While I'm thinking about my own personal problem, I scan the woman in front of me. My dick wakes up from its three-day sleep, and I lick my lips and focus on her face, tempted to look at her beautiful body once more, but knowing it's not right. Lusting after a woman other than Skyler is absolutely not on my agenda.

Regardless of what I said to Nate about things being over between me and Skyler, I need to tell the woman directly. It's the only fair and honest thing to do. I can't expect Skyler to be forthright and honest with me if I can't be so with her. I'm just not ready to deal with it all yet. Saying goodbye. Letting her go. Allowing all that we built between us to just disappear.

My gut churns, and my abdominal muscles tighten. I let out a heavy sigh while Alexis is none the wiser and answers my questions.

"I guess it would make more sense if the two problems were related, but it's just hard to believe that someone on my coding team could be part of that. Do something so blatant and behind my back to hurt me."

I huff and shake my head. "Well, I can tell you from personal experience, people are rarely what they claim to be." And it's as true today as it was when Kayla destroyed my heart, the feeling more intense now because of the deep connection I believed we had. I was stupid to believe that my relationship with Skyler would be any different. A downright fucking idiot.

"That's a very jaded way to view the people in your world, Mr. Ellis." Alexis frowns.

I cant my head and assess her piercing gaze. It's as if she's trying to look straight through me. I hate it. "Let's just say I've had my fair share of experience with people letting me down recently."

"People, or a woman you cared about?" She purses her lips and cocks an eyebrow.

"Would it matter?"

She lifts one shoulder and lets it fall. "I guess not. Though, I've vetted my team to the extreme. Made them each submit to a lie detector test, which every last one of them passed. I'm at a loss for how to proceed. Which is where you come in."

I plant my elbows on the arms of my chair so I can steeple my fingers under my chin. It's a move I've always subconsciously done but is now made difficult by my bandaged hand. I grind my teeth and remember why my hand is in this condition. Because the woman I love betrayed me and I lost control. Never again. I'll never let my emotions control my decisions when it comes to the opposite sex. That particular boat has sailed.

Alexis's pretty pink lips curve up into a sensual pout. "Do you think you can help me?"

I nod. "Yes, I believe we can, though it may take my entire team."

"In what way?"

"You said you had your team vetted." She nods as I continue. "That means whoever is doing this is cunning as hell. It could be anyone in any department leaking the trade secrets and only a handful of people dropping the viruses. Then again, we may have a team working together. One person doing the leaking, another accessing the system."

She grimaces and runs her hand through her long blonde hair. I loved running my fingers through Skyler's locks. They always felt like silk. I wonder momentarily if Alexis's hair is as soft as Skyler's, then mentally slap myself for even thinking about Skyler.

Focus on the work, Park. Not the woman.

"What do you have in mind?" She brings my attention back to the matter at hand.

"My assistant is a tech guru. We'll bring her in as a new hire in your coding and analysis department. Royce will come in as an auditor in the finance department. Bo will act as a new, very hands-on client who wants an application developed. Something related to photography perhaps. Do you think you could swing it?"

"Sure. There are a ton of applications you can create dealing with filters, lighting, sizing, instant editing, photoshopping. And you? What part will you play, Mr. Ellis?" She purrs my name as if it's a sensual treat she's about to eat up.

I ignore her. In another time, I would have been all over this woman like butter over a hot baked potato. With everything going on, though, I'm not sure how to react. I'm floundering between the professional and personal signs the sexy woman is tossing out. It's an uncomfortable, disheartening sensation I'm not sure how to take.

With a deep breath, I focus on the task. The work is what's important right now. Not the lengthy looks or subtle flirting happening from Alexis.

"I'm going to come in as a workflow-productivity consultant, which means I'll have to interview every employee, ask them about their job, what they do, that type of thing. I'm very good at reading body language and an individual's microexpressions. I can typically tell when someone is lying or being misleading. Plus, knowing you've got an auditor and a consultant digging into things might scare the person into making a mistake."

"Okay, how do we start?" She leans forward, and the material of her already-tight dress seems to expand further across her tits.

Don't look at her tits, Parker. Don't look at her tits.

Not cool, dude. Not freakin' cool.

However, I gotta admit to myself, she wouldn't wear dresses like that if she weren't expecting people to size up her form. My guess, with how comfortable she is and how tight fitting and short the dress is, she *wants* the attention. Possibly even craves it.

A muscle in my temple starts to flicker, reminding me that I should not be ogling this woman, even if I may be ending my relationship with Skyler. I haven't actually ended anything officially.

My stomach tightens into knots again, but I breathe through it and stick to the work plan. "My first suggestion would be to have Wendy come on board immediately, as in tomorrow." Her eyes widen briefly in what I can see is surprise, not complaint, so I continue. "We'll have you implement her right away so there isn't any suspicion of her position, and she can start connecting with the team and digging into your computer systems."

"Done."

"Next, we'll have you bring Bo into a meeting of the minds, including your application creation team, and he'll go over what he wants. He'll make a show of wanting to be where the action is, and you'll give him an empty office to work in."

She tilts her head. "Easy enough."

"I'll work with Wendy to pull the files I'll need on your staff. How many are on your team?"

"Twenty-two, not including me."

With that settled, I pick up the phone and hit the button to call Wendy.

"Word up, boss man," she chirps into the line.

"Did Royce have you do a full write-up on Stanton Cybertech while we were in San Francisco?" I gaze out the window, so I don't gaze at my client.

"Yessiree, Bob. I've got full files on all twenty-two employees and another on Alexis Stanton. Figured if something funky is going on at her company, you'd want all the info you could get your hands on."

I smile huge and turn around in my chair. "Excellent. Also, you're going to need to plan flights and hotels for all four of us."

"Four?" There's excitement in her tone that can't be denied.

"Yes, ma'am. You're going to be a new hire at Stanton Cybertech, starting tomorrow morning. We need to move on this and fast."

"Holy shit, boss! Rock on! I can't wait to tell Sir Mick! My first undercover mission. This. Is. *Awesome!*" She gasps the last word as if I'm making every last one of her dreams come true.

"Glad you think so. We'll talk more when I've finished here, but bring me the files."

"Righty ho!" she announces, and hangs up.

I turn back around to Alexis, who is taking me in. And when I say *taking me in*, I mean all the way *in*. The way a tiger scopes out a raw steak. She licks her lips and jostles her chest, wiggling in her chair. I have to bite down on the inside of my cheek not to take the bait and say something totally inappropriate.

"Okay, that's settled. Tell me a little bit more about the products you say were stolen."

3

Alexis Stanton's office is the exact opposite of ours. Where Team IG prides itself on crisp and sleek designs, Stanton Cybertech lives for comfort. Her office feels more like a home than a place of business. If it weren't set up in a multilevel warehouse on the outskirts of Montreal, I would have believed this could be her home. It's unsettling and bizarre. I stand up and walk around the space as Royce waits patiently in one of the deep-cushion, high-back chairs in front of a fireplace. Yep, a fireplace. Directly across from that fireplace are a couch and coffee table.

I look at Royce, and he smiles one of his shit-eating grins. I shrug. "Weird right? It's not just me?" I hook a thumb toward the other half of her office, which has an eighty-inch flat screen with an old beat-up wooden desk facing it. On top of the desk, a slim laptop, a phone, and a Tiffany-style lamp, complete with a flower pattern in the stained glass, are the only things that rest on the surface. A bookcase hugs each side of the flat screen.

"Different strokes for different folks, as Momma would say." Royce fingers his tie and smooths it back into place.

I walk over to one of the bookcases and scan each shelf. All of the pictures are of Alexis with a much younger man. A brother perhaps, since they share the same facial structure.

Alexis saunters in, carrying two cups of steaming coffee and wearing a smile. "Hi, boys. Thought you might want a shot of caffeine."

"Thank you." I reach for one of the mugs. Her thumb caresses mine as she pulls away. I glance up to find her smirking.

She offers a saucy wink and then brings the other mug to Royce. Her attire today is similar in fit and scope to what she wore the other day, though the black halter top is more revealing. Her double Ds are bulging against the deep V of the neckline, and the hem barely touches the top of her matching black slacks. There's a thin looped belt slung around her hips, bringing the eye to her hourglass shape. On her feet are my kryptonite: a pair of dark-red stilettos.

Sexy as fuck.

I clench my jaw and suck in a long, slow breath, waiting for the frustration to pass.

Royce glances my way over the mug he's sipping from and clears his throat. "Ms. Stanton—"

"Alexis. Please. We're all very informal around here. Everyone calls me Lexie, actually."

Roy nods. "Okay, Lexie, what does the team know so far?"

She stands near her desk, opens her laptop, and hits a button. The flat screen comes to life showing fifteen different squares. Each square is where a camera is planted in a different location in her warehouse.

"Well, as you can see on screen two, Wendy is sitting with Kidd, deep in training on our systems. According to him, she's a very quick study. More than that. Last night he told me it was strange that she wanted to work for us in a lower-level coding and analysis position, when he thinks she's a bit of a genius and could work anywhere. We might have to bring him in on our secret spy work."

I smile, proud of my own quick smarts in hiring Wendy. "Who's Kidd?"

This time, Alexis preens, her face taking on a beautiful glow. "My baby brother."

"Fella's name is Kidd?" Royce chuckles.

Alexis's expression completely morphs from one of happiness to annoyance. "Yes, our parents were *hilarious.*" Her words are laced with disdain.

Royce stands up, lifting his hands in surrender. "Hey now, Ms. Stanton, Lexie, I meant no offense. My name is Royce, not so common either. And the fact that his name is Kidd and he's your kid brother was humorous. I apologize for not being more professional."

She shakes her head and runs her fingers through her long tresses before going up to the bookcase and picking up one of the photos. "No, it's just . . . it's not your fault, okay? I'm protective of him. He's all I've got in the world, and he's been down a rough road. Our parents hated his mere existence, feeling caged in by having another baby late in life when they didn't want one. Later, he dealt with bullies in school, fighting until he was beaten bloody and everything in between. I'm his only family, and he's mine. We disowned our parents long ago. And now, he's doing so well, and he's only twenty-three."

"Royce meant no harm," I say, backing him up, and walk to her side to look at the image in the frame she's holding. It's the two of them back-to-back in front of the office sign.

She laughs dryly. "I know, I'm sorry, Royce. No harm done. Really."

Royce dips his chin and puts his hands in his pockets.

"Did you notify the rest of the team about our arrival?" I circle the conversation back around to work.

She nods. "Had a late meeting yesterday and introduced Wendy, which everyone seemed to take in stride. Then I mentioned we had a new client coming in tomorrow, and the two of you coming midmorning today. Royce, I'm going to drop you off with my CFO to start the evaluation of our finances. Parker, I'm going to set you up in one of the small cozy conference rooms to start your interviews."

I clap my hands together absentmindedly and hiss when the pain from my broken fingers and stitched palm ripples up my arm.

Alexis rushes to grab my wrists and cradle my hands. "Poor baby. How did it happen?" She leans down and places a kiss on the top of my hand the way a mother would her small child. Except when she's done, still hovering over my hand, she lifts her gaze and grins wickedly, blatantly flirting.

Jesus, what the hell am I going to do with this woman?

Royce jingles some change in his pocket, which seems to knock the client from her trance. She slowly eases her body up, making sure to jut her chest out for maximum cleavage perusal. It takes everything I have in me not to take the bait. I mean, I can look if I want. Skyler and I are done.

D-o-n-e.

At least *I* know we are. *She* should know after her betrayal, but I can't go there with Alexis, knowing I haven't broken it off with Skyler.

I don't even know if I'd want to anyway. For the first time in my life I'm not ready to jump into the sack with a hot blonde.

My chest tightens, and I swallow down the dryness in my throat.

"Shall I take you both to your spaces?"

I lift my hand to open the door. "After you, Alexis."

"Oh, no, no, I insist." She smirks and opens her office door for the two of us to pass through. We do, and as we walk forward, I glance over my shoulder to see she's definitely taking in our asses from behind. I stop abruptly, and she brings a shiny red fingernail to her teeth and bites it, smiling around the digit while maneuvering her body in front of mine, her chest just barely grazing mine.

She bats her eyelashes. "Sorry." Even though her tone is teasing, I'm gritting my teeth.

I bite into my cheek until I taste the metallic flavor of my own blood. The pain reminds me not to respond. I'm not getting into anything with Alexis. Hell, I'm not getting into anything with *any* client again. Ever. Been there, twice now. The first worked out aces, with me having my first ever female friend. The second tore through my heart, dropped it on the floor, and dug her spiked heel into it for good measure.

"Funny, Alexis, but we don't know where we're going," I remind her, doing my best to play along without leading her on.

"I know where I'd like to go," she states, scanning my suit-clad form up and down while wiggling her body enough to make her big boobs jiggle.

"Jesus," I blurt, and glance away from the show.

Royce's eyebrows rise up on his forehead as he covers his shock with one of his big paws.

"Just teasing." She chuckles, moving in front of us down the hall. "Come on, boys, we'll do the rounds. I'll introduce you formally to each department and give a reminder of what you're here to do. Then I'll leave Royce with my CFO and get you, Parker, settled into your own *private space* for the week." Her voice dips with innuendo on the last sentence.

Sweet mother of God. I cannot deal with a woman wanting my attention. Not now. Not this week, when I don't even know which way is up or down.

I clap Royce on the back and urge him to go ahead of me, adding distance between Alexis and me.

"Am I your human shield now?" he whispers under his breath as we follow her through the center of the warehouse.

"Is that a problem?"

His coal-like gaze shoots to mine. "Never, brother. I'll guard you with everything I've got. Whether it be tech goddesses or hot celebrity blondes, I've always got your back."

I purse my lips and nod tightly, letting the situation wash over me.

I'm not strong enough to handle what getting into anything with Alexis would entail, nor do I want to. I'm the weakest I've ever been, and if I'm being honest with myself, I'd just be using her to forget someone else. After the shit that went down with Kayla, I promised myself

I'd never treat a woman like just a warm body and nothing more. I've grown up. The man I was in college is not the man I am today. I'd like to believe I'm stronger, more mature, and I respect the female mind and body as much as my own. A night in the sheets with Alexis would feel good for the time it took to get off. Then reality would strike, and I'd be in the exact same position I'm in now, only with another hole in my notch-filled belt.

Right then my phone buzzes in my pocket. I pull it out and note the display.

From: Peaches
To: Parker Ellis

Just seeing her nickname, I feel warmth spread over my entire body like a blanket on a cold night in Massachusetts. I clench my jaw and take a deep breath while following Alexis and holding my phone so tight it might have dents by the time I get to wherever she is leading me. I don't read the message and shove the damn thing in my pocket.

Alexis introduces us to a slew of staff before dropping Roy off at finance and leading me to a corner of the building that seems outside of the action. It almost feels like she's leading me to the guillotine, though I'm sure it's the effect of the burning-hot coal in my pocket in the form of a message from my ex-girlfriend that's messing with my heart and mind.

"Here we are." Alexis opens the door to what looks like a reading room.

"You gotta be kidding me. This is a conference room?"

She smiles and shrugs. "I prefer to spend my time at work being comfortable. I'm here so much, I need things that put me at ease and in a good headspace to keep my muse happy."

"Your muse?"

Alexis leans her hip against the arm of the couch and crosses her arms over her massive chest. The effect has her boobs practically falling out of her halter. I can't help but take in the fleshy globes. They're practically calling out my name, waving a red flag to get my attention.

"Mm-hmm. You know what else keeps my muse happy?" Once again, her voice is sultry and dripping with a flirtatious flare.

My mouth goes dry as my body heats and reacts to her blatant sexuality, making me afraid to ask. "I wouldn't have a clue." The words come out sounding scratchy.

She smirks, knowing the kind of attention and effect her body, voice, and forward nature produce when it comes to the male species. Alexis Stanton is a man's wet dream incarnate. She looks like a Playboy bunny, dresses like a high-end escort, but speaks her mind like a man. I can't help but wonder if this is a facade. A mask she wears to throw off the opposite sex.

According to her background file from Wendy, she's not only at the top of her game and smart as hell, she's obliterated the competition in her field, all of whom were male competitors. She's been seen publicly with two of those men in what looked like romantic situations, but none have claimed to be in a relationship with her. At least none have *admitted* publicly to a romantic entanglement. Perhaps that's why her main competitor has scored her product information and released it early. They're going after her for personal reasons. It's definitely food for thought and something to look into more.

"Have a seat, Mr. Ellis, and if you're lucky, I'll show you instead of tell you." She lifts her hand, runs it down the side of her rib cage, and rests it delicately on a well-rounded hip.

As I move around her toward the couch, she reaches out that same hand and runs her finger down the center of my chest, stopping at the top of my slacks and belt buckle.

I jump back. "Ms. Stanton, Lexie . . ." I cough and raise my good hand between us. "Look, you are a beautiful woman—"

"I'm glad you think so." She takes a single step forward as I take one step back.

"I don't think this is a good idea." I gesture to her chest and then mine.

Her eyes light up with a mischievous twinkle, and my heart sinks. "Oh, but I think it's a very good idea. You see, I'm the boss, you're the boss . . ."

I shake my head. "I'm-I'm just coming out of a relationship," I state lamely.

She frowns. "Aw, that sounds harsh. Let me kiss it and make it feel better like I did your hand." She advances another step until my ass is resting against the round table in the center of the room.

"Alexis, as I said, you're . . . pretty . . ."

Her lips twitch. "Now I'm just pretty? I think you're trying to talk yourself out of touching me when you're clearly interested. I've seen the way you look at me, at my body. You want me as much as I want you. I'm rarely wrong as it pertains to chemistry between people. Your energy combined with mine . . . would be explosive!" She loops both of her hands around my neck and presses her boobs against my chest.

I keep my hands at my sides. "Jesus." My temperature rises along with my cock, and I feel dizzy, like I've had a couple of cocktails. "Another time, another place, you would be . . . hell, you would be the one up against the wall with your dress around your waist. Except, I'm not in the right headspace. I told you. I'm coming out of a relationship. It's uh . . . very . . . fresh," I finish lamely.

"Mm-hmm . . ." She runs her nose down the side of my cheek and down to my neck. A tremor ripples up my spine, goading me to take what she's offering as the heat of her breath tickles my skin. My dick perks up even more and hardens in my pants.

She smiles. "Your mouth is coming up with all kinds of excuses, but your body is responding to me."

I lick my lips, and her gaze drops to my mouth. Christ! She doesn't miss a beat.

She lifts up onto her toes, her body now fully flush against mine from chest to knees. I close my eyes and breathe through the sensation, desperately trying not to respond to her nearness, the scent of honeysuckle mixed with melon wafting in the air from her body, her warmth, those succulent breasts bulging so far out of her top that if I dipped my head a few inches, I could run my tongue along the fleshy surface.

I groan, finally bringing my hands to her hips. She smiles and hovers close to my lips. I can practically taste the coffee on her breath.

"Are you saying no?" she asks.

This moment. It's a moment I'll likely regret for the rest of my life. The moment I was offered a feast of carnal delights when I was absolutely *starved* for attention, for human touch, for the desire to just let it all disappear and gorge. Gorge on all the beauty Alexis is offering, but the knife wedged in my heart by Skyler is still there, dripping blood, making it hard to take a single breath. The blackness surrounding my soul isn't ready to leave, not even for a blessed moment.

I push her hips back. Her hands drop from around my neck.

"I'm saying, not now." I swallow the dust coating my throat.

She cocks an eyebrow and smiles sexily. "That's not a no. In my experience, that's an official *maybe*. I can live with that. When you're ready to have some guilt-free fornication . . ." She steps away and heads to the door, where she stops and taps the doorframe. ". . . I'm your girl." She winks and leaves me standing with a semi and a bleeding heart.

I close my eyes, take a few deep breaths, go over to the door, and close it.

What have I gotten myself into? I need to just tell her to back off.

I let it go too far.

Why did I do that?

Because I'm weak. I'm hurting. Worse, I don't know how to fix this empty feeling inside of me. The old me would have had Alexis naked and bent over the table in two minutes, tops. This me, the one who's still in love with my ex and can't stop being wrapped up in the agony of not having her in my life to take advantage of a good time, leans against the door, defeated and numb, before I remember she texted about a half hour ago. I pull out my phone and scan the text:

> I miss you. I'm not me anymore . . . without you. I'll be waiting. I think I'll wait forever.

"Fuck!" I grate into the empty room, the desire to destroy my new phone just as prevalent as it was when I smashed the old one against her kitchen wall.

Tension builds in my shoulders, and I start to pace like a caged animal.

She wronged me. Me! I didn't cheat on her.

Did she cheat on me?

The questions are endless, running a marathon in my mind, never stopping to take a break or a sip of water. Always just running and running. Making me dizzy, incapable of fluid thought.

I have to deal with her. Talk it out as the guys suggested. Kayla tried that. Lied her ass off trying to get me back. Greg, the same. The woman I loved and the man I trusted betrayed me years ago, then spent countless attempts trying to make it better, make me forgive their sins with excuses and rationalizations.

Well, I'm not buying it with Skyler.

She betrayed me!

With anger beating a heavy drum through my system, I bring up my texts.

To: Peaches
From: Parker Ellis

Stop texting. It's over. You cheated. We're done. End
of story.

I read and reread the message. That knife in my heart twists, dig-
ging in another centimeter deeper. My mouth salivates, and once again,
I want to toss my lunch like a little bitch. Taking several lungfuls of air,
I get my rage under control.

*This is it. You're telling her goodbye. Just click "Send." You can do it.
It's time. Let it go. Set her free.*

With everything I have inside me, I do it and click "Send."

My eyes mist over, and I rub at them with my fist.

I love her, but she was never mine to love in the first place.

My cell phone buzzes, and chucking it against the wall is really
starting to have some serious merit—business contacts, email, work,
and everything else be damned.

From: Peaches
To: Parker Ellis

Our story is never going to end. I didn't cheat. I can
see you need more time.

She didn't cheat.

Cheat.

Cheat.

The word *CHEAT* fills every inch of my mind, takes over my body,
pushing the knife deeper into my bloody heart.

"Fucking liar!" I bellow, hurling my phone so hard against the steel
wall that it shatters into shiny red speckles like blood spatter. The red

case I got at the airport did nothing to help protect the phone against my rage.

I walk over to the phone and stomp on the offender until there's nothing but shards left against the concrete floor.

"You are a liar. A no-good cheat. Just like Kayla. Like Greg. Like every fucking woman out there!"

I slump into the cushy love seat along one wall and rest my head in my hand.

"It has to be a lie." I shake my head and let the ugly in, invading my thoughts.

She's trying to save her own ass. But why? Why would she hold on? What is she fighting for? Skyler is a rare beauty. As perfect in real life as she is on screen. With her, what you see is what you get. Her body, her stunning face, there's no makeup needed. But makeup can't take away the blackness in her heart. I cringe.

"What's her motive?" I seethe through dry lips, and get up to pace once again.

With Kayla, she needed to be taken care of. I was her golden goose. Her family had money, sure, but her father wanted her to marry and be someone else's problem. I signed up, hand in the air, screaming, *Pick me, pick me!* Only I signed up for love. For a woman who would be there for me in all things. Support me in life. Raise a family. Work in a partnership in the things we dreamed of having together.

Kayla just wanted money and a lifestyle she was used to. The man didn't matter, which is why she was fucking me and my best friend Greg. It's also why she fought so hard for me over Greg, because Roy and Bo both backed my play. Kicked him out of our business plan to participate in the creation of IG, which meant he'd have to find a job at a corporation and work his way up to having money. This would take time, and Kayla was not a stupid woman. With Royce running our finances and investment portfolios, we were already on the verge of being self-made millionaires. Kayla wanted a piece of that pie and played the odds. She lost.

I guess in the end, I won because I got out of committing to a gold digger. Of course, it didn't feel that way at the time. It felt a lot like losing.

The thing is, Skyler has a hundred times the amount of money I have. What could she want? Why is she fighting so hard to save us?

In my swirling emotions and anger, the answer doesn't come. Instead, I take a half hour pulling my shit together and calling the first person on staff I need to interview.

It's time to dump my mind into the job. Let go of everything else that's controlling me and focus on the work.

Focus on the work.

Focus on the work.

I repeat the mantra in my mind a few times before the first staff member enters the room. It's Alexis's assistant. She's a shy speck of a woman named Molly. She looks like a librarian who's usually got her head stuck in a book instead of reality. And I can tell just from her body language that she's afraid to lose her job. This one is going to be a quick interview.

She's not our spy.

4

My eyes are blurry as sleepiness invades my mind. The room is too damn comfortable. Even the chairs she has around the circular table are plush leather, so soft my body sinks into them. The chairs also rock. Not exactly conducive to getting work done, more like screwing off or taking a snooze.

Across from the table and chairs are a TV and love seat. I'm surprised there isn't a fireplace in here. This looks like someone's small living room and dining area. The walls are painted soft beige with various tasteful prints and paintings meticulously placed on them. She's made a warehouse a home office with twenty-two employees who have their own sumptuous spaces. I think Alexis would give Google competition in a battle over who has the better work environment.

As I blink harshly a few times and stand up to move around, I note a ginger tabby cat walking along a wooden beam outside of the office, where I've left the door open. It stares momentarily from its perch, and I wonder to myself how a busy woman like Alexis can take care of a cat. I can barely take care of myself. Definitely not a pet. I'm not home enough. Even plants that are given to me as gifts end up in the trash after a few weeks of being neglected.

The cat jumps down and saunters into the office as though he owns the place. He pops up onto the arm of the couch and then the back, casually making his way to where I stand. When he gets a foot away from me he stops, looks directly at me, and meows.

I reach out my hand. "What is it, boy?" He rubs his head on my hand, demanding to be petted. I take the bait, because who wouldn't? He's a furry, cute entity rubbing his sweet head on my hand. I give him a few pets and scratch against his cheek. He starts to purr melodically.

A voice interrupts me and my new furry friend. "I see you've met Spartacus."

I turn to the man standing in the doorway. "It seems I have." I stop petting the cat to reach out my good hand.

He shakes it. "Kidd Stanton. I'm next on the list of interviews," he supplies helpfully. Alexis set the schedule so that the last person would notify the next person in line for their interview.

"So, you are. Come on in, have a seat."

I pull out his employee file from the folder on the table, as well as my tablet, which has the information Wendy provided on each staff member. I read them all on the plane ride over so I'm aware of what his "other" file states. The big surprise was finding out Alexis filed for guardianship when Kidd was fifteen and their parents didn't contest it, signing over their rights without ever seeing the inside of a courtroom.

Kidd sits down across from me, seeming perfectly at ease with being here. Probably because he knows his sister would never fire him.

He shrugs and starts off before I can ask a question. "What do you want to know, man? I'm an open book."

"Tell me about what you do here."

"I lead the coding and analysis team. Under Alexis's watchful eye, of course." He chuckles.

"Course." I smile, making sure to keep the conversation easy and my body language relaxed.

"Been coding under Lex's guidance since around the age of fifteen, so 'bout eight years. As my file there will show." He jerks his chin toward the file I'm holding in front of me. "Lex hired me right outta high school. I didn't have the grades or desire for college anyhow."

"And you took to the job."

"Like a drunk to a mickey, eh?" He laughs heartily.

The young man smiles a lot, seems to be comfortable in his own skin, and has a happy nature. His features mimic his sister's. Blond hair, blue eyes. His hair is more of a dirty blond than a golden hue. He has a solid day or two's worth of scruff on his jaw and a silver hoop in his left ear. Tattoos line his forearms, depicting a myriad of images. A lion on one, a sword on the other. A distinct red heart adorns his left inside forearm, and the word "LEX" in thick block letters is drawn in its center.

I nod at his tats. "Nice ink."

He pushes up his henley farther, showing off more artwork. "Yeah, I'm proud of it. Drew each design myself. Kind of a hobby."

I look closer and note the scars slicing horizontally underneath the ink close to the dip in his elbow. I don't say anything, for one because it would be highly inappropriate, and two because sometimes a person needs their secrets. The wounds look old, aged enough that the ink over them is a tad faded. My guess, he did those when he was a teen, before he was old enough to get the ink to cover them.

"Lex?" I ask, making note of the blood-red, vibrant heart.

His smile before was happy and unguarded; this one is sensational, inspired. "My sister. Alexis. Big boss lady."

I grin. "You tatted your sister's name on your arm?"

He nods with glee. No bullshit. Happy as a clam. "For sure. I know it sounds odd, but my sister is my life. My whole heart. Without her, man, I wouldn't be the me I am today. I'd probably be in jail or dead for fighting."

Without her. I wouldn't be me.

I'm not me anymore . . . without you.

I close my eyes as Skyler's words in her recent text come back to haunt me. Chills race up my spine, and I clench my jaw and breathe through the pain those words cause. I grip the pencil I'm holding so hard it snaps in half.

"Whoa. You okay?" Kidd frowns.

I blink a few times. "Headache. Sorry. Probably from the travel. I'm fine. Continue." I grab the water bottle that was brought to me earlier and swallow down half in one go.

"Yeah, well, what I was saying is"—he fingers the heart tattoo—"my sister, man, she's like my mother figure and best friend all rolled into one. We're tight as two sibs can be. I got this for her when I turned eighteen. See, if I pull my arm up against my chest"—he imitates the words by bringing his left arm up to his chest, inner forearm facing in—"it touches my heart. Right where she'll always be."

"Powerful," I offer, still shaken by his remark so closely mimicking Skyler's text.

Kidd leans back and rocks the chair. Not a care in the world. "I think so. Anyway, why are you here? We're not hurting for money or productivity. Lex would have given me a heads-up. There's not a lot we keep from one another."

On a split-second decision, I choose to give him half of the truth since I'm getting absolutely nothing in the way of nerves or fear of any kind coming off him. This could be because he's completely innocent of any wrongdoing, or a very good liar who is using his relationship with his sister against her.

"Then you know that the last three products have been leaked and released in advance by Stanton Cybertech's direct competitor."

He scowls. "Yeah, bunch of hosers, the entire lot of them."

I flatten my lips. "Be that as it may, we need to see what's happening on the production scale. Perhaps something is leaking into public knowledge without a person being the wiser."

"Or maybe we have a mole on the team?" he suggests.

Interesting how he went there first. "What would give you that impression?"

He crinkles his nose, his happiness dissipating instantly. "The coding and security is done entirely by Lex and me. We are the only two who know the back end fully because we created the damn thing from scratch. The rest of the team creates new codes and programs to work inside of it but could never break through a firewall we've created."

"And if there were a mole in the system, would you have any idea who that could be? New employees, anything could be helpful toward figuring out how your sister, your legacy . . . ," I add to see how he reacts. He simply nods and looks off into the distance. ". . . is being sacrificed. Anyone you have a strange feeling about or suspect might have a negative feeling about working here?"

He shakes his head. "There's a new girl, Wendy Pritchard, who was hired, but she's brand-new. No reason to suspect her. We actually have very little turnover. I don't think we've hired anyone new outside of Wendy in over two years."

Wendy Pritchard.

Looks like my office nymph changed her last name to her fiancé's. I'll bet she enjoyed the hell out of that. Probably created an entire life around the name too.

I nod and stand up. "If you think of anything, I'll be here all week evaluating the processes and workflow as well as the productivity of each member of the team in the hopes of figuring out how the information is leaking. I'm sure it's safe to say your job is secure."

He grins, the happiness he entered with seeping into his form once more. Kidd offers his hand and slaps the side of my bicep. "Hey, if you need a bud to hang out with after hours, get some drinks, see a little of Montreal, I'm your guy. I know a cool bar called Brutopia. They have great beers, good pub food, and often have some stellar live bands, if that's your thing. My girl and I would be happy to show you around."

"Your girl?"

"Yeah. My fiancée. Just asked her to marry me a few months ago. Best decision of my life, sharing it with her. She loves my sister—they're like two giggling little girls when they're together—and she looks up to Lex like a big sis same way I do. Can't wait, man. We're getting married next summer when the weather's nicer. Up in Old Quebec."

"Wow. Marriage."

Marriage. He's already found the woman he wants to settle down with. And me? I'm scratching the surface of thirty and have just lost the love of my life. An empty hollowness fills my gut, making it twist and churn.

"How old are you again?" My throat sounds raspy when I reply.

"Twenty-three. Smart enough to know when I've got a good thing and to hold on tight and never let it go, stupid enough to rush it. Me and my girl don't care. We're soul mates."

Soul mates.

I thought Skyler was my soul mate. A zing of lightning hits my stomach, and I curve my arm around myself protectively, trying to breathe through the sudden pain.

"You got someone, man?" He cracks a grin. "Aw, sure you do. Good-looking guy like yourself."

I shake my head. "Actually . . ." I swallow the lump forming in my throat. "We're uh, on the outs."

His body sways toward mine, and he locks his grip around my bicep again. "Sucks. You'll pull through. If she's the one, it will all work out."

I should stop the conversation where it is, get things back onto professional turf, but something inside me is screaming out, and I have to ask. "What do you think makes this woman your soul mate?"

Kidd purses his lips and rubs at his chin. "Well, for one, I had a girl I loved in the past. Had to end things with her to focus on the job. I was a punk kid and not paying attention to the responsibilities that Lex entrusted me with. My work was suffering, my life was turned upside down, and I hated the path I was headed down. Spent the next few years focusing on the job until I met Victoria. She adds to my life and doesn't take away from it."

"That's it, she adds to your life, unlike the first woman you scraped off?"

He shakes his head emphatically. "Naw, it's more that Eloise wanted all of my time and attention. That's my ex."

I nod, following along as though every last word is the last I'll hear. For the life of me, I haven't a clue why.

"With Victoria, she fits right in, you know? Like the last puzzle piece of a whole picture. She just fits. She completes me. When I'm down, she lifts me up. When I'm not with her, I feel her absence, right here, man . . ." He points to his abdomen. "In my gut. Yet I know she's thinking 'bout me and I her. Then, the times we are together, it's explosive."

I run my hand over the back of my neck, massaging the ever-present tension I haven't been able to shake since I left San Francisco.

Kidd walks over to the door. "Most of all, though, Vic is someone I can't imagine not being in my world. Like Lex. She's integral to who I am now. I appreciate who I am with her. She makes me like myself."

"Well, man, hold on to her and never let her go, because in my experience with women, I can promise you, a love like that is rare." Practically nonexistent, more like it. Though I don't add that, because he doesn't deserve my bullshit layered on top of his happiness.

"I know. It's why I'm going to make it mine legally." He waggles his eyebrows.

I chuckle, and he taps the doorframe the same way his sister did earlier today before leaving. I stare at the cat, who's now sleeping perched on the edge of the love seat back.

"What do you think, Spartacus? Are soul mates bullshit?"

The cat opens one eye, stares at me pointedly, and then closes it.

"Yep. It's what I thought. Total bullshit. I wish him luck, though. He seems like a good guy."

***

I've just sat on my bed and let my body fall back into a heap when the connecting door in my hotel room flies open, and Wendy bounces in.

"What the hell? Two phones in less than a week?" Her tone is shrill and grating on my last goddamned nerve.

"I dropped it, okay?"

She makes a face that tells me she's not buying it. "You dropped it. If that's the case, it would still be working, boss man. Not shattered into bits for the janitor to vacuum up when he cleans the warehouse tonight. You're lucky I went in there after you left and snagged the SIM card. Luckier still, it must have bounced off the wall, because I found it stuck in the threads of the area rug, away from the primary stomping you gave the old phone. You're also lucky I always keep a backup phone in my bag."

This piques my attention. "You do?"

She grins. "Yep." She hands me an exact replica of my last iPhone but with a plastic Rubbermaid-like case.

I slide my fingertips over the bumpy surface. The phone looks like it's been encased in an inch of rubber. "What the fuck is this?"

Wendy puts a hand to her hip. "It's an OtterBox. It's the thick one meant for men working in construction who drop their phones from high distances, et cetera. I figure if they can drop it from two stories up and the phone survives, this one should survive you catapulting it into a wall. I mean, your mom says you were a star baseball player, but really, Parker, this is phone number three. Give it a rest, okay? You're bleeding money in phone replacements outside of the warranty time frame."

I huff loudly, and she just bats her eyelashes, completely unfazed.

"I'm not using it like this." I hand it to her. "Remove that crap. The damn thing won't fit into my pants pocket."

Wendy inhales loudly and sighs even louder when she grabs the phone from my hand. "Fine." As if she had prepared for my refusal, she pulls a sleek metal case from her back pocket.

I watch while she removes the rubber childproof case and puts the sexy sleek one on, pocketing the old one. She hands it to me. "It's already loaded up with your contacts again, messages, voice mails, and emails."

"You know my password for the Google Cloud?"

She chuckles under her breath. "Sweetheart, I know your PIN on your debit card. I could probably get into your gym locker quicker than you. Never underestimate what I can and cannot do. Besides, you scared the shit out of me when you went off the grid today. I had to do a drive-by of your office pretending I was looking for a bathroom to make sure you were in that conference room."

"Wendy, really, you need to stop worrying about us." Guilt oozes into my mind, making me feel even more twitchy than I already do.

Her face flushes red, and she narrows her eyes. "Every time your temper flares, you do something insane. Destroy your phone, punch a wall. What next? You gonna drive off a bridge? This behavior is upsetting for those of us who give a shit about you. I may be your PA, but I'm also your friend, someone who loves you like family. This path you're on is dangerous and destructive."

"I'm sorry; it won't happen again." Even with the apology and declaration, I'm not sure it won't happen again.

"*Sorry* doesn't cut it, Parker. The three of us are worried about you. So much so, I read your texts from Skyler. If you want to fire me for invading your privacy, fine. I'll deal with it." Her chest moves up and down as though she's breathing fast. She's probably scared I am going to fire her, but honestly, I don't care.

My shoulders sink, and I lie back down on the bed and stare at the blank white ceiling. An empty void, just like my life without Skyler in it. "I'm not going to fire you."

She sits on the bed and brings her knees up, where she rests her chin. It's a move Sky did all the time. God! Why can't I just forget about the damn woman for one fucking day? Hell, I'd settle for half a day . . . an hour even.

Wendy grins. "Goody. Does that mean we can talk about what she wrote?" Her tone is hopeful.

"No," I state flatly.

"Parker, she said she didn't cheat. She's begging, freaking *begging* to talk to you. Hell, she's pleading to talk to *me*, and I've been ignoring her messages. And you know, *you know* how hard that is for me. All I've ever wanted was a bunch of friends and a big family. First, I scored Mick. Now I have you guys. And for a little while, I had a new best girlfriend."

Great. Now I'm hurting Wendy with my jacked-up relationship. "Guilt trips don't become you, minxy," I say dryly, rubbing at my tired eyes.

She eases her knees to the side and puts a hand to my shoulder. "Neither does avoidance become you."

"I'm not avoiding anything. She betrayed me." Why does it feel like I have to keep reminding everyone that I'm the one who got screwed over? Sky burned *me*. Just like Kayla. Just like all women I end up having romantic feelings for.

"She says she didn't." She shrugs nonchalantly as though we're not talking about the woman I gave my entire heart and soul to.

I suck in a harsh breath. "And you believe her. Even though he said they rekindled their relationship, and she was there. She spent the night with him, Wendy. There's no denying it."

"I think you want to believe that she hurt you. Why is that?"

"Because she did!" I sit up and stare Wendy down. "I was going to tell her I loved her!"

Wendy gasps, and her eyes fill with tears. She reaches out a hand to my cocked knee. "Park . . ."

I push her hand away, not wanting her pity or comfort. "No. I flew straight to New York to be with the woman I loved. To tell her to her face that I loved her and that me and my team were going to solve her problem with her ex. And what did I find?"

A tear slips down Wendy's pearlescent cheek.

"An empty fuckin' apartment. An empty bed that should have had the woman I love in it! Then I wake up to her ex in my ear and hearing her in the background. What would you think, Wendy? As a woman? Why would you have any reason to be in your ex's hotel room at shit o'clock in the morning, huh? Tell me."

Another tear falls. "I don't know. The only thing I do know is that I recognize when a woman is in love. And Skyler is in love with you. All of us saw it at Lucky's. Saw it in your eyes and hers. A woman in love would not cheat on her man. Not a good woman. And Skyler is a good woman, Parker, or you wouldn't have fallen in love with her in the first place!"

I get up and pace the room before heading to the bar and pouring myself two fingers of scotch. "You want?"

"Fuck yeah. No one should drink alone."

I pour her a couple of fingers and pass her the tumbler. She tosses the entire thing back like a pro. "Fuck!"

She holds out the tumbler. "One more. This time I'll sip. I like to get the buzz going right away."

Laughter spills out my lungs. I wouldn't have believed I could laugh right now if my life depended on it, yet this thin woman, who's pixielike for her size with big easy smiles, and fire-red hair that glistens when it catches the light, brings it out of me.

I pour her another and hand it to her. She clinks it with mine. "It's going to be okay," she remarks with such sincerity I want to believe her.

"You think?" I swallow down some whiskey and let it burn a fiery trail into my gut that can't seem to settle.

Her gaze settles on mine. "If you buck up and talk to her, yeah, I do."

I shake my head. "Not ready."

She firms her shoulders and straightens her back. "Well, when you are, I'll be there for you," she says instantly.

I smile softly, wanting her to know I appreciate her friendship more than I can possibly say right now. "You will, won't you?" I declare, allowing the words to sink into my heart, tugging that dagger back an inch.

She smiles wide. "That's what sisters are for, right? To help you with women. Tell you when you've got the wrong one on the hook. Call her a ho-bag. Remind you when you're being a stupid ass."

Once more, laughter bubbles up and flows to the surface.

"And Park?" she murmurs, before sipping her whiskey.

"Yeah, minxy?"

"You're being a stupid ass."

5

"Alexis, there's nothing in your financials that indicates any form of embezzling. Our gal pulled all of the financials on every employee, and not one of them has any fluctuations that are noteworthy." Royce sighs and puts the tablet down on the coffee table in her office.

She picks up the device and scans each document.

Two days of Royce reviewing Stanton Cybertech's finances and me interviewing sixteen employees have come up with jack.

Alexis inhales loudly and lets it out with a groan from her crimson-painted lips. Today she looks out of this world. Her golden hair is up in a messy chignon, and her lips are a glistening cherry red that match her top-to-toe red silk catsuit, or is it a *jumpsuit* the ladies are calling it these days? I'd have to ask Bo to be certain. Not that it matters. On her feet are the same pair of nude stilettos she wore when she met us in Boston. I lick my lips and notice her toes match her outfit at a siren red. The woman is sex on stilts.

Just as the thought hits me, Alexis places her hand on my upper thigh and leans forward. "What do you think, Parker?"

I clear my throat, grab her hand, and move it off of my thigh as subtly as I can, putting it on the couch cushion between us.

"Hate to say it, but whoever is doing this to you either isn't making a dime, or maybe they don't work here."

She frowns. "But I thought because the leaks were making my competitor rich, we'd find the source here."

I run my hand down my pant leg, straightening out any wrinkles in the fabric. "Ideally, that would make sense. We need to talk to Wendy, though, see if she's found out anything about the technology behind the scenes. Maybe we'll learn more about the potential leaks if we find out who's using the system to create viruses and manipulating your coding so you have errors. I can bring her into my interview like everyone else. Get some answers."

She nods. "Okay. I guess that's a step in the right direction. Royce, are you sure there aren't any discrepancies?"

He nods, leans back into the chair, and rests his ankle on his opposite knee. "Sorry. I've looked up and down, not to mention reviewed each employee's personal checking, savings, and investment accounts. Some are doing well in the stock market, but most are living off their salaries, which I find are very generous."

She smiles and winks at him. "I like to make sure my people are happy."

He clears his throat and adjusts his tie. "That is obvious. And you do it well."

Her gaze flicks to mine. "So I've been told." She licks her lips seductively.

I have to hold back from grinding my teeth and calling her out on her bullshit. There's forward, and then there's *forward*. Without sounding like a pansy-assed prepubescent teen, I'm getting a little tired of the innuendo and double entendres Alexis is firing off. She's like a dog with a bone. Once she sets her sights, it's game on. Almost as if getting me to submit is a challenge she must win. Then again, I imagine a woman like her doesn't get turned down often, if ever. It makes me think she may not even realize she's playing a game. Like a battle of the wills. So she gets a man she desires in her bed, then what? It's not like she's winning a trophy or an award. What's the endgame?

"Well, all right." Royce stands up. "I'm going to go back to finance and see what else I can drum up, if anything. Bo should be here any minute," he says, right as there is a knock at her office door.

"Lexie, a Bogart Montgomery is here for his three o'clock meeting," her receptionist says demurely.

Royce walks over to the door and sidesteps around Bo as though he doesn't know him. "Excuse me."

"Sure." Bo steps to the side as Royce moves his big body down the hall.

Bo turns to me and Alexis, his eyes widen, and he takes his time blatantly checking out our client from head to toe and back again.

My shoulders fall as if they're being pushed down by two metal robot hands. This is going to suck. I can already feel the drama of Bo being into Alexis unfolding. Tension coils in my back and up my neck, tightening the muscles.

"Well, hello, gorgeous." Bo shuts the door behind him and swaggers over to where Alexis is sitting. He holds out his hand.

She places her palm into his and cocks an unimpressed eyebrow as he leans down and kisses the top of her hand. He continues, "Am I awake? Because you look like my dream come true."

"Easy, tiger. This is our client, Alexis Stanton," I warn.

"Sexy name for a sexy siren," he purrs, ignoring my warning completely.

Ugh. I press my temples with thumb and forefinger.

Alexis's expression changes to one of confidence. "Now this is the type of man I'm used to dealing with." Alexis crosses her arms over her voluptuous chest, pushing her breasts up even higher.

"Ignore him. We do." I wave my bandaged hand in the air.

Bo plucks at his goatee; as he does, the buckles on his leather jacket jingle.

"Bo, to quickly get you up to date, Royce hasn't found anything in the finances of any employee to conclude that they're being paid for information. I haven't found anything in the sixteen staff I've interviewed, although I have seven more, including Wendy. Nothing they've said or the answers to my questions suggests they're unhappy or indifferent about Alexis and Stanton Cybertech. Each person is elated to be working here and seems genuinely baffled by the products leaking. Apparently, you're an exceptional boss." I dip a respectful nod her way, trying to make sure there's not even a hint of innuendo to my tone.

She grins and bites down on her plump bottom lip. "I'm exceptional at a lot of things when given a chance."

Bo groans. "Jesus! A woman after my own heart." In a dramatic move, he crosses his hand over his chest where his heart lies.

I ignore both of them and continue with my findings. "I've also reviewed all of the lie detector tests, and each person passed with flying colors."

Bo chuckles while he eases into the seat across from Alexis, his gaze never leaving her. "Lie detectors are a cinch to pass. The courts repeatedly reject the use of polygraph evidence because it's unreliable. You're far better at reading people than a lie detector. In my opinion anyway."

"Thank you. Still that leaves us at square one. You're up, buddy. When Alexis gets you into a room with a bulk of the team members to work on your application, feel them out. You know what to do."

He smirks. "I always know how to work a person, mentally or *physically*." His tone is filled to the brim with innuendo and pointed directly at Alexis.

Sighing, I get up and move to the door. "On that note, I'm going to go back to my room to get the rest of the interviews out of the way."

"Awesome, I thought I'd never be left alone with the most beautiful woman alive." Bo leers and smiles wide.

Heck, maybe having Bo on-site will give Alexis a dose of her own medicine. Couldn't hurt at this point. If her focus is on him and not me, I won't have to deal with the sexy temptress coming after me anymore. Not that I can't handle her . . . maybe, probably. I've thwarted her attempts so far, which means in this game she's playing, I'm winning. Not something I imagine she's used to, which is almost a double whammy win for me.

Alexis laughs out loud, stands up, and goes over to open the door for me.

I glance over at Bo where he's moved to the couch, both arms spread out along the back, legs wide, settling in as though he's about to sit and watch a football game. "He's mostly harmless. Forward, but harmless. Put him in his place if you need to."

She grips my tie and runs her hand down the length of it, her fingers brushing along my chest. Ribbons of heat spread out from where her fingers touch and along my skin, settling hotly between my thighs. My dick takes notice, coming up to half-mast. I stare at her cherry-red lips and wonder for a brief moment if they'd taste like the juicy fruit. Okay, maybe she's winning the game at this point.

"Oh, I'm comfortable with forward. What I want to know is when are *you* going to be comfortable with the idea of you and me?" She places her hand on my waist and leans against my body.

You and me.

Those three words are like throwing a bucket of ice water over my head, putting out the flicker of arousal that was budding inside of me.

The only "you and me" I can even fathom is with Skyler. We talked a lot about being a "you and me" and an "us" for that matter. Now she's gone. We're over.

The knot in my stomach tightens and twists, and I grit my teeth against the pain. If this ache and strangling sensation keep up, I'm going to need to visit my doc back home. Something's gotta give.

As politely as I can, I ease Alexis back. "I can't. I'm sorry."

"But . . ." She starts to push, but out of nowhere, a big hand cups Alexis's shoulder.

"He really *can't*, beautiful. Me, on the other hand . . ." He grins, and she shrugs his palm off her shoulder. Bo backs up with his hands up in a gesture of surrender. "Okay, okay. I see my charm isn't working, but honey, with Park, you're barking up the wrong tree."

I fling my gaze to Bo's and wince. "Back off. I've got this under control."

He shrugs and saunters back to the couch, where he drops onto it like a sack of potatoes. I cringe and focus my attention on Alexis.

"Why?" she whispers softly, her expression changing to one of concern, though I can also hear a hint of insecurity.

I bite into my bottom lip and frown. "It's personal. And I told you, I'm coming out of a relationship."

"You know what they all say?" she murmurs, the sound more like a humming purr.

I close my eyes, knowing she's going to say something to the tune of "the best way to get over someone is to get under someone else."

"A night of guilt-free fucking can cure all?" she says, smugness rife in her tone, any speck of insecurity gone in an instant.

Bo snaps his fingers and raises his voice enough so that both of us can hear him. "I've actually heard that one and believe in it wholeheartedly!"

I tip my head back and laugh at the sheer ridiculousness of it all.

Fighting the attraction between us.

Guilt over having not yet talked to Skyler about what she's done.

And my wish to not be in this predicament in the first place.

If Skyler hadn't fucked me over, I'd be able to brush Alexis off with nothing more than using the *g* word and *committed relationship*, but it would serve her right if I hopped into bed with Alexis.

Hell, I could take pictures and send them to her. She likes sending texts. *"Here are a few of me and another hot blonde. Hope you had as much fun with your ex as I'm having with this bombshell."* Yeah, that's what I'd do. Hurt her the way she hurt me.

Then the thought of Skyler hearing about how I'd stepped out the same way she did makes the acid in my stomach swirl and clench so hard I might end up getting sick. No, I'm better than that. Better than banging anything hot with legs just to piss off my ex, or soon-to-be ex, depending on who you ask.

Fuck! I can't think about this anymore. I've got work to do.

"Look, it's a very nice offer, Alexis, and a different me would be more than happy to take you up on the incredible experience I know we'd have. But, I can't. I just . . . It's not happening." I turn and head down the hallway, leaving her and Bo to a battle of the sexes.

When I get back to my interview space, I note Spartacus is curled up in my chair. "Hey, buddy, what are you up to?" I lift the cat and place him in my lap. Surprisingly he curls right back up and plants his head dead center of my stomach. I run my fingers through his velvet-soft fur. "You understand what it's like, right? To love someone so much and not know how to let them go?"

Spartacus yawns, stretching his mouth open wide, and rubs his head against my abdomen. His warmth and gentle purring presence start to allow the tension in my body to seep out. With every long stroke across his furry body, another bundle of negative energy leaves me until, eventually, my eyes close, I lean back in the chair, and for the first time all week, I can finally take a full breath. My stomach isn't as knotted, and I feel at peace.

Fuck.

I need to get a cat.

***

Two hours later, I've interviewed another individual and Mrs. Wendy Pritchard is entering my office.

"Go ahead and shut the door, Mrs. Pritchard."

Her lips twitch with a smile she's holding back. The padlock around her neck gleams in the light. She's wearing a pair of royal-blue leggings, suede ankle boots, and a black-and-white checkered top that hits midthigh with a yellow belt hanging at her hips. She's got silver hoops in her ears and a soft pink color on her lips. On her hands are fishnet fingerless gloves.

A style icon in her own right. Every time I see her clothing I wonder if I like it or not. Regardless, it always works for her.

"Hey, boss man, how goes it?" She sits down, spins in a 360-degree circle once, and then stops her spin by catching herself on the table.

I chuckle. "You know I called you in here like a regular interview so we can hash out some of this crap and the others wouldn't become suspicious, right?"

"Totally."

"And . . . Mrs. Pritchard?" I cock an eyebrow.

She beams, her happiness like a ray of light bursting straight from the center of her chest and lighting up the room. "Isn't it awesome? Sir Mick spanked the hell out of me for it."

I frown. "Why? He didn't like you using his name?"

She jerks her head and tilts it to the side. "Uh, no. He liked it *very much*. Duh, that's why he spanked the hell out of me. Reward. Heeeellllooooo?"

I spend a few moments mulling that information over.

Wendy purses her lips. "That's right. I forget how vanilla some of you guys are. I'm sure Bo would have gotten the joke. Though don't you dare tell him. He'll come up with an endless number of spanking-related things to bother me with for a solid week." She groans. "Man never shuts up. Sometimes I want to ball gag him and weld the damn ends together so he can't get it off."

"Duly noted."

She preens as if we weren't just talking about spanking and ball gags. When the hell did my relationship with Wendy change so dramatically?

"Since we don't have a lot of time, let's get right to the point." I move forward with getting the information I need.

"Okay, boss. I'm ready." She sits on the edge of her seat, rests her elbows and hands on the table, and waits for my next response.

"Royce found nothing in the financials. I've found nothing in the interviews, and I only have a handful left."

"Even Kidd Stanton?"

I pause and sit back in my chair. "What about Kidd?"

She takes a deep breath and lets it out as if she's gathering her thoughts. "I've been going through his code. There's a distinct method in which coders write. Almost like a fingerprint. There are idiosyncrasies that I can see between the way Alexis codes and Kidd's coding. His isn't nearly as advanced or secure as hers, but he's damn good."

"All right, what else?"

"Based on the bit of digging I've been able to do in between the projects and training, I've found at least three places that were funky. One was a bug in the system that looked like it was placed there. The coding matches Kidd's style. Another was wonky coding—and let me be clear, even the best of us screw up sometimes when we're tired or whatever. This . . ." She shakes her head.

"What? Just say it."

She winces. "This looks intentional. As though he meant to write something that was going to trip up the system. Worse, it's so blatant that the average techie would skim right over it. Kind of like it's so amateur, it's hidden in plain sight in a way. Does that make sense?"

I lean back in my chair and tap my lips with my index finger.

Why would Kidd Stanton write bad code that his sister could easily find? Why would he bug the system?

"It doesn't make sense. I sat with the guy. He has his sister's name tattooed on his arm."

"Yeah, I saw that. It's pretty cool. I'd like to get something with Mick on it."

"Anything else? Another staff member in the department doing strange things?"

She shrugs. "One chick is kind of standoffish. Kind of like she's put out that I was hired to be on the team. Even made the comment that she didn't know why I was there when she could easily pick up the department's slack."

"Who was it?"

"Eloise Gagnon. Worked here several years."

I thumb through the leftover stack of files on my desk and pull hers out. "I haven't interviewed her yet."

"Seems standoffish, but it could be she wants a promotion or something and is bummed that I was brought on instead of giving her the promotion."

I nod. "Perhaps. I'll find out for sure. Good work. Keep digging into the other coders. Make sure to get into those products that were leaked and evaluate the coding there."

"Got it. That was my next step anyway." She runs her fingers through the hair at her temples.

"All right. You can go back. Tell this Eloise she's up next."

Wendy pushes her chair back but doesn't rise. "How are you doing today?"

I glance up and into her clear blue eyes. "Wendy . . . not at work."

She looks chagrined, and her cheeks flush pink. "Sorry . . . I just . . . Have you called her yet?"

I sigh. "No."

Her lips move into a flat line. "I don't know how to do this." She worries her fingers in her lap.

"Do what?"

She lifts one shoulder and lets it drop. "Be okay with the fact that I know you're wrong. And you're hurting. And I hate it. I hate it so much because I feel like it would be so easy to fix if you would just call her." The words leave her mouth in a rush, but once they do, I can see the second she realizes all she revealed. "I'm . . . oh my God. I'm sorry. I shouldn't . . . it's not my place."

The knife that's skewering my heart digs a little deeper, stealing my breath right along with it. My heartbeat becomes erratic, and my entire body warms. I clench my good hand into a fist on top of my leg, trying to manage my out-of-control feelings.

"No, it isn't."

"Parker . . ." Her voice cracks, and with it, a lightning bolt sizzles straight into my stomach, singeing muscle and tissue in its wake.

"Wendy, I know you mean well, and you are a godsend to the IG team. You are one of us. That isn't going to change. But you have to stop."

God, please make her stop. I can't deal with her hopefulness on top of the overbearing dread filling my soul.

I think for a moment and then take a different approach. "Look, I'm dealing with what happened between Sky and me the only way I know how. This is not the first time a woman broke me. Okay?"

"What?" she gasps, her hand flying to her chest.

Dammit. I did not want to go there again. I'm trying desperately to leave her in the past. Deal with this new hurt and move on.

Wendy sits absolutely still, waiting for me to continue.

"Fine." I sigh. "I'll give you the CliffsNotes version. I was engaged in college. Kayla McCormick. She used me and betrayed me by fucking my best friend, Greg, while wearing my ring and doing so in our bed."

Her eyes turn the size of coasters. "Ho-bag . . . ," she growls through her teeth.

I grin. "Undeniably. And since then, I haven't trusted a woman with my heart until . . ."

"Skyler." She closes her eyes as if the information is slamming into her and breaking her heart into little pieces the same way it's done to mine.

"Yeah." I lick my lips and try to clear the sudden emotion swelling around us.

"I didn't know."

"You had no way of knowing. It's not something the guys or I talk about. With good reason. Because that was a shit time in my life. Right now, what I'm going through is another shit time."

Her hand shakes as she reaches out and puts hers on top of mine. She squeezes it. "I want to help you. How can I help you?"

I embrace her hand firmly. "Just be my friend, Wendy. Be there like you promised you would." I shake my head. "But don't try to fix me. You can't. This is not something you can do for me. I have to find the right way to get past it."

Her lip trembles. "But . . . but, what if the right way is to give Skyler a second chance?" Her eyes fill with such hope and love it's hard to look at her without crumbling or alternately punching another wall.

"How's about I promise to think about it?"

That light I saw when she walked in flickers back on. "Really?"

"Really." I squeeze her hand once and let it go. "Now get out of here. I've got this interview to finish tonight, and then I need to let off some steam. Now that Bo is in town, maybe the four of us can head out. Away from this side of town of course."

"Righteous! I'll find a place."

"I actually have been recommended one called Brutopia. And it's Wednesday night. They might even have live music."

Her entire face glows beautifully. "I love live music." There's awe coating her tone.

I grin. "I know you do, minxy." I wink. "Make sure the guys are on board. I'm heading out in an hour."

"Will do, boss man."

"See you later, Wendy."

She grins, and her shoulders go up to her ears. "I can't wait to tell Mick I'm going out for a night on the town with the guys."

"Uh, do you think that's wise?"

A wicked smirk slips across her lips. "Oh yeah. It will mean serious punishment when I get home. I may not be able to walk for days after. I can't wait!" She shimmies in her heels, wiggling her tiny booty.

Again, in her presence, I can't help but laugh.

"Glutton!" I tease as she opens the door.

"For my man's lovin', you know it." She maneuvers her fingers into the shape of a gun. "Bang, bang, I'm out!"

I snort and lean back in my chair. Once I do, an orange fluff ball lands on my lap, forcing me back to a normal seating position. Spartacus looks at me as though I've disturbed him and not the other way around.

"You think you own the universe, don't you, cat?"

He looks at me as if we're having a stare-off. I blink first, after which he pushes his head against my gut and starts to purr.

Before I can move the cat, Wendy's back at my door.

"Hey, Eloise left early today. Doctor's appointment. It was on her calendar." Her voice dips. "I checked."

"Of course you did." I'd tell her that she's done well, but then she'd get a big head. "Well, looks like I'm out of here. If this cat will ever let me up." I point down to my lap where Spartacus has deemed me the perfect napping spot.

"Aw, so cute. You know . . . cats have an innate sense of good people. Also, studies have linked lowered stress levels in people when they are petting a cat or snuggling up to a kitten."

I raise my hand and point to the door. "Out."

"It's true, though! Fine. Bye!" She scampers off.

I look back down at Spartacus and run my hand through his fur several times. "You're a pain in the ass, getting my slacks all furry with your orange hair, but"—for this, I lean down close to him and run my chin against his soft head—"you do make me feel better. Thanks for keeping me company."

6

Brutopia is a hip-looking western-style bar in the heart of downtown Montreal. You have to go up a set of rickety wooden stairs to get to the heavy door. Inside, the place has a healthy number of patrons eating and drinking beers and cocktails. The place seems small from the inside, but as the four of us move closer to the lone bar, we can see there's a small stage where musicians are setting up their instruments with a small dance floor and seats all around it. Farther back through a cutout in the wall, I note a much larger back end to the bar. A hint of a pool table can be seen from where I stand.

Wendy shimmies in like a colorful butterfly flapping its wings. "This place is righteous!" she says with awe.

Roy looks around, placing his hands in his pockets. "Glad I changed."

I grin and assess his attire. He's still wearing his dress slacks, only he's paired them with a thin long-sleeved shirt made of white cotton. The white against his ebony skin seems to glow under the low lights in the bar. I clap him on the bicep. "Too true. Should we start with a drink, find a seat, and order?"

"Hell yeah." Bo claps me on the back, eyes scanning all the women in our immediate vicinity as he heads to the bar. "Shot of tequila and whatever's cold on tap you recommend."

Wendy raises her hand. "Ooh, ooh, me too! Same."

I glance at Roy, who gives me the side-eye and grins in agreement. "We'll have the same."

Bo's eyebrows rise up. "Is that so? We're doing this, then. Getting shit-faced."

I run my hand through my hair, messing it up even more than it already is. It's overly long and needs a cut, but I don't care. I don't care much about anything right now. "Yep."

Royce shakes his head. "Not sure I'm going to get shit-faced, but the night is young, and I saw a trumpet and a trombone setting up."

Wendy turns her head to look around Roy's large form. "Killer! This is going to be so fun!"

The bartender sets four shots of tequila on the counter with a wedge of lime on the rim. He then proceeds to draw four pints into what look like chilled glasses.

He sets the four glasses near the shots. Bo passes out the shots and pints to each of us. "What should we drink to?" He smiles wide, his goatee and mustache trimmed to perfection.

I'm plumb out of anything positive or motivational to say. Wendy holds up her shot glass, and we all follow her move in a game of monkey see, monkey do.

"I think we ought to drink to . . . trusting your heart. Let our hearts lead us to our very own happiness."

My own heart clenches like a vise is around it, the invisible dagger Skyler wedged there still lodged deep. I close my eyes and take a breath.

"Hear, hear." Royce clinks his glass with hers.

Bo does the same. "Cowboy up."

I open my eyes and focus on each person's gaze one at a time, proud that I'm standing right where I am, that I have the support of these three people to help me find my way.

"To trusting your heart." I clink my glass, suck back the shot, and let the blessed heat of the alcohol slide down my throat and warm my gut for what feels like the first time in ages. The tightening of my heart abates a little more as I wash the shot down with two long pulls of the cold beer.

"Let's find a seat near the band," Wendy says excitedly. The woman is barely containing her exuberance. It's refreshing to see someone enjoying themselves every day. Using every minute God gives them to appreciate the goodness in their life.

"So, tell us your story, Wendy." I sit down in the booth as she dips into the center, Bo sitting next to her, Roy in the one chair across from her. The booth only fits three and is an odd curved shape.

She blurts, "We're gonna need another round of shots for that to happen."

"On it!" Bo smacks the table and gets up, shucking off his leather jacket and putting it on the hook near our table.

Royce eases his chair to the side so he can see the band setting up behind him. "Looks like a seven piece. This ought to be good. Haven't heard horns live in a while."

"Yeah." I sip my beer. "And such an eclectic mix of individuals." I nod to the black guy in the center setting up his mic, dressed exactly like a wannabe Michael Jackson from the 1990s. His outfit is complete with high-water dress slacks, a tight white T-shirt, and a sparkly glove. Even his hair is cropped in close curls at the sides.

"I don't know 'bout all that." Royce runs his gaze up and down the lead. "But if the brother sounds anything like Michael, I'll be happy."

Bo comes back, holding four double shots of tequila this time.

"Doubles?" I chuckle.

"Go big or go home, right?" He laughs heartily.

"Guess so." I take one of the short glass tumblers.

"For you, my lady." He passes one to Wendy.

"When are you going to learn I'm Mick's lady, not yours, not ever," she chastises while accepting a glass.

Royce wraps his long fingers around the glass. It looks minuscule in his giant hand. "What do we drink to now?"

Before one of them can wax poetic about trusting your heart again, I jump in. "To friendship . . . and family. New and old."

"Friendship and family. All right," Royce murmurs, clinking his glass.

"Hell yeah," Bo adds.

"Family." Wendy's voice cracks when she brings her glass to the center of the table where we have our hands stretched out. "I love you guys," she whispers.

"Ugh! Wendy!" I groan.

"Woman!" Royce mutters.

"Not that kind of family, God willing." Bo slices the air dramatically.

"I'm sorry! Jeez Louise!" she huffs.

"Tink, you're with the guys, your brothers from another mother. You don't get all mushy," Bo warns.

"My man Bo's right, little lady. If you're gonna roll with the big bros, you gotta lay off the sweet, ya hear?" Royce adds.

She rolls her eyes. "I'm just sayin' I love you. You act like I'm writing you love poems and promising to name my firstborn after you."

"Bo is the perfect name!" Bo fires off instantly.

"No way! Parker is hip!" I toss mine into the ring.

Royce shakes his head. "Gentlemen, I got this. Royce is classy. Elegant. Definitely a leader."

"What about Michael?" Wendy blinks prettily and drinks her beer.

All three of us groan again.

"Just do your shot!" I demand with a laugh.

"Fine! To family!" She clinks her glass, and we all toss the doubles back.

Now the heat in my belly is swirling like a boiling hot tub at the exact perfect temperature for soaking. I ease back into my seat, running my finger over the rim of my beer. "All right, minxy, you've had your shots. Tell us about you. Where did you grow up?"

"Sacramento."

"California. The land of fruit and nuts. Makes total sense," Bo jokes.

She grins. "Met Sir Mick when he was staying at a hotel for a conference. I was bartending the event. We spent the night together, and two days later he had my shit-hole studio apartment packed up and me on a plane to Massachusetts, where I've been ever since."

"Shee-it, brother's got moves. Get a woman to drop her life and move across country in two days." Royce shakes his head and runs his hand over his bald scalp.

Wendy smiles. "I fell in love at first sight. Add the fact we're both in the lifestyle, and everything clicked into place for us. Before him, I had nothing. A couple of friends. A shitty job and was struggling to make ends meet. No high school education, though he did make me get my GED online. And look at me now. I've never been happier." She takes a long pull from her pint.

"Wow, Tink, what happened to your family?" Bo's facial expression turns into one of concern and compassion. The loving guy behind the leather and man-whore ways.

She shrugs. "I don't have any. According to what my social worker told me when I was a teen, my mother had been a drug addict and there was no father on record. When I was about five, child protective services was called because I was walking myself to and from kindergarten, and I was malnourished. Teacher made complaints, the social workers came in, and I never saw my mother again. She never even tried to get me out of the system. Then I bounced around from one crappy foster care home to another until I was fifteen and decided I'd had enough."

"Fifteen?" I put my hand over her shoulder. "Wendy." My throat clogs at the image of a tiny redheaded little girl being moved from home to home. How could anyone do that to her? She's amazing.

She rolls her lips inward. "Yep. I already topped out at a high IQ and had the hacking and lying skills to fake an ID stating I was eighteen. I left school and went to work. Started waitressing at a diner. Rented rooms or stayed on friends' couches when I could to save money. And then finally, my knight showed up."

"What do you mean?" Royce asks, leaning into his large forearms on the tabletop, as engrossed in her story as I am.

The bar around us is buzzing with activity, people laughing, drinks being shared, hoots and hollers coming from the back room, but the three of us are glued to our seats and solely focused on our pretty red-headed sister.

That bright smile I've gotten used to when it comes to Wendy breaks out from behind the dark conversation. "Back to the hotel bar I was working when I was twenty. Michael came up, ordered whiskey, sneered when it wasn't a good year or brand, and proceeded to share his thoughts on the stuff. I happened to have a secret bottle of Macallan stashed in the bar for when I needed a real pick-me-up."

"Guuurrrlll, you are smooth." Royce smirks.

She waggles her eyebrows. "Don't I know it!" She holds up her hand and high-fives him over the table, lightness leaking back into her story, pushing aside the sadness from revealing her past.

Bo flicks his hand. "Then what happened? Don't leave me hanging, sweetheart, it's a heavy weight to bear, if you know what I mean." He grins wickedly, cocking a brow.

She turns and punches his shoulder.

"Ouch!" He rubs at the burn. "I hate when you get me with those knobby knuckles."

"You're lucky I don't invest in a pair of brass knuckles!" She holds up her small fist like a little Italian grandma would when threatening her grandchildren to keep in line.

He rubs at his sore bicep, pouting. "Just continue the story, Tink."

She licks her lips and leans into the table. "Well, I told Mick that I'd hook him up with the good stuff if he didn't tell my boss."

"Risky." I suck in a breath through my teeth.

She nods. "Yeah, but he was handsome, and I swear the way he looked at me, like he could see straight through to my soul, destroyed any resolve I had. I wanted nothing more than to please him. Be his everything so he could be mine."

Royce whistles. "Damn. Now why can't I find me a woman like that!"

"Because you're not looking in the right places, dumb ass." Bo chuckles.

Royce frowns. "Bull. 'Sides, coming from you, King of the Chicklets . . . ," he scoffs. "I wouldn't believe a word you had to say about the subject. Park, on the other hand—at least he found a good one."

This time I scoff, "Shit. You're looking at the wrong guy. I couldn't hold on to a good woman if my life depended on it. I think I have a sign in invisible ink written across my forehead, one you can only see under a black light, that says 'Cheat on Me' or some shit."

Royce shakes his head. "Not true. I don't believe for a minute Sky cheated, and the sooner you accept it and give the poor thing a chance to explain, the better off we'll all be."

I grind my teeth and wish I had another shot of tequila to wash down the instant lump in my throat.

Bo glances away and pretends to be interested in the server placing food down at a table near us.

"Is that what you think too, Bo? Wendy already hit me with her suggestion today, you might as well get it out on the table right now."

Bo shrugs. "You sure you're ready to hear what I think?"

"I'm certain I don't want to be surprised by you dropping the bomb later. We're all here, and sharing is caring, right? Lay it on me." I feel like a peacock whose feathers have been ruffled. Frustration, irritation, and sudden anger are burning a path through my veins, looking for any way to be let out.

Wendy puts a hand to Bo's forearm and glances up at him. He tilts his head. "Okay, fine. I think you're scared."

Not something I expected him to say.

"Scared? Of a hot blonde? Seriously? That's your play?" I huff out a harsh breath and wait for him to continue.

He plucks at his goatee and taps his bottom lip with his thumb. "You're scared of what it means to love someone the way you love her. Scared that she'll do exactly what Kayla did . . ."

I widen my eyes and slam my drink on the table. Thankfully I drank most of it, so it doesn't slosh out of the glass. "She *did* do what Kayla did. Sky stayed the night in Johan's hotel room—"

Bo lifts his hands. "I get that. I do. Except you can't prove she cheated based on his word alone. Look, all I'm sayin' is the girl I met, the girl I hung out with in New York, was wild for my best friend. All in. Your dream girl. Then she comes to Lucky's and spends time getting to know all of us. Opens herself up to our family. Talks about moving to our town. What reason would she have to give that up?"

"She likes hard cock? Girl likes to fuck. Know that firsthand. And she's *damn* good at it. Maybe she wanted a reunion with Johan's dick." The thought of Sky getting anywhere near Johan's puny pickle has me squeezing the pint glass so hard I just may break it.

Royce's head drops down toward the table. "Aw man, you had to go there."

A powerful burst of anger speeds through my system, making me hot all over. I grind my teeth so hard I hope I don't crack a molar. *They don't get it. They don't freakin' understand what she did!*

"Yeah, yeah, I went there. Because I *need* to know that my team, *my family*, is there for me. Me! I should be your priority, not the woman who fucked me over!" My voice gets raspy and raw, and I suck down the rest of my beer. "I need another fuckin' beer." I stand up and head to the bar, needing a minute of peace. Some time to cool down before I explode on the outside the way I'm imploding on the inside.

Fuckin' hell. Are they backing her up?

They're supposed to be my friends. My family. Not hers. Then I remember, Sky doesn't have any family.

Images of her flutter through my mind as I wait for the bartender to come take my order.

Sky's nervousness over meeting my parents.

Later, Skyler laughing at my mother and father bickering.

My girl exchanging phone numbers with all the guys over beers and pulled-pork sandwiches.

Sky and Wendy talking wedding plans.

My girl promising to attend the wedding . . . with me.

Sky telling me she was thinking about moving to Boston.

What if she's telling the truth?

Johan is a master manipulator. He could have easily built up the time he spent with her. Lied to me. My heart starts a rapid-fire beat, and my stomach clenches. I clutch at it and take a couple of deep breaths. I need more beer. And another shot of tequila.

"Beer or tequila?" the bartender asks.

"Both. A round of four pints and four more double shots of tequila. And you can send a waitress over. We'll need to eat."

"Good idea, band is about to start." He lifts his chin at the seven piece standing up on the stage.

The guitarist is strumming a lick, and the keyboardist is warming up his fingers. As I wait for the refills, the horn players run some scales, and my heartbeat starts to ease once more. It's probably more from the liquor making its way into my bloodstream, but whatever it is, I'm thankful.

Royce comes and stands in front of me. "I'm sorry, brother. What you're going through can't be easy, and it's not my place . . ."

I shake my head. "Naw, man, it's cool. I need to hear it. If not from the people who care about me, then who?"

"You gonna take our advice?"

I shrug. "Not sure what I'm going to do just yet. All I know is, for the rest of the night, I just want to let loose with my team. Is that okay?"

He grins wide, his white smile extra bright against his dark skin and his white shirt. "Yeah, that's all right." He puts his hand around my neck and leans forward so that our foreheads almost touch. "No matter what, though, you always have me, Bo, Wendy. We're your people. We got your back. Still, it's our job to kick your ass sometimes. Help you see things in a different light in the event you're blinded. Say like when you think a good woman stepped out on you."

I laugh even though he's still pushing, but I get why. "You like her for me." I lift my gaze to his dark one.

He does a half shrug. "Yeah, I like her for you. Think she's the whole package. 'Sides. I wanna see my boy happy. I've never seen you happier than you are with her."

His words hit hard, slamming into my subconscious and mixing up the messages my past is telling me about my future. "I was happy. More than that. I was in love."

He squeezes my shoulders hard. "Brother, you're still in love. It's why it hurts so bad."

And he's right. Regardless of what I believe Skyler may have done with Johan, it doesn't change the fact that I'm head over heels in love with the woman. And I didn't even get to tell her to her face. Maybe if I had, she would have waited for me to get there to deal with her ex. Maybe then she wouldn't have thought she was alone.

"Christ!" I run my hand through my hair. "Brother, I'm a fucking mess."

Royce turns me around to face the bar where the bartender has placed the four beers and four double shots. "Yes, you are. It's okay. We got you."

He grabs two of the beers in one hand, two in the crook of his elbow wedged against his body so he can grab two of the shots. I grab the last two in my good hand and bring them over to the table.

The second I put the drinks down, Wendy catapults into my arms. The side of her face presses against the side of mine, her breath in my ear. Her coconutty scent fills my nostrils, displacing the dank greasy smell of the bar and replacing it with something more pleasant, comfortable even, as I've become more familiar with her scent.

"I'm sorry, Park. I never want you to feel like we aren't Team Parker. No matter how much I like Skyler, you'll always be my priority." Her fingernails dig into my back as she tries to imprint herself on my skin.

I rub her back and enjoy her hug for a moment, letting the feeling of having this woman's care and concern seep into my aching, tired body. "Thanks, Wendy. I'm sorry too. To all of you. I was a schmuck there for a moment. I'm working through it all."

"Well, I wasn't going to say anything," Bo mutters under his breath, but it's loud enough we can all hear him.

Unfazed, I continue. "How's about for the rest of the night we just have fun. Eat, drink, and be merry. Yeah?"

Wendy eases back, her eyes a little watery, but she holds her tears in check, for which I'm thankful.

"Shots up." Royce holds the tequila high over the small table.

The three of us follow suit.

"To never letting anything get between what we have. We're Team IG, all the way!"

"Team IG!" Wendy cheers, and Bo follows.

"Now *that* I can drink to." I smile, letting go of all the baggage I entered the bar with. The band starts up with one of Michael Jackson's biggest hits, "Billie Jean."

Wendy screeches out her excitement with a yelled "Woo-hoo!"

Roy pushes even more to the side so he can see fully. The keyboards kick off, and by the time the chorus hits, we're all singing along at the top of our lungs.

Team IG, all the way.

7

The door to my conference space opens with what seems like a thundering creaking sound, hitting my hungover mind like a hammer banging against my temple. I grind my teeth through the pain and swallow down the bile that wants to come up.

Eloise Gagnon enters. "I believe I'm next for my interview," she says in a small voice while opening the door more fully.

I nod. "Yes, come in. Have a seat, Ms. Gagnon."

"Eloise is fine." She smiles slightly, but there isn't much sincerity behind the gesture. Almost as if she's done it out of habit, because it's what someone does upon meeting a new person.

The woman is petite and thin, very little curve to her form, which is shown clearly through the jeans and long-sleeved V-necked shirt she's wearing. On her feet are a pair of simple ballet flats. Her brown hair is pulled back into a tight ponytail at her nape. The black-rimmed glasses actually add to her appeal rather than take away from it. She looks young, just out of college, but her file puts her closer to my age.

"I'm Parker Ellis. I assume you know why I'm here?" I ask the same question I've asked every employee so far.

"Yes. To discuss productivity, but I imagine it has more to do with the fact that there've been some pretty serious product leaks."

I narrow my gaze. "And what would make you think that?" My spidey sense has taken notice.

She shrugs. "Makes sense. Company loses a lot of money because of our competitors launching a similar product before us, so it would stand to reason that we have an internal problem of some kind."

I lean back in my chair, dragging my fingers along the pencil I'm holding until it falls to the table's wood surface with a whack. Once it's down, I pick it back up and repeat the process. It's a technique I mastered back in Harvard during a course on interrogation techniques. I had a real ball-busting business analysis class. I've found the practice tends to annoy people, which can cause them to slip up and reveal information they were trying to hold back.

Her gaze flicks to the pencil as I repeat the same process over and over. She flinches when it smacks the table again, but I pretend not to notice by making a show of skimming her file.

"And what do you do here?"

"I'm one of the coders."

"Oh, then you work with that new hire, Wendy."

I lift my head to watch her facial expressions. A look of disgust comes across her face, then disappears in an instant. "Yeah, I guess."

"Sounds like you have some feelings about the new hire. Anything you care to share?"

She purses her lips. "Just not sure why they hired her when I could have taken on the extra load, worked with Kidd directly."

"Kidd?"

"Yeah, the director of the department. We always used to work together perfectly."

Interesting. There's something in the way she speaks that has needle pricks prodding at my temples, but the pain from last night's escapade is clouding my thought processes a little.

"So, you've worked with Kidd for a long while?"

"We started at the same time. I was just out of college, and he was just out of high school. He's brilliant. Didn't even go to college, and his knack for the coding language is as good as his sister's. We were the best team. Perfect in every way." She frowns and then looks away. "Then Alexis separated us, and I got relegated to the boring side of the business. Maintenance. No longer working on product creation."

"That must have made you feel bad. Did something happen?"

Glaring, she turns her face back toward mine. "No. I guess I wasn't as good as they were. No longer capable of hanging with the big boys. But I've worked my way back up to the coding team. And now I have to compete with Wendy. The new IT girl."

Oh, I see what's happening. Her negativity is about *Wendy*. A zap of pain bolts through my head, and I grind my molars and try to breathe through it. God, my head hurts.

Too much booze.

Next time we have an IG team "Kumbaya" get-together, we need to do it *after* the job is done. The fluorescent lights above feel like they're burning right through my retinas.

I swallow down the dryness in my throat and reach for the water bottle.

"You okay?" Eloise asks. "You look green."

I suck back most of the water, letting the fresh, cool feeling coat my empty stomach. "Just tired."

She snickers. "Looks like you tied one on last night."

I breathe through my teeth, allowing her to catch me in a little bad-boy behavior to see how she responds.

"Be careful. She might fire you. She can be a real bitch if she wants to." She leans over the table, moving closer, and scowls. "Don't let her bombshell body and movie-star face get to you. That woman is a she-devil underneath all that fashion and glamour."

Damn. That was harsh.

"You don't sound like you care for Alexis much. If that's the case, why do you work here?"

She squints. "Because Kidd is amazing, and I've learned more under his mentorship than I ever did in all four years of tech school. I'd do anything to keep my position here." She waxes rather poetic about a man who, for all intents and purposes, is her boss. There's a tinge of something more there, something I can't grasp in my tired, hungover brain.

I need to sleep.

For a year.

"Was that going to be all, Mr. Ellis? I really have a lot to do. I've been reviewing the errors in Kidd's coding."

"Errors?" Wendy mentioned yesterday there were errors in the coding that matched Kidd's style.

She nods and runs her fingertip in a circle on the tabletop. "I think it's his new girlfriend." She leans forward as if she's going to tell me a secret. "Ever since he started seeing her, his work has suffered. I'm trying to clean up the errors, so no one finds them. Eventually, he'll get rid of this woman and start thinking more clearly again."

Whoa! That's a damning statement if I ever heard one.

"Let me get this straight." I rub and press my fingers to the back of my neck and work them up the back of my skull, trying to relieve the tension a night of drinking laid upon my dome. "You've been going into Kidd's work and cleaning it up?"

She nods. "Yeah, it's a mess. He's making really obvious mistakes. Things that could put the system at risk for a security hack."

Ding! Ding! Ding! Ding!

The alarm bell is ringing in my head.

"Like I said, I'm fixing it, so don't worry. I'm taking one for the team until he gets his head out of his bum regarding that girlfriend of his."

"Girlfriend?"

"Yeah." She sneers the next word. "Victoria. She is no good for him. He needs to kick her to the curb, fast."

"Actually, I don't think she's going anywhere, since he said he asked her to marry him and she said yes. Planning a wedding next summer. I'm surprised you didn't already know that."

Eloise's chair flies backward and falls to the ground in her haste to stand. Her entire body is ramrod straight, her nose and chest flushing red.

I stand up and lift my hands. "Hey . . ."

"He's marrying that tart!" Her voice is a barely restrained screech.

I try to swallow, but my mouth is the Sahara desert right now.

"He'll never get better! She's ruining a genius!"

"Calm down, Eloise."

Eloise.

Eloise.

Her name pounds a beat in my head. I know that name. It's unusual, but I've heard it before. Recently.

"It's more that Eloise wanted all of my time and attention. That's my ex." Kidd.

Could this be his Eloise? His ex?

"I've got to go." Eloise shakes her hands like she's flinging water off them.

Before I can stop her, she's out the door.

I fall back into my chair, and Spartacus jumps into my lap, pressing his small paws directly into my aching stomach.

"Jesus, buddy. I'm already green around the gills. Don't make it worse." I finger behind the cat's ears, petting him.

Spartacus meows, then settles into my lap, ready to take a nap.

"Glad someone's getting some sleep," I state dryly, and finish off my bottle of water, drinking the rest down in one long, blessed go. Once done, I fling the bottle into the recycling bin, making a three-pointer. I pinch the bridge of my nose, let the chair dip back, and close my eyes, trying to figure out how all of this information relates.

Eloise is fixing Kidd's errors in the system. Covering up for him. Why?

Because she's in love with him? Maybe.

Kidd stated he had an ex named Eloise. It's not that common of a name. And they work together. Kidd is getting married, and Eloise freaked out. Maybe Kidd is accidentally leaking the information, which is why there's no payoff money in anyone's financials. Because it's unintentional.

I pick up my new cell phone and bring up Wendy's contact info.

To: World's Greatest Assistant
From: Parker Ellis

Have something for you to check out. Call me.

I click "Send," lean back in my chair, and close my eyes again for a few minutes before my cell phone rings.

"What's up?" Wendy says, sounding breathless.

"Where are you?"

The sound of street traffic can be heard in the background. "Told Kidd I needed to take a walk down the street for a coffee run. I'm getting Starbucks, and you'll never believe what I just walked past. Straight up this awesome, gothic-looking church. Literally walking to get coffee and I'm slam-bam-thank-you-ma'am blown away by this stunning building that looks a million years old!"

I grin at her excitement. At least someone still has some positivity this morning. "It's the Notre-Dame Basilica."

"I thought the Notre-Dame was in France, or in Indiana if you're the Fighting Irish!" She cracks up at her own joke.

"It is. The one you're seeing is called Notre-Dame Basilica, versus *cathedral* in Paris. *Basilica* means *church*, but in the Catholic religion, it's a church given special privileges by the pope. The architecture is the

Romantic Gothic style you see in a lot of the churches from that era. The coolest feature is the stained-glass windows. If you can take a moment to pop in, you'll notice that the windows are not biblical; rather, they depict the history of the city of Montreal. It's really fascinating."

"Wow, you know a lot about this."

"Yeah, studied a lot of it in college. Visited with my family too. Oh, and last I heard, they were doing this intense light show where the lighting technicians from Madonna's concerts created a performance using the inside of the church's spires, curves, windows, and paintings to create an experience the likes of which you'll remember forever. Maybe we can all go when the case is closed," I offer, thinking it would be a good idea to show Wendy a little bit of Montreal's rich history.

I've always loved this city, though I'd love to drive her up to Quebec City and show her Old Quebec, stay in one of the historic hotels, and ride on the ferry to get the best view of the islandlike city.

"Cool. I'm in. So what do you got for me on the case? I'm at Starbucks now."

Coffee sounds awesome right now, but I can't have her pick me up anything, or it would cause suspicion. I sigh. "Well, I just had the meet with Eloise."

"Delightful, isn't she." Sarcasm drips off each word.

"About as delightful as my stomach feels right now."

"Aw, poor baby. You can't hold your liquor," she teases.

I scoff, "How the hell are you so chipper? You were round for round with the rest of us."

She snorts. "Yeah, but there's a few small differences. In between my drinks, I pounded a glass of water, then sweated my ass off on the dance floor. Plus, I ate my weight in fried food. You just kept drinking."

Ah. Food. Water. Yeah, that would have been a good idea. Hell, that would be a good idea now.

"Sure was a blast, though," she continues. "I've still got 'Man in the Mirror' in my head. They killed that song last night." Her voice lowers, sounding farther away as she places her Starbucks order.

Once I hear her finish, I respond, "The band was great. Anyway, back to work. Eloise told me that she's been cleaning up errors in Kidd's coding. She made it sound like she's been doing it for a while."

"Really? Hmm."

"Yeah, and on top of that, I think they used to date. When I mentioned he was getting married, she flew out of the office like fire licked at her heels. A woman only does that—"

"If she's in love and it's unrequited. Shit." She thanks someone, and then the sounds of the street can be heard in the background as she huffs and puffs as if she's walking at a brisk pace. Wendy always moves fast. Part of me wonders if it's because she doesn't want to miss a single second of life.

"Yeah."

"But how does that solve our problem? If anything, it builds a bigger case against Kidd."

I rub at a knot forming in my shoulder. "Yes, it does."

"You have to tell Alexis. Maybe if she looks into it too, or straight up asks him?"

"You see, that's the thing. If he did do it, it might have been unintentional. Hence the reason there's no financial record of a payoff in the system. Maybe someone's hacking from the outside and all of Kidd's errors in the coding are making it easy to get in?"

"Maybe. I'll do a full check of the firewalls and see what I can find."

"Thanks."

"You got it, boss man. And I'm loving being undercover! I feel like a Charlie's angel!"

I laugh. "Signing off, angel."

"Bye, Charlie!"

***

A fluid pressure runs the length of my scalp, rubbing and teasing the overly long layers that are curling at the top. Skyler loves running her fingers through my hair. I sigh into the feeling, sleep still clinging to my mind as I hook an arm around her waist and tug her onto my lap.

"Ooh!" She giggles, but it sounds muffled, deeper as her body rests against mine. "Parker . . . ," she sighs, and I tip her head and take her mouth without opening my eyes. A wall of warmth flattens against my chest. I grin around her lips and run my hands up her back. Sleepily I enjoy the feeling of Skyler being generous as my body slowly comes awake. Of course, "the beast" is first to rise. I thrust my hips up and feel a swaying, rocking sensation. I'm in the office chair, leaned back. Skyler's mouth lands on mine again, wet and soft. I kiss her with all I have.

God I've missed this.

Her succulent mouth on mine, tongue invading deliciously. I grind up against her heat, and she moans. It sounds far away and different. A lower rumble than I'm used to hearing from my girl. I caress my way up her back and note a lot more of her than normal.

Huh?

The bright lights invade my tired eyes and hungover brain as I blink them open. And when I do, I'm beyond shocked at what I see.

Alexis.

In my lap.

Her tongue in my mouth.

Shit! I did this. Pulled her into my lap and kissed her. I wrap my hands around her rib cage and push her back enough so she lets go of my mouth with an audible plop.

"What the fuck!" I shake my head, trying to force the last vestiges of sleep out of my brain. My dick realizes the change in woman immediately, shrinking down to half-mast.

Alexis wraps her arms around my neck. "Your lips are as soft as I thought they'd be."

I swallow around the taste of her lipstick and coffee on my tongue. Arousal at her body's proximity hammers through my chest, heading south.

Jesus, what have I gotten myself into? "Alexis. You are beautiful, sexy. Any man would want you . . ."

She grins wide. "Fantastic, because I want you!" She slams her lips against mine, and for a weak moment, I kiss her back, dipping my tongue in, swirling with hers until I've got her taste imprinted on my taste buds. She moans and presses her large breasts against my chest. I slide my hand down to her ass and grind against her core. The beast comes back online, standing proud and ready for some guilt-free action.

For several minutes, I kiss the living daylights out of Alexis, pouring all my anger, hatred, and disgust for what Skyler did into my own actions. Taking charge. Controlling my destiny. Kissing the hell out of a beautiful woman I've been dancing around all week.

Until reality bursts in like a beacon of light shooting into the sky as Alexis goes for my belt. She gets the belt undone, the button open, and the zipper down. I groan and press up into her movements. Except the second she wraps her hand around my hard length, an arrow of poison shoots straight into my gut. I cry out and push Alexis back and off. Standing up, I quickly button my pants and do up my zipper.

She sits on the table nonchalantly with a sensual smirk and kiss-swollen lips.

I run my hand over my mouth, trying to wipe away her taste. It's going to take a lot more than the back of my hand.

Without realizing it, I start pacing and tugging at my hair.

"Fuck me. Fuck me. Fuck me!" I growl.

"That's what I was trying to do before you so rudely interrupted me." She laughs.

I sigh and turn toward the sexy blonde. "Alexis—"

"If you're about to say it's not you, it's me, I'm afraid I'll hurl, lover boy. Men don't turn me down. Not ever. And the steel rod in your pants proves my point."

My entire body feels weighed down by a wrecking ball, with the need to just fall into bed and sleep . . . for a year. My body is in agony, but the emptiness within my heart is far heavier than anything I could possibly imagine. It's debilitating, this need for her. For Skyler.

I clear my throat. "Alexis, I'm sorry. When I say I just got out of a relationship, I mean a week ago, I was in love with a woman, seriously committed. Now . . . fuck, I don't know what I am. What we are. And it's unfair of me to go there with you when I haven't settled things with her. Do you understand?"

She closes her eyes and crosses her arms and then her legs over one another where she's perched on the table. "I guess. Though I'm offering you nothing but a physical release. Two bodies coming together in a heated night of passion. No one has to know . . ."

I groan in misery, running my hand over my clenching stomach. "I'll know."

She huffs. "I had you pegged all wrong. For some reason, I suspected that you lived and breathed sex. You exude it, I can feel the physical waves coming off your body. I'm disappointed to hear all that bundled-up heat and energy is wasted on someone you're brooding over."

"Doesn't change the facts. My heart is still with her."

"Yes, but your body is here, and for a moment it was hard and wanting . . . *for me.*"

I suck in a long, slow breath, trying to calm the anxiety and nerves bristling all over my skin. "Like I said, you're a beautiful woman . . ."

"One who could make you forget all about your long-lost love . . . at least until you go back to the States." She cocks an eyebrow.

I shake my head. "'Fraid not."

She sighs and smacks her lips. "Pity. I was really hoping for a wild romp with the hot American."

I chuckle and look up at her, pairing our gazes. "I'm sorry if I made you think I was willing otherwise . . ."

She laughs, and it sounds like music. "Oh, honey, you didn't lead me on."

The word *honey* rolling off her lips makes me wince. The only woman I want to hear that endearment from is Skyler, and I'm suddenly afraid I never will again.

My gut churns, and I swallow slowly, breathing in and out in even, measured breaths, attempting to get my body back in line. I need sleep, water, and food. Not necessarily in that order.

"Guess I'm not used to a man saying no. Sorry I came at you hard." She grins sexily.

"No, you're not."

Her smile is coy as she gets up off the desk. "No. I'm not."

"Can I ask you a question?"

"Does it start and end with 'Never mind; I was wrong. Can you take me home with you?'" She waggles her brows.

I shake my head. "Alexis, why do you do this? Play this game?"

She pauses for a moment before answering. "What game?" She grins, knowing exactly what I'm talking about but not copping to it.

"You don't have to do this." I point to her attire and gesture around the room. "Play up your sex appeal, have an unrelenting nature when going after a man."

Alexis tips her head. "And why the hell wouldn't I, if it gets me what I want far quicker than my intellect alone? Besides, if I'm the one who makes the rules, I also determine the prize. Sometimes it's a fantastic roll in the hay with a sexy American; other times, it gets men to see me as an object. Then, while they're looking at my tits and ass, I'm buying out their company shares, taking over their products ultimately, and setting up a bright future for myself."

"Alexis . . . game playing is not the answer." I frown as a wave of self-realization washes over me. In the past, I'd been known to play a game or two.

"Isn't it? When I always come out the winner? It's not my fault if men see me as a walking fantasy with no brain cells and just big boobs. It is, however, their fault when they think with their dicks and not with their brains during business negotiations. And frankly, this"—she waves her hands up and down her form—"works every time. I rarely follow through on the fantasy a man sees before him, unless I want that man under me. My choice. My game. I win."

I gesture between us. "Not this time, sweetheart."

"Perhaps I'll have to review the play-by-play and figure out where it all went wrong . . . or maybe there's still a chance of it going my way?" She cocks an eyebrow.

"Not a chance." I laugh. "Get out of here! Go find another unsuspecting soul to tarnish."

She chuckles. "Won't be hard. Your partner is not exactly sloppy seconds."

I shake my head and grab my blazer from where I left it folded over the couch.

"Nope, and he would be a willing player in your game. Not only that, he understands the rules because he has the same ones."

She taps her smudged lips, and my heart sinks, remembering my lips did that. My tongue was in her mouth in my eagerness to get at more of her taste.

"Doesn't make the game nearly as fun."

"No, but it makes it honest. Think about that before you move on to your next target. They should know what they're getting into."

Her jovial expression falls flat, and she purses her lips.

I slow my roll so that I don't run into her body as I pass her, heading out of the small space. "Think about it."

"I will," she says, and with the weight in her tone, I believe her.

Once I've made my way through the back of the building and down the stairs to street level, I wave down a taxi, get in, and rest my tired head all the way back to the hotel, staring out the window at the intricate buildings and architecture. Wendy was not wrong in her excitement about the mixture of old and new in the city. There are buildings crafted out of metal and bright colors right next to those built with stone that look to be a few hundred years old. The combination of the old with the new makes the city uniquely special and pleasing to the eye.

As I gaze out, the city starts to blur and fade while thoughts of Skyler start running a marathon in my mind.

What is she doing right now?

Is she sad?

Does she still miss me?

It's been days since her last message.

How do I move forward from here?

I get to my room, toss my jacket over the chair, drop my slacks, and pull off my shoes where I stand. Next, I unbutton my dress shirt, pull back the coverlet, slide my boxers-clad body in, and hit the button on the lamp for the lights. I grab the remote sitting on the end table and flick on the TV. The first thing that comes on is an entertainment news program.

Skyler's face appears on the screen, Tracey standing by her side, an arm wrapped around her shoulders. A microphone is thrust in front of her face. She looks tired. Black circles paint the spaces under her eyes. She smiles her fake everything-is-roses smile for the bloodsucking paparazzi.

"And how is SkyPark doing?" one nosey man asks.

I sit up in my bed and hold my breath, waiting for her answer.

"Fabulously. Parker's on business right now, but I very much look forward to his return."

The crowd bum-rushes her with a bunch of questions. She runs her hands through her hair and glances around as the next question flies at her.

"And what is the first thing you're going to say to Parker when you see him?"

Skyler closes her eyes, and I can feel the pain like an invisible blow to the solar plexus. I rub at my sternum and wait for her to respond.

Her eyes open, and they are a brilliant blue. The only color I want to see first thing every morning when I wake up. She locks her gaze right into the camera, and I swear, if I didn't know better, I'd believe she were speaking right to me.

"When I see Parker, I'm going to tell him how very much I've missed him, and I love him more than anything on this earth."

"Miss."

I miss him.

"Love."

I love him.

"More."

I love him more than anything on this earth.

She loves me. Skyler loves me. Skyler loves me, and she admitted it on national television for the entire world to hear and see.

Holy. Fucking. Hell.

8

I'm a mess. I didn't sleep a wink last night after I saw the entertainment piece. I tossed and turned, trying to figure out what to do.

How do I respond to this?

Skyler loves me.

Loves me.

The thrill of her admission rushes through my bloodstream, gifting me with a warm, liquid sensation that seeps deep into my bones, coating my frozen soul. It's as though I've been encased in ice this past week. Lost to the chill of cold hatred and betrayal.

She loves me.

I close my eyes and let the truth in. My woman admitted on national fucking television that she's in love with me. Energy licks at my heels, and I start to pace the hotel room, not knowing what to do with the extra kinetic energy pumping through me. It's as though I'm a live wire, all synapses firing a hundred miles an hour with nowhere to go as I wear a hole into the carpet.

The connecting door flies open.

"Oh. My. God. You have to watch this new piece about—" Wendy starts as she rushes in, holding her laptop open and at the ready on the entertainment news station.

I shake my head and hold up my hand, not wanting her to come any closer. "I've already seen it. I watched it on television last night."

Her eyes widen, and the blue of her irises seems even lighter than normal, more like the sun-filled sky right after a heavy rain. "Then you know." Her voice lowers to a gentler, less excitable timbre. And understanding sizzles within the space between us.

"That she loves me?" I croak out the words, each one filling an empty part of my heart. The dagger eases, giving me a moment's reprieve from the pent-up pressure and dull, aching emptiness that's been there all week.

Wendy nods, slams the laptop shut, and flicks her hand. Her gaze turns wild with excitement, eyes bulging as energy bustles around her petite form. "Yes! Oh my goodness, Park. This is so awesome! See, I told you she loves you!" Her smile is huge and beaming.

Someone pounding on my door calls my attention. Knowing it's one of two people, I fling the damn thing wide and walk away from it to continue my pacing. My mind is filled with flickering thoughts running around like chickens with their heads cut off.

Why would she admit she loves me on TV?

How does this change what's happening between us?

"Shee-it, brother," Royce says as his large suit-clad form enters with a gentleness in his expression I absolutely do not want to see, because it means he's seen the piece and is expecting me to lose my shit.

I *am* losing my shit, but I don't need the guys to know that. However, with the wild thoughts about Skyler dashing through me, not to mention where I went with Alexis yesterday and the guilt that comes with it, I have no chance in hell of keeping my cool.

"Brother . . . shit just got real!" Bo chuckles, coming in behind Roy and shutting the door.

The three of them stand before me like the three amigos.

"Guys . . . I . . ." I lose my train of thought as the one thing, the single most important question that's been plaguing my every movement, assaults me. "Is it possible she didn't cheat? I mean *really*. You know my history . . ." I go back to pacing the room, though the space I now have to do it is significantly decreased by three additional bodies.

"Um, I have an admission . . ." Wendy holds up her hand. I glance her way, and her cheeks pinken as she averts her gaze.

"Uh, yeah, brother . . . me too." Royce clears his throat and shifts back on his heels and then to his toes, back and forth in a move I've seen him do a thousand times. He's got a secret that's making him uncomfortable.

"No way are you guys going first!" Bo cuts in, anxiety and irritation clear in his scratchy tone.

Before my eyes, the three of them look at one another and then start bickering . . . loudly, as if I wasn't even in the room.

"I have to tell him first!" Wendy demands with a childish foot stomp.

Royce shakes his head. "Naw, no way, nohow. My boy deserves to hear from me, true?"

Bo makes a choking sound. "Absolutely not. I've known him longer . . ."

"By an hour. You had one class with him before the class we all shared," Royce fires back, and crosses his arms over his massive chest.

Wendy groans. "I'm the newest. I could be fired!" she says, wading back in, her voice reaching hysterical levels.

"We're not going to let him fire you," Royce states flatly.

"Don't worry, Tink, I'll take care of you if you're out of a job. You can manage me, if you know what I mean." Bo waggles his eyebrows.

Wendy's face contorts into an expression of disgust. "Gross! This is not the time to joke!" She points at Bo, her cheeks turning beet red.

I wade in between them. "Will the three of you shut the hell up! Criminy. I need my best friends right now. The woman I love—who I believe *cheated* on me with her ex, stayed overnight with him, put herself at risk, paid off said asshole's debts—just stated on national

television that she's *in love* with me. And . . . I kissed Alexis last night."
I let the final admission spill out of me as though I'm purging the ugly
truth from my heartbroken soul.

All three of their heads turn toward me. Expressions of . . .

Shock . . . Wendy.

Surprise . . . Royce.

Irritation . . . Bo.

"What!" The word sounds so loud when three people are screaming it.

"How could you?" Wendy chokes back the emotion as if I'd cheated
on her.

"Aw man . . . you done fucked up," Royce adds.

"Totally fucked yourself." Bo nods. "And I wanted Alexis for myself,
dammit!" He scowls.

I fall back on the bed and hang my head, cradling the heavy weight
between my palms, elbows to my knees. Guilt, shame, and fear are
the predominant emotions spiraling through my system. Then, out of
nowhere, there is the pinprick of happiness, excitement, and anticipation as I remember what Skyler revealed. The woman I love loves me
back.

I should be elated.

Should be shouting my joy from the rooftop of the tallest building.

Falling down on my knees and thanking God for bringing me "the
one."

Only I can't. The knife she stuck in my heart pierces a bit deeper,
more blood pouring out, filling me with dread.

How can she love me and cheat on me at the same time?

Wendy falls to her knees at my feet and places both of her hands
over my bicep. "I've been texting with Skyler." Her voice shakes. "I-I
uh, I asked her point-blank if she cheated," Wendy admits in a rush,
her eyes clouding with tears.

I blink slowly and focus on her gaze. "And w-what did she say?" I hate myself for needing to know, needing to hear her reply like a dying man receiving last rites. All I can do is wish and hope against all odds my initial response is wrong. At this point, I'm so far down the rabbit hole, I'd rather spend my life apologizing to Skyler and making it up to her than live a life without her love in it.

Wendy licks her lips and peers up at me from her position at my feet. She looks so small, delicate, honest. "She swears she didn't cheat." Matching tears fall down Wendy's cheeks at the same time. I wipe the first away and then the second.

Roy clears his throat. "She told me the same. Except I called her."

My head flies up as if it's being self-propelled. "You spoke to her?" My voice cracks.

He nods. "Yesterday. After our night on the town, I couldn't help myself. You're hurting too much, brother. Too much. And every day seeing you like this kills me. I was angry. Mad that she had such control over my boy. Upset that she could break my brother's heart. I wanted her to feel pain. To tell her how much she screwed up."

I swallow down the Wiffle-ball-sized lump in my throat. "A-and?"

He shakes his head. "She admitted she went to Johan's hotel in the hopes of settling their dispute herself. Promised me she didn't cheat." Roy bites into his plump bottom lip and rubs it with his thumb, I imagine to soothe the ache. "Man, I believe her, but I'm not going to tell you what she said. You need to hear it direct from the source."

I close my eyes, and the pain of not being with her and the possibility that she didn't betray me roll over my body like a gust of warm air. Opening my eyes, I focus on Bo. "You too?"

He tips his head, lets out a long, tired breath, and puts his hands into his jacket pockets. "Well, I figured since she was available, I'd ask her out on a date."

I laugh loud and hard at Bo's absurdity. The brother means well, and his go-to method of making someone feel better is to crack jokes.

Royce smacks the back of Bo's head so fast I could swear it was magic propelling his arm.

"Ouch!" Bo growls. "I hate it when you do that! You're messing up my perfect coif."

"I'll give you perfect coif with my foot up yo' ass! Tell the truth, and stop with the wisecracks. Can't you see Park's hurting?"

Bo rubs his head, and his dark gaze meets mine. "She called, I answered. She wanted to know how you were doing."

Anticipation squeezes my chest like a vise. "And what did you tell her?" I'm hanging on his every word.

He rolls his lips between his teeth. "Told her you were doing fine. Better than ever," he says flippantly, even haughtily.

"Really?"

He scoffs, "Fuck no! I told her you were hurt. Pissed off. Angry. And if I found out that she did cheat, I was going to find a way to make her pay for fooling you, me, all of us." He waves a jaunty arm around the room.

I narrow my gaze and tighten my fist, straightening my spine, ready to charge. I can feel my nostrils flare as anger ripples along every nerve ending. My body heats up, and my gut clenches tight. "You did not say that to my woman!" I glare at him, protectiveness for Skyler still running strong through my veins.

He nods. "Yeah, yeah, I did. Because when she hurt you, Park, she hurt all of us. We all accepted her into our arms. Into our team. And if she fucked us over, I wanted her to feel that hurt too!" he snarls.

"Christ!" I run my hand through my hair and drop my head back down, clenching my teeth so hard I could crack diamonds with my molars. "This is such a clusterfuck."

"Sure is. Now tell us about why the hell you kissed Alexis Stanton?" Royce demands, crossing his arms over his massive chest. "Were you thinking at all?" Royce's tone is weighted with disappointment.

Bo, at the complete opposite end of the spectrum, chuckles. "Yeah, he was thinking all right. With his *little head* and not his big one."

I point at Bo. "You leave the beast out of it."

"Ew . . . the beast." Wendy blanches and makes a gagging sound from the back of her throat. She murmurs a few other choice words and eases back onto her heels, petting my thigh back and forth in a show of her support.

I spend a few moments thinking about why I finally gave in. "I don't know why I kissed her. She's been all over me since we got here. And at the time, I was vulnerable, okay? Missing Skyler, feeling hungover, lost, tired, all of the above. Hell, I don't know. The old me would have jumped into the sack with her in a minute flat. The woman is sex on legs . . ."

"She really is." Wendy nods frantically. "I'd kill to have her body. All boobs and hips and long legs. Golden hair. Plus, she's extremely smart. Knows her stuff."

Royce sighs. "I'll give you she's a honey. Doesn't give you an excuse to give in, though, especially when you're trying to work shit out about your feelings with Skyler. Bad move, brother. Bad. Freakin'. Move. Because if you clear this thing up between you and Sky, and I have no doubt that you will, you're gonna have to come clean about Alexis."

I groan, hating every second of the idea that I'll have to admit to my weakness with Alexis. Then again, if it weren't for Skyler's own betrayal, it would never have happened in the first place! "Yeah, got it. I'll deal with it when the time comes. For now, I need to figure out what I'm going to do about Skyler."

Bo inhales loudly while plucking away at his goatee. "Surprise her again. Head to New York when the case is over. Have it out once and for all. And if you still believe she cheated after talking to her, hearing her side, then by all means, cut her loose. We'll back your play all day every day." Bo holds out his fist.

I knock the top of his with my own, and he repeats the gesture.

"We got you. No matter what you decide. Yeah?" Royce holds out a fist turned sideways.

I bump his fist.

Wendy eases up onto her knees and grabs my hand, squeezing tightly. "We're here for you." She leans forward and kisses me on the cheek.

I hold her in a close hug, enjoying a female's comfort. I pat her back and let her help me stand up.

A rush of solidarity and pure love fills my chest as I look at my three friends, two old, one new but no less important. I hold out my arms. Wendy hooks me around the waist and snuggles against my side. Bo takes up position at my other side.

"You know I never give up the opportunity for a bromance," he jokes, clapping me on the back and squeezing the top of my shoulder where my neck and clavicle meet.

Royce sighs and rolls his eyes. "You're going to fuckin' make me do this, aren't you?" He looks down at his shiny name-brand shoes.

I wiggle my fingers. "Come on, brother, group hug. Take one for the team."

"Goddamn team, I'm always taking one for the team," he mumbles stubbornly, but moves against my front and dips his head, so my forehead touches his, not our chests. That would be a bit too far for Roy. Wendy hooks him around his waist and presses herself against both of us, her coconut scent filling the space between all of us. Bo curves his body forward and nudges his head against ours.

"I always wanted to be on the football team. I imagine this is what it was like during the group huddles, only a little less stanky." Bo chuckles.

"Shh! You're ruining the moment," I grit through my teeth. "I just want to say, thank you. From the bottom of my heart. Thank you."

***

"What you're suggesting is ludicrous! My brother would never screw up so badly that a product launch set to make us millions would be at risk."

I clasp my hands over my waist and look at Alexis with compassion. "I can only give the information my team has assembled and allow you to decipher what we've found so far. We're not done with our investigation by a long shot; nevertheless, the evidence we've found so far is damning."

"Yeah, toward my kid brother!" Alexis paces her big office, her stilettos making clacking noises on the concrete floors, the sound disappearing when she walks on one of the many area rugs scattered around. She rests her arms on the back of the couch Bo is sitting in. Royce is in the chair opposite me.

"Alexis, we're not saying your brother is intentionally trying to hurt you. As I told you before, we have found nothing in any of the employees' financials, including Kidd's, to suggest a payout of any kind. However, we can't ignore the bugs in the system and the bad coding Wendy's found that matches your brother's unique style."

"As someone who knows coding inside and out, who mentored and trained him in the art, I'll need to see the evidence myself. Exact locations." For the first time since I met Alexis, her gaze is piercing, her tone agitated, and her jaw tight as a drum. She is not happy that we are suggesting her brother might have something to do with the leaked information.

I stand up and place a tablet on her desk. "We figured as much, which is why we had Wendy scout out some locations for your review and verification. There is one more concerning issue." I say this with as much professional tact as I can muster.

"Which is?" She flicks open her laptop and brings up her system. She glances at the tablet and pulls up a section of her back-end coding that Wendy marked.

"Apparently, Eloise Gagnon has found a bunch of errors in the system and has been cleaning them up, fixing the coding on Kidd's behalf."

Alexis's eyes narrow into slits. "Why in the world would she do that?" She turns back to her big screen and pulls up a section that has a black background with a bunch of numbers and letters. The image on the screen reminds me of something out of the movie *The Matrix*.

"I get the impression that they used to be an item and she still has a fondness for him. She did not seem happy about his pending nuptials."

Alexis huffs. "She wouldn't be. I helped split those two up years ago."

"How do you mean?"

"They were a couple the first year Kidd started here. Except Kidd was young and dumb. He led with his dick, not his brain."

Bo chuckles from where he sits. "Can't blame the youngster."

Royce bats the zinger right back at him. "The youngster? Hell, brother, you're one to talk."

Bo smirks. "'Tis true. Only I've learned along the way."

Roy sucks in a breath through his teeth. "Shoot, I'll believe that when I see it."

"If you two are quite finished . . . ," I chastise them.

Both sets of eyes seem to grow bigger. Royce scowls, miffed that he got caught being unprofessional. His professionalism is something he prides himself on, so even a simple slipup is going to hurt, especially after the Rochelle debacle. In this circumstance, though, I can't blame them. Alexis keeps a chill environment where pretty much anything goes. Especially if you take into consideration the number of times she's attempted to pick me up. Although since our chat yesterday, she seems to have gotten the hint that, even though I find her attractive, I'm not willing to go there with her.

Which reminds me of what I still need to do with Skyler. I'm itching to get this case over with so I can do as Bo suggests. Hightail it to New York, show up at her door, and demand answers. And so help me God, she will listen to me, and tell me every last sordid detail of what went down with Johan if she has any hope of a future together.

A future together.

My heart bleeds at the thought. I'm so close to getting some answers and settling this emptiness inside me. I just need to be done with this case. Part of me is considering leaving the details up to the rest of the team and catching the next plane out, but it wouldn't be right. I can't leave my team hanging in the wind when we're so close to solving this case and leaving Montreal with a happy client. Or at the very least, a satisfied client.

"When you say you split them up, how did that go with Kidd?"

Alexis shrugs. "He was fine with it. He'd been spending too much time following Eloise around. She's a few years older, and honestly, she had way too much control over him. I put a stop to it. Separated them by putting her in a different department and suggested if he were serious about his job with Stanton Cybertech, he'd cut the woman loose and focus on the work. He made his choice. To be honest, I was proud of him. Kidd never went back on the decision either."

"Huh, that's interesting." I crack my neck, allowing some of the day's tension to ease.

"How so?" Alexis asks but stares at the monitor, her fingers flying over the keyboard.

I cross my arms and cradle my healing hand. It feels a whole helluva lot better, but it's still sore, and the two fingers will be splinted for quite a while yet. "She claims to be fixing his errors that she finds because she thinks he's lost focus due to his girlfriend."

"Really." She laughs dryly. "I sincerely doubt that. Kidd has been on top of his game since he met Victoria, not wanting to let history repeat itself. If anything, he's more focused on work and securing his future for the family he wants to create with her."

"I'm guessing that means you're a Victoria fan?" I prod.

Alexis nods. "Absolutely. She's done wonders for him. He's more passionate, eager to go home at quitting time, which feeds his muse. Plus, I love the girl. She's like a little sister to me. I couldn't be happier that he found her."

"What feeds your muse?" I ask, knowing there be dragons in such a question.

She grins, flicks her gaze over her shoulder, focusing her pretty eyes on me. "Hot, meaningless sex." Did she learn anything from our chat? Anything at all?

Before I can respond, Bo stands up and juts his hands out in a T shape. "I offer myself as tribute for the cause."

Royce and I both howl with laughter, but it's Roy who responds through his guffaws. "Sit yo' ass down, man. She doesn't want you."

Alexis turns fully in her chair and sizes Bo up, from his shitkickers and faded, tight-fitting jeans to his ever-present leather jacket. "Oh, I didn't say that." She picks up a lock of her hair and twirls it around her finger. "I usually prefer the chase, not my prey served up on a silver platter." She licks her lips and cocks an eyebrow. "But"—she gestures toward me—"since this hunk of beef won't play, I could be persuaded to go for something a little more willing."

Bo blows Alexis a kiss from across the room. "I'm all in, sugar plum. Tonight, we dance."

"Good Lord, help us all." I rub at my temples, a new headache stirring. One thing I learned from my wading into Royce's deal with Rochelle is not to. Therefore, I'm not going to say shit about anything involving Alexis and Bo. They want to bone the rest of the time we're here, so be it. At least she's finally gotten the hint that I'm not going down that rabbit hole with her.

Alexis goes back to the coding and frowns.

"What is it?" I lean a hip on the edge of her desk.

She shakes her head. "The coding looks like Kidd's, but there's something off. I'm going to need some more time with it in order to put my finger on what's missing."

"All right, we'll leave you to it. I have two more staff interviews. Wendy has her leads and is working the coding to see if she can find anything that connects the leaks with the viruses. Royce, if you want to go back to the hotel and work on our other cases for a while . . ."

"Yeah, man, I really do. We've got a prospect in London who is bidding now, not to mention I've got to review Sophie's end-of-quarter financials."

Sophie.

Shit. With all of this going on between me and Sky, I haven't checked in on her and the new development Wendy mentioned about Gabriel potentially popping the question. By now, he may have already, but I'd like to think she'd call and give me a heads-up.

Pushing thoughts of my friend to another recess of my mind, I point to Bo. "Bo, you're up. Bring out your brand of crazy at the tech application meeting and see if we can shake any wack-jobs loose."

Bo grins, shakes his jacket out, and smirks. "*Crazy* is my middle name."

9

"Explain to me what you found that has Alexis poring over her keyboard." I pinch the bridge of my nose and lean back in the office chair. I took a chance and came down to the coding area after hours and found Wendy and Bo shooting the shit discussing the case, or rather bickering about it. Everyone else besides the three of us and Alexis had gone home.

It's been two more days on this case with very little to go on. Royce is flying home tomorrow, his part of the case complete. Bo has made the coders and tech team jump around to create the most impossible application under the sun. Every single thing you shouldn't do with an application, he's asked them to do. Which means everyone here hates him. Everyone aside from Alexis. Apparently that situation has worked itself out. Once Bo went home with her, she made a complete three-sixty over wanting me. Now she's up Bo's ass and begging for more. Guess she likes his brand of crazy in the sack too.

"We do not agree." Wendy gives Bo the evil eye.

Bo sighs and rests his chin on the back of the computer chair. He's straddling the thing backward, his big legs dwarfing the chair.

"What's the problem?" I lift my feet onto the desk in front of me. A blast of muscle relief ripples down my legs in the process.

"I believe Kidd is the leak," Wendy states emphatically. "And that's based on the new code he wrote today. He left some serious holes, ones so huge any hacker worth their salt could easily exploit them to steal every single thing in this place and make it their own."

I frown. "How so?"

She points to the computer. I get up and peer at the numbers and letters as if they can tell me what she's seeing. Unfortunately my degree is in business, not computer information systems. "Minxy, you'll have to give me more than a screen filled with the alphabet."

"I'm telling you, Wendy. Kidd. Didn't. Do. It. The sooner you start believing my instincts and looking elsewhere, the sooner we'll find out who did." Bo flaps his hand down against the back of the chair. "What did you say, that weird chick, the coder El-something . . ."

"Eloise," I supply for him.

He snaps his fingers and points at me. "Yeah, her."

Wendy groans. "Her coding looks totally different."

"Just hear me out. I get that her coding is different, but what about this. She dated him in the past. Right?"

She sighs and flips back to her computer and types away. "Yeah. I'm listening."

"You're not looking at me," Bo notes dryly.

Her demeanor changes to annoyance. "I'm multitasking. Get on with what you were going to say."

Bo twists his lips and taps his fingers on the back of the chair. "Here's the thing I can't stop thinking about. Alexis said she told Kidd to break it off with Eloise back in the day. He did. Maybe this whole time she's been pining away for him. Then you, Park, told her that he's marrying his current girlfriend, one you already told us she didn't like, and she responded the other day by fleeing the interview room, needing to get out fast."

I frown. "I'm following. What does that have to do with anything?"

He tugs at his goatee. "You know how there's something about a woman scorned? Maybe Eloise is still holding a torch for this guy."

"If what you say is true, she wouldn't be telling us about his mistakes." I toss the figurative ball back to him.

"And she wasn't beforehand. Up until we came to town and she needed to cover her own ass. Alexis wasn't told anything about what was going on with Kidd and his supposed mistakes. Does he seem like the type of guy to make these errors she's claiming he made?"

Wendy turns back around. "Not really, no. He's extremely focused and super passionate about this company. And he loves his sister. I don't see him giving anything but a hundred percent, but it doesn't change that the coding looks like it's his."

My mind is humming with possibilities, but I can't seem to cling to any of them. It's as if the answer is right there but it's slipping through my fingers. All I can focus on is my need to get to New York City and confront Skyler about her time with Johan.

Wendy's phone rings while we're sitting here thinking out loud. She puts it on speaker. "Parker, Bo, and I are on. Find anything?" Wendy questions the caller.

Alexis's voice comes through the speaker. "Yeah, a lot actually. The coding does look like Kidd's but not exactly like his. There's a subtle difference, a little flair that I have never seen in his work before. It's really small, but it's still there. I think someone is making it look like he's the one creating these errors."

"Tink, send a chunk of Eloise's coding to her so she can do some comparisons," Bo requests.

"On it!" Her fingers speed across the keyboard once more.

"Don't. Even. Bother. You twit!" A low, deadly voice comes from the doorway.

The three of us turn around to see Eloise just inside the door. Her arms are out straight in front of her, and a big black gun is between her palms, her fingers wrapped around the trigger. She shoots at one of the servers, and the thing splits into pieces. "Stand up, all of you!" she screeches.

The three of us hustle to stand. I start to move around the desks to get in front of Wendy.

"Don't you fucking move!"

I stop where I stand, my heart pumping as adrenaline dumps into my nervous system. "I'm sorry, Eloise. I meant no offense."

"You!" She points the gun at me.

Wendy cries out, "No!"

Eloise waves the gun back at Wendy. "Shut up!"

"Hey there, darlin', no need to point the gun at us," Bo says in his most charming voice.

Eloise's eyes bulge, and her face reddens from what I can only assume is anger. Without even sparing a second, she points the gun at Wendy and fires.

"No!" A yell blows through my system and out my mouth so furiously it's like a tornado touching down on dry land.

Bo jumps toward Wendy to intercept the bullet, but it's too late—she's been hit in the right side of her chest. Blood oozes out just above her breasts, painting her yellow blouse crimson from a dark hole in her shirt. Her life source seeps out the hole and down her front. Wendy's eyes go wide in recognition for a brief second before her body falls harshly against the table and down to the ground in an uncoordinated heap. She lies flat on the ground, her pale hand over her gunshot wound, blood pooling in a giant circle along her chest. Bo scrambles to her side, knees to the concrete floor, where he puts his hand over hers to staunch the blood flow.

"Wendy, baby, no!" Bo cries out, his body hunkered over hers.

I try to go to her too, but another shot rings out, and I stop in my tracks. A blaze of pain races from my shoulder and down my arm.

"Christ!" I grab for my arm and look down at the bloody horizontal slice against the top of my shoulder where the bullet grazed me, taking bits and pieces of my suit coat and shirt and pieces of my flesh with it. I hold the seeping wound, thankful she didn't get me anywhere more serious.

"I said, don't you freakin' move! Why are you not listening to me? Nobody listens to me! First Kidd, then Alexis, and now you three!" She waves the gun around like a lunatic. Well, technically, she is a lunatic, and my next approach needs to be better if I'm going to talk her down.

I lift my hands in a show of surrender and lower my voice even though my entire being wants to see to Wendy.

"Come on, Tink, stay with me . . ." Bo's voice is a low, agonized rumble. "She needs an ambulance! She's losing a lot of blood and gasping for air."

I look down where they are about fifteen feet from me and see pink foam coming from Wendy's mouth, which scares the living hell out of me.

"I'm listening to you, Eloise," I answer the woman with a gun.

She laughs, and the sound is eerily devoid of any emotion. "Guess you figured me out, huh."

I shake my head. "Not really, no. We realized you were involved somehow."

Her arm goes out toward me again, gun pointed directly at me. "Who are you anyway? How do you all know each other?"

I swallow down the fear for Wendy's life and try to rush through it. "We work together out of Boston. The three of us. We were called in to investigate the product leaks and bugs in the system."

"Wow. The head floozy actually called in a team of people. To figure out what little ol' me has been doing to her system. Go figure. That's actually a compliment." She tilts her head back and laughs. I move a couple of feet forward, leaning across the desk closer to her. I have to find some way to get the gun away from her and get Wendy some help.

"Park . . . Wendy's not doing so hot. We need help!" Bo's agonized voice rips through the heaviness in the air.

"I. Said. Shut. Up!" Eloise screeches like a banshee and fires off a shot at the desk next to Bo's head. He ducks, putting his body protectively over Wendy's prone one.

"Hey, hey, I'm eager to hear what you have to say. Tell me how you did it all. And why."

Her head jerks back, and her pupils turn a scary shade of black. "Why?" Her tone is scathing. "I'll tell you why. Revenge."

"Revenge?" I whisper.

She huffs. "Kidd left me high and dry four years ago. Alexis told him to break up with me, and she moved me to another department to make it easier on her little baby brother. Blech." She makes a gagging sound and leans the hand holding the gun against the top of the desk nearest her.

"But you didn't sell the secrets," I say to keep her talking.

She snorts and looks up at the ceiling. "Why would I do that? I don't want her money. I want her to lose everything to her competitors. And I wanted to show up Kidd. Show him what he lost. How good I was. What he could still have if he apologized and made it up to me."

I take another step closer to her while she's distracted. Wendy makes a gurgling, hacking sound, and I peer over to see blood and froth coming out of her mouth as Bo holds her on her side, letting it spill out on the concrete so she doesn't choke on it. A hammer pounds against my brain, and sweat breaks out all over my body. My chest feels like it's taking in air like a marathon runner at the very end of a race. Fast and instinctive.

Eloise continues, "Then you tell me he's marrying that *woman* instead of me. We could have been so happy together! We were perfect. And all this time I've been waiting for him to remember, to see what it could be again. Us working together and living together. Victoria doesn't deserve him!"

I shake my head. "No, you're right. She doesn't. As for you, you deserve better. I'm a professional at finding women their mate. I did it in San Francisco right before we came. Right, Bo?"

Bo's voice is nothing but a scratchy whisper. "Yeah, he's the best." Tears fill his eyes.

I look down at Wendy, and she's unconscious.

"Is she still breathing?" I ask, fear permeating my words.

"Yeah, but barely." He sounds as if each word is killing him slowly.

"How's about you and I go find you a mate, eh?" I offer Eloise.

She tilts her head to the side and taps the gun on the table. "That could be fun, and you're right. Kidd isn't worthy of me or my talents." The woman lifts her head in a prissy move while my friend lies bleeding to death on the floor.

As another bout of loathing and panic rushes through me, I note the cavalry has arrived. Behind Eloise there's a wall with two windows separating the room from the stairwell and hallway. Two police officers skate past, arms out and guns drawn. They sneak up to the door of the coding office.

How the hell did they know we were here? Maybe Alexis heard the gunshots?

I glance over at the phone and note that Wendy never ended the call. Alexis must have heard it all.

While I hold my breath, I try to keep Eloise's attention on me. "So, what do you say?" I swallow as the door behind Eloise slowly opens. "I'd be happy to set you up. It would be so easy—"

The two cops stand behind Eloise, weapons trained on her. "Put your hands up in the air!" one of them hollers.

Eloise's eyes are blazing daggers of anger as she turns around, gun pointed up. "No!" she growls. Her hand twitches once before both cops drop her with two bullets apiece.

I crouch low and crawl to where Bo has Wendy in his lap, cradling her. His lips are against her forehead. "Come on, Tink. Don't leave us!" he cries.

Her body doesn't move.

***

The hospital was a madhouse when we were carted into the emergency room, Wendy on a stretcher, nonresponsive but with a shallow pulse.

The paramedics said something about a collapsed lung and the loss of a lot of blood. I called Royce and told him to meet us at the hospital and to call Michael.

Now I'm sitting on a bed while a resident stitches up my flesh wound, telling me I'm in shock. I can't even feel the pain. Everything is numb.

Bo stands to the side of my bed as if he's standing sentry. An hour has gone by since they rushed Wendy to surgery.

Royce runs into the ER, suit coat flying in the wind like he's a member of *Men in Black* and he's come to save the world.

"Brother." Roy puts a hand to my other shoulder. His voice is deep, much deeper than normal. "You okay?"

I nod, not capable of saying anything more.

"Flesh wound. The bullet just grazed his shoulder," Bo answers on my behalf.

Roy nods and then takes in Bo's attire. He's bloody from chest to waist, his white T-shirt coated red from Wendy's blood.

"Jeez-us. Are you hurt too? What the hell happened? Do we know anything more about Wendy?" He fires off what feels like a swarm of questions I can't even assimilate in my current mental state.

Bo shakes his head. "It's not my blood. Wendy was taken right into surgery. Collapsed lung, gunshot wound to the chest. You called Mick?"

His voice is a shallow husk, nothing like his normal joking, exuberant, loving tone.

Roy nods. "He'll be here in the next hour or two." He runs his hand over his bald head. "How could this happen?"

I shrug. "I didn't see how unstable she was. My head wasn't in the game. I should have caught the connection. Something—" I start, self-loathing and shame filling my mind with all the things I should have, could have, done better.

Bo puts his hand on my back. "Don't you dare try to take this one on. All four of us were on this job making the connections, and we had it, we were putting the pieces together when she went loco. This is on that psycho, not on you!" Bo points a finger at me.

"If Wendy dies . . ." My body is trembling so hard even my voice is shaky. Tears fill my eyes and fall unchecked down my cheeks. "She can't die," I whisper.

Bo presses his forehead against my back, and Royce grips my shoulder hard. "Brother, you have to have faith. Have faith in our strong girl. She'll come back to us, and just think, she'll have one helluva story to tell."

I laugh through my tears and wipe my nose and eyes with the back of my arm. Wendy loves a good story. "Yeah. God willing."

"That's right. God willing. You gotta believe in order to receive his blessing." Royce rumbles his truth, and I let it sink into my heart.

***

"Where the fuck is she!" Michael Pritchard storms into the hospital waiting room, a desperate man on a mission. His navy pinstriped suit jacket flails behind him in his speedy strides.

He comes up to where I stand in the waiting room, fury mixed with anguish written all over the hard lines of his face. He's not much older than the three of us, but he exudes barely contained power the likes none of us have ever seen. He grits his teeth and speaks through them.

"Where. Is. My. Woman," he growls, and I can feel the vibrations of his torment rippling off him in scorching-hot blasts of fury.

I swallow and stare into his light eyes.

His darken as my gaze intensifies. "If she dies, I hold you responsible," he warns with a sneer.

I nod. "She's not going to die. Wendy's strong—"

"You think I don't know that?" he snaps. "I'm the one who plucked her out of her horrible, rat-infested apartment and crummy job unworthy of her goals and talents. I helped her get her education. In turn, she gave me life. Her life *is* my life." He pounds on his chest. "She may be your assistant, even your friend, but she's my *everything*. My world revolves around her wants, her desires, her love. So, I *know* Wendy's strong. *My* Wendy—and every perfect inch of her *is mine*—is nothing but strength."

Royce puts a hand on the man's shoulder, and Michael snarls at the contact.

"Doctor's here . . . ," Roy says, and points to the waiting room door.

"You the family?"

"Yes," all four of us state, much to Michael's aggravation.

"I'm her fiancé. Please, tell me, how is she?" Michael says, emotion thick in his tone.

The tall dark-haired doctor clasps her hands in front of her. "She did well. The bullet went in through her chest, penetrated her lung, and ricocheted off her scapula. The lung was collapsed when she arrived. She lost a lot of blood. We've repaired the lung, removed the bullet, and put her into a medically induced coma until we can get her vitals back to desired levels. It's going to be touch and go for the next twenty-four hours, but I have every reason to believe that, provided her stats keep rising, she'll do very well."

"Can we see her?" Michael requests.

"Once she's out of recovery and settled in ICU, we'll notify you."

"Thank you, Doctor." Michael swallows, his voice cracking while his shoulders sink.

Behind the doctor, a nurse comes out with a clear bag and approaches Michael. Inside are Wendy's diamond engagement ring and her padlock and collar. "I, uh, thought her family should hold on to these."

Michael takes the bag and cradles it in his large hands. Tears fall onto the plastic as he falls to his knees.

"They cut her collar off." He holds himself up with one hand braced on the floor, the other still holding on to the bag.

Royce and I crouch down and help lift him up and to a blue plastic chair a few feet in front of us.

"They cut it off." He gulps, and more tears fall over his stoic face.

The leather band was cut cleanly near the loop and lock on the collar. He must have had the thing made for her with the two ends welded to loops that were connected by the dangling padlock. I move to finger the package, and he crushes it to his chest and glares at me.

"Sorry. I meant no harm." I rip my hand away as if it's been burned.

Michael pulls the collar out of the quart-sized bag. He tugs his tie loose and then undoes the first button of his dress shirt. Next, he pulls out a long beaded chain, similar to one you'd see dog tags hanging from. At the end is a silver key on which Wendy's name is engraved. He takes the key, inserts it into the lock, and releases the silver padlock. He removes it from the destroyed collar, snaps the lock closed on his chain, and secures it into place before tucking the lock and key back under his shirt against his chest.

"She's going to be okay," I offer, squeezing his forearm in support.

He swallows slowly, and his gaze focuses straight out at the blank white wall, almost unseeingly. His voice is a low snarl when he responds, "She better be, or there will be hell to pay."

10

"Why isn't she waking up?" Michael's barely contained rage is slipping every minute that Wendy stays in her coma.

The surgeon stands stiffly, waiting while Michael breathes and attempts to get himself under control.

"She's been asleep for two days," Michael says.

"We tried to wake her this morning," the doctor says. "She is no longer receiving any form of sedative to prevent her from waking. We believe when she was shot, she also endured a concussion in her fall. Her body and brain are healing from the trauma. She has normal brain activity, so there is no fear of any brain damage. However, the brain is a tricky thing. Your fiancée will wake when her brain and body tell her to do so. All we can do now is take care of her current injuries and wait."

The doctor reaches out a hand to Michael's forearm. "I understand you are eager for her to open her eyes. We all are. Unfortunately, *she* is not ready. Just talk to her, let her know you're here and ready for her to wake up."

Michael's entire body bristles at the doctor's orders. He grits his teeth and speaks through them. "Fine." He spins around and moves back to Wendy's bedside, where he's been for two days without leaving to shower or change clothes. He's still in the same suit he arrived in, even though his assistant arrived yesterday with his luggage and set him up in the hotel next to the hospital.

"Hey, Michael, why don't you go get some food in you, shower, change clothes," I say.

He shakes his head stiffly and holds Wendy's hand to his lips, staring at her face with a pleading expression.

I put my hand on his shoulder. "Man, she needs you. More than ever." I hold back the emotion that wants so badly to spill out. With her upper body wrapped in bandages, an oxygen tube in her nose, her normally pale skin almost see-through, she looks so peaceful, though none of us are. We're four strung-out males ready to lose our minds if our girl doesn't open her pretty blues and nail us with one of her smart remarks.

"Which is why I'm not leaving . . . ," Michael growls.

"Mick . . ."

He turns and snarls, "Don't. Call. Me. That."

I swallow against the dryness coating my throat. "I'm sorry. I can see that you are too far gone to be any help to her. You need to go to the hotel, eat something, shower, and change. If you could nap, that would be even better. You are no use to her or anyone running on empty. Please, man, do this for her."

He presses her hand against his cheek. "I can't leave her alone."

"She won't be alone. I'm here. The guys are coming soon to relieve me, so I can do the same in a couple of hours. Whether you like it or not, we're her extended family now, and we take care of our own."

His voice cracks, and he closes his eyes. "Why won't she wake up? I need to see her eyes, hear her voice to know she's going to be okay."

"Doc said she's going to come out of this aces. You, on the other hand, won't be worth anything to help her heal if you're down for the count. Go. Freshen up. Eat. Shower. You stink."

"I do not." He narrows his gaze.

I chuckle lightly so he knows I'm playing around. "No, you don't, but you will if you wear that suit one more day."

He sighs deeply and dips his head over Wendy's form. My gut clenches and my heart pounds. It's almost wrong to witness this man's pain and suffering, but there is real beauty in his devotion to his woman. He's a man lost at sea, the woman he loves his lock on land. Without her, he will allow the tide to carry him away.

My feet start to feel heavy, laden with the burden of my own lost love. Michael stands abruptly. "You're right. You'll stay with her?"

I nod.

"I'll be back soon, Cherry. I'm going to refuel, change, and I'll be back soon, my love." He kisses her on the forehead and then on the lips before looking at me. "You've got my number if anything changes. And I mean anything. She wiggles her fingers, I want to know about it."

"You have my word."

He nods curtly and leaves me alone with her.

I sit by her side and grab her hand. "Hey, minxy." I squeeze her hand and wait for a response, but there's nothing. She's lost to dreamland. "I wish you'd wake up. Your man is about to have a coronary waiting for you to open your pretty blue eyes." I stare at her and hold my breath. Nothing. No movement. I hold her hand between both of mine. "I'm so sorry, Wendy. So fucking sorry you got hurt. It wasn't supposed to go down like that." I shake my head and allow the guilt and shame that's been hiding just under the surface to spill out now that I'm alone with her.

"Aw, Wendy, won't you wake up? I need to see you're okay. Need to hear you tell me it's all going to be okay, because right now, I'm drowning, honey. Drowning in a sea of uncertainty. You're hurt. Bo and Royce are beside themselves. Your man is about to strangle the next person he sees. And I'm a goddamned mess. Straight Looney Tunes. I haven't talked to Sky, and I know you want me to. I did text her. Told her you'd been hospitalized here in Montreal with a gunshot wound.

She didn't respond, and I don't know why. Maybe because she hates me for not calling her sooner about our crap." I hang my head. "I need you to wake up, sis, wake up and yell at me. Tell me what to do. How to make everything better."

"I don't hate you, Parker." A whisper reaches my ears, and I slowly turn around.

She's like a golden halo of light. Her blonde hair falling in glowing waves around her face. Her caramel-brown gaze reaches straight into my chest and locks around my heart.

"Skyler . . ." I choke out her name and stand up.

Tears fall down her cheeks in a river of torment. She licks her lips. "I could never hate you. I love you."

"Jesus, come here." I hold out my arms, and she runs the ten feet it takes to get to me before plowing into my body. She wraps her arms around me tightly, and I'm engulfed by her warmth.

The scent of peaches and cream fills the air, replacing the bleach and antiseptic smell of the hospital with my favorite smell in the world. I burrow my face into her neck and hair and inhale long and deep. Her body trembles against mine, and her nails dig into my back. They graze the wound in my shoulder, which stings and burns, but I don't care. Nothing could prevent me from holding this woman.

"Honey, I'm so sorry . . . for everything." Her voice turns into sobs against my neck, her tears wetting my long-sleeved shirt.

I tunnel my good hand into her hair at the base of her skull and hold her to me, soaking up every ounce of her being plastered against me, alive, and in the flesh.

How did I live without this?

Without her.

I tighten my grip on her body and close my eyes, letting our bodies connect for a minute, two, ten. I don't know how long we stand there just holding one another. And then reality seeps in.

Hurt.

Dishonesty.

Betrayal.

Gritting my teeth, I push her back and away, swallowing down the bile that rises with the act of putting space between us. My mind swirls with the need to get her into a private space and interrogate the hell out of her, or toss her over my shoulder, throw her on the bed, and fuck the sins out of her.

"Park . . ."

"What are you doing here?" I clear my throat and take a step away.

She lifts her arms over her chest and rubs at her biceps, seeming suddenly chilled, though I think it has more to do with the space I put between us than the temperature.

Skyler frowns. "What do you mean? You told me Wendy was hurt." She lifts her hand toward Sleeping Beauty. "Wendy's my friend. She's like a sister to my boyfriend. Of course I'm going to drop everything and be by her side, by yours."

"I didn't expect you to come all this way."

"Parker, we have to talk. I am not the enemy. I'm the woman who loves you."

Loves you.

Her words shred my resolve, and the last two weeks pour over my body like acid, burning its way through flesh and bone.

My anger at her for being with Johan.

My love for her battling against what she did.

Alexis clamoring after me.

Wendy being shot.

It's all too damn much, and I feel like a volcano ready to erupt.

Bo takes that moment to enter. "Whoa, howdy." He glances from me to Skyler to Wendy and then back to me again. "Uh, should I come back?"

I clench my jaw and stare at Skyler, taking in her flowy dress, simple sweater, and knee-high suede boots. She's my living dream come true and, at the same time, my waking nightmare.

"You need to stay with Wendy until Michael comes back. Contact him if there is any change whatsoever. I promised him. I need to deal with *her*." The words are like poison on my tongue as I stomp over to Skyler and grab her hand and drag her out of Wendy's room.

"Where are we going? Where are you taking me?" She tugs on my good hand, and it pulls against the stitches in my shoulder. I wince but grip her tighter. No way in hell I'm letting her go.

There is no stopping this train. I'm out of my mind right now, and I need peace and quiet in order to deal with the raging emotions swirling like a vortex inside of my mind and body. "Hotel attached to the hospital. You wanted to talk. We're going to talk."

She keeps up with my pace, though mine is more of a jog than a fast walk.

The second we reach my room I insert the card, push her in, and shove the door closed with my foot. She whirls around, her chest lifting and falling with her labored breaths. Her eyes are a wild mixture of brown and caramel, and her cheeks are pink. She's never been more beautiful.

Fuck!

"Parker . . ." She licks her lips, and I lose it.

Gone.

I grab her at the waist, spin her around, and press her up against the hotel door, smashing my body into hers. She gasps at the contact, and I take full advantage of her open mouth, kissing her. She tastes of mint and madness. Or maybe that's me. Whatever it is, I lick deep, suck her tongue, and swallow every last one of her moans. Her tongue dances with mine in an illicit rhythm that has every one of my nerve endings heating and popping.

I grind against her and cup her ass, getting closer for more friction. She rips her mouth away, sucking in much-needed air. "Oh God . . ." She tips her head back, and I run my lips down her throat, biting and nipping, not caring if I mark up her pretty skin. She deserves it, the bite of pain. I want her to feel what I've felt.

"You like this, Peaches. Me losing my mind over you." I nuzzle at the scoop neck of her dress and push up her tits, not caring that my hand is killing me. I bite down on the fleshy globe of her plump breast, and she cries out at the pinch.

"Yes. You've made me crazy!" She battles, tugging at my shirt, lifting it up until she can get her hands on my abdomen. Her knuckles trace the square ridges of each abdominal muscle, and it's like a direct shot of arousal to my dick. The beast stands at attention, swelling and growing harder with every sigh from her lips, every flutter of her fingers against my bare skin.

I ease back and pull my shirt over my head and push off her sweater. Her dress would take too much time. Her fingers are quick at my slacks, opening them and dipping both her hands in to cup and fondle me.

Ecstasy.

Pure heaven.

Her touch is molten lava against my skin as I thrust into her palm. "Please . . . ," she pleads, a desperation I know all too well.

I slip my hand under her dress and find a lacy thong. "You wore this scrap of lace for me?" I growl and take her mouth in a deep kiss. The lace is flimsy enough I'm able to rip it easily with one fierce tug.

She cries out at the pinch on her sensitive skin, and I pull the shredded lace from her body and tuck it into my pocket, pressing my hard cock against her while I ease my hand up her thigh.

"You wet for me?" I lick up the side of her neck.

She moans. "Always."

"Hmm, guess I'm going to have to find out myself." I palm her center possessively; her desire coats my hand. "Did you get this hot for Johan?" I grit through my teeth, and press two fingers deep inside of her.

Her mouth opens on a silent cry, and she shakes her head. "Never for him."

I finger-fuck her, grinding my palm against her wet clit. "He touch you like this when you went to his hotel? He put his fingers in you, make you scream his name?" I ease my fingers in and out in a rapid, torturous move that I know will keep her excited but isn't hitting the right spots to make her go off.

"No!" She smacks my chest with her hand. "I wouldn't do that to you. To us!" Her eyes flare with white-hot anger and disgust. It does something to me. Something I needed more than I could ever voice.

It gives me hope.

I remove my fingers from her slick heat, and she cries out, "No!"

"Wrap your arms around my shoulders and hop up," I demand.

She doesn't hesitate for a moment before she responds. I catch her with my good hand on her ass and press her harder against the door. She holds on as I push up her dress up and maneuver my cock to the slippery center between her thighs.

I hover with just the tip inside. It kills me not to power home, but I need to know. She squeezes her legs, trying to get me to move, to sink inside, but I can't. Not until I know for sure.

I look her right in the eyes and hold her gaze. "Did you sleep with him?"

Her lips twist into a grimace. "No." Her eyes shimmer with unchecked tears.

"Did you cheat on me, Sky? Tell me the truth."

Her gaze sparkles with ire and then softens. "I swear I didn't. I love you."

"Fuck!" I slam into her, letting almost two weeks of anger, hatred, and uncertainty bleed out of me as I pound into her perfect body. "You.

Are. Mine." I thrust hard, grinding my pelvis against hers, wanting to go deeper, harder, until I'm wrapped up in nothing but the woman I love.

"Honey, God, I missed you. Missed us!" she cries out on a gasp.

It's too much. Everything that is Skyler and me together is too much to bear. I'm hanging by the strength of a single strand of hair.

"Get there," I growl, pounding into her body as she tightens around me, the walls of her sex a sacred home I never want to leave.

Sparks and pinpricks move over my body as I take in all that is Skyler and me.

The haven between her thighs, welcoming my every thrust.

Her arms holding me tight, as if she'll never let me go.

The serenity of having her lips on mine, her breath and taste in my mouth.

Her soul coming home.

"I'll never be the same," I whisper against her lips, taking us both higher and higher with each blessed thrust. Our bodies joining, minds melding, hearts healing with every breath.

"Honey . . . ," she moans, and licks her lips, licking mine in the process.

The touch of her tongue sends another ribbon of ecstasy between my thighs, swirling around my groin until my eyesight wavers, my thighs lock in place, glutes tightening painfully. Sweat breaks out over my body, and a buzzing euphoria spreads out from my lower back, drawing my nuts up tight as they slap against her ass with every pounding thrust.

I hold her face with my busted hand, using my thumb and forefinger around her jaw. "You've destroyed my world. I can't be without you. Without this. I love you, Skyler. I fucking love you so much it burns in me."

Tears fall down her cheeks as her body locks down, arms shackled around my shoulders, heels digging into my ass. She slams her lips to mine in a crushing kiss.

Her kiss is love, honesty, and truth. It heals me from the inside out as my own body soars to the stars.

***

Her hair is so soft as I run my fingers through the strands. After the wall fucking, we made it into a heap on the bed, still half-dressed, me in my opened slacks, no shirt, her with her flimsy dress on. She did take the boots off, much to my sadness.

I glance over at the clock and realize we've been gone for two hours and not a lot has been solved besides soothing the ache in our physical bodies.

"We have to go. Wendy could wake up." I let her hair fall through my fingers one last time and sit up, heaving my body over the side of the bed.

"Honey, we need to talk. Really talk." She places her hand on the center of my bare back, and it burns against my skin.

I nod and stand up, unable to handle more of her touch right now. If I let it, I could so easily go down the rabbit hole and disregard everything else in my life and lose myself in her warm light.

"And we will."

She gets up onto her knees. "But do you believe me?" Her voice shakes, and she eases back on her heels, perched on the bed like a needy puppy awaiting its next treat.

I look at her sorrow-filled face and honest eyes. "Yeah, I do. That doesn't mean I'm not still hurt and angry for what you did. Going to him."

She rushes to speak. "I had to try and fix it—"

I cut her off. "We can't do this now, Sky. I need to get back to Wendy. She needs us. All of us. Do you understand?"

She bites her lip and nods before crawling out of the bed and putting her boots on. "I need to pick up my suitcase." She gestures to her lower body where, under her dress, I know she's going commando.

"Yeah, okay."

Her gaze falls to the bandage on my shoulder as if just seeing it for the first time. "What is this?"

"Gunshot wound. Was grazed by a bullet the same day Wendy was shot."

Her eyes widen and fill with tears once more. She reaches for my wrist above where my hand is now bandaged from where the ER doc replaced a few of the stitches I busted this past week. The ring and pinky fingers are still in their splints.

Her voice is raw and so low I can barely hear it when she whispers, "And this?"

I try to pull my hand back, not wanting to tell her what I did to myself. "Let it go, Sky."

She brings my wounded hand to her face and kisses my palm. "And this?" she repeats.

I close my eyes and rustle up the courage to admit my pain. "I had it out with a wall and a beer bottle. You should see the wall."

"When?" A tear slips down her cheek.

"Sky . . . ," I warn, but her voice rises.

"I said when?"

"The same day you woke up in another man's bed."

Her eyes close, more tears slipping out. "Parker, I didn't sleep with him." Her words hold even more conviction now because I'm not balls deep inside of her.

I straighten my shoulders and my resolve. "I believe you."

SKYLER

Parker's hand is warm in mine as he leads me through the halls of Montreal General Hospital. I watch his profile and stare longingly at his handsome face. His jaw is hard and scruffy from what seems to be a few days of going without his daily shave. The high cheekbones and straight Roman nose are a sight for sore eyes, though it's his eyes, or rather the dark circles underneath those baby blues, that have me worried. I squeeze his hand, reminding him that I'm here and thanking every deity known to mankind that he's allowing me to be by his side.

Together.

It's all I've prayed for the better part of two weeks without him. Our coupling earlier was an angry crash of bodies, limbs, and mouths. A fever that swelled and crested with the most beautiful crescendo but ended with doubt and uncertainty of where we stand now. I can only hope it will be enough until we have the time to talk, truly work out what happened.

We reach Wendy's room to find Michael speaking with a blonde woman and a younger blond man. The blonde looks like she could be splashed all over the Victoria's Secret website. Either that or a classy version of *Hustler*. Her hair is hanging around her shoulders in bountiful big curls. She has on a skintight royal-blue dress that looks like she was sewn into it and is the exact opposite of my simple maxi dress and sweater. She's wearing sky-high stilettos, and her lips are painted a glossy pink. She looks like she could have just come out of a nightclub, only it's just ten minutes past noon. The man sitting next to her has similar facial features, hair, and eyes, and is wearing a pair of jeans and a T-shirt. Definitely not a couple but very likely related.

"Parker!" The woman jumps out of her seat and plasters her voluptuous body all over my man.

Parker lets go of my hand and pats her back in a gesture of support and concern, but thankfully, not more than that. Still, I cringe and grind my molars together.

"Alexis, what are you doing here?" He looks over to the blond man. "Kidd." He nods.

"Well, we came the first day and again yesterday, but we must not have crossed paths. We're heartbroken over what happened to Wendy, and by someone working for us." She sniffs, getting teary before she presses her forehead to Parker's chest, her hands to her face, and sobs, letting her tears run.

He pats her back and swallows. I can see his Adam's apple moving slowly. Parker glances at me and frowns. I'm not sure what it means or why he did it. Maybe because there's a strange woman crying against his chest. Maybe he doesn't want me to see him console her.

"It's okay. Wendy's going to be fine," he coos into her hairline, and nods his chin at the man standing next to them, who looks rather uncomfortable and out of place. He eases the crying woman into the man's tattooed arms, and he takes over easily, comforting her within his embrace.

She lets out a whimper, pulls her head away, and takes the hankie Michael holds out toward her. Ever the gentleman, Wendy's Michael is.

"Who is she?" The blonde points to me, wiping under her eyes and nose. Not a speck of her makeup is smeared, which makes me want to hate her for being so perfect even when she cries.

Before either of us can respond, Michael glances my way. "She's Parker's girlfriend."

Her eyes widen, and a devilish smirk appears across her glossy lips. "Pretty. I can see now why you wouldn't take me up on my offer," she says, addressing Parker while sizing me up.

Take her up on her offer?

What the hell kind of offer did she make?

A violent wave of jealousy washes over me, and I narrow my gaze at her and tighten my fists at my sides. My heart pounds a bass drum-beat so hard I can barely breathe. Butterflies take flight in my nau-seous stomach; I'm two seconds from tossing my cookies in the hospital wastebasket.

"Ouch. Those daggers you're sending are lethal." She runs a hand through her hair, a nonchalance in her movements I've never quite mas-tered. "Don't worry, he didn't accept my offer. Well, not completely." She winks, which might as well be seen as nothing short of a point being marked on a scoreboard.

"What the fuck does that mean, Parker? Who is this woman?" I lose my lock on my filter and glare at Parker. "Do you have something you need to tell me about Miss Big Boobs over there?"

Parker runs a hand behind his neck. "This is Alexis Stanton and her brother, Kidd. They're our clients. The shooting happened at their business. They're here to see Wendy. And no, I don't have anything more to say. The rest we'll deal with *later*." The emphasis on the word *later* brooks no argument. Even though I feel like I'm coming out of my skin, and beads of sweat are forming along my hairline, I tighten my jaw and keep my mouth shut.

"You look familiar. A dead ringer for that actress Skyler Paige," the blonde says.

Parker sighs loudly. "It's because she *is* Skyler Paige." He looks down at his feet, the awkwardness of the situation clearly weighing him down.

"Wow." Alexis blinks rapidly as if she can't believe her own eyes.

Inside, I want to fist-bump the air and call out a *"Take that, Barbie bitch!"* Win for me.

Michael comes over to me, and I take his hand in both of mine.

"Thank you for coming, Skyler. Wendy would be pleased. You should talk to her. I believe she can hear you." His lips flatten into a thin white line of irritation as he leads me over to Wendy's prone form before glancing back over his shoulder. "All of you."

Seeing her lying so still, bandaged up, darkness smudging around her eyes and cheeks, my stomach plummets. I slide into the chair next to her bedside and grab for her hand.

"Wendy . . . it's me, Sky. Your new bestie, remember?" I swallow down the sudden clog in my throat. "Hey, you have to wake up, girlie. You have a wedding to plan, and we have bridesmaids' dresses to pick out. Remember? We were going to have a girls' weekend in the city?" I lean my chin against her arm and look intensely at her face, willing her to wake up. "Please wake up." My voice sounds like I've swallowed razor blades, and my throat feels just as bad.

A warm hand comes down on each of my shoulders. Parker.

"I didn't know she asked you to be in the wedding."

My nose starts to run, and I sniff, not caring if Miss Big Boobs sees me breaking down. I can't care about anything when my friend is lying in a bed, fighting to wake up and come back to those who love her.

I clear my throat. "Yeah, when you left for San Francisco. She called, and I said yes." I gaze intently at Wendy's face. "I said I would be thrilled and honored to walk in your wedding." My voice rises in hopes that Wendy can hear my commitment all the way in dreamland or wherever her mind is floating.

Time ebbs and flows around me, but I stay where I am, holding Wendy's hand, willing my friend to open her eyes.

Just open your eyes.

I chant the phrase in an ongoing loop as hours go by.

She never moves or opens her eyes.

Sometime later, Parker's warmth seeps deep into my knotted shoulders where he places his hands like he did earlier. He leans down and kisses the crown of my head, and I wish for a moment that we could stay in this happy, loving place for a bit longer. The place where we're a couple who loves and cares about one another with no lies and half-truths between us.

"Time to go back to the hotel. Visiting hours are over." His voice is a rumble against my hairline.

I blink as if I'm suddenly awake from a hypnotic trance. Opposite me, Michael sits holding Wendy's other hand, staring desperately at her pixielike features. I don't remember when he moved to that side or how long I've been sitting, but my back aches, and my knees and hips are stiff as boards. Parker grabs my hand.

"Come on." He urges me up and out of the plastic chair. I squeeze Wendy's hand one last time.

"Please wake up," I whisper, and turn around to leave.

Bo and Royce are standing like sentries at her door. That drop in my stomach from earlier happens again at the sight of Parker's best friends. Bo's features are hard, a grim expression on his face. Royce's is not far from that, but I'm uncertain if it's because of me or Wendy's condition.

"Hi, guys." I shuffle forward, Parker leading me by the hand.

Both men clock our clasped hands.

"Skyler," Bo says flatly, not a hint of happiness at seeing me.

Royce isn't much better with a nod and a rumbled, "Girl."

I close my eyes and dip my head down, following the white linoleum squares along the hallway floors while the chill that came off their two forms freezes me to the bone. Briefly I wonder if I'll ever get back in their good graces.

***

Parker doesn't say a word as we pick up my luggage at information, and he leads me back to his hotel room.

Numbly I set my luggage on the couch and rummage through until I find a pair of shorts and a cami, along with my travel toiletries. Clutching my pajamas and bag in my arms, I wander to the bathroom. As I shut the door, Parker is on the phone ordering room service. He knows what I like, so I don't bother giving him my order. Not that I could eat anyway. I've got no appetite and a tightening stomach to contend with. It's as if I've just gotten off a roller coaster, the waves of nausea and dizziness overcoming my movements.

Between being nervous for Wendy and my own insecurities over whatever happened between Parker and Alexis, I'm a mess. My heart is heavy and my chest is strung extremely tight as I set my pj's on the vanity and look at myself in the mirror. Long, unruly blonde waves run over my shoulders and down my back. The little bit of makeup I wore today has already been rubbed off. Even still, I wash my face and moisturize, needing the break from the man in the other room.

I don't know what to say to him. How to get him to trust and believe I would never betray him. He says he believes me, but if he does, why isn't he talking to me? Why is he avoiding what must be said? And what the hell happened between him and Miss Big Boobs?

An idea forms, and I don't know how it's going to go over with him, but I feel as though I'm standing on the edge of a building. Down below is the busy street, cars zooming past, citizens going about their business, and then there's me. High up on a ledge, teetering between being saved and letting myself fall.

A flash of my mother's kind eyes comes to me, a memory swirling around me and taking me back to a time long ago.

I was sixteen, and a boy I liked in the movie I was filming had hurt my feelings. I was standing in front of a mirror. My beautiful mother stood behind me, running her fingers through my long hair.

Her chocolate-brown eyes were on me, sending love and compassion through our mother-daughter bond.

"You know what to do, my precious girl." She smiled softly and pressed her chin to my shoulder.

I shook my head, and tears filled my eyes. *"No, I don't, Momma. He hurt me, and I don't know if we can be anything more than friends."*

"Oh, I didn't teach my daughter the act of forgiveness for nothing."

I smashed my lips together and frowned.

"Did he apologize?"

"Yes, but I'm not sure I believe him." My voice shook through the admission.

"Well, my precious girl, it looks like you're going to have to use the best advice my mother gave me at about your age. Especially when it pertains to boys."

"What did Grandmomma tell you?" I asked, hanging on her every word.

My mother was always the wisest, most loving woman I knew. I wanted to be just like her when I grew up.

"You just have to follow your heart. It will always lead the way."

With my mother's words in my head and my heart in my throat, I dig through my travel bag and find a dark-pink lipstick. I uncap the lid and set it on the counter while I lift up onto my toes and write my own message to Parker in my swirling text. Something for him to remember and hopefully understand.

Trust your heart.
Love you,
Peaches

When I'm done, I put on my pajamas and open the bathroom door. The scent of hamburgers and fries assaults my nose, and my mouth waters, my stomach grumbling.

Parker chuckles and points down at the food on the table. "That was fast."

"Peaches, you were in there for ages. I thought maybe you'd taken a bath."

"Guess time got away from me," I mumble.

"Yeah?"

I nod.

"Well, come eat." He holds a chair out at the small table for me to sit in.

I let my bare feet take me to the chair and sit down. He helps push it toward the table before going to his own seat. When he sits, he lets out a world-weary sigh, one I can feel all the way down to the tips of my toes. What I wouldn't give to ease his tension, though I fear I'm part of the cause.

"Are we going to talk?" I blurt out, knotting my fingers in my lap, my food untouched.

He sets down his hamburger without having bitten into it. "Yeah, baby, we're going to talk. After dinner, in bed, when I can have you in my arms. We'll talk then."

"You promise?"

"Have I ever lied to you?" His question seems to have a double meaning, as if I've somehow lied to him when I haven't. And he needs to know and believe I never would.

"No. You haven't." At least I hope he hasn't. Even with the issue of Alexis hanging over my heart, we still have to deal with what happened between Johan and me. That's a priority, but I can't help the gnawing fear clawing at my insides.

He tilts his head. "And I'm not going to start now."

"Did you sleep with Alexis?" I ask, not capable of waiting until we're done eating to ask.

He sighs and presses his thumb and forefinger into his temples. "I thought we were going to wait until after we ate and were in bed to talk."

My throat goes dry, but I scratch out the single plea. "I have to know."

He shakes his head. "No, I didn't sleep with her. Now eat your burger. I fear it's going to be a long night."

"As long as I know at the end of this we're still together. Can you promise that?" A tear slips down my cheek, and my heart pounds. Goose bumps rise on my flesh, and I wish we were already in bed, that his arms were cradling me in the safety of his embrace. "Parker . . ." The word comes out as a choked cry.

He lifts his face, and his baby-blue gaze locks onto mine. "I don't know what the future holds, Sky, but I know I want you in mine."

The end . . . for now.

If you want to read more about the guys—Parker, Bo, and Royce—from International Guy, get your copy of *London: International Guy Book 7*.

In the seventh installment, Parker heads to London, England, to assist an international bestselling author with a massive case of writer's block. With Wendy still in the hospital, the guys up in arms, and Skyler back in the picture, Parker's life is spinning out of control so fast he can't seem to catch his breath. Maybe a trip to London is exactly what he needs to find his peace.

Helping author Geneva James, a beautiful brunette at the top of the heap in the publishing world, see her gifts for the natural talent they are shouldn't be too difficult. Until Skyler is invited by the client and Bo ends up crashing the case, falling instantly in lust with the pretty author.

ABOUT THE AUTHOR

Photo © Melissa McKinley Photography

Audrey Carlan is a #1 *New York Times* bestselling author, and her titles have appeared on the bestseller lists of *USA Today* and the *Wall Street Journal*. Audrey writes wicked-hot love stories that have been translated into more than thirty different languages across the globe. She is best known for the worldwide-bestselling series Calendar Girl and Trinity.

She lives in the California Valley, where she enjoys her two children and the love of her life. When she's not writing, you can find her teaching yoga, sipping wine with her "soul sisters," or with her nose stuck in a steamy romance novel.

Any and all feedback is greatly appreciated and feeds the soul. You can contact Audrey through her website, www.audreycarlan.com.